Angela Fournier
Adventure Thriller Series
Book Two

Darkness
After
Midnight

John F Russo

John F Russo Fictional Novels

The Perplexity of Engram
(A futuristic fable)

Enjoy *Angela Fournier*
Adventure Thriller Series
in
Tabula Rasa - Book One
Darkness After Midnight – Book Two
Compromised Interests – Book Three
Le Journal – A Novella – Book Four

Other titles in this series coming soon!
Whiteburn – Book Five
(Including excerpts from Le Journal)

Books2Read: E-books and Printed
https://books2read.com/ap/8prE7z/John-F-Russo
Instagram: @johnfrussoauthor
Facebook: JF Russo
Website: johnfrussoauthor.com

Disclaimer

Angela Fournier — ATS Book Two - Darkness After Midnight is a work of fiction. Names, characters, businesses, organizations, places, events and incidents are the products of the author's imagination or are used fictitiously. Any resemblance to actual events, locales, or persons, living or dead, is entirely coincidental.

Paperback ISBN-13: 978-1-7346457-4-3

E-book ISBN-13: 978-1-7346457-5-0

Dedicated Always

To

My loving wife, Lori Russo

And

Our Family & Friends

In Loving Memory

To my cousin, David Pence and his son, Nicholas, through a senseless crime were gunned down by a seventeen-year-old as they sat in their living room.

AND

To my dear friend of twenty-eight years, Jimmy Sentes, who survived one bout of cancer to surrender to another, whose character—only in name and livelihood—will be forever remembered in my book, Tabula Rasa. To you, I also dedicate this book.

My darkness after midnight...

Acknowledgements

Thank you to my wife, Lori for her continuous input and endearing support and to my father-in-law, Hank Bielefeld for his insightful criticism. I am forever in debt to Jeanne Adams for her keen eye and gracious compliments.

Lee Massee, for his friendship and technical guidance.

Mark Senmartin, owner of Cash Flow Guns and Ammo, Marathon, Florida.

Google ® Maps pg. 82; Wikipedia ® pg. 412;

Barrett ®; Beretta ®; Glock ®; Smith & Wesson ® Chenowth ®

A special thank you to my friend and writer, Tom Cuba for his comments and support.

2024

I want to sincerely thank my editor, Malory Wood of The Missing Ink LLC, for her diligent work, her comments, and her friendship.

FB: /themissinginkwritingservices

IG: @themissinginkllc

LinkedIn: /the-missing-ink-writing-services

Content

Chapters

Day 1, Wednesday - Charlie 1100 Hrs.   1

Day 2, Thursday - Charlie 0530 Hrs.   35

Day 3, Friday - Charlie 1300 Hrs.   60

Day 4, Saturday - Charlie 0100 Hrs.   81

    Map of South Sudan, Uganda, Kenya   86

Day 5, Sunday - Charlie 0545 Hrs.   139

Day 6, Monday - Charlie 0600 Hrs.   166

Day 7, Tuesday - Charlie 0700 Hrs.   190

Day 8, Wednesday - Romeo 0120 Hrs.   212

Day 9, Thursday - Charlie 0300 Hrs.   269

Day 10, Friday - Charlie 0630 Hrs.   282

Day 11, Saturday - Charlie 0730 Hrs.   312

Day 12, Sunday - Romeo 0530 Hrs.   322

Day 13, Monday - Charlie 0730 Hrs.   347

Day 14, Tuesday - Charlie 0600 Hrs.   372

Day 15, Wednesday - Charlie 1200 Hrs.   402

Day 15, Midday - Charlie 1800 Hrs.   412

The Author   422

Interesting Facts   423

Military Time Chart   424

From the Author

During eighteen months of research for this book, I had to stop the writing process four times as I could barely handle the atrocities I was reading about in South Sudan, and then two months of reconstruction after my hard drive crashed, yet the people of South Sudan, the 193rd UN sanctioned country had been at civil war since December 13th, 2013 to February 22, 2020. I pray for their salvation.

Introduction

Poignantly brutal from the harsh African lands notoriously known for their complete disregard of women's rights and human dignity. Lives wasted for the profiteering from a few for mineral rights of a country at war with itself. Four million have been displaced, tens of thousands have been murdered and raped, the innocence of children has been stripped from them, and forced into military slavery by civil conflict created by two men who took an oath to protect and uphold the constitution of this adolescent country South Sudan, born July 9, 2011.

Lt. William 'Billy' Clark had to make a decision and then live by it as he was sent in to eliminate one of the leaders of the warring factions. An over-compelling fear of being set up made his choice, and then he took to the heartland as he was hunted down as a governmental scapegoat by PAG.

His loner life changed when he met 'Maysa', a young woman who had been banished from her village after being raped by an elder, and together they forged through, saving thousands of lives with little consequence to their own.

Unfortunately, the offices of CTA at the Pentagon had other plans—terminate the threat to save their foreign interests.

Serendipitously, Angela Fournier was thrust into the equation. Would she be able to help in time? And, who else would be at personal risk, and at what costs?

The Nile River

The mineral-rich landscape of South Sudan is virtually untapped with only a few foreign countries pumping oil from the northern states. The diverse terrain could support a flourishing tourist trade, if security was not an issue. The White and Blue Nile are tributaries of the renowned Nile River, which splits off at Khartoum, Sudan, and heads south. The Blue Nile crosses into Ethiopia while the White Nile runs through the fertile land of Juba, the capital of South Sudan. The misconception is that the Albert Nile River flows into Lake Albert. And from there, the tributary flows along the west border of Uganda, through the southern Rift Valley, past the countries of Rwanda and Burundi and finally into Lake Tanganyika which borders the Congo and Tanzania.

The fact is that Lake Victoria, being the second largest fresh-water lake in the world, although south of the Equator, flows north. Mostly fed by rainwater, it flows up the Victoria Nile to Lake Kyoga, west through Uganda, through the Murchison Falls, into Lake Albert. The Albert Nile River then turns into the White Nile, at Juba. The Nile flows all the way to the Mediterranean Sea.

War waits for no man!

It is the innocent that drowns in the misery of greedy, power-struggling men. To escape, one needs an invisible force that believes in the truth. Angela Fournier and her foundation believe that truth needs to be liberated. But can she fight Washington, DC? Can Angela and her team devise a plan in time to save a betrayed soldier?

Day 1 - Wednesday

South Sudan

Charlie 1100 Hrs.

He waited in the heat of the rising noon-day sun, entrenched in his own dug grave. A musty stench permeated his nostrils—the ground still devouring the previous water from the end of their wet season. He lay motionless and undetectable to any who might be returning from the growing fields or observed from the sky. He was invisible from satellites. Even drones equipped with metal or thermal imagining cameras could not detect him. One had buzzed him earlier—he did not dare raise his head to see if it was friendly or enemy. As far as he was concerned, they were all enemy. He was alone—he was used to it. His whole life had been spent on the outside looking in—the drifter, stigmatized as a biker with a questionable background. Why? He knew why. He saw things differently. Life wasn't about money, greed or power. It was simple to him—life was about honor. *They* didn't bother him, the establishment with their meaningless stares. He was where he felt most comfortable and where his government felt he was most needed.

The toes of Lieutenant William 'Billy' Clark's Israeli-made boots had gouged an indentation in the granular mud hollow. Obtrusive roots he had cut—still bleeding their sap—dripped into a pool beneath him. A bead of sweat had formed on his lip and his usual tireless sight-eye blinked twice on him. What was so different this time? He had been in plenty of situations like this before. That is why they picked him—the 'Iceman'.

Lt. Clark's target dialed in at 1408.8 yards away. Not his longest shot, by no means. But, by the time his mission played out, the news propagated from his actions would have the world organizations dedicated to peaceful solutions in an uproar. The criticism of this type of intervention would be monumental. Perhaps though, hundreds of thousands of lives would be saved! Maybe, just maybe, children would be free to be children, and mothers who feared the abduction of their children and forced to join lethal groups of brainwashed militants would be spared.

Governments always waited too long before getting involved when they knew damn well genocide was occurring. The Red Cross pleaded for help as did CFAFW (Citizens for a Free World) and UCARV (United Countries Against Radical Violence) who had signed petitions from their members and presented them to the world leaders to relieve the bloodshed and human sacrifices. Words echoed at the UN like: protocol, exaggeration, physical facts, and sanctions always seemed to slow the process. And let's not forget political agendas.

Rwanda was an embarrassment to the modern world where an estimated one million Tutsi and Hutus opposed to the violence—died. Syria was embroiled in a civil war, which already had led to hundreds of thousands of innocent citizens dead and millions displaced. The Russian-lead split of Crimea from Ukraine almost led to WWIII and still might with Russia's current made-up war. This time, however, the E.U. and the U.S. were seeing eye to eye, but each felt their involvement could lead into another world crisis. Thousands were paying the price with their lives, while the world leaders debated intervention. *How sick!*

Lt. Clark knew something was different about this mission. He had been on too many not to have suspicions. Lying there—waiting, time ticking slowly by, he recalled the events from eighteen hours earlier when a blacked-out SUV had driven a quarter mile down his sand road and turned into his property in the panhandle of Florida during his supposed leave. Looking up, holding his sharpened axe, drenched in Florida humidity from trimming a fallen tree, a uniformed man slipped out of the passenger seat and approached. There was little talk—just, "Lieutenant William Clark, we need you now, sir." His kills had earned him a commission, which he found funny, in a strange way. Any other time he had gotten in trouble as a youth, it had landed him in jail. Now he was getting decorated for it.

There was little to pack and no one to say goodbye to. He locked the door of his house behind him and left in the SUV.

~

The lieutenant had been patted down before his flight, another unusual procedure, he thought. Many of his peers with his type of talent sometimes carried lucky charms or other paraphernalia they felt necessary for their survival. No one interfered with their idiosyncrasies. His boots were the only part of his uniform he was allowed to keep. Lt. Clark noticed these camouflage khakis had an Indonesian tag sewn in, his watch was removed and he was re-issued a similar military-style one with a chrome ring and florescent face. He was told not to bring his rifle of choice, a McMillian TAC 50, and was not issued the standard Barrett M82A1 (M107). Instead, Clark was given one mag of 50 caliber cartridges for, and by the look of it, a modified SV-98 Russian-made rifle. A 15-shot Beretta M9 with NATO issue 9mm FMJ replaced his lighter-weight Glock G19, with 15-shot mag and JHP rounds, used by him and some of his teammates for up-close and personal work.

~

Lt. Clark had been piggy-backed in an F-15 Strike Eagle fighter where strict radio silence was the stated protocol. They even made an in-flight refueling instead of landing at known U.S. bases. There was no question in his mind that this mission was definitely off the books. When they finally did land, it was at a makeshift landing field, and as soon as the lieutenant disembarked the plane, it immediately took off. He was left standing and looking at absolutely nothing. No one—nothing—nada. He had been abandoned. Lt. Clark waited all day in the heat with only a canteen of water. As night fell, so did the temperatures. He wasn't prepared.

Clark waited patiently in the desolate-chilled darkness—goose bumps dared beneath his sleeves. He was sitting cross-legged fiddling with his new watch when finally, in the near distance, he saw a cloud of sand coming out of the blackness. Within seconds, they were upon him. Clark was motioned to step into one of the recognizable Chenowth buggy, three in all, and heavily accessorized. They sped through the night air.

No one spoke—again, very abnormal not to have a little chit-chat. Usually, at least, 'Where were you from? How about those Tigers?' Or even, 'Go fuck yourself'. Nothing. He could play their game, and probably better than them.

As they drove in silence, rocking back and forth on the dusty road, Clark thought of the time he was on a mission in Somalia. His team of six had been taken down the Red Sea in a Special Ops high-speed boat and then dropped off just south of the city of Djibouti. From there, they hoofed it over to Ethiopia and then paralleled the Rift Valley for a distance of 250 km. Then they caught the Shebelle River and headed towards Mogadishu, Somalia. It was a grueling mission. They hit every type of weather, from freezing snow over the mountains to flood conditions on the Shebelle River. The stench from the mud-strewn river hampered every move they made. Ten days it took them to trek the 1550 km to reach their coordinates after dodging farmers, children swimming in the river, militia, and snakes. They rarely spoke, only surviving on training and intuition.

When the six men arrived within the designated kill zone, Clark divided his men up into three teams of two and each team was to dissect the kill zone into a circumference-like spokes of a wheel through a ninety-degree arc. Each shooter had their own wingman to scope for distance, wind speed, and deviation. The mark looked like a pinwheel, spinning, as each sharpshooter landed his shot. One team didn't make it out. They were quickly beheaded with an accompanying video aired for future terrorists' intervention by unwanted world powers. The message was well understood by our governmental establishment—each party blaming the other side of the aisle for the indiscretion and loss.

"We felt the loss, but we knew the possible consequences of the mission. We are soldiers and each of us shares the responsibility of lost lives. It's not up for discussion like you fat-cat politicians thinking you need to warm the air with your oratory skills to further jockey for favor by the American people. You have no idea of all the

situations we are involved in. And it's better that way. There is less chance of failure without you knowing ahead of a strike. You have loose lips that get our men and women killed," he remembered saying at a congressional hearing.

Clark's thoughts were quickly aborted as the Chenowths slid to a stop outside a low-lit, make-shift Quonset hut. Clark looked over to the goggled driver who indicated with his gloved hand pointing, *your exit, buddy.* An aide rushed to Clark's side and ushered him into a back office. He had no idea who his escorts were—personally that is—but no doubt, part of the Seals or Special Ops. No one wore insignias, stripes, or stars. No one saluted.

A fit, blond-haired man wearing aviator glasses sat at a desk beyond an opened curtain. He looked up as the soldier entered. The blond-haired man shared no smile or handshake, just a nod as Clark approached.

The room was sparsely furnished as noted by Clark. A map of the area bearing only co-ordinates was pinned to the canvas sides, an SAT phone, a computer, and a small printer. Lying on top of the man's desk were two small photographs of two different men, neither familiar to Clark. One of the photos showed a man wearing khakis garnished with foreign chest metals; the other photograph showed a more casually dressed man. A hand-drawn map with coordinates and a red circle lay beneath the photographs and an extraction written in military time was set at 2200 hours. The blond-haired man looked at his watch and handed the athletic, six-footer Lieutenant Clark the map.

"You have forty-five minutes, soldier, to gear up and six hours to get to your spot after we drop you off. Your strike will be at 1200 hours. Sorry, but we can only take you the first hundred miles, and then it is up to you. Any questions?"

"Which one?" asked Clark, wondering who this Russian-accented man was.

"Either one," he replied.

The aide touched Clark's arm for them to go. Clark walked backward for a couple of steps keeping his eyes on the instructor and then turned to follow the aide. Clark's mind was spinning with questions but knew he wouldn't get any more information than what was in his hand.

The aide brought the lieutenant into another room where just enough equipment was arranged on a desk to satisfy Clark's immediate needs, and nothing more. He managed to pick up a couple of extra magazines of 9mm rounds for his Beretta, some dried food, and night glasses. A collapsed shovel was secured to a backpack along with a steel survival knife and head gear with a radio. Inside was not his usual stealth camouflage but a poncho similar in design to the uniform that he was wearing. Clark packed his disassembled Russian rifle and the one mag of five rounds into the new pack, looked at the aide, and then said, "Let's go. I got enough."

~

The three same Chenowths dropped the lieutenant off according to their orders. He now had six hours to run deep into the countryside across no-man's land to his designated site location. Clark had calculated with his normal running speed, weight of equipment, and heart rate, he should have a half hour to spare before sunrise. If he dropped the extra forty-five pounds of gear weight, he could run faster—a speed he could keep up all day, if needed. A fact, the lieutenant just might need.

As Clark ran with his night-vision glasses, he took notice of the surrounding terrain. Thatched roof huts dotted the landscape as he darted unnoticed. Different scenarios ran through his head and were filed in case of future need. Clark travelled quickly on the gritty red-sand road that wound through a mixture of tall grasses and low scrub trees at an altitude of two thousand feet. He wasn't going to take anything for granted; everything seemed too surreal, too... He couldn't put a word on it, but nothing like he had ever experienced. Clark had a daunting thought of being set up—a scapegoat for whoever authorized this mission.

The lieutenant was surprised to hear the blond-haired man even apologize for not being able to take him farther into the strike zone. If the blond-haired man was the actual commander-in-charge, his hands must be tied by someone higher, thought Clark. Usually backup tried their utmost to accommodate a shooter's mission, whether it was watching their back or keeping communication open. Command had never sent him in cold like this—and alone.

~

Coming down the hillside from the mid-plateau, easing through gouged troughs carved out by previous rushing rainwater, the lieutenant stopped and looked at his watch. He was at 1800 feet of elevation. He kept up his pace and ran for another twenty-minutes before he came alongside a river's edge. It flowed in a surprisingly northward direction with a fairly strong current and was only about a half-mile wide at this particular point. Clark knew if he jumped in here and swam diagonal with the current, he could cross the river with less effort and without the loss of too much ground. Clark swung his pack around to his front and without hesitation, jumped in. He cradled his pack and steered his way using his left arm like a rudder. He safely reached the other side, wet, but according to his map, on target. He started his run again.

The lieutenant treasured his boots. On his first assignment, Clark met a *military advisor,* GT, a big Black guy with a deep voice who was stationed in Israel overseeing a covert operation. GT, a master sharp-shooter himself, gave him a pair of Israeli-made boots to try out. They became friends, and on one of many of GT's lectures, he had told the young lieutenant to always watch his back. *"Kid, even our own could turn on us to protect their interests. Always give yourself an escape route,"* he had said. 'Kid', for 'Billy the Kid' was what GT called Clark.

The boots were special—no metal at all. Even the eyelets were carbon fiber, and the best part—secret compartments in each heel. His friend had given him a special shock-resistant compass—a liquid-filled internal needle enclosed in rubber, which eliminated any detection from metal-seeking scanners. GT also told him to ditch the traditional steel blade knives and get ceramic blades, again undetectable. Luckily for Clark, they hadn't demanded him to remove his boots. They housed his five-inch long ceramic blades, which were sewn into pockets along the pattern of the stays.

Seven and a half minutes later, the lieutenant ran into another river, but this time, it was more of a stream. Waist deep, he forged through to the other side. Cautiously, he knelt as the radio's preset with the GPS coordinates started to transmit a series of slow beeps to his earbuds. According to Clark's new watch, he was right on schedule. Possibly another hour would have him already dug-in and waiting for 1200 hours—then the party would begin.

The lieutenant's map was not very detailed. It looked more like something you would cut out of a kid's cereal box. Why not just tell him, *"Go straight for the first 40 miles, cross a river, and then hang a left at a mound of dirt."* He chuckled to himself, *It's all dirt and scrub.* Clark thought back to when he first moved to his property in the panhandle of Florida while trying to find the DMV. Even the post office employees, including the mail carrier, couldn't come up with the DMV's street name. Rather, they told him to turn left at the old high school and then a quick right. Maybe they drew the map?

He continued in a northerly direction until the GPS-enabled radio sounded with a continuous low resonating beep, Clark quickly checked to catch the coordinates. It briefly flashed 4.52° N, 31.36° E. It went black.

Where the fuck am I? Instantly, he remembered the coordinates his team had during a past assignment as they floated down the Shebelle River. *I must be in South Sudan, and I bet the light on the horizon is coming from Juba. A political debate? It must be; otherwise, why would these two men show up at this one particular location?* It made sense to him. There had been a lot of chatter in his corps about the turmoil that had been taking place in this young country of South Sudan.

Clark quickly dug his hole in the soft sand-embedded soil, which had already borne the growth of tall grass-shrubs and scrub trees brought on by the end of the wet season. His location gave him good cover but as Clark sighted his scope toward the coordinates on his map, his line-of-sight seemed to compromise his position—leaving him exposed. The lieutenant wasn't going to take any chances. He searched discriminately throughout the tall stalks of bamboo and chose the sturdiest. He dug this hole a little deeper than usual and constructed a bamboo gird with sharpened tips pointing upwards. Clark then tied his steel knife to a tripod of stalks—he was almost ready. He reached for his boot's heel, twisted it open, and unraveled a fine filament line. Forming a slip knot, he placed it outside his hole, and waited.

It wasn't long before Clark heard the rustling of the plains grass and the delicate steps in between moments of quietness. *A small-range deer,* he thought. His baited trap of Juniper leaves lay within his filament loop. He waited for the unsuspected to enter its grasp. It was getting closer. He heard the munching on the new growth of leaves hidden amongst the taller grass. The animal was almost in his grasp, and then—he pulled tight and fast, lassoing the hoofs of the young deer. He burst from his branch-covered hole and grabbed the frenzied animal and applied pressure to its neck. The animal fell unconscious into the lieutenant's arms. Clark untied its hooves and placed his new heat-signature gently curled into a ball into his hole alongside the bamboo trap and the GPS radio. Would all this be necessary? He hoped not.

Cautiously, Clark who was hunched over and moving closely to the ground was watchful of his decoy's sightline to a distance where he felt comfortable—closer to the river. His new position suited his needs for a clear shot, and observance of his dictated coordinates as relayed on his GPS radio. In the distance, he saw an outside light flicker as daylight was almost upon him. It appeared to be a hangar. *The airport. Of course!* He dug in at his new location, a mere thirty feet to the river. *Do I dare a fifteen hundred-yard run of open terrain or a quick slip into the river?* It was a no-brainer. Clark planned his eventual escape as GT's words echoed in his mind, *"Watch your back."* The lieutenant tossed his steel shovel into the river, assembled his rifle, attached the scope, and snapped in the .50 caliber magazine. The seasoned sniper cast his filament line once again. He was ready.

~

The lieutenant had a couple of takers slip through his filament line but he resisted as it was too soon to secure his new diversion. Clark needed his prey as fresh as possible. He didn't want to attract bigger game by its blood-scent too early.

Clark's sight-eye was focused but his mind drifted to his hometown, to the first time he visited after his first tour of duty. He had recovered from a poacher's bullet, who had mistaken Clark for a game warden in the wild lands of the Kenya Reserve. Animals were being slaughtered in inconceivable numbers just for rich collectors. Rhino horns, elephant tusks, lion heads, and zebra skins were only a few he saw with the carnage left to rot—as he was. After he received the green light from the medical staff to return to his home country for a furlough, the lieutenant made a quick three-day reconnaissance of the Reserve. He found a group of poachers one night who were sitting around a fire drinking home-made moonshine. By morning light, the five men were sprawled in their own blood. Although there were words circulating around the Canadian compound, no one confronted Lieutenant William 'Billy' Clark with his whereabouts or the found note showing the location of those dead men and their trophies. He flew home.

~

Clark was a ghost in his own town. No one recognized the once long-haired biker who now sported a military-style haircut and decorated uniform. He even got a nod of respect as he walked past one of the cops who had arrested him on charges of distributing cocaine. A plant, Billy had voiced in court, but to no avail. The authorities took him away. But, in the courthouse that day, a man dressed in civvies watched as the proceedings barely held water. Billy's past reputation of reckless behavior convicted him of a crime he hadn't committed. The mystery man wielded his influence with the courts and had Billy transferred to a secretive military training site.

Billy held no malice for the cop, Willard Owens, as it was probably the best thing that happened to him. Billy had been taught to channel his aggression with precise and deadly consequences, for which he now had a chest full of medals for his accomplishments.

As Billy walked along the crowded street, commonwealth flags flew freely in the light breeze. The elite parade of who's who, decorated floats, and the queen of the parade sitting on the back deck of the Cadillac dealership's newest convertible model, all brought cheers. In the crowd, Billy couldn't help but notice the bulging figure of an old flame, Mary Catherine. She was standing beside, he assumed, her nerd husband who was wearing a sleeveless Argyle cardigan. Billy chuckled to himself, *Stylish? He must teach at the college.* No one else would dare wear that in his town of Aylmer, Ontario.

Mary Catherine used to tempt Billy as he sat on his Harley outside of the BP gas station where he worked part-time. MC, as Billy used to address her, was prim and proper from a well-bred and notable family, but she had a devilish streak that poked at him like a sharp stick. At every opportunity, MC would prod him to take her for a ride. One day Billy obliged and that was the first time Owens pulled him over. The officer wrenched MC off Billy's bike and made her sit in the back seat of the patrol car while he berated Billy for his obvious misjudgment. A warning, Owens had said, shaking his finger at Billy. But, to much of Billy's delight, he shrugged Owen off and continued on his way back to his dad's farm. There was talk at the high school of MC's daring motorcycle dalliance with that guy—Billy Clark.

~

Clark checked his watch that he had hung over a root and faced toward him. It read: 1130 hours. He adjusted his weight, and watched a bug crawl over his fingers and then burrowed its way adjacent to a cut-off root. He again slipped into his past.

The second time Billy returned home, he had switched uniforms and countries. His talents had been observed, qualified and obtained while visiting one of the USAMU shooting competitions held by the U.S. Army. There were delegates from all branches of the military participating in this world competition of marksmen. Clark's mind was sharp and his mild and controlled manner intimidated some of the U.S. marksmen to the point of them missing a shot or two. Clark had capitalized on their overzealousness to be the best. They had succumbed to his patient and precise skill.

One of the competitors had questioned his austere manner. He remembered replying simply, *"My grandfather."* They were not satisfied with Billy's two-word answer so Billy had to relay his story. He told them that his grandfather had trained commandoes during WWII out of bases in Campbell River and Vernon, British Columbia. He had told Billy: *"Just relax and think. It's not personal."* Clark's Canadian training and discipline had served him well as he was welcomed into their ranks along with his nickname, 'Iceman', from where else but Canada.

On that trip, Billy had dropped by his dad's farm and rolled out his old Harley. He spent a full day just cleaning it, priming it, and tuning it to its deep, earthy, unmistakable sound only a Harley can make. He threw on his old colors and went to visit his sister. She used to have the most brilliant deep brown eyes, which shone with life itself. Even though she was married and had a couple of kids, her luster had been taken from her by the drunken jocks headed by Owen's younger brother, Shawn. *"An unfortunate mistake,"* as the judge remarked about the attempted rape and the ultimate beating of Shawn by Billy.

Shawn, after he recovered and was released from the hospital, was shipped out to an uncle in Alberta while Billy sat in a jail cell for a year. His sister was never the same but she was still his shining light.

~

Clark re-focused on the activity at the decorated stage as local dignitaries filed in and took their seats. *Thank you,* he thought. *Building that stage gave me another four feet of elevation.* His scope indicated the top of the stage was 1516 feet, and he lay at 1505 feet of elevation. If he was at a higher elevation like his original co-ordinates, the situation would be completely different—but as a man stood, that little bit of difference would save his life. Through his scope, Clark saw that there were two podiums set only a few feet apart, which the security teams were now hovering around. He thought, *whoever these two men were, they must have arrived.* Everyone's eyes turned to their right. Clark waited.

A man dressed in traditional tunic and kufi with shifty eyes walked to one of the podiums and started to address the crowd. He bowed out of respect as one of the statesmen wearing a western-style dark suit, a black cowboy hat and dark-rimmed glasses stepped to one podium and another dressed in military attire sporting a lit cigar, approached the other. They were the two men in the photos given to him by the blond-haired commander. *"Either one,"* he had said. Clark studied their movement and mannerisms as they spoke; he alternated back and forth. The rimmed-glassed man seemed frustrated with the wild gestures from the cigar-smoking man who pointed indignantly towards the other.

Clark studied the reactions of each local dignitary who was sitting on stage as each statesman spoke—their faces as stoic as a gambler's. One statesman would re-unite the country while the other would be self-serving. *Which one? Would the military man do it by force and then maintain that fear for allegiance or would the rimmed-glassed man bring the opposition together with debate and constitutional reform? Who would the US government trust? Who would they side with as an ally?*

Clark had seen the supposed meeker turn tyrant and the stronger be overthrown by yet another faction. *How can they put this choice on me?* Millions of people waited for Clark's decision. Do they return home or do they keep on running for fear of a genocide cleansing?

Clark counted backward. Five, four, three, two... He gently pulled back on the trigger and fired. This time he counted one one-thousand, two one-thousand, three one-thousand, four one... Through his scope, Clark saw his mark's face go blank as his head snapped backward and spurts of blood sprayed onto the faces of the local dignitaries. Chairs scattered as the red-speckled crowd raced around in a frenzy. Lost in the chaos, they tripped over each other as they scampered off the stage. Bodyguards ran to the side of the opponents with guns drawn as they scanned the perimeter and prepared for another violation. The minds of the security were on securing safe passage as they hovered over their prone statesmen.

Clark pulled tight on his filament line and stabbed at the surprised, wild dog, as it had approached too close with curiosity. He rolled out of his shallow hole and looked over to his predestined location. Clark watched as a jeep with three military soldiers, of which two hopped out and ran to the thermal index of his coordinates with guns drawn. If everything that Clark had gone through with the silent treatment wasn't enough of a sign of betrayal, this certainly put the icing on the cake. *Come on,* he said under his breath. *A little closer together... Now move to your left.*

He fired—he counted—the bullet travelled through the neck of one soldier and into the other. They collapsed together into the hole impaling upon the supported survival knife. The young deer jumped from the warmth of its confinement, darted—scared, and zigzagged past the amazement of the jeep's driver. The driver hurriedly turned around on the rutted, dirt road and headed back to the town of Juba, past the commotion of the airport.

Secured in the thought after watching the comical display of the Jeep driver that it would be a while before anyone returned, Clark disassembled the rifle, wiped it down, and buried it beneath him, minus its scope. It was made out of a carbon fiber composite. He deactivated his watch and left it hanging on the protruding root as a message to whoever might find it. The only metal on him now, was his 9mm and he wasn't about to give that up.

Clark placed his sacrifice on top of his grassy, stick-supported hide-out and tied it down to prevent any vultures from stealing his diversion. He slipped underneath his spoils, face up with a ceramic knife in hand and his 9mm resting on his chest. He waited for night fall.

Clark assumed if Command ran thermal imaging, they would pick up the two dead soldiers and a possible beeping transmitter. And fifteen hundred yards away from this known location, they would find one dead dog. If they sent in drones with metallic calibration, they would again find the dead soldiers—and with any luck, the dead dog's warm fluid would block any transmission from his location.

Clark had plenty of time to sort out this fucked predicament while he waited. Later, he would worry about who set him up. He imagined he was probably flown into a friendly location in northern Kenya and then the Chenowths brought him farther into South Sudan, to as far as they dared without being seen. *Not a good idea to head back that way*, he thought. *If I head south along the White Nile,*

I will have more cover along the shoreline than open grass lands and scrub trees.

He knew of a Canadian base on the west side of Kenya on Lake Victoria. If it remained, that meant going right through the center of Uganda. *Some crazy motherfuckers there,* he rambled in his mind. *At least I understand their craziness, which is a point in my favor. They won't be looking for me there, too dangerous for an escape route with no predetermined extraction.*

Clark lay still and listened—tall grass mixed with river reeds was rustling and then a branch cracked. Someone or something was approaching. He grabbed the Beretta off his chest and held it at his side pointing upward. Whatever it was, was taking their time. It had to be an animal; humans weren't as patient. He tried to concentrate on the numbers of the intruders and their direction. He had splayed the animal open to hopefully hide Clark's scent. *An easy supper for the hungry,* he thought. At least three, he sensed, and then the river reeds of his make-shift hut started to tense under their weight. Their chosen steps indicated no fear of what lay beneath their salivating jowls. They approached, heads down, sniffing and then—the tearing of flesh. The smell was rancid from their filthy fur drenched in sun-dried blood from previous killings. They ripped Clark's diversion apart.

The unmistakable groan from a predator drone only momentarily recoiled the savages from digesting. Obviously, the distraction had been picked to the bone when a second pass from the drone sent the scavengers scattering in different directions. And then—silence. Time will tell if the drone picked anything up, he had no choice but to remain until the cover of the night. Clark eased his weapon to his chest and relaxed. He slipped back into his memory.

~

After leaving his sister's place, the second time he returned home, Billy took a ride through town just for curiosity's sake. Walking down the street with her three-year-old daughter, MC's swagger was a delight to see. He pulled over, shut off his bike, and stepped up to her. Her startled expression from seeing a ghost from the past was also shared by her once, pigtailed, braces-wearing sister, Janie, who now stood tall, shapely, with long flowing golden hair, and a perfect smile. Billy remarked on seeing MC pregnant on his first return to town. How time had flashed by. Janie was still unencumbered by anyone's grasp and was poised to take over old Doc. Elliot's veterinarian practice. Before Billy returned to his bike, Janie placed her hand on his arm and said, "Take care of yourself, Billy. Some of us have always believed in you. Come back soon when you can stay longer. Promise me?"

He had looked into her eyes and said, "I doubt there is anything here for me."

"I'm here," she had said.

Billy smiled and cranked over the bike. Janie watched him leave and as he looked into the handlebar mirror, he muttered to himself, "Maybe one day, Jane. Maybe one day."

Lt. Billy Clark smiled at the thought as he lay buried beneath his sacrificial lamb.

The Pentagon - Arlington, Virginia
Romeo 0900 Hrs.

The deep overtones of fashionable wood panels steep in tradition, housed ornate-framed classics of past generals sitting on their steed, black-framed photographs of recent presidents filled with propaganda handshakes, and colorful lift-offs of Apollo missions. Bookcases, floor-to-ceiling, stacked with unread hard-covered books occupied the other two walls, and a row of windows brightened the interior from behind the heavily carved wood desk. The office of Director Jack Tomlinson of CTA (Counter Terrorist Agency) was in an uproar.

"Where is he!?" shouted Director Jack Tomlinson as he sat dressed in his blue suit and red tie—loosely knotted, pounding his fists on his desk. Even his closely trimmed hair seemed to shiver in his outrage.

"We don't know, sir. He made the shot and then disappeared," replied Petty Officer Derrick Smyth.

"What do you mean disappeared? How could he? We have drones, we have satellite, we have thermal imaging, and we have 'PAG' and everything else. God damn it! Explain?"

"He was dug in at the precise coordinates. And by all reports, he should still be there..., except one of the extractors said two of his men were taken down and then a fawn vaulted from this location and ran right in front of him. When he gathered enough men to go back, all that remained were two dead team members, our man's rifle, his watch with the tracking device crippled, and his communication set still beeping."

"Did they scout the area?" the director questioned, intensely.

"It was getting dark. They'll go back at first light," informed the petty officer.

"First light? They've had six fucking hours!" scoffed the intense man. "Who the fuck is handling the coordination over there?"

"Colonel Dimitri and his team were to handle the extraction, sir. But locals were to handle the detention."

"That doesn't sound like Dimitri's work to use locals. Dig, Smyth, dig. I want answers, and I want them now! Set up a meeting. You know who needs to be there. We need a counter plan, ASAP."

"Yes, sir. I'm on it."

"By the way, who did he take out?"

"That confirmation hasn't been relayed as of yet, sir."

"What a fucking screw-up. Could it have been any simpler?"

"No, sir."

"Yeah, right. Obviously, it was above the intelligence level we had on the ground. You still here, Smyth?"

"No, sir."

Petty Officer Smyth left the angry man's office at CTA and headed down the long white corridor past framed pictures of glorified wars. His dark skin was perspiring under his white uniform as he rushed to a solid door with a key-pad entry. His hands were shaking as he pressed a sequential set of numbers. Smyth's request for entry was affirmed. The door clicked open and he quickly stepped in. The room was small, possibly holding four men at the most. The P.O. set his chin on a scanner and stared straight ahead. An inner door clicked open and he stepped through.

The room was bustling as Derrick entered. A few chosen programmers diligently hammered away at computer terminals. The huge wall-mounted monitors displayed graphs with colored imagining, some streaked with sound waves, while others displayed close-up satellite images of grasslands dissected with roads and rivers. Each sector was meticulously scanned for human sound, thermal imagining, and visual characteristics. Villagers stepped in and out of frame, and huts were dissected for possibly harboring a man of 'Particular Aura Generation'. Nothing had come up.

PAG's abilities had been tested in a kidnapping case earlier that year in Los Angeles, but this was the first time for a military application. It functioned somewhat like DNA or fingerprints, except it was done without physical limitations. In governmental—or in its first case, a specialized personal locating firm who were aware of PAG's project had their employees scanned as part of their security implementation program and sent these values to SAS as part of PAG's original instrumentation. These scans identified each employee's aura and then these values were stored within PAG's AI. As per the kidnapping case, a Special Ops team made a successful extraction of a scared young woman.

Petty Officer Smyth walked over to the 40-ish director of SAS who was wearing a white lab coat, stylish make-up and long black hair rolled into a bun. Lieutenant Colonel Samantha Jones turned to the P.O. as he whispered, "He is not very happy."

"I told them 1200 hours was the wrong time. We had predicted the sun flare but they wouldn't listen."

"I'm just telling you as a concerned friend, ma'am. Jack wants heads and he wants to find that soldier, come hell or high water," informed the petty officer.

"We are doing our best. We need more time. There's lots of land to cover."

"He wants a meeting ASAP with you and other interested parties of his cadre. What time should I set up?"

"Christ's sake!" she angrily blurted. "Tell him..." she looked at her watch and started to calculate, "...there's eight hours difference, so it will be 1800 hours there. So tell him 1400 hours. That's the best we can do. If we get something, I will let you know. Oh, thanks, Derrick for the heads up."

"Don't mention it, Sam. Literally, don't mention it," smiled the petty officer.

Petty Officer Smyth took leave of Lieutenant Colonel Samantha Jones, U.S. Army, the Director of SAS (Strategies and Statistics). Exiting the secured laboratory, he headed down the hall through a door, down two flights of stairs, and to his office, located off what they called 'The Flight Path'. If no one was running down the Flight Path due to a military emergency, then the world was standing still, in which case, neither a good thing. He swiped his ID card and pushed several buttons. The security was not as heightened in his area as low-level messengers and assistants resided here at their meager computer stations— a perfect spot to conceal his advanced security status. No one expected this group to have knowledge of much more than the dietary needs of the senior personnel. Once in a while, one of them might be asked to pose for propaganda pictures, but mostly, they handled insignificant details for tourists or visiting school bands.

Smyth headed to his private cubicle at the end of the row. An old storage cabinet once used for ink and perforated printer paper sat next to him, unencumbered. There was no reason for anyone to come his way, or without him noticing. He sat down at his terminal and logged in. Smyth typed a barrage of numbers and cross hatches and then opened a tag left arrow with <8768253> and ended the tag with a right arrow. He hit enter. He quickly got out of his secured screen and brought up a log calendar to set up the meeting that Jack Tomlinson requested.

South Sudan, Juba
Charlie 1930 Hrs.

Lt. Clark felt the heat of the day had passed and there had been no return of the drone. He moved aside a couple of the entwined reeds and saw the reddish glare of the sun was disappearing fast. Nighttime had a different personality than the daylight hours. The nocturnal animals came alive and their sound travelled farther in the cooler, thinner air. He removed several of the stick-reed supports and started to slip out of his cocoon.

Lying on top was the remains of his cleverly designed distraction. Strangely, no one had been back to gather or even investigate the two dead soldiers. Obviously, they did not want to connect the two incidents together—at least not now, without a scapegoat to hand over. No, they had to come up with another plan if they were going to take Lt. William Clark out, and they had better come hard and fast.

~

As Lt. Clark remembered, a Canadian base resided on the west banks of Lake Victoria, Kenya. In his mind, he was going to take the treacherous trail south.

The waterways formed many of the commercial routes, which Clark knew. He had to stay relentlessly alert to disguise his movements along the way, whichever one he chose. Anyone—man, woman, or child could give him up to authorities even if they intended no malice. Just the sight of a white man in a camo uniform was enough to raise interest and talk.

Clark reached for the heel of his boot and pulled out his compass. He slipped on his night-vision glasses, gathered his filament line and headed south by southeast to find his escape route.

South Sudan, Mang – Battered and Alone

She had been beaten, stabbed, stoned, and was lucky to be alive. Even her influential, teary-eyed father had cast stones at her. The elder who stripped her of her innocence was politely asked to move to a different village but he put up such a dogmatic defense as to blame the young girl with her 'tempting his will' with liberal talking and pro-European desires. He was allowed to stay but she had to go. She left, leaving her family in shame.

Nine months later, she bore a beautiful little girl in the ruins of a bombed-out school. She had no means of support and she frequently was passed from shopkeeper to shopkeeper in exchange for food for her child. When insurgents raided the small northern border village of Mang, they tossed her around like a child's soccer ball and then left her in the red dirt—deflated.

She was one of the few girls from her home village who actually attended school; however, her education had not prepared her for such abuse. Nonetheless, she was quickly gaining the essence of survival. Her intimidations were lessening as she grew in strength, experience, and handling a knife. She had watched an insurgent, while they had her lashed in humiliation to a post in Mang's small square, wielded his knife against the throats of several elders of the village. His action was smooth and deliberate as he spilled their blood for others to see and fear.

She was prepared to pay with her body for gratitude for food, but any violence detrimental to her put the violator into the same gasping of air as she had been forced to witness. She moved often.

With her slight of step, the young woman was learning to steal fruit and milk stray goats rather than giving her body for payment. She had little to no communication with

25

any of the thousands of IDPs who were fleeing the atrocities of warring sympathetic tribes. The fear of association had everyone weary of forming connections or knowing ones name. The young woman made her way south with the determination of a lioness protecting her cub.

. . .

He was a survivalist and a trained assassin. Clark wasn't bothered with what he had to do to survive. No, what ate at him was the betrayal. As he cautiously left a footpath and approached the welcoming sound of the river, he overheard the chatter of men escaping from the tall reeds along the riverbank. Clark knew he would find what he needed, and he did. A small punt lay in the river's reeds just down from a gathering of fishermen who were circling a fire, frying their fish. He slipped quietly away, paddling up the river's edge in the shadows of the night.

Kenyan Border

Charlie 2000 Hrs.

The Special Ops compound was quiet. A few men were chit-chatting amongst themselves while cleaning their weapons; some were resting—all waiting for their next mission. The radio operator removed his 'ears', left his station, and ran over to his superior's Quonset hut.

"Sir!," said the aide, his chest heaving as he approached the blond-haired man, Colonel Dimitri, who had his head buried in his hands, deep in thought—planning his next move. He looked up. "Yes, soldier."

"They are asking... I should say, demanding answers, sir," relayed the aide.

"What was your reply?"

"I sent a generic response that we couldn't confirm the hit because of mass hysteria."

"Well done. How long do you think we have?" asked Colonel Dimitri.

"Possibly, until daybreak," answered the aide.

"Send Reynolds in. Oh..., and Jake as well, please," instructed the Colonel.

"Yes, sir."

The Colonel stood and with a slight limp, walked over to his displayed map of the area. He was studying it as the two men were escorted into his office by his aide, Jacobs.

"Colonel," acknowledged the men.

"Gentlemen. Step over here. You as well, Jacobs. We are one unit here. Our Lt. Clark is very clever. Where do you think he is headed, and tell me why you think that?"

The men stood next to the Colonel and scanned the most likely escape channels. Jake spoke first.

"I met him during a training course at Fort Benning. That is why I chose not to be around when he was escorted in. He is very calm and calculating. His pain threshold is extremely high and his focus is unchallenging; therefore, in my opinion, we may never find him if he doesn't want us to."

"Not quite what I wanted to hear, Jake."

"I understand, sir, but I thought we needed to lay it on the line. Our choice of understating his mission and security breach played well with his instincts. He survived," Jake stated, matter-of-factly.

"I hated to see him go out like that, as well, sir," remarked Reynolds.

"They are demanding answers, gentlemen. We can't stall them much longer. If they fear we compromised the mission, they will send others."

"Why would they think that, Colonel? We stayed true to their orders. There is no possible way they could conceive how we implemented them. If Lt. Clark wasn't as perceptive as he is, the outcome could have been different. He might be on T.V. as a renegade conspirator right now," shared Reynolds.

"I agree," acknowledged Jake.

"Jacobs, is your contact trustworthy?" asked the Colonel.

"I would put my life on it, sir."

"Good and his benefactor?"

"That remains to be seen, sir."

"Well, some information is better than being blind. Now, more importantly, where should we look, gentlemen?"

Corporal Jacobs spoke up. "Sir, he was stationed at a Canadian Exercise Command hub in Kenya, which, according to the Canadian Operational Support Command (CANOSCOM), it doesn't exist."

"Like us," laughed Jake.

They all raised a brow and smirked at Jake's comment, which slightly eased the tension in the room.

"That would be a dangerous move, sir, and he would know that. If he went through Ethiopia to the Red Sea, he would have more of a chance to contact friendly sympathizers," stated Reynolds.

"Sorry, Rey, I don't believe he is looking for the easiest route. He doesn't trust anyone at the moment. Lt. Clark has probably figured out we dropped him off within running distance of Juba, so he won't chance coming our way in fear of us tracking him down in the Chenowths. With his talents, I would attempt crossing Uganda to Lake Victoria and then to the imaginary Canadian base in Kenya," related Jake.

Colonel Dimitri listened quietly to his comrades as they debated Lt. Clark's options.

"Gentlemen, I appreciate your input. First, we will need to satisfy command with our search and progress. At daybreak, we will strike camp and move to Lake Turkana..." he pointed to the map, "...along the northern border of Kenya, the Rift Valley, and Ethiopia. SAS will be able to track our movement. And Jacobs, you will send a message to confirm our intent. Jake, I want you to follow your instincts and take two men with you. That is all we can spare, sorry," instructed the Colonel.

"Thank you, sir."

"Don't thank me yet, Jake. Besides, side-stepping the Boko Harem, LRA, the Al-Shabaab, and the Ugandans, the toughest part will be to convince Lt. Clark that you have his best interests. Our initial contact with him wasn't so friendly. He might not take too kindly to your intervention. So, be very careful," elaborated the Colonel.

"Sir?"

"Yes, Jacobs."

"Who should we say he took out?"

Pentagon - Boardroom

Romeo 1400 Hrs.

They—Jack and his loyalists plus one other—all had gathered in the plush boardroom and sat around the impressive, highly polished Rosewood table. Microphones were turned off but a center piece resembling a spaceship with a dial pad blinked green indicating Jack Tomlinson's foreign partners were present. He controlled the meeting.

"Gentlemen and ladies, I will skip with the formalities and get right down to business." He paused so his words could be translated. "We underestimated our device. He is being sought out, as we speak, by a team of professionals." He paused once more. "We are concentrating our efforts on the most logical and the preferred direction of the team leader." Pausing... "With all of our resources, we will jointly ascertain and extract the device. We are assuming our cigar man has been snuffed out by our device and a more casual approach will lead to constitutional reform to sanction our interests in developing resources and of course, our protected trade route. We will keep you informed as we learn the situation. Thank you for your time."

The green flashing light turned red. The attendees, who sat at the table with Jack Tomlinson, stood with pretentious medals dangling on starched suits and surly faces avoiding eye contact, started to leave—all except...

"Director Jones, may I speak with you?" asked Tomlinson.

"Yes, sir."

"I will not have to recant my words, will I?" he said in a low direct voice.

"We are doing our best, sir," reassured the Lt. Colonel. "Our system only allows for a level of intense magnification of a square mile at a time for a preliminary bleep, and then we have to zoom closer for direct identification. It all takes time, sir."

Tomlinson flashed a phony smile as he nodded to the departing attendees. He then hung onto Samantha's arm tightly. Jack turned into her.

"I don't want to hear how you fucked this up and let him vanish into thin air. You promised your equipment could pinpoint anyone. Now do it!"

"You're hurting my arm. Let go!" she demanded glaring back at him.

He relaxed his grasp, "Thanks for dropping in, Director."

Another attendee, Nigel Redman, a strong man with piercing blue eyes, handlebar moustache, and a heavy Scottish brogue, was about to disappear through the door.

"Nigel... May I have a word?" Jack said, cordially.

The director rubbed her arm as she left the two men in the boardroom. Steaming, she rushed through the maze of hallways.

"How dare he blame me!" she said, sounding off under her breath, pissed off. "I told him it was not a suitable time."

As she stood at SAS' solid exterior door ready to punch in a code, a familiar voice called to her.

"Samantha! Samantha, wait!"

She turned to see an old admirer, Admiral Chauncey Stone. He was a distinguished man, six feet tall with dark to greying hair. He smiled as he slipped next to her.

"I saw you come out from his war room. You didn't look too happy. Is everything okay?"

She smiled and looked up into his concerned eyes, "He is an arrogant son-of-a-bitch, but it was his lobbying that helped to obtain some of the financing for my project."

"Which, I still don't know what you do, exactly," smiled the Admiral.

Samantha looked in each direction before she put her hand on Stone's chest, "You know I can't say..."

Interrupting her, he said jokingly, "Yes. Otherwise you would have to kill me."

"Don't say that too loud around here. Strange things are going down." She then added, "How is Barbara?"

"You know Barbara. More concerned about her social status than what she has pushed away at home."

"Chauncey, I can't do it this way, you know that."

"I'm not asking, Sam. I... I just miss you and want you to know that if you need anything, I am here for you."

"Thank you, Chauncey. I truly appreciate your concern. I'm sorry but I have to get back to work." She placed her hand on his arm and said, "Thank you."

"Anytime, Samantha... Anytime."

The lieutenant colonel looked at her watch and punched in a new code as every two hours the code changed sequentially. She stepped inside the outer room. The exterior door clicked shut behind her. Samantha paused and cleared a tear from her eye before resting her chin on the retinal scanner's pad.

Admiral Stone returned down the hallway from the direction he came. He passed the war room where Jack Tomlinson and Nigel Redman entered the same hallway.

"Lost, Admiral?" said Tomlinson sarcastically.

"Haven't changed have you, Jack? Still the same asshole."

"Admiral, just wanted to offer assistance to an old friend," remarked Tomlinson.

"It will be a cold day in hell before I call you a friend."

"I had nothing to do with those pictures reaching the Admiralty. By the way, how is Barbara?"

The Admiral turned to Jack—face to face.

"What, Chauncey? Want to duke it out right here?"

Nigel interfered, placing his hand between the two. "Not the place gentlemen, and not the time."

"Watch your step, Jack. The world does not revolve around you."

"Jesus, Admiral, I thought it did."

The three men parted ways. Jack and Nigel turned into Jack's office as Admiral Stone made his way through the labyrinth of hallways.

"Jack, you really shouldn't threaten an Admiral. Did you have something to do with his de-commission?"

"Ah, he is a pompous motherfucker. Not my fault he couldn't control his pecker. Now where were we?"

~

Upon entering the offices of SAS, Lt. Colonel Jones was greeted with concern by her friend and colleague.

"Director, are you all right?" questioned Marsha Jean Atworth, Navy Lieutenant JG, a thirty-three-year-old senior researcher, and PAG's co-author.

"Yes, Marsha, thank you," replied the director as she rubbed her arm. "Anything yet?"

"We have been following the recovery team and as their communication stated, they believe the hostage was taken into the mountains of Ethiopia," informed Atworth.

Gently guiding Marsha to the side, the director quietly explained, "Marsha, we have worked on many projects together in the past and we have enjoyed a professionally mutual degree of success. What we thought we were designing PAG's abilities for..." The director paused to find the right words. "...appears to be quite the opposite. They are using our system to hunt a man, not to save him."

"What!?"

"Shh, this is between you and me. Let me know when the recovery team makes their base camp. Oh, and Marsha, do you think any of the others here believe as we do?"

Marsha looked around with a different interest and stopped at each researcher. She tried scanning her own memory banks of each résumé she had read and believed she had the good sense to have picked the best.

"Samantha, let me review my notes. I will get back to you tomorrow. I can't tell you how disappointed I am in hearing this. I really thought we would be up for a Pulitzer for humane survival, not arrested for human liquidation."

Samantha squeezed her friend's hand, "I know. We can't let our feelings show to the others until we know for certain who is on our side."

"I agree. You know I have your back, right?"

"Marsha, you are the last person I would ever suspect of this madness."

"Thank you, Samantha."

Marsha Jean, a pretty woman, with green-blue eyes who always wore her long brown hair in a bun, lived alone. Her friend Samantha, who held a higher rank than her, always treated her with respect. On several of their combined papers, Marsha was afforded the same accolades as Lt. Colonel Jones. But, living with the "don't ask, don't tell" policy, she had repressed any affection that would compromise her friend. She would do anything her friend would ask of her.

Day 2 - Thursday

South Sudan

Charlie 0530 Hrs.

As the sun broke through the darkness with red and orange whispers of color, Lt. Clark had set his punt amongst the tall grass reeds of the river, out of sight. It was too dangerous to travel along the river in daylight hours. He needed rest and then to find something to eat. Like a cat, Clark climbed a tree and hid in the cover of its foliage. It also gave him a vantage point to scrutinize the traffic on the river in this area. He imagined, as he approached Lake Albert, villages would be more plentiful. The lieutenant knew he needed to find a more bustling town, other than Juba, where one could possibly find support for cell service. The river people might not have a need for such a device, but the towns' people had a different opinion of themselves. They wanted as much Western influence as their government would permit.

The modern Sudanese wanted satellite T.V., cell phones, and microwaves even when their floors were still in dirt. It was this technology that raised them out of third-world country mentality and their feeling of despair. China and India were investing heavily in their economy with everything from plastic buckets to mopeds and cars. The Sudanese still needed to harness more of the available hydro-electric power and water reclamation plants for potable water, like at Jinja, Uganda. But such expense would have to be initiated by a collective government, not one in turmoil. Other conglomerates only wanted to steal their natural resources, like they had repeatedly done to other rising countries. The people were left out in the cold and still impoverished, while under-the-table deals and paybacks lined the pockets of the very few.

Nothing was different and nothing had changed, even after millions in the U.S. had lost their jobs and homes in the burst of the economic bubble. The rich made more money and their politicians, who should have been responsible to the citizens, carried on without prosecution. The only asphalt roadway in South Sudan came from the border town of Nimule to Juba, a mere 120 miles. It cost the U.S. taxpayers $230 million while roadways in the U.S. stayed unpaved and dangerously potholed. Another $180 million in humanitarian aid from the U.S. was slated for the starving, due to the on-going conflict from opposing tribal leaders of this newly formed country.

Clark's mind wandered as he watched the slow transaction of commerce float up and down the river. The shirtless father in a laden punt pointed to an interesting peculiarity in the river. His son gleamed with delight over this simple gesture and filed this knowledge in the back of his mind for later generations. Lt. Clark watched the simplistic nature of the past float by, as 'civilization' raped its innocent.

It was time for real change and Clark hoped his kill would rock those who were instrumental in developing such change. If he was captured, what would he be allowed to say? Or would his voice be digitally manipulated to say what message the US government wanted the people to hear? It was all a game. No winners, just losers being played over and over again to a different sound byte. Clark liked the easy mannerisms of the river, but he imagined even here, greed and violence played out. *Would this young boy make it to manhood or would he be stripped of his innocence and forced to mine gold or diamonds or don fatigues to enforce rhetoric he didn't understand?* He laid his head against the tree and closed his eyes.

Tonight's new moon would offer Lt. Clark full darkness after midnight—and another chance at survival.

. . .

The young mother lay quietly in the early light, amongst the tall grass near the Kenyan border with her baby suckling nourishment from her, as three strange vehicles and two large rubber-tired machines silently made their way inconspicuously past her. They disappeared into their surroundings, but briefly and only for a moment, they quickly re-appeared as if it was an aberration. She had not seen anything like that before. *How could they move in machines across the ground, but yet, not be seen?* The only visible indication was the movement of grass, as if the wind was blowing. *What if I ran into these? What would happen to me? Would I be swallowed up?* The young mother decided to be more cautious and watchful of the grass before she made another move.

. . .

Lt. Jake Alderson had picked two fellow soldiers, Ben Peterson, alias BP and Thomas O'Rielly, to go on this mission. Each stood out for their particular talents, which Jake thought might be necessary for their success of this mission. Each had over five years in Special Ops, but Peterson, among his deadly talents, was also a linguist, who spoke many Nilo-Saharan dialects. Although English was the official language throughout this region, there were many dialects spoken, which would be to their benefit to understand.

O'Rielly, who they called *MacGyver* or 'Mac' for short, was a whiz kid. He could turn anything into something that could go 'bang' or any other practical application one might need.

Jake was silent but deadly. He admired Clark for his talents and his personal integrity. Jake was not afraid to voice his opinion when their orders came down to assist Lt. Clark on his mission. "Clark's betrayal you mean!" he had said, scoffing at the orders and declaring his displeasure to his superior officer, Colonel Dimitri. He felt proud the Colonel had trusted his input and foresight into this situation. It was up to him now, to rectify the wrong that had been dealt to a fellow, respected soldier. Jake knew his Colonel had connections outside of his command; although, he never came out and actually spoke of those connections with direct names.

Jake's Colonel was an honest, but cunning man and his loyalty was never in question. Jake heard, the Colonel was secretly 'acquired' while he held the post as head of the Russian crime unit against drug trafficking. True believers 'of truth' transcended any propaganda any government could have inflicted on its citizens. Jake was proud to serve under him.

Before the main team had shipped out, Jake's team had secured rapid-fire, silenced automatic M4A1 rifles, stealth ghillies, with an extra one for Clark, and communications that Mac had modified. They traveled light on foot along the Kenya-Uganda border. Jake knew if Clark took to the river, his travels would be swifter than theirs. But at some point, Uganda's center would have to be crossed, which gave his team time to intercept him, if they were lucky.

. . .

The young mother had no idea how far she had walked, only that she was now in Uganda. She, however, felt fortunate to land a ride in the back of a flatbed truck with a family who was moving to safer lands farther south. Eventually, the family hoped their travels would land them at the capital of Kenya, Nairobi. It was a dusty trail but the young mother was thankful for their hospitality. The wife, who had emerald-green eyes, had been the one who made her husband stop; she took compassion on this poor young mother. As she too had a breast-feeding infant and she knew too well, the dangers associated with women of their circumstances. A young boy sat in the front seat with his father. He watched the young mother.

After a short distance, a couple of miles at most, past the town of Arinyapi, Uganda, the young mother was able to adjust her body's cramped state as her young child awoke and stretched from under her wrap. Within a split second, as she was repositioning herself, she glanced past the gully of the road and noticed more shimmering aberrations moving slowly, but this time, on foot. She stared off with a smile, not wanting to give startle to the compassionate woman with emerald-green eyes. For some reason, the young mother felt no fear but wondered in her silence.

Virginia

Romeo 0730 Hrs.

It was Thursday morning in Virginia, almost 0730 hours and Marsha had been at SAS already for twenty-four hours. She couldn't let the news Samantha had confided in her rest. The first shift was now tracking the recovery team, which was eight hours ahead of them. Marsha had promised Samantha she would review her notes; however, they were locked up at Marsha's home in a safe place. Although against protocol, the notes were private and of no concern to the military machine. Terry Tanega was a proficient researcher and quite capable of handling the helm while she went home. Marsha gathered her bag and signed out.

The hallways were crowded as shifts changed. She dodged the bright-eyed morning dwellers and their optimistic "Good mornings". But as she stepped outside and took her first breath of fresh air, she sighed with delight. *Nothing like fresh air to clear the mind.* Marsha jumped onto the commuter and rode it to the secured lot where her car was parked. Fumbling with her keys, she clumsily dropped her bag, and as she was about to unlock her door, a kind man who was walking by, stopped to give her assistance.

"Are you alright, Lass?" he asked in a thick Scottish brogue.

Marsha looked up and acknowledged his concern, "Yes, fine. Thank you."

"Very good. A pleasant day to ya."

Marsha smiled back at him, inserted her key, and the lock clicked open. She pulled up on the handle of her race-engineered, metallic-blue Miata supporting high-intensity lights and Pirelli tires—she slid inside and turned the key.

. . .

Jack Tomlinson was sitting at his desk seething with contempt over the failed mission. His telephone rang jarring him out of his agitation. He looked at his watch: 0745 hours. Only five minutes since the last time he looked. He answered, "This better be good, Smyth. What do you have?"

"He took out Tahir Aldama."

"He took out who?" shouted Jack Tomlinson.

"Tahir Aldama," said the petty officer.

"I heard you. What the fuck? How did that soldier know Tahir was one of our guys? What other agencies are involved in this?" questioned Jack Tomlinson.

"I don't know of any."

"Somebody knows! Jesus fucking Christ! This is getting worse. Can they trace anything back to us?"

"I don't believe so, sir. Everything went through the proper channels and decisions were made on reputation."

"Yes, but it was our money that inflated his reputation. Who could have turned him?"

"Tahir?"

"No, stupid... Clark? How did he know to take out Tahir? His mission was one of the other two fuckers. Not our man! No one over there knows about our alliance, so there couldn't be a leak from...? Get me Nigel. We need to fix this. We have spent too much money over there supporting the rebels and building their infrastructure just to be back at square diddly squat. That Castro want-to-be is an idiot, the other guy, we might be able to manage. Where are they?"

"On ice at the embassy," stated Petty Officer Smyth.

"Why Jesus for?"

"Nowhere else to go. The general wanted to kill everyone and the majority leader believed it was the general who set this up."

"Okay, maybe with a little tweaking, it could work to our advantage. Let me know when Nigel gets here."

"Yes, sir."

Petty Officer Smyth was about to hang up when he heard Jack call him, "Smyth."

He placed the receiver back to his ear, *"Yes, sir."*

"Where is Dimitri?"

"Headed for the Ethiopian border, sir."

"Has the director confirmed anything yet?"

"No, sir."

"Stay on her. She needs to understand the urgency of all of this."

"Yes, sir." The petty officer hung up.

Jack muttered under his breath, "Well the taxpayers just inherited an extra $5 Million. Not much from the $1 Billion we have already spent over there. I wonder what Tahir did with the first $5 Million?"

Jack tapped his fingers with a pencil as he glared out at the manicured lawns through his plush office window.

. . .

Deep in the maze of the Pentagon's labyrinth, Lieutenant Colonel Samantha Jones' phone rang in her private office. "Hello...hello?" The line *clicked* then went dead. Nothing surprised her since she accepted this secured space at the Pentagon, through Jack's insistence. Samantha looked up and saw Derrick entering through the security door. He looked around and then spotted the director who waved for him to come to her office. He nodded hello to some of the researchers who briefly looked up from their terminals. He ascended the three stairs and entered her office.

"Good afternoon, Director."

"Afternoon, already?" she questioned looking at her watch.

"Yes, ma'am."

The director offered the petty officer a chair to sit on while they talked. His back was to the lab.

"Sam, don't get excited when I tell you this, but Jack is in a bind. He thinks someone is setting him up, or at least, interfering with his project. He is at a loss right now. He wants to pressure you into finding the lieutenant. Jack has some very nasty men working for him that I believe, will stop at nothing to get the answers."

"I can only do what I can do. We need direction of some sort. Colonel Dimitri sent us coordinates but we haven't had any luck."

"I hate always bringing you 'heads up news' but Jack is pissed."

"Do you think Colonel Dimitri knows what is going on? Is he an ally to Jack?"

"I believe Colonel Dimitri is a righteous man, from the little I have heard. I cannot believe he would send a man to his death, but I don't make the decisions or issue the orders."

"Derrick, you are a fine young man. Don't let the politics shadow your vision of what is right and wrong."

"Yes ma'am. I think I have a good grasp on political bias. Ma'am without being obvious, is anyone watching our conversation?"

The director flushed her questioning stare from her face and stood to get a file from one of her cabinets. She stood briefly thumbing through a file folder before handing it to the petty officer. Samantha casually scanned the lab. No one looked out of place. She sat back down and leaned in toward Derrick, "What is on your mind?"

"I was just wondering how you were doing and if there has been anything unusual happening?"

In a low whisper she said, "My phone just rang and no one answered."

"Did you hear a slight click before the call ended?"

"Yes. Why do you ask?"

"Your phone is tapped, Samantha."

"What!? This is supposed to be a secured line," she said with a denial tone.

Derrick rendered a half smile at Samantha's "secured line" statement. He shifted in his chair and lightly tapped on her desk with his finger to make a point.

"Samantha, I am telling you, it is tapped. Get yourself a throw-away phone from Walmart. Only give the number to your closest friends. People you trust."

"Derrick, can I be so bold and ask you a question?"

He settled back into his chair—attentive.

"By all means."

"Are you caught up in all of this somehow? Are you who you say you are?"

"Samantha, I am a believer as you."

She chuckled. "Derrick, you sound like me when you say that. I put my trust in you, you know that, right?"

"Yes, ma'am. I will not let you down. I promise. I have worked hard for my position, maybe harder than most. I have been privileged to see a bigger picture, if we can leave it at that for now."

"Yes, of course. One other question. You had a deployment under Admiral Stone, correct?"

"Yes, ma'am. I had the privilege of serving under Admiral Stone before his de-commission."

"Do you know why he was de-commissioned?"

Derrick again shifted, this time a little uncomfortable in answering the Lieutenant Colonel's question.

"I have no authority to review the Navy's transcripts, ma'am."

"But, in your heart, you know."

"There are always two sides to every story. I do believe he loved you, ma'am, no matter what the cost to him personally."

With a tear budding in her eye, Samantha said, "Thank you, Derrick, for being so direct with me."

"Ma'am, for what it is worth. Don't give up on your dreams."

"Thank you, Derrick. You have no idea how your caring makes me feel. I wish I could give you a hug."

Derrick stood to attention. "Ma'am, I salute you." And whispering, he added, "I can feel your warmth, Sam."

He turned and left the director's office with a file folder of blank paper clutched in his hand as if it were *top secret*.

Uganda Outback

Charlie 2230 Hrs.

Jake and his teammates, BP and Mac, staged their camp in the shape of a triangle with a point man hidden in a tree. Their rotation was every hour, which gave each man a total of two hours of sleep before they continued with their journey. They had a lot of ground to cover and little time to do it. Mac whispered over his radio into the ear buds of his teammates.

"Did you notice the young girl with the baby in the flatbed? I know she saw us, but she just smiled and turned away. What do you make of it?"

"As if she had recognized us," stated Peterson.

"From where? And how?" questioned Jake. "Keep a watchful eye for her, anyway. Could be trouble if she gives us up."

"I don't know, sir. She seemed to find comfort in seeing us," replied Mac.

"Wake me in 55 minutes, Mac."

"Yes, sir."

The thought of a civilian seeing them, had Jake uneasy. *How could she spot us? Drones can't even find us.* He tried to fight his restlessness and get some much-needed sleep. *Maybe Mac was oversensitive of his observations, but I will not assume anything. We'll need to be more careful of our movement.*

Jake had learned not to question another soldier's perception, especially on recons. He had seen other commanders with a point to make, fuck up because they refused to listen to an enlisted soldier. They were a team. What one felt, the others needed to be aware. He would not lose a man over ego. Their survival depended on it.

. . .

Although the time was late and the night was pitch-black, the young mother felt she had exhausted the kindness of the traveling family. She would make her own way and thanked the woman with emerald-green eyes for her compassion. The truck pulled over and they bid farewell.

The young mother knew she had to find nourishment, for soon, her baby would want more than her disappearing milk. Farmlands were plentiful in this area. She left the road in search of food.

. . .

Clark eased the punt past the river reeds into the open water. He had seen all sorts of floating debris go by while he was resting. No one seemed to bother with the water-soaked cargo, and just let it pass. The river people had probably learned that anything floating could be a potential disease for their village or worse, lost cargo from the cartels—best to let it be. Unoccupied punts, on the other hand, could serve them well. He needed to find a disguise to blend in or make his punt look like any other floating by with strapped-down cargo or draped in fishing nets.

Clark scoured the riverbanks as he paddled along. Finally, he spotted a dwindling fire at a fisherman's camp. He directed his punt and silently went ashore. To one side of the campsite laid two wooden fish traps, propped up nonchalantly, by a rolled-up discarded net. On the other side and next to the sleeping men were AK-47s and boxes of medical aid with Red Cross stamped on them. These men were not fishermen. Clark crept quietly past them, cautiously looking back at the sleeping men. He raised the traps, but the net held fast to the ground by weeds growing through it.

He replaced the traps back down and reached for one of his ceramic knives from the stay of his boot. Just as he had freed the net, a third man came out of the woods, zipping his pants, still sleepy-eyed, and by the time he reached cognizance—it was over. Clark laid him back down into the foliage from where he had appeared. It was survival—his survival. Clark had no remorse for his actions; he wasn't trained for that. He gathered what he needed and headed back to his punt and set off.

. . .

The young mother stopped in her tracks as she heard the rattle of gunfire in the near distance and immediately thought of her traveling friends. She clutched her baby tight with the thought of overwhelming anxiety. Her face twitched with the realization of what could happen. She had witnessed it before.

With her baby well secured, she abandoned her search for food and ran down the road through the blackness. Fifteen minutes later, she stopped short as she felt the heat whip at her. Raising her hand to shadow her face, she observed what she had feared—a fireball engulfing an over-turned and bullet-riddled flatbed truck. The young mother investigated cagily, knowing firsthand the capable horror one might fall into. A man's arm protruded from underneath the truck, but no others seemed to fair the same injustice.

As the young mother moved away from the crackling noise, she heard the faint scream of a woman farther down the road. Holding her baby tight once again, she ran alongside the edge of the road until she came closer to the wailing cries. She turned into the tall grass. The screams of a distressed woman, inanely hollowed, pierced the night air. The young mother kissed her baby's forehead and laid her baby down in her protected wrap among the tall grass.

She slipped into the night, past the audible sounds of crickets, towards her friend's frantic misery.

As she approached, she squatted, and through the tall grass she saw three men sitting around a small fire, a hundred meters from the road. Listening to their conversation, she understood their Arabi-Juba mix dialect and by the sound of the continuing screams, another man was inside a make-shift tent from where the screams were emanating.

The young mother crept closer, protected by nocturnal sounds and undetected by the merciless men. One of the men, who was sitting on a log next to the fire, got up and walked into the tall grass to relieve himself unconcerned about what awaited him. The young mother stood silently in front of him. His eyes were looking skyward, wearing a pleasurable smile until she plunged her knife deep into his throat and turned the blade dragging it across his jugular. He gurgled with an incoming breath as his hands reached for his spewing blood—his eyes fixed on hers as he sank into the young mother's arms. She laid him down. Warm red liquid soaked the ground each time his heart pumped—until it didn't.

The man who was in the tent came out, adjusted himself, and waved for another to take his turn. They all laughed as he sat down by the fire.

There was too much open space for the young mother to hedge out of the tall grass and take them by surprise, so she slipped around to the back of the make-shift tent. Her bare feet caressed the red dirt—silently. She slowly approached until she saw her friend lying in loathsome violation upon the boxes of her family's stolen possessions—her head dangling, her emerald-green eyes staring into an abyss. The man on top squeezed out her milk and caught it in his mouth—laughing. His eyes were as black as the night.

The young mother stepped into her friend's abyss and stared down at her. The young mother put her finger to her lips warning her friend to be silent. The young mother stood strong above the disgusting man and as he looked up for a moment of relief exposing his tightened throat, his face drained in disbelief at seeing a young woman in front of him. She lashed out, precisely. He, too, collapsed in gasping oblivion.

The young mother pushed the smuggler off of her friend and gathered the dead man's revolver from his crumbled pants that were draped around his ankles. She walked to the front of the tent. And she stepped bravely out without a sound. Raising the revolver clutched with both hands, she caught the last two men off guard. She screamed in a 'lingua franca' dialect, "Cochons! ... Cochons!" The young mother then emptied the revolver rotating one to the other until the hammer *click—clicked*.

From behind the young woman, the battered, emerald-green-eyed friend limped out of the tent, naked. Her face was pale and expressionless as she staggered over to the dead men. The fire crackled. The emerald-green-eyed woman stood above them, hesitating for a moment, before she bent over and picked up one of her rapist's gun. She looked over to the young mother, eyes glassy and forcing a smile, cocked the hammer, put the barrel into her mouth, and pulled the trigger. She fell lifeless to the ground.

The young mother stood in silence and leered at her compassionate friend. The emerald-green-eyed woman's family had been stolen from her and her body had been violated. She had nothing left. The young mother had witnessed this sacrificial devotion before. The young mother dropped her emptied revolver at her feet into the reddening soil. Solemnly, she returned to the tall grass. Her—darkness after midnight.

. . .

Peterson, after the third watch was over, whispered over his radio to Jake and Mac. The two shook off their sleep and immediately readied themselves. The three men gathered as Jake set a small light under his ghillie to illuminate their map. He held out his watch, flicked a button and turned it into a compass. He pointed in a direction as the other two synchronized their watches. A third button would set the GPS, something they did not want to do. Their location would most definitely be compromised, which would send alarms back to the watchful eyes of Command Central.

The three soldiers quickly geared up in their stealth ghillie suits and headed out. Their refractive surface blended well with every nuance of landscape surfaces, unlike the old-style non-refractive material. Jake thought of the movie *Predator* with Arnold Schwarzenegger when the creature ran through the forest and blended into its environment to unexpectedly kill its prey. *Amazing how fiction translated into reality.* He smirked as he blended into the tall grasses.

The men stopped every two hours for five minutes and then, at four hours of travel, they stopped for ten minutes. They could keep this pace all day as long as no one was shooting at them. The three men had paralleled a road for almost ten hours when, in the distance, a smoldering, over-turned flatbed truck lay on its side in the ditch. They scanned the area and looked for any signs of life before approaching cautiously.

Peterson took point, his weapon drawn and scanning as Mac and Jake continued. Through the bullet-riddled windshield, they saw the body of a man. There were droplets of blood on the deck but not enough to be from gun fire. The two women who had been sitting in the back were gone. Their possessions had been picked clean. Jake looked at his watch, it was 1400 hours. He deduced it must have happened in the early morning, as the smoldering tires had a chance to burn out.

The three men headed back into the tall grass scouting the area for signs of life. They found a patch of grass that had been flattened and then followed a set of shallow footprints left in the soft soil until they came upon a campsite of deadly consequence. The men had noticed one man lay in the tall grass with his throat slit. Peterson continued to follow the footprints around behind the tent as Jake and Mac went directly to the center of the camp where they found two dead men, shot, and a naked woman with a gunshot to her head. Peterson walked out of the tent and informed Jake of one dead inside who also had his throat ripped open. Turning over the two dead men, each had been shot three times. The revolver at the entrance of the tent was empty. Taking out their camp shovels, they proceeded to dig a grave for the violated woman draping her body in her torn clothes. Mac fashioned a cross and placed it as her head stone.

They dusted their tracks and took to the tall grass with the thought of the early morning horror.

Mac questioned his teammates. "Do you think it was the young mother who revenged the older woman's abuse?"

"Abuse?" questioned Jake. "How about rape? Indignation? I would put money on it. That flat spot we found was probably were she laid her baby before she stalked them and took revenge." Concerned, he said, "All the more reason to keep a watchful eye for her. She obviously can be a very dangerous young individual."

Mac felt around his neck and shuddered.

"Let's go, soldiers. We have a long way to go and time to make up," mustered Jake, instilling their duty.

"Jake?"

"Yeah, BP."

"We saw a young boy in the cab of the truck when they passed us. There was no sign of him at the crash site."

Mac added, "And, the woman we buried was lactating. Where is her baby?"

"Gentlemen, I know what you are thinking. Our mission is to find Lt. Clark. Copy?"

The two men acknowledged their mission. Jake hated sounding so cold and thought it was possible the young mother had found the other children and taken them with her. He knew though, if they came across a gang of human traffickers, nothing and nobody would be able to stop him from reaping justice. He also knew his men would stand right beside him.

Washington, D.C. - Suburb
Romeo 1530 Hrs.

Terry Tanega, a respected researcher and programmer of SAS, sat duct-taped to his kitchen chair with blood flowing from around his swelling eyes. His mouth puffed from the repeated punches, and his punisher was not giving up. The tormented man had walked into his bungalow, just off from his morning shift into a nightmare of horror.

"Tell me, Mr. Tanega, you little faggot, what I want to know and all this goes away," said the burly man in a thick Scottish accent.

Tanega, spitting blood from each word, managed to say, "I don't know what you want! There is no conspiracy. We are doing our jobs with the parameters we have been given. It all takes time."

"That's not what I want to hear, Mr. Tanega. Millions have been spent on this program and we were promised results. But you have refused to give us any. How I shall proceed, is up to you, but you are trying my delicate patience."

"I can't tell you what I don't know. We are all working hard to locate this man."

"Not hard enough, Tanega."

"No... No!" screamed Tanega.

"Hold still or I might miss and take your whole arm. Is that what you want? Now tell me what I want to know!" The burly man raised the hatchet to the forced, out-stretched hand of Terry Tanega.

"Please!" he screamed. "I don't know anything. I didn't pick these people."

"Okay, Mr. Tanega, we are getting somewhere now. Who picked them?"

"The director and..."

"And who?" taunted the heavily accented man.

"Marsha... Marsha is the head assistant. I don't know anyone else."

"Here's your cell. Call her."

. . .

Marsha, standing by one of the terminals at SAS reached into her pocket to retrieve her vibrating private cell phone. She answered, "Hello?" She could barely understand the person on the other end.

"Marsha?" he said in an unrecognizable voice. *"I'm in trouble."* Her face went pale as she listened. *"No, wait please. No...!"* he pleaded. She heard a THUD! And then a horrifying scream, *"AAAHHHHHH!"*

54

The phone went dead.

Marsha lost her composure and collapsed to the floor. "Marsha!" shrieked one of her teammates as they rushed over to her. They checked her pulse and shook her, tapping her face lightly, she remained still. The director looked up from her paperwork and noticed a huge commotion in the main lab. She opened her door and rushed to the center of it. Before her, lay her friend.

"Marsha!"

"Shall I call for help?" asked a young researcher.

"Wait, go get the first aid kit. Let's see if we can bring her around. Marsha! Marsha, can you hear me?"

The researcher dashed over to the first aid station and pulled a bag from its cabinet. She rushed back to the director with bag in hand and placed it beside the prone Marsha.

"Here, Director," said the researcher.

"Are there any smelling salts?"

"Yes ma'am. Here you are," she said after rifling through the bag.

Samantha opened the bottle and passed it under Marsha's nose.

"Marsha, it's me, Samantha. Can you hear me?"

Marsha choked and moved her head side to side.

"Marsha, are you all right? Speak to me."

Marsha lay there looking straight up. Tears flowed down her cheek.

"Come on. Help me get her to the couch in my office."

A couple of the men helped Marsha to stand and then aided her in negotiating the stairs to the director's office. Her legs were like rubber. They laid her down gently.

"Thank you, Paul and Raj. Let's give her some air. Do you hurt anywhere?" asked Samantha of her friend.

Slightly stuttering she replied, "I... no, I'm not hurt. I am sorry for that display."

"Nonsense, Marsha. What happened?"

Marsha looked around the room.

"Please, everyone. Thank you. I'll handle it from here," instructed the director.

They all returned to their terminals and talked among themselves as the director closed the door.

"What is it, Marsha?"

"It's Terry Tanega. He could barely speak. He was being tortured. I heard a thud and him screaming," cried Marsha.

"What?" The director's face lit up, eyes bright with concern.

"He was warning me and then the phone went dead."

"Hang on." The director went to her desk and picked up the phone and called the emergency line. She instructed the emergency responder to get someone over to Mr. Tanega's place immediately. She returned to Marsha's side on the couch and put her arms around her.

"Why would they hurt Terry? He is a kind man. We have nothing here that would elicit such action as that," stated Marsha, tearfully.

"Shh..." Samantha rocked her friend. Marsha put her arms around Samantha's waist. How could such pain bring such reward?

"Why do you think he was warning you?" asked Samantha.

"I don't know. What's going on, Samantha?"

"I am sure we will have answers soon, my pet."

She didn't want to let go of her friend. She longed for her embrace.

. . .

At 1620 hours, Petty Officer Smyth had received a message from the officer on duty at the back entrance of the Pentagon informing him that a guest was waiting to be signed in. Smyth rang Jack Tomlinson of Nigel Redman's arrival.

"Sir, Nigel just arrived at check-in."

"Good. Go sign him in and bring him to my office," instructed Jack Tomlinson.

"Yes, sir."

Smyth wound his way through the busy hallways and headed towards the 'special guest' check-in entrance. He was only a hundred feet before the check-in when his Blackberry buzzed in his pocket. He was surprised as he looked at the number. *Shit, I will have to retrieve the message, later,* he thought. He quickly put it back into his pocket. It was not private enough to answer it. He arrived at the check-in, nodded at the soldier and then placed his hand on the identification pad. The soldier verified his scan and then he printed out a visitor's badge for the gentleman who was waiting to see Jack Tomlinson.

Nigel Redman had done this a hundred times, and each time, he had a new joke for the soldiers on duty. He always left them with a slight smile on their faces. It was protocol for Tomlinson's assistant to escort Redman to the chief's office, even though the 551 steps to Tomlinson's office could be accomplished by Redman in the pitch of blackness.

"You look a little anxious, my friend," said Redman.

"No. I'm fine. Just a busy day for me," replied Smyth.

Most of the conversations between Tomlinson and Redman were private and the P.O. hadn't been privy to any of the subject matter. Sometimes, he preferred it that way, but at times, he welcomed the chance to be a fly on the wall—which he could arrange. Smyth was more anxious to retrieve his message than to eavesdrop on those two. It was unusual to receive this message over his Blackberry. Smyth dropped Redman off with Tomlinson's secretary in the outer office as protocol dictated and then the P.O. headed to his private cubicle.

Upon arriving, Smyth sat down, opened his Blackberry and retrieved the message. He then plugged it into his computer and synced his Blackberry to confirm his authenticity. Message read: One of ours found dead this morning. An implication of hate crime was left at the scene as cover-up. Intruder <64435#733626*> believed hired by CTA, relay through E-scram.

Holy fuck! exclaimed the P.O. in his mind. He quickly disconnected his Blackberry and set his keyboard singing with an encrypted message to his friend in the field. *I've got to be calm when I go see the director. She has to tell me. What's my excuse—another heads up?*

. . .

The director's desktop phone rang startling the director and causing her and Marsha to release their embrace. Samantha sat back momentarily and looked at Marsha's face and welcoming the return of her natural color. Samantha, feeling somewhat relieved, got up and as she reached for the receiver, wondered if this was another unsolicited call. She answered, questioningly, "Hello?"

"Sam, it's me, Chauncey. I am told Terry's preliminary cause of death appears to be a hate crime. Men's gay

magazines were found in his house with some photos of him at a gay bar. The police are handling it as such, even as gruesome of a crime scene as it is. NCIS has no jurisdiction as Terry was an independent contractor. I'm sorry, Sam."

"Thank you, Admiral. We'll talk soon."

She turned to Marsha, "Could you hear that conversation?"

In a low voice, Marsha questioned, "Hate crime? Gay? No way, Sam. Terry was not gay. He told me just the other week that someone wanted to meet and discuss something of importance with him, but never showed. He didn't realize until he got inside that it was a gay bar. He waited for a half hour and then left."

"They are trying to hide their tracks, Marsha. Why would Terry call you?"

"Sam, there is something I need to tell you..."

The director cut Marsha off, "Later, Marsha." She rolled her eyes around the room as if trying to say something without saying it. "Let's return to our jobs, Marsha. There will be time for all of this after we find the missing soldier," she shared somewhat convincingly.

"Yes, ma'am. We need to push even harder now," said Marsha, as she followed her friend's direction.

"Yes. We'll let the police do their job so we can concentrate on ours." Sam took out a single piece of paper and wrote on it and slid it across her desk to Marsha. It read: "After work, come to my house." The director slid the paper off her desk and into the shedder.

"Yes, ma'am. I will expand our parameters."

"Very good, Marsha."

Marsha straightened her uniform, left the director's office, and returned to her terminal to the comforting well-wishes from her team. She sat down and initiated satellite repositioning.

Samantha picked up the phone and dialed Petty Officer Derrick Smyth's line.

"Hello. Petty Officer Smyth," he answered.

"Petty Officer Smyth, this is Director Jones. I have some sad news. May we meet in the hallway, say in ten minutes?"

"Yes, ma'am. I'll be right there."

Day 3 - Friday

South Sudan, Near Nimule
Charlie 1300 Hrs.

As Lt. Clark picked up his scope, he noticed on the far side of approaching rapids, what appeared to be, a brickyard factory before the river took a hard right, and adjacent to that a bridge, with a constant flow of traffic. He decided to ditch the punt that most likely would not have held up to the rapids anyways. This was a good sign, he thought. He was getting closer to a town. There were many stick and reed huts spotting the river's banks as well, with indigenous men fishing off the sandbars. He figured they were merely following in their ancestors footsteps. They didn't look like typical South Sudanese.

Navigating on foot through the brush and rock formations, he came upon a road sign indicating the town of Nimule, South Sudan. *Ah,* he thought, *last town before Uganda.* He stayed out of sight as he crept along past the UN compound occupied with thousands of tents for the IDP's. Clark noticed while some families were talking among themselves, a dozen white-coated technicians with clipboard in hand were interviewing family by family. *A horrible situation.* As he moved closer to the border, he observed two smashed buses at the side of the roadway, set nose-to-nose as monuments with many little stations of crosses and dried flowers propped up against them. *No doubt a testament to be careful,* he thought.

The roadway south was unpaved but looked like it had been recently graded and waiting for asphalt. Clark spotted huge rolls of fiber-optic cable sitting idly by. He assumed farther south he would be able to get a good phone connection with what he had just seen. He needed to dump the khakis and find something more suitable to wear. His backpack was not a U.S. Military issue so it blended in, which was in his favor.

Idle thought momentarily flooded Clark's mind as he propped himself up amongst the rocks within sight distance of a haberdasher's store. *Were his dune-buggy escorts trying to tell me something? But why not just talk to me? Possibly, they felt if they did say something, it would compromise orders and by remaining silent, I would suspect a betrayal. Maybe those guys saved my life.* A thought he would embellish on later. That night, however, his plan was to rid himself of his camos. This was a busy road for civilians as well as commerce. He had witnessed all

61

nationalities traversing up and down. This was his chance to integrate, maybe as a road engineer.

. . .

Jake and his team were making good time as they blended in with the landscape and paralleled the roadway. But all of a sudden, Jake stopped. The other two men instinctively took up positions.

"What is it?" softly asked Mac over his 'PRS" (low-range personal radio service) scanning the area as he watched a convoy of UN trucks filled with IDP's drive by.

"Sorry, just a thought. What if the lieutenant ran into trouble? It could cost him time and to maneuver slower than our pace. Remember, we were situated a lot farther south than he was. He might be behind us."

"What do you want to do?" asked BP.

"Fuck, I hate second-guessing," stated Jake. *"Let's head over to where the Nile crosses the road south of Palenga, Uganda. We will be at a higher elevation so we will be able to sight both the road and the Nile through our binoculars. Sorry guys."*

"Jake, it's okay. Don't you think we are having the same thoughts? It's important to all of us to find the lieutenant. He's a man I want beside me, not behind me or in front of me," remarked BP with a slight hint of humor.

"Mac, are you sure they can't monitor our frequency?"

"Not that they can't, they aren't interested in hearing English. As soon as their scanners pick up English, they move to another channel. I have ours set to just below the UN channels, so even if they do, they will think it's cross-talk and that we are part of the UN contingent," reassured Mac.

"Well done, my friend. Let's move out."

. . .

The young mother felt the rumble through the red dirt roadbed. She turned around and saw a cloud of dust heading her way. Instinctively, she tucked her baby from sight as she watched the dust cloud increase and felt the rumblings growing stronger. She noticed on the high-tarped stack bed, the white UN letters stood out clearly. One rambled past before she got completely off of the roadway. Then another swished by. She turned to protect her face from the suffocating dust. A third came to a screeching stop—the driver swerved. His eyes were affixed on the young girl, at first through his front windshield and then in his side mirror.

She stood on the side of the roadway covered in red dust. Coming to a dead stop, he relaxed his grip on the steering wheel and made a sign of the cross. Screams of annoyance mixed with terror engulfed its back passengers. A UN volunteer peered out of the back through the settling dust to the sight of a young woman standing covered in red grit with a baby in her arms. She motioned for the girl to climb aboard.

"Sweet child, what are you doing out here by yourself? Com' on get inside," she demanded.

With a smile, the young mother accepted. She stumped her feet, shook her wrap, and hoisted her baby to the open arms of the volunteer. She climbed into the back of the already full truck. They continued on to Gulu, Uganda.

Pentagon

Romeo 1630 Hrs.

Nigel took a seat in Tomlinson's outer office as P.O. Smyth took leave. He seemed anxious, thought Redman.

"Sir, Nigel Redman is here to see you," announced the secretary.

"Send him in, Patty."

The double insulated door opened and in stepped Nigel. He closed the door securely behind him.

"Well?" asked Jack Tomlinson as he turned from admiring the steeds of historical generals.

"Nothing. He either was well trained or knew nothing."

"Is that your professional opinion or your gut feeling?"

"He endured a lot of pain. He gave up Marsha Atworth as a prime candidate."

"You think? He gave you nothing we don't already know. The director and Atworth have been partners on several joint programs. Of course, he said her. It's an obvious fact."

"Well then... he was well trained," restated Redman.

"Jesus fucking Christ... are you all stand-up comedians? He blew you off! He knew you wouldn't spare him. Yes, I would say definitely well trained, but by who?"

Re-thinking his next move, Tomlinson said, "I need you to go to the Embassy in Juba. Sniff around. Talk to those two idiots we have on ice and watch out for ISIS. I hear they have a faction growing down there. See if anyone made contact with the shooter beforehand and find out who our next bitch is?"

"Should I make contact with Dimitri?"

"Hell, no! He's in the field anyway. Stay away from him, understand? What happened between you two anyways?" Jack walked over to behind his desk and sat down. Nigel stayed standing.

"A long story."

"Fine, I don't have time for bedtime stories. Go through regular channels... shouldn't be a problem. You are there on CTA's dime. I'll have Patty draw up a dossier for you."

"Yes, sir."

"Nigel. Try and keep the body count down, will ya'?"

Nigel smiled. He left Tomlinson sitting with cathedral hands, fingers tapping index to index while his elbows rested on his desk, contriving.

. . .

Marsha sat in her car and rummaged through her purse looking for her cell phone. She paused, trying to remember what she had done with it and the last time she used it. She had received Terry's call and then she blacked out. *My phone must have slid under a terminal,* she thought. As she was about to open her door to go back and retrieve it, a knuckle tapped on her window.

She looked up startled and then rolled down her window.

"Good day, lass. We seem to have aligning stars as I catch you again at your car as I pass by. My name is Nigel Redman," he said extending his strong hand to meet hers. "And you are?"

Marsha looked up into his steal-blue eyes and said, "Marsha."

"Marsha... is there more or are you a one-name person like that woman singer...?" He stumbled for a name.

"Madonna?" she said.

"Yes, quite right. Madonna," smiled Redman.

"Atworth... Marsha Atworth," she informed, hesitantly.

"My pleasure, Miss Atworth. Maybe some time you can take a drink with me?" he said in his thick Scottish brogue.

"Mr. Redman, you presume that I do drink and that I am single."

Redman laughed still holding onto her hand, "Well then, Lass, please correct me if I assumed wrong."

"You are a charmer, Mr. Redman. No, you are right on both assumptions. Perhaps one day when those stars align again, but unfortunately, today I have a previous engagement," replied Marsha politely.

"Well then, Miss Atworth, maybe when I get back into town, we can gaze upon the stars together. Have a good evening, missy."

Marsha watched Redman through her rearview mirror as he walked behind her car and disappeared into the sea of vehicles in the secured lot. She had kept Samantha waiting long enough, so she decided to look for her phone the following day. She needed to go home first to change and freshen up. It had been some time since she had been at Sam's house. She remembered—it was for a fourth of July party for all the team members from their previous project. *What shall I wear?* She looked into her rearview mirror once more, and then, took down her bun and shook out her long wavy brown strands. She started her car and left the parking lot.

"Marsha Atworth, you say lass..."

. . .

Meeting in the hallway, although not as private as what Samantha wanted, felt it would be best to keep this new revelation to as few as possible. She didn't want to attract undue attention or impact the others on her team. Derrick came up the stairs and turned down the hall. Ahead he saw Samantha leaning against the main door to SAS.

"Thank you for meeting me, Derrick." In a whisper, Samantha said, "I feel like someone is watching me, or at least listening to me. Do you know how or know of someone who can test my office for any device?"

"Yes, of course, Sam. I'll set up a sweep tonight as an 'RMS'. You are over-due anyways."

"What's a 'RMS'?"

"Routine Maintenance Service. We don't say sweep but it is part of the program. All the offices routinely go through it," informed Derrick.

"It won't raise eyebrows?"

"No, not at all."

"How will they get in past our security?"

"Someone will call and then whoever is on duty will have to let them in. We don't have passwords to anyone's offices."

"Yes, about the person in charge." Samantha lowered her eyes and waited as two conservatively civilian-dressed ladies, one carrying a sealed cardboard box and the other a briefcase, walked by—heels clacking. Samantha raised her eyes and watched the two ladies as they turned right into Jack's office. They looked like a lawyer and her assistant. She continued. "Terry Tanega was found dead at his house this afternoon."

"Terry! Oh my God!"

"They say it was a hate crime because he was gay."

"Gay? Terry? No ma'am, not Terry. He was quiet, but not gay. He has a fiancé in Japan. I know she was planning a visit when this project was over," related the petty officer.

"I didn't know. Well, I should say, I don't remember that from the interview. Marsha handled most of them. I must have skimmed over his personal information when approving his qualifications. Maybe that is why he made that call to her?"

"Terry called Marsha, ma'am?"

"Yes. I imagine before... before he was killed. I'm sorry for laying this on you, Derrick. I have to go."

"Ma'am, don't worry, I will take care of things for you."

"Again, thank you, Derrick. I have very few who I can trust."

"Oh... Ma'am, where is Miss Atworth now?"

Samantha leaned into Derrick and whispered, "Coming over to my place."

"Sam, let me send a couple of agents over to your house. At least for the next couple of days, just to be on the safe side."

The Director looked at Derrick with inquisitive eyes. *How does a petty officer have such clearance and resources?* She kept her questions to herself and added, "If you believe it is necessary, I will allow it. But they must be discreet."

"Yes, ma'am. I'll look after it," he said reassuring her.

Northern Kenya

Charlie 1330 Hrs.

It was slow going as Colonel Dimitri and his team crisscrossed the landscape toward safer grounds in northern Kenya. They had encountered many IDP's (internally displaced people) who were flooding the borders to take refuge wherever they could. The many UN camps Dimitri's team saw along the way were overcrowded, had poor sanitation, and lacked a continual supply of food. The threat of savage retaliation by either warring party was real and ongoing.

Colonel Dimitri and his team had to be discreet in their movement even with their stealth camouflage. If spotted, however, their appearance might be viewed as a mirage by some, because most refugees were suffering from malnutrition, which impaired their vision. Colonel Dimitri hated to think that the IDP's suffering was his salvation. The money his government was spending to find this operative could have fed a lot of these people. Dimitri had to keep telling himself he was a soldier and although he made no direct misconduct, others might not see it that way. Dimitri was following protocol and unless they had received orders contrary, they were on the logical path. Just like an American football game, someone in the booth was calling the shots even if the quarterback had a different vision on the ground.

Colonel Dimitri had never met the Director of SAS, personally, but had seen her at a fundraising event for her well-received program. The 'PAG' project was enabled to aid in the rescue of lost hikers, skiers, journalists, boaters and mariners, and even army personnel who had gone missing. Another tier to the project was for anyone who thought they could be at risk or just for reassurance, could get their aura spectral-gammed, which was then stored in the SAS computers. An interesting concept, Dimitri thought at the time. It had many humanitarian applications. Of course, there was always someone who thought of a more military utilization. And now, he was living that nightmare.

Eyes were continually on them, from the sky and the ground. In Dimitri's opinion, his team was the best, as each person had been hand-picked for their special talents. He had chosen wisely because not all situations were written in a playbook. His team had to have the ability to improvise. There were no pre-games to work out the bugs.

Dimitri's Corporal Jacobs was his spy in the sky, so to speak. He handled the communications between command and his team. And whoever was his contact in Virginia, he knew Jacobs trusted them. When they received the encoded 'trouble' message, it gave them enough time to re-organize, and Jacobs, assured a seamless response to command. Lt. Clark's reaction was, at the time, undetermined, especially slapped with no support. The lieutenant had, however, performed as Dimitri hoped and he looked forward to the day when a bottle of Vodka would be shared between them. A man with Lt. Clark's observational awareness would be welcomed on his team. This type of man could save lives. Dimitri hadn't questioned Jake's input but hoped the lieutenant would give his man a chance to explain the situation. Dimitri truly believed if two men confronted each other but held the same belief, the outcome would be a positive one. He had to believe this would happen.

A ping from their point scout, Andrews, startled the Colonel and warned the team of approaching militants. They immediately stopped. Dimitri ordered high alert—they sat and waited. Two pickups, the second one with a mounted .50 caliber machine gun followed by a flatbed truck with troops in the back, slowed. The men all jumped out except the driver of the first pickup. They stood to the side of the road, twelve men on Dimitri's side and eight men on the opposite side. They started to relieve themselves. In the back of the staked flatbed, four young girls were hooded and bound with ropes.

A shiver engulfed the Colonel. He had seen too much mistreatment in the Ukraine and Bosnia to let this pass. He tapped one short and two long pings (W — meaning wait) across their 'PRS'. Andrews, who was on the far side of the road, confirmed eight men on his side. Reynolds pinged in and verified twelve men on his side. Colonel Dimitri pinged two long and one short (G — meaning GO). His men instinctively dispersed among the mirage of the brush.

A man with a red beret stood an arm's distance from Andrews. He had a machete hung from one side of his belt and a holstered 44 Magnum with white pearl handles on the other. As the red-beret man turned to talk to one of his men, his stream of piss followed and splashed on Andrews' stealth poncho. The sound was different than the plants— more hollow. The eyes of the militant leader grew wider and whiter as he looked down suspiciously.

Andrews sprang from his crouched position, dug his knife deep into the man's chest, and swung with his drawn 9mm, and took out the driver who sat in the first pickup truck. The Colonel took out the man who jumped onto the second pickup to operate the machine gun, while Reynolds and his team released a burst of quiet fire disabling the rest. Within seconds the precise maneuver was over without one shot being delivered from the un-muzzled guns of the militia-dressed traffickers.

Reynolds jumped into the back of the flatbed and removed the hoods from the four young girls. Their eyes were bruised and their lips were split from apparent abuse.

"Are you all right?" he asked.

"We will be," said a scared, teary-eyed girl, thankful.

"Thank you!" cried another.

Reynolds untied the girls as the rest of his team remained hidden and alert. It was their protocol. As long as there was no immediate danger of lost life, only one man made contact.

"Can any one of you drive?"

"I can," stated one of the girls.

"Is it safe from the direction you came?"

"They raided our little family camp," one cried. "They killed everyone, except us four."

"I'm so sorry, little one. Is there anyone you can go to?"

"Just back to the UN camp in Apoka... but there are so many people," said the older one who could drive.

"Can we go with you?" sobbed the young one as she hugged Reynolds tightly.

Reynolds returned her hug and said, "I am so sorry, little one, but I have to go on by myself. Let me help you turn the pickup around."

The young girl did not want to let go. "Come, Manisha. We are your family now," stated the older girl. She touched the young girl's arm. Slowly the teary-eyed girl let go of Reynolds and accepted the hand of her new sister.

Reynolds jumped out of the flatbed and paused a moment to regain his composure. Proceeding to the front pickup, he swung open the driver's door, grabbed onto the dead driver and threw him out into the gully of the road. Reynolds' jaw was tight and he was trembling with heartache as he turned the truck around—stones slashing at the inner wheel wells.

Reynolds stepped out of the cab, returned to the back of the stack bed, and helped the girls down. "Okay, my brave little girls..." He handed them a couple of rifles and a machete as they stepped inside the bloodied truck. "Please, be careful and get to a UN camp. Please do not say anything about meeting me. Okay?"

"God be with you, kind sir," stated the older girl. She shifted the lever into first gear, released the clutch, and jerked the truck ahead in bunny hops. She then pressed in the clutch again, and shifted into second gear, and chugged along until it built up power. Reynolds stood and watched them disappear in the dust.

Dimitri's team came out from hiding. Nothing was said—nothing needed to be said. Colonel Dimitri put his hand on Reynolds' shoulder with a 'proud of you' grip.

Bodies were dispersed into the undergrowth, trucks were pulled into the ditch, and distributor caps and wiring were ripped out. Then they dismantled the firing pin of the 50 caliber as well as the other assortment of rifles and AK-47's. Dimitri and his team left the scene in silence, but each a little prouder of being able to have, hopefully, saved the lives of four young girls.

. . .

Lt. Clark didn't know if it was a mandated curfew or a safety issue as to why the store clerk closed at dusk. But as the orange glow of the sun cast long shadows on the dirt-road town, commerce concluded. Clark waited until darkness fell before he broke the weak lock off the rear door of the closed shop. On the street side of the building, an outside porch lamp barely lit the inside as he searched for pants, shirts and a ball cap. He also picked up a small camp shovel, since he had discarded his in the foxhole, a flashlight with extra batteries, and a notebook. Clark looked for a phone but only cheap Chinese radios lay in plain sight. He didn't dare look through the glass cases that faced the large glass display windows. There would be another occasion, he was certain. Clark had grabbed what he immediately needed. If he took too much at one time, it could send off the wrong signals.

Clark replaced the broken lock so as not to look so obvious of a break-in. He quickly returned to his hiding spot, dug a hole and buried his khakis. His choice of clothes was limited but serviceable. He couldn't hide the fact he was white, but as he had seen in the short time he had been hiding out, other white men had been milling around the large earthmovers with dockets in hand. All he needed now was a company truck.

Clark pulled the ball cap over his forehead, swung the backpack over his shoulder, and headed south paralleling the roadway at a safe distance.

. . .

It was midnight by the time Colonel Dimitri decided they had put enough distance between them and the militants' convoy. They stopped and all took a much-needed stretch. Reynolds and his men set camp and secured the perimeter. Jacobs had received a ping on his E-scram, which he immediately retrieved. It was not good news.

He went to the Colonel. "Sir?"

"Yes, Jacobs."

"An E-scram, sir. Not good," he relayed.

"What is it?"

"One of ours has been compromised."

"Do we know who?"

"Not in transmission, sir. But intruder is (6-mno), (4-ghi), (4-ghi), (3-def), (5-jkl), hmm... Nigel..."

"Nigel Redman?" flared the Colonel.

"One second, sir... hmm yes, that's what I get."

"Motherfucker! I should have taken that Scot out in Donets'k twenty years ago when I had the chance," angrily stated the Colonel.

"You know him, sir?"

"Yes. All too well." The Colonel felt his leg. "He thinks he is a ladies man, but he would slit their throat if they didn't respond to his funnyman humor. He is a real asshole... and ruthless. He's looking for answers, and probably us, and Lt. Clark. Are we still secure with home base?"

"Yes, sir."

"We can't have Redman interfere any longer. Send a message to your contact: TERMINATE."

"Yes, sir."

"Damn it. I was hoping one day, it would be my pleasure."

The Colonel looked off into the dark night as his haunting memories flashed in his mind like it was yesterday.

Washington

Romeo 1800 Hrs.

Marsha pulled into her driveway, set the parking brake, and almost forgot to shut off the engine. She had a lot on her mind and being invited over to Samantha's house had her excited but a little confused. She ran to her door and as she was about to put the key into the lock, the door swung open on its own. She hesitated before walking in—listening. It had not been a good day for her co-workers returning home from work.

Marsha pushed the door ever so slowly. Even in the dim light of the room, she could see the horrific mess. Carefully, she stepped in farther, poised and ready as she inspected the damage. Everything had been overturned, including her couch with its bottom fabric ripped open. Drawers were emptied and turned upside down, shades from her lamps lay on the floor, and her laptop was missing. Marsha picked up a screwdriver off of the kitchen floor and walked into her bedroom. Marsha's clothes closet was barren except for a few empty hangars and the rest of her clothes strewn on the floor. She remained calm as she scoured the rest of the room.

Empty luggage was lying on her bed with the lining slashed and her framed pictures had all the backs removed. Marsha knew what *they* were looking for. After checking all the rooms for the possible perpetrator, Marsha was satisfied, whoever it was, had long disappeared. Stepping towards the bathroom and with a screwdriver in hand, Marsha removed the built-in medicine cabinet and carefully unattached a rear wire. She reached inside between the 2x6 studs and pulled out two by one gallon-sized bags. She carefully replaced the cabinet. Marsha looked around through the mess for her backpack. Gathering some clothes, she placed them and the two by one gallon-sized bags into the pack. She threw on a pair of khaki shorts and a white tank top.

Marsha didn't dare call Samantha from her house phone. Whoever did this probably had her phone tapped and hanging around was not an option. Someone still might return for her.

Closing the door behind her, and before she got into her car, Marsha scanned her street to see if there were any unusual cars or SUV's parked nearby. Confident nothing looked out of place; she slid into her car and left at a normal speed. She didn't want to attract any undue attention. There were plenty of straight roads were Marsha could watch for anyone tailing her and there were plenty of streets where she could lose them. In her mind, Marsha knew, whoever did this, must be the same person who killed Terry—that was a certainty. And if they knew her address, they knew Samantha's as well.

Once on the freeway, she left her tranquil driving behind her. Marsha weaved through the traffic like the Indy 500, swerving over from the outer lane to an off-ramp jetting past blaring horns and screeching brakes. At the end of the ramp, she looked in her rearview mirror. No one followed. When the light turned green, she went straight through and back onto the expressway. After 20 minutes of playing cat-and-mouse, Marsha landed at Samantha's with a thought on her mind: *I need to tell her.* She looked at her black-faced military watch and clicked a button. She quickly returned it back from Charlie time to Romeo time.

Samantha had been pacing up and down and frantically calling Marsha but every time, the phone went to voice mail. "Where is she?"

Just then Samantha heard a car pull into her driveway. She looked out the window and saw Marsha's little blue Miata. Marsha stepped out and threw her backpack over her shoulders, the straps stretching the white T-top's jersey material tight, which emphasized Marsha's well-toned body. Samantha had forgotten how beautiful her friend's hair was when she let it down. And Samantha noticed Marsha's shapely figure.

Samantha rushed to the front door and swung it open. Her friend had barely stepped in before Samantha had her arms around Marsha in a hearty embrace.

"Oh my God, I was so worried about you. I tried calling but kept getting your voice mail."

Marsha thought she would return Samantha's weakened moment and tenderly returned her hug.

"I must have dropped my cell phone in the lab," she whispered in Samantha's ear. "I am so sorry to have worried you."

"That's okay," Samantha assured, warmly, "...you are here now." Samantha felt relieved as she held her friend and stroked her long wavy hair.

There seemed to be a mutual hesitation in their release as each shared this bonding moment. Marsha was noticeably aroused by this unsolicited endearment by Samantha.

"Phew, I think I might need a cold glass of water," remarked Marsha slightly embarrassed as she cupped her hands over her protruding nipples.

"No, don't," insisted Samantha as she grabbed Marsha's hand and led her into the kitchen. Marsha was confused and was not sure what to think.

Samantha went to the fridge, pulled out a Brita filter jug and poured Marsha a glass of water. "Ice?"

"Yes, please, Sam."

Samantha still dressed in her Army uniform said, "Come, talk with me while I change into something more comfortable."

Marsha momentarily detoured to lock Samantha's front door. She then stepped into Sam's bedroom while Samantha was in the bathroom with the door partially open. Marsha sat down on Sam's bed—the water was running.

"My house was ransacked when I got home today," she told Samantha over the noise of the water rushing into the tub.

"What! Why?" shouted Sam.

"Sam, I need to tell you something, but it cannot go any further than you."

Samantha came to the bathroom door, naked. "It's okay. I believe I already know. Come, take a bath with me."

Marsha was stunned. She could feel her throat gulp and hoped it wasn't too noticeable. Marsha felt like those pervs at a strip club, eyes wide open ogling the girls' bodies. Sam was beautiful. Samantha held out her hand, and with an inviting smile, waited for her friend. Marsha nervously stood and walked over. Sam slowly removed her friend's tank top over her head, unbuckled her shorts and let them fall to the floor. Marsha was as naked as she was. Sam tenderly ran her hands over Marsha's erect nipples and down her flat stomach to her muscular thighs. Samantha escorted her friend to the scented, bubbled tub. They stepped in.

The warm bath ended with them exploring in each other's arms, cuddling on Samantha's bed. Affectionately, she declared to Marsha, "I never thought at forty-two years old, I could feel comfort in another woman's arms. You've opened my eyes to something I have imagined but never thought conceivable. Your body is so smooth, it just feels right."

"I have known about my interest in a woman's touch for as long as I can remember. I have had a few relationships in college, but not since I joined the Navy."

Samantha turned to face Marsha. "I didn't know what to expect. I wasn't sure if you had any inclination as you had never approached me."

"I wasn't sure you were receptive to even going there. You are, after all, my superior officer and after your... Well, after the thing with Admiral Stone, I thought for sure I would have you only in my dreams, not lying here in my arms."

Marsha, hesitated in changing the subject or to leave Samantha's side, but she noticed the time on Sam's clock-radio read 2230 Hrs. Her sense of duty was biting at her. She had to interrupt their soiree.

"Samantha, I need to go to Terry's house... tonight."

"Why? It feels so nice just being here with you, in your arms."

"Listen, I have fantasized about this longer than you can imagine. I won't be long, but it is something I must do," shared Martha.

"Okay, I'll get dressed and go with you."

"No! I mean... it is not necessary. I'll be in and out in a flash. Just need to see if Terry left me anything."

"What would Terry leave you?"

"Samantha, I... I have been trying to tell you something..."

Samantha interrupted Marsha, "Look, if you are in any trouble, or if it has something to do with our program, I want to help. I am not as frail as you might believe. Besides, Lieutenant, I still out-rank you in the real world," smiled Samantha.

"Ma'am, I would feel more comfortable if you did not."

"I understand. Now, let's get dressed," instructed the director.

Day 4 - Saturday

Uganda

Charlie 0100 Hrs.

Heavy earthmovers, compactors, mechanical shovels, dump, and pickup trucks were all staggered between trailers and camp buildings along the newly graded roadway, just south of Atiak, Uganda. Huge concrete pipes and box culverts lay in fenced yards with razor-wire affixed to the top. Generators running halogen lights, kept the storage yards lit and a few well-placed safety lights ran from building to building. S&W logos were plastered on everything—even the yellow flashing safety stands and orange barrel cones. Lt. Clark decided this was his chance to secure a truck.

He eyed the under-construction roadway in both directions—shadows lurked from behind equipment without any movement. Feeling safe, he dashed across the roadway to the side of one of the pickups that lined the fence. He tried its doors—locked. The first three pickups were all locked but on his fourth attempt the handle lifted all the way up and within a split second, he was in. He reached around the steering column, grabbed the wire loom and pulled the wires from under the dash. Clark used his talents of his past life and quickly stripped the power wire going to the key and re-attached it to the other main power cable. He then pulled the two brown starter wires from the panel and sparked them together. The truck started. He quietly pulled out of the parking area and headed south once again.

Inside the truck, Clark noticed a white hard hat. *That might come in handy.* He relaxed as he drove through the night. *Much easier than floating upriver*. He hoped his S&W disguise would carry him through roadblocks, if he came across them, otherwise his path was secured.

. . .

The young mother stepped out of the back of the crowded UN truck with the rest of the IDPs and entered one of the many compounds that were located just on the outskirts of Gulu, Uganda. The food they offered was nourishment to her body, but she knew this was not a permanent stay. For tonight, at the hour it was, she was thankful. The UN volunteer had been very pleasant to them all and reassured them of their safety at the camp. Safety in numbers was not always the case as the young mother knew too well. Without weapons or the men to use them, this compound filled mostly with women and children was as much at risk as walking down the road. Before the pregnant young girl was expunged from her village, she had learned of three hundred schoolgirls who were captured from their village's schoolhouse and remained missing to this day as far as she knew. So much for safety in numbers without weapons.

The young mother's baby was almost one year old, which meant she had been on the road for twenty months. *Almost two years,* she thought, and life was not showing any signs of improving. In fact, more people were now running for their lives and traffickers were making money by preying on the abandoned mothers while their husbands either joined the militia or were killed. Their rich farmland had all gone to seed as there was no one to take care of it. The young mother couldn't make any sense of it. Her dreams of becoming a teacher lessened with each dusty step she took. Her only joy was the smile she got from her little baby. Her only reason for remaining strong was to protect her little one and to bring justice to all who had suffered so inhumanely.

. . .

On the horizon, Clark saw a halo of dim lights and as he swooshed past a sign, it read: Gulu 40 km. He felt the excitement stirring in his body with the anticipation of locating a cell phone. He had people who could help him; at least, that's what they had promised him in the past.

Clark figured it would take him about forty-five minutes to go the 40 km, which was about double the time it would take on an American highway. Even though the roadway was freshly graded, there was still a lot to look out for. There weren't any signs posted indicating 'sharp turn' or 'crossing animals' or even 'bump ahead', which there were still plenty.

The lights of Gulu were getting closer and brighter. "It won't be long now," Clark said out loud. And as the words came out of his mouth, he slammed on the brakes. Just ahead were two trucks, nose to nose, with forty-five-gallon barrels set at each side, blazing with fire. The men standing there on each side had guns.

Clark slowly proceeded forward. He had no other choice. One man, who was wearing a green beret, approached his driver-side window, while another went to the other side. Clark drew his backpack closer and with the flap opened, he slipped his hand inside.

Stopping, Clark rolled down the window to the gesture of the soldier.

"You are out late," stated the man who wore a green embossed beret.

"Yes. I have an early meeting at headquarters in Gulu," said Clark.

"You have papers?"

"My papers? Yes, my papers." He looked around like a lost puppy. "I'm sorry. I got up so early I must have forgotten them at my trailer in Atiak."

"What are you?"

"An engineer," replied Clark.

"You're not an accountant to bring us money to pay for the road you are putting through the middle of our village?"

"Sorry, but I have nothing to do with that arrangement. I make sure your road is safe. I don't design it or indicate its path. I just make sure the contractor is using the right equipment and installing the correct pipes."

"Until we get paid, this section is closed," said the gun-toting man.

"But, I have a meeting I must attend. How shall I pass to Gulu?"

"Go around." He pointed to the grass and shrub treed outback.

Lt. Clark looked at the landscape and knew very well, if he took the path proposed by the gun-toting man, Gulu lay hours away. He smiled at the man and nodded. He reversed his truck to clear the burning barrels and then went forward and took the alternative path as instructed. Clark was leery; this would be a good spot to get ambushed. His truck rolled and heaved over the bumpy terrain. A cart path at best, maybe even a goat trail. As his headlights illuminated the thatch-roofed brick huts in the pitch blackness, they seemed to spring up in front of him like cardboard targets at a shooting range. He drove through their backyards and tried to follow the path. The wet season had only ended a few weeks prior; the dirt path was still soft and slippery. He estimated his time for arrival to Gulu before daybreak was unrealistic. Perhaps it quadrupled at his current pace.

The lit barrels that lined the roadway of the small village gave Clark a reference point as he traversed through the darkness. If he eased so slightly towards them as he passed the village, he thought, without serious detection the graded road would again be his.

A dog, lit by Clark's headlights, stretched and let out a bothersome bark as he passed. "Shut up, you fucking dog!" shouted someone from inside a hut. The dog turned to the hut and yawned before it flopped back down. Clark slowly moved closer to the roadway. He sympathized with the gun-toting man at the first blockade. *With all the wide open space, why had they graded so close to the village's huts? No wonder they were pissed off.* His thoughts continued, *Some unknown engineer probably told the government if the road was straight, it would cost less to build, without any consideration for the people who lived along its path. And, why this town? The rest of the road even skirted around trees.*

Eminent domain, he scoffed. *That's what they call it back home. And it sure pissed off a lot of people when they built the Toronto Expressways. Why should it be any different here? Maybe the chief of the village pissed someone off?*

Clark felt a new compassion for the people who were trying to get paid for what they had lost. He pointed his truck back down the bumpy road, through back yards, slid sideways in the slick mud potholes, and bounced like a child in a fun house. He speculated he could walk faster than what he was traversing by driving, but it was his cover—and so far, it had worked.

MAP OF SOUTH SUDAN, UGANDA, AND KENYA

Google Maps ©

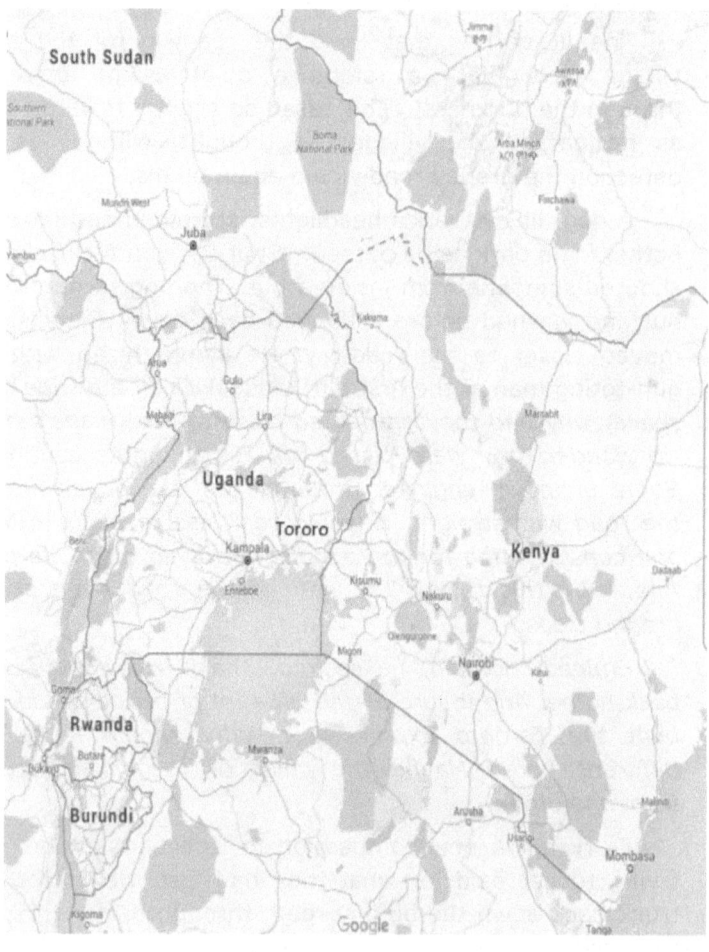

Uganda – UN Camp

Charlie 0530 Hrs.

The young mother woke early to the sound of the wind on the grasslands. She walked over to the UN camp's chain-link fence, placed her fingers through the twisted wire pattern, and gazed outward. She barely got any sleep with the constant coughing and moaning from the small children camped around her. The young mother felt trapped, corralled, defenseless, and vulnerable to the whims of the militants' oppression as they swept in and out at will. *A candy basket*, she thought, *"...nicely wrapped for them to divide up and share to the highest bidder."* She had heard virgins were sold to the leaders as wives and the older women were sold for less than 10 U.S. dollars, or just killed.

The young mother looked back over her shoulder as others started to stir. *How could God let this happen?* She looked at the desolation in the faces of the women. *One more day,* she thought, and then on her own again. She needed to get her bearings.

The troubled northern Ugandan town of Gulu had a long history of turmoil and strife from the warring LRA (Lord's Resistance Army). They terrorized the region for over two decades and were direct contributors to thousands of kidnappings and outright murder. The concrete walls of downtown buildings still displayed the chipped-away bullet holes. Burned-out buildings now housed patched-together families. Pieces of tin roughly supported with branches made temporary roofs. The future was bleak as the women talked among their cadre.

A UN representative tried to uplift their spirits as she told them of the much-needed field hands. Their combined labor could be instrumental in rebuilding their small community's commerce. The representative told the women about the shortage of food in South Sudan, which had caused a need for their direct exports going to feed the starving who remained in their country. Storekeepers needed help and new stores needed to be opened.

The young mother looked around at the women who sat with their children with their hands out. Promises had been made to them before, and yet, here they sat with not enough money between them to open a can of soup. The young mother decided she would walk to town that day and see for herself. She would love to settle down but if everyone else was struggling, what chance would she have?

. . .

Lt. Clark had arrived in Gulu just before dawn broke as he had anticipated. He ditched the pickup a few miles back and took up residence at one of the many abandoned buildings on the perimeter of town. The two-story concrete building had been gutted and was void of doors and windows with barely a roof. There was a counter with broken shelves behind it and a few busted chairs on the perimeter of the main floor.

In the middle of the floor, old tires and the remains of a burnt-out fire with melted glass and rusted cans mingled with the ashes. Off the main room was what he thought to be the warehouse. As he inspected it, he found a deep hole in the concrete floor—he assumed from an RPG. A set of concrete stairs led to an upper floor. He cautiously went up the steps to the second floor where he found nothing but more crap. It looked out; however, above the one-story neighboring buildings and had a clear view of the town's clock tower. Through one of the upstairs' windows on the opposite side, he saw cell towers with power lines draping from pole-to-pole stretched throughout the community.

One of the upstairs' rooms had a steel bedframe minus its mattress—it called Clark's name. *At least I will be off the filthy floor and in a position where I will be able to hear if someone comes up the stairs.* He laid his weary bones down for a quick nap.

Later, he thought, *I will head to the center of town and somehow barter for a cell phone.* His eyes closed.

Washington - Friday Night
Romeo 2345 Hrs.

The two women, Samantha Jones and Marsha Atworth, after skirting Derrick's security team, pulled up into the back lane, a short distance down from Terry Tanega's house. Neighborhood dogs instinctively barked as the crash of a trash can piqued their interest. The two women quietly stepped out of their vehicle wearing black dungarees, black pullovers and black hooded masks. Their movement was stealth-like, blending into the shadows as they headed towards Tanega's house. They bent under the police yellow crime scene tape and proceeded to the back door. Marsha carefully opened the back screen, anticipating a squeak. She pulled out a steel-wedged bar, placed it in the door jamb, and gave it a quick pry. It popped and Marsha pushed the creaking door open. They entered, unnoticed. Samantha closed the door behind them.

The kitchen was a foray of dried splattered blood, a chalked outline on the floor, and a wooden table marked with more chalk circles drawn around a deep groove. They couldn't help it; they paused and imagined the horrific scene that must have taken place. Marsha tugged on Samantha's arm so her friend would not fixate on what she saw. A streetlight offered the only illumination streaming through a partial depression in the large bay-window curtains. Ornate Japanese figurines were well placed throughout the living room. A decorative, six-foot-tall, three-panel screen acted as a barrier as one entered through the front door. The rest of the house looked like a bomb went off. The same M.O. as Marsha's house with the exception of painted slurs on the walls.

Marsha took out a small flashlight and focused its dedicated beam to the floor. They stepped gingerly towards the bathroom. The linen closet had been emptied with towels, sheets and blankets strewn everywhere. Marsha led the way focusing on where they stepped. Broken glass lay on the old black and white square tiles next to the tub, while shattered glass from the medicine cabinet partially filled the vanity sink.

Marsha motioned to Samantha to hold her light while she unscrewed the medicine cabinet. Carefully and cautiously, she removed the screws and then wiggled it out slowly, just far enough to reach her hand around to feel for a trip wire. She detached the wire from the cabinet's back and pulled it the rest of the way out. Whispering to Samantha to balance the medicine cabinet on the vanity, she gathered up between the studs what the intruder missed. Secured safely in her hand, she lifted the prized possessions, and placed the articles in her backpack. Marsha refitted the mirror. As they retraced their footsteps back to the living room, they heard a noise from the back door. Someone had jimmied it open.

They quickly scrambled behind the decorative screen at the front door. Two figures entered the mud room and now stood looking around at the mess of the kitchen.

"Fuck, mon, watcha think happened?" said the dreadlocked man.

"Quiet, motherfucker! And look around for anything we can fence."

"It's all Chinese junk, mon. No one wants this shit."

"It's Japanese, stupid."

"Whatever... Look at this place. Someone got here before us."

"Look over there on the shelf and grab those dolls."

"This is stupid, mon. I ain't fencin' no dolls. We'll be laughed out of the hood."

"They might be expensive, asshole."

"Look it, motherfucker... Don't be calling me names. I'll cap your ass," threatened the dreadlocked man.

"All right, Jerome. Just get a pillowcase over there and fill it up."

"And don't be calling me by my first name neither."

"I told you not to smoke crack before we came over here."

"It's not the crack, mon. It's you, fucker. Ordering me around like I was your dog. I'm not your dog."

"Okay, Okay... Will you keep it down?"

The dreadlocked man shone his RayVac Mag light at the screen.

"What about this folding wall?" asked the dreadlocked man.

"And how would we carry it?"

"Yeah... right. Com'on, this fag's place gives me the creeps."

"Will you turn off that blasted spotlight, for fuck's sake?"

"That's it. I'm outta here you albino snake."

"Jesus Christ. Why did my sister hook up with you?"

The dreadlocked man bulled through the house and his partner trailed behind him. Samantha took a deep breath and wiped the sweat from her brow. Marsha was calm and collected as she slipped past the screen to the back door. She looked out the curtained window at the two men who were still arguing. They stepped into their Mercury Marquis and pulled away. Marsha unscrewed the silencer off her Glock and put them both in her pack.

Samantha and Marsha waited ten minutes after the two men departed before they ventured out. Silence prevailed as they journeyed back to Samantha's house. She felt her heart. It still pounded with excitement. She reached for Marsha's hand and placed it on her beating chest. Marsha smiled at her and then turned her concentration back to the traffic in front of her. She also kept her trained eye on her rearview mirror for any unwanted distractions. Samantha looked at Marsha and knew there was more to her friend than what she saw on the outside.

When they arrived safely behind the locked doors of Samantha's home, Marsha mentioned cleaning up her house that morning. She said she would have to replace some of her furniture, like her mattress for one, as it had been cut up. Her couch might be salvageable and some of her framed pictures. Marsha didn't want anyone to know about this attack on her. She made Samantha promise.

Samantha, on the other hand, was not convinced it was such a good idea to tackle such a large job so soon. She had plenty of room and Marsha could have her own bedroom if she wished. Samantha was still waiting for answers from the Police and from Admiral Stone as to what the real reason was behind Terry's hideous crime. Plus, the weekend would not only give the ladies time to plan their strategy, but also time to discuss whatever their personal future together might hold. Marsha agreed to wait but was worried her presence might also endanger Samantha. Samantha would not hear otherwise.

Uganda, Gulu - Saturday

Charlie 0800 Hrs.

The early morning air was still fresh as the young mother prepared her baby wrapping her in a carrying shawl. A UN representative had dropped by and had given her a few shillings to buy some much-needed toiletries or other products she might need. The young mother was grateful for the act of kindness. She set off on her walk towards the streets of Gulu.

Along the way, she passed the four-sided clock tower in the center of town and strolled past dry goods stores, several mechanic shops, and an all-in-one hardware store, one of many, that seemed to be in the majority. She had noticed that many of the young men, besides being of darker skin, were just milling around, doing not much of anything, besides kicking a ball back and forth, or just gabbing.

She was much fairer in skin tone and her bright blue eyes sparkled in the sunlight. Her mother had told her their ancestors actually came from the Mediterranean area and had an influence from Northern Europe. She loved that expression: 'an influence'. What she really meant was some bastard from Europe raped her great grandmother and now it seemed every other generation had the deep blue eyes and fairer skin. It also seemed to her that the rich and powerful could do what they wanted against the less fortunate but never included them in the sharing of wealth manifested by the hard work of the indigent.

Her baby was starting to stir. On her right, the young mother approached one of the many markets where she could buy some fruit. Her baby loved plums. She had no idea what fruit sold for as she had been stealing it for the last, almost two years. She held out her hand and displayed the money. The shopkeeper looked into her eyes, folded her hand back up, and gave her an extra plum, all with a kind smile. She bowed to him and thanked him for his generosity. She did, however, buy a bottle of ice-cold water from an ice-filled bucket. The young mother turned down a small, vandalized vacant street and headed back toward the camp. On the way, the young mother decided to stop and take refuge in a two-story concrete building that was close to the perimeter of town and out of the sun, so she could feed her baby daughter.

She had felt the uneasiness of stares as she had walked through the streets. She didn't know if it was the invasion of IDPs into their area, or the community's fear of losing the few jobs they had to intruders, or if it was just her paranoia. Some actually said "Good morning" to her. Had she hardened in her travels and turned into such a despondent person that she couldn't accept acts of kindness? Her friend's blank stare as she raised the gun to her head had sealed the young mother's heart from anyone entering it.

The building was much like every other one she had taken refuge in. The same story of suffering, the agony of lost family, the torment of not knowing, and then the self-imposed realization fate had spared you while destroying everyone you loved. She lamented over what she was dealt through no fault of her own. Old tradition was meant to be grown upon, but not intended to be practiced in this changing world. She wiped the tears from her eyes and placed her baby on top of a counter. Her child looked up at her with a big smile as the young mother tucked her wrap around her baby to keep her from rolling off. She pulled out her knife, peeled the skin off the plum, and placed the fleshy orb to her smiling baby's lips.

From outside, three red-beret men who sat in a battered Nissan truck had watched a young mother walk into an abandoned building. Hidden in the tall grass at the end of the street, they waited for a moment before they slowly emerged onto the red dirt road. Two men jumped out and quietly eased alongside the building. One took a quick look through the missing window and then darted between it and the open door, the other followed suit. The man in the truck drove past the open door disguising any noise from his fellow attackers.

The young mother quickly glanced up but was satisfied the truck was merely driving by. She smiled at the delight of her daughter as she held the plum in her two little hands and sucked on the juices.

~

He awoke—startled. Leaping to his feet, Lt. Clark went to the front window. He saw a pickup parked, still idling, a few buildings down as if it was waiting for someone. And then— he heard a commotion coming from the floor beneath him. He knew instinctively what was going on. He heard the cries of a baby and the screams of a young girl as she struggled with her assailants.

Clark climbed through a half-bombed wall and ran down the hall where he jumped through a window onto the thatched roof of a one-story building. The palm leaves caved in with his weight and he fell onto the floor below. As he rolled to his feet, he reached back to his boot for one of his ceramic knives and then raced to the front door. Without hesitation, he dove through and plunged his knife into the neck of the unsuspected driver—swift and precise. He went around to the back of the building, hopped onto the loading dock of the warehouse, and through its large missing doors.

At the interior door of the main room, he quickly glanced at the situation—only two men. They had a young girl sprawled on her back attempting to rape her as she kicked back in defense. He darted in, and to their surprise, he sank his knife deep into the back of one and kicked the other in the head. The knifed man fell, reeling upward and forward. Lt. Clark had the other man's head in his hands and gave it a quick snap. The young mother scrambled to retrieve her knife off the floor and swung at the throat of the knifed man as he attempted to reach back at his pain. He fell to the floor, eyes bulging and blood spewing.

The young mother looked at the white man with deadly blue-grey eyes, watching every move he made. She swayed like a cobra in a striking stance to take on this one as well.

Lt. Clark raised his hands as if he was surrendering to her intentions.

"Ma'am, it's all right. I mean you no harm. Please, put down the knife."

"No!" she shouted, her adrenaline was pumping.

"I'm not going to hurt you, I promise. But I do need to take care of business outside before suspicions arise. Do you understand me?"

"Of course. I understand your language, if that is your reference, but not your intentions," she said in perfect English.

"Please, don't do anything crazy. I'll be right back."

The lieutenant rushed to the open door, scanned the street, and then darted out to the idling pickup once he saw it was clear. He shoved the dead driver to the side, pulled the truck between the buildings, and parked it in the back lane.

He jumped onto the loading dock and went through the warehouse to the main room. The young mother had her baby wrapped in her shawl and her knife was drawn.

"Look. We will need to get rid of these bodies. I will not harm you."

"Why should I trust you?"

"I just saved your life."

"I can take care of myself," she argued back.

"Well, not from where I was standing."

"I have fought off worse than these two."

Clark momentarily smiled.

"Maybe so, but it looked like you needed a little assistance this time."

She was confused. Her eyes darted from the open door to the white man who stood in front of her. He had kind words but so did others.

"Did you follow me?"

"No. I was taking a nap upstairs when I heard the truck drive by. There's not much traffic down this street, so it woke me up. I heard you screaming and could tell you weren't going easily so I took out the driver first before coming in here to rescue your ungrateful ass."

"You are American?"

"Well, depends. Let's say I am Canadian and previously employed by the U.S. Military."

Lt. Clark felt she was starting to ease her intensity but after watching her wield her knife like a surgeon, he wasn't taking any chances either.

"Let me dump these bodies into the hole back in the other room. We can pile some of this old concrete on top to hide them for a while, at least until they start to smell."

She eased up and tucked her knife into her waist band. She bent over to give Lt. Clark a hand.

"I can do this if you want to attain to your baby."

"I am not a weak little flower."

She insisted on helping Clark dispose of the bodies in the shell-ripped hole of the warehouse. Clark grabbed the body from the truck and dumped him in as well. The young mother walked out of the warehouse and over to the counter. She picked up the fallen plum and poured a little water on it to clean it. Her baby, still slung in the shawl around her mother's neck, smiled once again as it suckled on the fruit.

"What's your name?" asked Clark.

She smirked. "Why do you ask?"

"Well, it is only polite to ask."

"I have been traveling with my baby for almost two years and no one has asked my name. I have almost forgotten it myself." She paused a moment. "It is Maysa."

"Maysa, a pretty name. I believe it means you are honest and responsible but have a strong will."

"How do you know this?"

"I had the pleasure...well for the most part, of training in Kenya and one of the housekeepers name was Maysa."

"What do you call yourself?"

"William...but everyone calls me Clark. It is William Clark."

"What are you doing here?"

"Sorry, but that information I cannot divulge. Let's just say I need to leave as quickly and quietly as possible."

"You are in danger? Someone after you?"

"You are very perceptive. How old are you?"

She paused. "Almost sixteen and a half years."

"And your baby, I presume, what is her name?"

"I have heard a lot of mothers are naming their baby girls 'Nyaring', meaning 'running'...as most of us had to be on the run or die. But I did not want my baby to carry that stigma throughout her life. I call her 'Ateefah', meaning 'passionate' and 'one who follows her heart'. I hope she finds that in her life."

South Sudan

Charlie 1100 Hrs.

Nigel Redman's plane touched down at the Juba airport. Two blacked-out SUVs waited as he disembarked. He was a big man, casually dressed but walked with determination. A man in uniform saluted him and then opened the door. They headed straight to the U.S. Embassy.

When they arrived at the Embassy's compound, Redman was not directed to the incumbent Ambassador of South Sudan, Thomas Hushek's office, but to another building across the compound's lot. The uniformed man pressed a series of buttons and the two stepped in. Another man came from down the hall and excused the escort. They walked down the hall from the direction he came, through another security door to the desk of Robert Blakely. Redman handed the man his dossier.

"Morning, Mr. Redman."

"Morning." He paused and looked at the man's name plate. He let out a robust "Ro-bert." The name twirled in his Scottish brogue.

"Which one do you want to see first?"

"How about the cowboy?" Redman looked toward the Embassy. "Does he know anything?"

"No. The Ambassador has no idea what we do here and we want to keep it that way. FYI, the 'cowboy', as you call him, refers to himself as 'Mister President'."

"We all have crosses to bear. Let's talk to him first, then with the Castro wanna-be."

Blakely, a CIA agent got up from his desk and motioned to Redman to return to the hall. They walked down to the end, through a door, down two flights of stairs, through another door and down a dark hall, where a soldier stood on guard. The soldier moved to the side as Blakely knocked and then pressed a series of buttons. The two walked into a well-appointed suite built thirty feet underground.

The President, Salva Kiir Mayardit, the founding leader from the time of South Sudan's independence in 2011, was a big man with a rugged face. He stood with a cigar in his hand while his infamous black cowboy hat, given to him by President George W. Bush in 2006, sat on his desk.

"Are you my warden?" asked the president.

"You are lucky I am not," stated Redman, boldly.

"Gentlemen, if we can skip the pleasantries. Let's get down to business," cited Blakely.

The president scoffed, "My business is for you to let me out of this stink hole so I can return to my people."

"Your people, Mr. President? I heard they took a potshot at you and hit some poor sucker."

"It would not have been directed at me, but at the imposter."

"The imposter, your opponent—your ex-Vice President? Come on, mister, let's face it. The fighting between you two from since when? December of '13. Your bickering has caused too much strife for your people and us. You are destroying your country and our interests. Your little civil war does not make us feel very happy; especially with all the money we have poured into your little shithole. Now, I really don't give a throne's shit about you, but you need to convince me we can cooperate together. If not...do I have to spell it out?"

"You are an obstinate bastard, mister!"

"Oh! That so hurts me," Redman said as he put his hands to his heart, laughing. "So I take it then we do understand each other. Nice talking with you Prez."

The two men turned to leave the suite. Redman glanced back at the fuming president.

"By the way, Mr. President... How do you like the Cuban-rolled cigars?"

Blakely and Redman continued their walk down to the next man's holding suite. The soldier stepped aside as his counterpart had done. Blakely knocked and then punched in a set of numbers. He pushed the door opened.

Redman stepped in before Blakely and didn't waste any time with his interrogation of Dr. Riek Machar.

"Don't bother getting up, Rieky. Let me put it to you this way. You are a fish—you flip and flop and flip-flop worse than our politicians. Your degrees don't mean anything to me except you are a learned man, and that scares me. Everything that has happened to you lately, you have done to someone else—like in Sudan. Do you remember that and all the money we gave you and your asshole buddy? Don't bother to answer. Just to be clear—we need peace, that's it in a nutshell. No warring on the Dinka. If we help you gain control, we need to be assured our interests remain intact. No taking back the oil refineries or dams our money built."

"Who the fuck are you to come in here and talk to me like that?" Reiky's eyes, bold and black widened in deep resentment.

"Whoops, wrong answer, Rieky boy. What happened to that nice Presbyterian upbringing? Think about it, big boy, or we might let the two of you duke it out instead of killing anymore people. Not that I am opposed to that, but even my hands are tied, somewhat, if you catch my drift. I'll be here for a couple of days and before I leave, you better have an answer that sits well in my stomach." Redman paused. "I think your cowboy buddy next door looks better in his black suit and cowboy hat rather than fatigues, don't you?"

Redman and Blakely left the astounded man steaming as he sat gripping the bolsters of his easy chair. Blakely remarked to Redman, "I don't think you won any brownie points with either one."

"I'm not here for their fucking cookies. I'm here for results—and I promise you, I will get results. Now, who is our next bitch in the line-up?"

Nigel Redman did not mince his words but came straight to the point. He was big enough, mean enough, and well-connected to literally say anything he wanted, as long as the results were in his clients' interests.

Uganda, Gulu – Lira Highway

Charlie 1300 Hrs.

Jake and his team had set camp up on the high rock-face overlooking the Nile at the crossroads from south of Gulu and the roads that went east to Lira and in the opposite direction, west to Pakwach. Hidden among the trees, they had easy access for scouting in either direction or spotting anyone crazy enough to traverse the Murchison Falls along the Nile. At this point in time, they had not ruled out anything.

Mac had been eavesdropping on Gulu's local radio station, 'Mega FM 102.1', for any news that might tip the whereabouts of the lieutenant. The British-financed radio station mostly informed and tracked rebel LRA militants, but clearly stated the government's position on amnesty for those who choose to give themselves up and for the release of all the abducted children. Not one or two, but 30,000 children had lost their childhood and forced to be killers or be killed. There was a news spot on an allegedly stolen S&W truck, but it was later found just outside of Gulu. *Obviously someone on a joy ride,* commented the announcer. He also mentioned three LRA's had allegedly been spotted on Friday just north of Gulu but had not been seen so far this Saturday.

Mac shook his head as he listened to the news of all the atrocities these poor people had to endure. He relayed the news to Jake and Petersen. They sympathized, but all they could do was just sit and wait. They had their orders, and as they sat having some dry food, the talk of the circle was the same—they had better not see these injustices on their watch, or hell will be paid.

~

Colonel Dimitri and his remaining men finally made camp beside Lake Turkana, Kenya, at a point next to the Ethiopian border. Corporal Jacobs had sent a message back to command of their current position and added a comment: They felt confident the lieutenant had left South Sudan. The message also stated for SAS to begin their 'PAG' surveillance from their coordinates. Reynolds came into the colonel's private make-shift office and closed the curtain behind him.

"Colonel, you wanted to see me?"

"Yes, Reynolds. Please sit."

"The other night, the corporal informed me one of ours had been terminated in Washington. I didn't want to alarm any of you at that time, but I feel you need to know. Now that we are stationary, I'll have the corporal find out who it was."

"Do we know who did it? Or whether it was a coincidence?"

"Transmission stated Nigel Redman," informed the colonel.

"That fucker," gritted Reynolds with a tight fist slamming it down onto the Colonel's desk. "Excuse my language, sir."

"Nothing I haven't said, I assure you."

"Has our mission been compromised?"

"I don't believe so. We will know more after Jacobs has a chance to communicate with 'Black Hawk'. As far as command is concerned, the mission is a go."

"I hate just sitting, sir. Not knowing or having communication with Jake makes me uneasy."

"We all feel it. We have to believe and trust in our gut and rely on our training."

"Yes, sir. You know, Jake and I go back a lot of years. Our wives are friends as well."

"I saw that in your dossiers and I was a little concerned. If I had any reservations at all, Jake would not be in command of that mission. But as you know, he is a dedicated man and well-trained for any circumstances. I know he will do right by us."

"That means a lot, sir, to hear you say that. May I speak candidly, sir?"

"Of course, Reynolds."

Standing, Reynolds looked directly into the Colonel's eyes and said, "I...we, the men...all of us, sir, hold you in the same regard. We are honored to be serving with you, sir."

"Thank you, Lieutenant, I appreciate your words. Our countries have not seen eye to eye for many years. It's the people who suffer, not the governments. If we can strike a blow to the corruption of both countries, I would be satisfied as a soldier and a human being. Lieutenant, if you don't mind, keep a lid on this until we find out who was hit."

"Yes, sir."

"Has the camp been secured?"

"Yes, sir. And the AVSBOs' (Advanced Vehicle Stealth Battery Operation) are being charged up and we fixed the momentary glitch in the stealth mode on all of the units."

"Good. Tell the men to take some R&R, they can use it. The lake looks very refreshing."

"Yes, sir, they will appreciate that."

Lt. Reynolds took leave of Colonel Dimitri's make-shift field office and informed his team of the issued R&R orders. His team comprised of twenty-five men including the CO.

They were highly trained, highly disciplined, and highly motivated. They appreciated their colonel's strong leadership but more than anything, his logical mind. Too many officers were afraid to deviate from the book, while Colonel Dimitri learned to re-write it. They were the elite of the elite from all factions of the military and from several different countries. They moved with precision as they had when they took out the convoy a few nights prior. Each one was hand-picked and then given the free will to accept their mission. They were promised one thing—they *would* make a difference.

Out of the ten dispersed teams around the globe, two teams at a time were on a rotating leave, several were stationed in Africa, another two in and around Iraq, one in Pakistan, two in South and Central America, while the other one was privately funded and could be almost anywhere. But their ideology and mission were the same—to protect and serve the people of the world against tyrants and persecution.

Colonel Dimitri had himself, been hand-picked while on a brief assignment to the Russian Ambassador in Washington. While attending a fundraiser for the 'PAG' program, he had been sent a private message to meet with a man who appreciated his talents. His admirer was introduced to him as an associate of the "Swan." The Swan, as far as Dimitri's intelligence could find out, had a long history, and as told to Dimitri in private and shared with a sense of humor, "almost antediluvian" and invisible. Dimitri accepted the associate of the Swan's terms who had persuaded the colonel his talents would be best served to join his organization. Although militarily based, their actions did not report to anyone other than the Swan's associate. He, the Swan's associate, was obviously a passionate and a convincing speaker as two months later,

Colonel Dimitri was secretively ushered into a secured training ground.

Whoever was in control, whether it was the Swan or not, had deep pockets and connections as Dimitri still held a Russian passport, but under his new name, Colonel Sven Dimitri.

Washington - Saturday

Romeo 0600 Hrs.

Her phone began to ring and woke Samantha from a pleasant sensual dream. Beside her lay her friend, who also stirred from the injustice of the early morning intrusion.

"Hello," she grunted.

"Director, sorry to bother you so early on your day off, but we have had a transmission from our recovery team. They wish for us to switch our coordinates closer to the Ethiopian border."

"Has the transmission been authenticated, Carmen?"

"Yes, ma'am."

"Then do as they ask. We...I will drop in later today to sign the order. Make sure the time of request, the change of coordinates, and the time of our conversation are included on the DAT form. Thank you, Carmen."

"You are welcome, Director. I know you wanted to be informed of any changing variables."

"You did right, Carmen. See you later."

"Yes, ma'am." The call ended.

"We switched coordinates to the Ethiopian border?" questioned Marsha.

"Yes, it seems the colonel has moved location and wants us to track a different swath."

"Sam, may I use your computer?"

"Of course. I'll make coffee. I doubt either one of us will be able to get back to sleep."

Sam slid out of bed in her full awareness and headed to the kitchen. Marsha picked up her backpack and searched for one of her plastic bags. She pulled out a Blackberry, plugged it into Sam's computer, and typed a memorized set of keystrokes. She quickly sent an encrypted message. She heard Samantha in the kitchen clanging pots and the run of water and then, silence. She looked up from the computer—her face had gone ghostly white. Marsha unplugged the Blackberry and reached for the other bag and pulled out her Glock.

She tip-toed to the bedroom door and listened. Nothing. She raised her gun and slowly eased toward the kitchen, each step as silent as the last. Marsha darted a look around the corner to the L-shaped kitchen. She couldn't see Samantha as daybreak was starting to stream through the windows. Suddenly she heard a commotion at the back door. Marsha rushed to the sound, with gun drawn and rounded the corner to the back door. Samantha looked up in horror, her face stripped of her smile.

"Marsha!" screamed Sam as she eyed down the barrel of Marsha's drawn gun.

"Samantha, what are you doing?"

Marsha lowered her gun.

"I went outside naked to pick some fresh herbs. I've never been outside naked before," she confessed with a bitter-sweet smile.

"You threw the fear of death in me. I thought something happened to you," said Marsha as she relaxed her grip.

"I am fine." Samantha eyed the Glock. "Marsha, this is twice in less than 24 hours I have seen you draw that weapon. Is there something you need to tell me?"

Marsha placed the gun on the counter and walked to Samantha's side. She embraced her. Samantha's body was chilled from the early morning air. Marsha hugged her tightly.

"Yes," she whispered. "But let's have coffee first."

Uganda, Gulu

Charlie 1330 Hrs.

The warehouse wasn't safe, and Billy knew it. He had the pickup that he had stashed behind the building that he commandeered from the three guerilla fighters—they wouldn't need it.

"I have transportation if you want to come with me," Lt. Clark announced to Maysa.

"Where are you going?"

"To Kenya. There is a Canadian training base near Kisumu where we can hopefully, get you and your baby help."

"What about you?" asked Maysa.

"I will know after I talk with someone who I can trust."

"I have a few things at the UN camp I will need to get. I will tell them of my traveling plans so they don't send anyone after us. Shall I meet you back here?"

"Yes. We can leave tonight from here without suspicious eyes tracking our movement. See if you can get a map or simple directions. Tell them you want to go to Nairobi. I don't imagine there will be too many routes."

Maysa smiled. "What?" asked Clark.

"If you would have told me you were an American, you just gave yourself up as a Canadian."

"What do you mean?"

"You said route. Americans say 'root' like what a tree has. Our teacher taught us the King's English, not American colloquialism," quipped Maysa.

"Whoa, aren't we the snob?" laughed Clark.

"Snob? No! Americans think we are uneducated because we are poor. And it is true some of us have not had the chance to complete higher education but in primary school, we have learned the proper use and pronunciation of the English language in spite of our difficulties. I speak four languages, plus a few dialects. How many do you speak?"

"Um, a little French to get by," he said, a little embarrassed.

"Exactly!"

"You are not going to be like this the whole trip are you?" asked Clark, smiling.

"I am who I am, but I will not ridicule the man who... 'saved my ass', as you put it," indulged Maysa.

"Oh boy! You are. Okay, I will give you the language thing but I need you to understand that when I tell you something, I need to know you will not hesitate. It could save your life and your baby's. Are we clear on this?"

"Yes, sir," she responded with a salute.

"Go on and get out of here. Don't give our position up," smiled Clark, shaking his head.

Maysa smiled back at him, and although she wanted to say something to him, she just turned, gathered her baby, and headed back to the UN camp. She knew she would have to wipe the smile off her face when she approached the camp, but at the moment, it felt good.

Clark went out into the back lane and checked out the pickup. In the bed of the pickup was a large green box with the letters 'RPGL' written on the side. Several other boxes lay in the bed as well. Upon prying the lids, several AK 47's and several canisters of ammunition were packed in foam. Before dumping the three soldiers into the pit, Clark had removed the gun belts, which he now placed behind the seat. He searched inside the cab for any maps or written directions indicating intersecting roads that might help their cause.

Their cause, he thought. *How did I get mixed up with a young, intelligent, obviously dangerous girl... with a baby, no doubt? I must be crazy.* But he wasn't about to leave her to survive on her own. Not after what he saw from those two militants who jumped her. No one deserved that. They would make it or he would die trying. He thought of his sister and how her episode had changed her. How could this young mother do it? He was in awe of her strength and determination to be tackling this journey all by herself. He won't let anyone harm her again—that, he swore.

. . .

Juba, the capital of South Sudan, and more importantly, the US embassy had not seen anyone like Nigel Redman. He was a rugged, unrefined individual with a craggy voice who meant what he said. There was no room for interpretation.

"Take me down to the airport where those two were facing off," demanded Nigel Redman.

"There's nothing there," assured Robert Blakely.

"Just humor me."

The two men jumped into one of the blacked-out SUV's. A designed driver and another soldier dressed in full combat military gear with a communications set accompanied them.

"Nice rifle you got there, soldier. A forty caliber?" asked Redman.

"It's a M4A1 5.56x45 caliber, sir, with a *Barska* scope."

Nigel smiled. He knew full well what the soldier carried. He looked out the window as they bounced along the rutted roadway. The airport lay on the east side of town with only one road entering and leaving it. They stopped on the tarmac near where the stage was set. The two men and the soldier got out. Blakely showed Nigel exactly where the stage was set up while the soldier took point. Redman looked around and found a few splatters of blood on the tarmac close to the hangar doors. He asked the driver to turn the SUV around and back it into the stage's location. Redman opened the tailgate and jumped on. He scanned the area from where the coordinates had been issued and then he looked back at the splattering of blood.

"Was this where Jack's snitch got hit?"

"More or less."

"Well, which is it... more or less?" said Nigel with a glare in his eyes.

Blakely sensed Nigel's displeasure with his comment, so he clarified his answer in more detail.

"Yes, he would have been right here. The other podium was set over there and Rieky was standing here."

"Better," said Nigel. He raised his arm and swiveled from the issued coordinates and then looked back at the blood pattern. He then swiveled once again, and positioned his arm, like he was stuck on the semaphore letter 'R', to the opposite side of the field that lay before them. This particular view was only a short distance to the river.

"Have your men checked over there?" said Redman pointing to the direction of the river.

"No one has indicated to me an alternative location," responded Blakely.

"Of course not, Ro-bert," patronized Redman. He turned to Blakely, "If you were on a covert operation and you had...let's say, somehow realized you had been set up, would you stand where that order jeopardized your survival?"

Blakely looked at Nigel with a questioning stare, "I... I..."

"Yes, quite right, Blakely. Driver, take me over to those trees by the river."

The men all jumped back into the SUV. The driver took them to the grassy plains next to an outcrop of trees near the river's edge.

"Keep going," instructed Nigel. He eyed the purposed shoot site and when he felt they were at the perpendicular arc to the hangar, he shouted to stop.

"Come gentlemen, time to go for a walk," informed Nigel.

"What are we looking for, sir?" asked the soldier.

"A hole the size of a man—like a shallow grave."

"A foxhole?"

"Exactly, soldier, exactly."

They slowly examined the area. Nothing looked out of place other than wild dog footprints and a dead carcass. Nigel bent down.

"Soldier, give me your scope."

The soldier removed his scope and gave it to Nigel. He lay on his belly, put the scope to his eye and made a small adjustment. He got up and moved farther back and over to where they spotted the dead carcass. He lay down again and drifted his stare over to the original coordinates. He quickly removed the scope from his eye with a questioning look on his face. The other men watched him. Redman got up and eased over to the dead carcass. He lightly tapped the ground with his foot. He moved closer and tapped once more. This time, his foot penetrated the reeds. He almost lost his balance but stopped himself from falling into the hole. Down on one knee, he flashed a bold conceited grin, and said, "Gentlemen, I think we have found something."

Redman felt in the dirt for the ends of the bamboo supports. Finding then, he threw the twined reeds and bones to the side to expose Lt. Clark's holdout. "There, gents, lies our sniper's rathole."

He tossed the scope to the soldier. "Soldier, get down in there and give me a reading."

"Yes, sir." The soldier re-attached his scope and slipped into the foxhole. He adjusted the eye piece and read out, "1408.8 yards, sir. Approximately 8/10ths of a mile to the hangar's doors." Dangling off a cut root, the soldier caught the shimmering of a watch.

Nigel smiled—one of the few times. He offered his hand to the soldier. "Well done, soldier." He looked at the other two. "Okay, gentlemen, I would say our sniper took to the water after he made the shot. He might have waited here until nightfall, probably why the diversion of the dead dog.

Let's go back to the embassy. There is nothing else here for us," instructed Nigel Redman.

"Sir..." He raised his hand displaying a military watch.

The quick ride back was quiet as Nigel tried to imagine the lieutenant's plan for escape. He slipped out of the SUV as soon as it came to a stop in the embassy's compound. He wasted little time in heading to Blakely's office.

"Do you have a secure line?" Redman asked sternly.

"Yes, of course."

"Get me CTA, STAT!"

Pentagon - SAS
Romeo 1300 Hrs.

The Director, Lt. Col. Samantha Jones, and her senior team leader and design collaborator, Marsha Jean Atworth entered SAS headquarters and the origin of PAG. They were speechless as they looked up and saw a different tracking sequence displayed on their big screen plotters. Carmen ran over to them with an apologetic look on her face.

"I am so sorry, Director, but we were just handed these coordinates ten minutes ago straight from CTA. It has been signed off by CTA's Director Jack Tomlinson."

Samantha looked over the paperwork and then handed it to Marsha.

"What's going on?"

"It says 'reliable intel'."

"Reliable intel?" questioned Marsha.

Samantha Jones was pissed. This was her project, not Jack Tomlinson's.

"I'm sorry, ma'am. I had to follow orders," said Carmen.

"Yes, quite right, Carmen. I'm not questioning you or your duty," stated Director Jones.

At that moment, the office phone rang. Samantha picked it up. "Hello."

"Director, this is Jack Tomlinson. Could you be so kind as to have Marsha Atworth report to my office immediately?"

"What's this about?" she asked demandingly.

"Well, quite frankly, we are concerned about finding Ms. Atworth's cell phone underneath one of your terminals," he replied smugly.

"Fine! I will send her up as soon as we have finished here. Now, let me ask you. What is going on in having my staff change the coordinates of PAG? You know it takes hours to re-position the satellite."

"You are so defiant, Sam. Get over it! And send Ms. Atworth up here; otherwise, I will have the guards come and get her."

She put her hand cupping the receiver so no one else could hear, "You are a bastard, Jack."

"Oh, Sam, you are hurting my feelings," he said in a patronizing voice and then he came down hard on her. *"I don't give a fuck what you think. Now do as I say!"*

She slammed the receiver down to the astonishment of the other team supporters. They had never seen her so upset. She took a deep breath and then turned to Marsha and calmly said,

"The Director of CTA would like to see you in his office ASAP. Something regarding your cell phone."

"Oh...my cell. The one I dropped the other day. Not a problem, Director, I promise," smiled Marsha.

"Do you want me to go with you?"

"By that last conversation, I think I can handle him."

"I'll wait here for you," said the director in a professional manner. "We have coordinates to go over."

"Yes, ma'am," acknowledged Marsha.

~

Marsha Atworth arrived at the outer office of CTA. She was immediately announced and asked to step into the director's office. This was the first time she had been allowed to enter Jack's hallow sanctuary. His office was as plush as any of the congressmen on the hill. He sat behind his man-desk. *An obvious replacement for his exaggerated ego and lack of personal providence*, thought Marsha. Jack raised his eyes and saw a pretty and shapely woman dressed in form-fitting civvies with long wavy hair. He had never seen her, other than formally dressed in her Navy uniform. And her obvious long hair was usually worn in a bun.

"You wish to see me, Jack?"

Surprised at her lack of respect for his position and her forwardness, he stumbled, "Uh, yes. Please sit." He motioned to an ornate leather chair that resided prominently in front of his lavish desk. Marsha sat and ran her hands along the carved wood bolsters. She was quick to comment.

"I never imagined a man of your position would have such an ornate piece of furniture displayed in such prominence."

"What?" he answered confused.

"Your furniture does not emphasize your personality," she said tauntingly.

"What do you know of my personality?" he shouted. "We are not here to talk about me. It is you who needs to explain this..." He threw her cell phone across his desk and as it flew into the air, Marsha grabbed it like a first-base man, without a blink.

"Thank you, I have been looking for this," she stated calmly and antagonistically.

He glared at her momentarily, which allowed Marsha to go on the offense.

"Director, let's not mince words. You have called me in here to berate me, or at least try to intimidate me into a hysterical emotional turmoil over a simple misplacement of my personal cell phone. You have obviously had it scanned, dissected and prodded. You have lifted every number and name in it and found nothing. So what is this charade all about?"

Tomlinson was taken back again by this insolent woman. He went on the attack. "You fucking bitch! Who do you think you are? Who do you think you are talking to?"

"I don't report to you, so let's get that straight. You were gifted this position; it wasn't earned. Your JAG career was in shambles and filled with corruption. To save face, they promoted you to here." She stood up with a smirk on her face, leaned on his pompous desk, and stared right into his eyes. "Don't fuck with me, Jack. And don't fuck with my director. We'll play your little game of hide and seek, but if anyone else from our team befalls any accident..." she hesitated long enough for this to register in his egotistical brain, "I'm coming for you." She ended her volatile spiel with a tight fist pounding on his desk.

Jack's eyes swelled with anger as he looked at this pretty thing threatening him. His face turned red and he blathered out, "Get the fuck out of my office! You better be the one to watch out."

"What, Jack? You going to have someone rip apart my house again?"

Marsha turned on her heel and charged out of the room.

~

Marsha laid her chin on the retinal scanner in the inner sanctuary of SAS. The door clicked open and she walked proudly through it. The director had been working closely with her staff to re-position the satellite to the coordinates dictated by the Director of CTA. They all turned their focus to the opening door. Their concern for Marsha's stressful encounter with the head of CTA had them all unnerved. To their amazement, her face was bright, almost beaming.

Samantha asked, "Are you all right? Have you seen the director?"

"Yes."

"Well?" she said with palms pointing upward waiting for the book version.

Everyone's eyes were on Marsha. "He muttered what he had to say, and I said what I needed to say. That's all."

Samantha looked at her with a questioning stare and a doubt in her mind with Marsha's 'that's all'. A conversation with Jack never ended with a 'that's all'. *What was she holding back?* After their eye-opening conversation during their morning coffee, Samantha could only imagine what was said. She had seen Marsha as cool as a cucumber when those two thieves broke into Terry's house, but Jack was not some dumb thief. His ego stuck out like a rhino's horn and his temper flared quicker than a firestorm driven by the Santa Ana winds. Her questions for Marsha would have to wait, for now, but she felt proud of her friend and supportive of anything she might have said to Jack.

"Marsha," called out Nina, another chosen programmer, who was working on the coordinates handed down by Jack Tomlinson. "These don't make sense. These coordinates are for Gulu, Uganda. Our last transmission from our recovery team would set their coordinates hundreds of miles away, near the Ethiopian border."

Marsha looked at Samantha. She went over to Nina to confirm the location given to them.

"How long before we can re-position the PAG satellite?" asked the director.

"We were in mid-stream of re-positioning it to the recovery team's coordinates. It will take at least twenty-five minutes to receive any data from the new location," stated Nina as she feverishly re-coded the computer. "Sorry ma'am. It all takes time."

"You are doing fine, Nina." She looked around the room to the other technicians. "You are all doing just fine. And thank you for all your support," said the director with real admiration.

"Director, should I send a transmission to the recovery team of this new development?" asked Carmen.

Samantha looked at Marsha. "What do you think, Marsha? Do you think these new coordinates would benefit our recovery team or do you think it is a wild goose chase?"

"Our team has been following protocol." Marsha turned to Carmen. "Carmen, send an apologetic transmission to our RT Commander and inform him of the transgressions that have been taking place. Inform him of the Director of CTA's decision to change location and cite 'reliable intel'."

"Yes, ma'am."

Marsha looked at the director with a positive grin and nodded. She turned and refocused on Carmen. "Carmen, also mention a possible hostile environment might present itself."

"Yes, ma'am."

"Anything else, Director?" asked Marsha.

"I think you are handling this with precision and detail. Carmen, can you, Nina, and Phillip handle all the tasks at hand? Marsha and I have some other business we need to take care of."

"Yes, of course, Director. Ah, ma'am, where is Terry?"

The director slowly looked around the room at the faces of her staff. She saw the concern in their eyes as Carmen's question resonated like an earthquake. She looked at Marsha and then said, "I have some bad news. I have been waiting for clarification from the local Police and NCIS but..." She paused. "...Terry was involved in a horrific accident, and unfortunately, he didn't make it. I am so sorry to be telling you all this."

Marsha intervened. "We had Paul take over Terry's position provisionally until we heard more. We were going to make this announcement on Monday, but no time like the present. Carmen, the Director and I feel you are quite capable of being team leader when we are not present and you have the experience to coordinate any variables with Paul, who will remain team leader on the second shift. Just today, you have shown your commitment to the team and to protocol."

Carmen was flushed with the news of Terry but also elated with her new position with PAG. Nina and Phillip applauded her appointment with genuine approval.

The director added, "Now that Marsha has her cell back, let's all stay informed of any other changes. It seems command is going through some troubling times, but we must adhere to our protocol. Is that understood?"

The team acknowledged the director's wishes and returned to re-establishing PAG. The feel in the room had lightened as they busily reconstructed their grids to plot the landscape and accept the satellite's information. Marsha and the director took leave of their motivated team.

As they walked through the hallway, the director said to Marsha, "We have a good team, don't we, Marsha?"

"Yes. Loyal and trustworthy as well, Director."

Uganda, Gulu – Saturday

Charlie 1800 Hrs.

Lt. Clark stood on the second floor of his concrete building and looked out the window periodically as he waited for the return of Maysa. In his mind, he reflected. *She has been exposed to such horrible shit in her life, yet when she looks at her baby, it is all love and joy. I hope, if we survive, I'll be able to offer her a chance for a better life in Canada.*

As he had noticed the last time he was home, the faces had changed to a more cosmopolitan flavor and influence. And then there was Janie. *A sweet gesture, if I read her right. But for me to settle down after all I have done, I just can't see it. It could be a great place for Maysa to raise her child and my father could use the company and help around the farm. My sister would feel a certain compassion for her, which might settle her trauma.*

The sun cast long, golden-red spears of light as it started to settle in the west. Maysa would be back soon and when the sun dropped, they would head out. He heard some commotion in the street and quickly moved over to the glassless window—he peered out. Two young boys were playfully kicking a soccer ball down the street just as Maysa turned the corner. She stopped and spun backward. They hadn't noticed her and kept bouncing the ball from building to building pretending they were opposing players. They turned right at the next street and headed north, towards the main road. Clark watched Maysa as she darted in and out of doorways; she always checked back and forth for any detection. He smiled and thought to himself, *She has done this before.* Within minutes she entered the old warehouse. There was still too much daylight to leave unnoticed. Clark thought, to pass the time, he would teach Maysa some release techniques.

The lieutenant had her grab his shirt with both hands as if to throw him to the ground and as she did, he gently reached over the closest hand and grabbed her hand on the opposite side and twisted it upward. She bent to the force and with her arm in a backward position. Clark told her, one could place a hefty elbow or stomp at the shoulder to dislocate it. Maysa smiled. She liked that maneuver. Men had approached her in the past and ripped open her dress, leaving her bare and violated. Now, she could crisscross her body and with one hand and disarm the unexpected intruder. Maysa practiced and practiced until even Clark was getting tired of having his arm bent backwards. She wanted to learn more. Clark couldn't remember the last time he had such an enthusiastic student.

He showed her several quick kicks and a couple of in-close punches. Clark then showed her how to hold the knife so she was still able to punch and maintain control of the blade. She was like a sponge, absorbing everything he said and every movement he made. Maysa was a natural, and at her young age, very limber. She told him of the TV shows she watched as a girl when her father was not around. Clark told her that type of martial arts was just for show. A high kick to the head left you very vulnerable to all of your bleed-out arteries; not used in survival fighting. Maysa listened intently and watched as he demonstrated. She had found a friend.

It was time, and the lieutenant felt a little anxious. The sun had set, and now they had to head south. Maysa produced a map, hand-drawn, that was created by the kind gentleman who had given her the plums. He had wished her luck with her travels and offered a blessing. She was very appreciative of his kindness.

The map showed a tee in the road about 60 km south of Gulu. To the right, it headed through the Murchison Falls National Park, and to the left, he said that it would take her to Lira. There, she could catch A104 south, which would eventually take her all the way to Nairobi, Kenya. Clark knew the A104 was too far east for their intentions but the map definitely helped to get them started. There were only a few towns pinpointed on the map. Maybe at one of these towns, Clark thought, they could nab a cell phone and directions to Kisumu.

Kenya, Lake Turkana
Charlie 2020 Hrs.

Colonel Dimitri and his men's stay at their make-shift camp allowed for maintenance and some R&R. But they were also anxious to conclude their mission. Jacobs had received an encrypted message and he rushed to his colonel's side. He knocked on Colonel Dimitri's make-shift canvas door.

"Colonel?"

"Yes, Corporal. What is it?"

"Sir, you need to read this." The corporal produced the latest transmission from SAS to the Colonel. He read it. "What the fu..."

"Exactly, sir. The shortened encrypted message from earlier now makes more sense."

"Yes, Jacobs, indeed. Redman must be in Juba and found something that made CTA change their focus. Where's Reynolds?"

"I sent a message for him to meet you here, sir."

"Very good."

No sooner had the words left the colonel's lips when Reynolds charged through the raises canvas curtain into the colonel's office. "Sorry, sir, for not knocking. The men and I were just finishing up a football game," said the winded soldier.

Colonel Dimitri handed Reynolds the transmission. He read it carefully and then said, "The earlier transmission from 'Hourglass' now makes sense, sir. Redman has to be in Juba."

"That's our understanding as well. This could work to our advantage. We will be able to legitimately offer support. Our orders have been changed, gentleman. We will strike camp and head south. If Redman follows his gut, maybe I will have my wish after all," calculated the colonel.

"We don't know if he is staying or heading back to the States, sir. He could just be here to gather intel and then leave."

"True. But don't you think, with his ego, he will want to be part of the kill? I think he will wait to see if PAG picks up a ping and then he will pounce like a cat at night. Let's not waste any time in turning our mission around. We will be able to receive data as quickly as he can."

"If he is as ruthless as you say, he will not want to stick around in Juba. Might he go further south to the embassy in Kampala on Lake Victoria?" queried Reynolds.

"Very good, Rey. Kampala is almost due south of Juba. An easy flight in a single engine where he can fly close to the ground and parallel the Nile. Tell the men to be fully loaded; we leave at 0530 Hrs."

"Yes, sir," saluted Reynolds as he turned and took leave of the colonel.

"Jacobs, stay on top of your man. We need pinpoint information as soon as it becomes available."

"Yes, sir."

Colonel Dimitri looked at his map, but what he saw in his mind, was Redman slitting the throat of an innocent female friend. A tear budded in Dimitri's eye as he remembered lying on a cold concrete floor, in a drug-induced state with a gun to his head, some four years prior. This was twice now that Redman had inflicted pain. He swore there would not be a third.

Uganda, Gulu
Charlie 2130 Hrs.

Lt. Clark was trained to follow his intuition—it started to gnaw at him. And Maysa was as intuitive as he. "What is wrong Mr. Clark? You look very anxious."

"I have this sixth sense. I can't explain it, but we need to leave Gulu. Now."

Maysa did what she was told, just as Lt. Clark had asked of her earlier. No questions asked—just do it. They had previously packed the pickup with the little they had. Now, the three settled in. Unfortunately, the only road out was through the center of town. They passed the square clock tower with its shattered glass faces that stood in the middle of a roundabout that directed traffic as a hub of a wheel to other locations in town and also to the north-south highway of A104.

No one seemed to take notice of them as they emerged south from the last row of houses. People were milling around and Clark's non-descript pickup looked like every other one that passed through. The night air was starting to cool down as they pierced the darkness.

The roadway was decent enough, at least by African standards, and the wind from their open windows had a fresh flowery scent. Only when a commercial truck passed by, were they forced to wind up the windows to alleviate the surge of dust that blanketed their vehicle. Maysa recalled the UN transporter, and how it had stopped for her, leaving her in that same cloud. The taste of dry dirt mixed with her saliva forced her to spit out the mud concoction; her baby sneezed with the same objection.

Clark had his elbow propped on the open window and thought about his 'crop dusting' teenage days. He and his buddies had bought a case of beer and drove down all the gravel roads that surround his little farm town. The drunker they got, the more interesting the topics seemed. The art of 'shooting-the-shit' solved all the world's problems. He had a smile on his face—his anxiousness eased.

At their current speed of 80 km/h, the T in the road lay less than an hour away. As he eyed his rearview mirror, commercial trucks with high-intensity lights raced to the rear of their pickup and then passed wildly, blowing a friendly toot of their horns. Their blaring music came and went like a sonic jet. Not much different than any other part of the world. Someone was always in more of a hurry to die.

As they neared the stop at the tee in the road, red brake lights lit the roadway like an airport landing strip. Some trucks went right, some left and some stopped at the corner at the combined fuel dock and food depot. Maysa had brought some water and a rice dish that was offered to her at the UN camp. There was no need for them to pull over at this well-lit intersection. Clark stopped at the flashing light. He looked left, then right, and then turned left for the last leg of the trip to Lira.

Up high on a wooded hill, Mac shouted out, "Holy shit! That's the lieutenant in that pickup. He has someone with him."

Jake looked through his night-vision binoculars. "Are you sure?"

"Fucking absolutely I am," reconfirmed Mac, somewhat dramatically.

Jake quickly grabbed his flashlight and pointed it to the direction of the lieutenant's pickup as it headed east down A104. He started to flash Morse code. Four short, one short, one short – long – one short, one short. He paused, one long, three long. He paused again, four short, one short, one short – one long – and two short, one short – two long – one short. Jake repeated the sequence one more time.

Clark noticed a flashing light in his rear outside mirror coming from a higher elevation. He adjusted his inside rearview mirror and thought someone was playing a joke on him.

"What's wrong, Mr. Clark? What do you see?" Maysa quickly turned her head and looked out the rear window.

Clark watched intensely as he felt a chill on the back of his neck.

"L, P," he said. "Wait," he spelled out the letters. "H, E, R, E – T, O – H, E, L, P. Here to help?" he said, confused.

"Someone has spotted us?" Maysa now looked directly at her friend.

"I don't know how, but someone is sending us Morse code. 'Here to help'," he said one more time.

"They must be friends of yours?"

"Not friends of mine. No one knows where I am," he said convincingly.

"Well, someone knows where you are. I don't know anyone who knows Morse code in all of Africa."

"It's okay...settle down. How far to Lira?"

"Maybe 50 km."

"All right, here's the plan. We will gas up in Lira and then keep on going south until daybreak. We will re-adjust our thinking at that time."

"And what money are we going to use to pay for petrol?" questioned Maysa.

"If we can find a closed station, we can steal the gas. If not... Well, we will have to improvise."

"You are not going to hurt anyone, are you?" feared Maysa.

"Not if I can help it. I'll leave an IOU, if that makes you feel better," he said briefly, smiling. He remained at his current speed as they headed towards Lira.

"What is an IOU?" asked Maysa.

"A piece of paper, usually signed and dated, saying you will repay someone for something you received."

"That is very commendable of you," she said.

Clark looked at her amused. She seemed to accept his intentions of leaving a promissory note. He smiled at the thought. *A stealth sniper leaves IOU for gas as he runs for his life.*

~

Scrambling to gather their stuff, Jake ordered, "Let's go guys! We can hitch a ride on one of those trucks down there at the truck stop."

Mac and Peterson understood what Jake meant without any further explanation. The three men hopped, jumped, slid, and bounced down the hillside towards the well-lit fuel dock. There were enough abandoned vehicles stacked along the perimeter to conceal their movement once they arrived. Most of the vehicles had either front-end damage or side damage. It was obvious the stop sign had little influence on their driving habits.

"*Do you think he saw the Morse code?*" asked Peterson.

"*I am hoping he did,*" replied Jake.

"*His speed didn't seem to change. He either didn't see it or he doesn't want us to know he saw it, which might make him concerned of our intent,*" remarked Mac.

"*We will have to deal with that after we catch up with him,*" said Jake.

Mac was a little concerned the lieutenant might not be so agreeable to their presence. "*If we catch up with him or at least spot him, I think we should just hang a bit to watch his maneuvers. If he knows it is us, I would wager he will have a welcome party not to our liking.*"

"I have no doubt you are correct, Mac. But let's zero in on him first. If he has a hostage, we will have to deal with that as well," related Jake.

"I can't imagine the lieutenant would take a hostage. That would slow him down. He is helping someone," shared Peterson.

"I'm with BP," said Mac. *"But he is still a threat until we can convince him of our intentions."*

"Off the PRS, guys. And find us a vehicle."

They crept silently along the trashed cars, observing every movement in front of them. One at a time, they scurried to the next hold out. Each observed for the others next go-ahead and each poised to protect their movement. A stolen truck would attract too much attention. They needed to commandeer their ride quickly and quietly.

A three-ton, vegetable-laden stake truck sat idling on the side of the road. 'Papas Farm's' fading moniker was scripted on the doors in white rust-peeling letters. The lone driver stepped from the fuel dock chewing on dried beef and holding a drink container. He casually walked through the lit parking lot to the shadows of his waiting truck. The three men watched as he got closer. Peterson and Mac held their positions as Jake moved in behind the shadow cast by the truck body. The man opened the door—Jake stepped to him and into the driver's seat and maneuvered the right-hand drive truck to his waiting men. They pushed the disabled man to the floor out of sight as they headed east towards Lira.

. . .

Redman, after informing CTA of his findings, requested a plane to take him farther south. A flight plan, he thought, would have to be filed with Uganda and he had Blakely initiate the request.

"Will the plane be fueled and ready for take-off at 0600?" asked Nigel Redman.

"Yes," replied Robert Blakely. "And I have informed Kampala that you should arrive in the next day or so. Here is a radio for you so you can contact the embassy. It is set for Malcom Coleman's frequency. He will be able to help from that end."

"Thank you Ro-bert, I appreciate your help. Take care of yourself." Redman offered his hand to Blakely.

"What do you want me to do with those two?"

"It's only been four days since this all went down. A week cooling off won't hurt either one. After that, cut the bastards loose."

Virginia

Romeo 1730 Hrs.

Samantha and Marsha each sat relaxed in silk pajamas on her living room couch. Samantha was caught up in a book and Marsha searched the web as their bare feet unconsciously played flirtatiously. Startled from her bliss by her vibrating cellphone, Sam placed her book down and answered it. "Hello."

"Director, it's Paul. We are about to go live from Gulu, Uganda. Carmen brought me up to speed with everything that has happened. I am truly sorry to hear about Terry. He was a good and honest man."

"Yes, he was, Paul." She paused to gather her thoughts. "We have no other coordinates than the base units. I suggest you scan south, let's say a five-mile swath from the main roadway until we hear the contrary."

"Yes, ma'am."

"Do you have the map of the area up?"

"Yes, ma'am. It is up on monitor two. Not much out there. West of the main roadway A104, is the Nile River. Ma'am, may I suggest narrowing our path to, say two miles on either side of A104."

"Your reasoning?"

"Well, ma'am. If they, that is CTA, choose Gulu as the pinpoint, may we not surmise that our kidnapped person of interest and his capturers would stay close to the roadway? The half-mile on either side of our swath would be inconsequential and would gain us an extra sector every four miles of southern inclination."

"Sound reasoning, Paul. Log it. I'll sign off tomorrow. And Paul, thank you for being there."

"You are welcome, Director. I know how much we all have given to this project and all of us wish it to succeed. I know Terry did."

"Thanks again, Paul. And share my appreciation with your team, please."

"Yes, ma'am, goodnight."

"Goodnight, Paul."

"Everything okay?" asked Marsha.

"Yes. Paul had an idea of narrowing the swath, which will give us quicker results."

Marsha laughed. "I think Paul has that spy mentality type mind. Like a chess player anticipating each opponent's move."

"Something like yours?" smiled Samantha.

"Does my vocation offend you?"

"Offend? I find it exhilaratingly dangerous but also alluring," purred Samantha as she slid across the couch to Marsha's side.

"So, I am your pussy cat now?"

"I wouldn't say pussy cat, maybe my..."

"Don't say it."

"My...Jasmine Bond!" laughed Samantha as she rolled on her back, pinned under Marsha's control.

Uganda, Lira
Charlie 2430 Hrs.

Lt. Clark was uneasy with the Morse code event even if it stated that *they* wanted to help. Who were *they*? Another set-up? He eyed his gas gauge.

"Keep your eyes peeled for a closed gas station or anything that might look like it contains gas," instructed Clark.

"Peeled? Another American colloquialism?" interpreted Maysa.

"Girl, you will get stoned if you keep correcting Western English," joked Clark.

"Stoned! I have been stoned. Even my father threw stones at me. He ordered me out of my home, away from my mother, brother, sisters, and my village," combatted Maysa.

Billy Clark looked over at her bewildered and apologetic.

"I'm so sorry, Maysa. I didn't mean literally. I can't imagine your pain. Please, forgive my insensitivity. I didn't realize..."

"Realize what? Why a young girl with a baby would be on her own? Why she would give up her dream of teaching?" Maysa exploded as tears filled her eyes. Clark quickly pulled over. She cried as she retraced her horror, "Why I would let filthy pigs rape me... for a cup of rice, or a bottle of water?"

She darted out of the pickup as it came to a stop. Clark jumped out after her. She turned to him and ripped open her wrap-around tied dress, revealing her scarred body.

"Look at me!" she screamed. "Would any man want me now?" She withered to the ground in tears.

Clark saw the multitude of scars that crisscrossed her body. He saw her despair and felt her pain. He went to her. Clark knelt at her side and put his arms around her and held her tight.

"I am so sorry, Maysa."

Maysa accepted his strong arms as she released the tears of her injustice that she had been harboring for the last twenty months. She had never let anyone get remotely close to her. She held onto Clark's arms—she cried uncontrollably.

~

Jake and his team saw the lights of Lira. Only once had Peterson needed to subdue the driver after he started to regain consciousness. He sprawled, wrapped around their legs like a sleeping dog. A stenciled fluorescent sign northwest of Lira pointed to a bypass road that indicated a southerly direction to Soroti.

Jake quickly veered to the right causing a partially opened pineapple crate to fly across the road to the delight of some pedestrians. The three soldiers continued to follow the paved road south until Jake noticed the fuel gauge's needle was starting to ping on empty. Obviously the driver was more interested in feeding his face first before re-fueling. They needed either to find fuel or ditch this truck and recon another—and soon. Their focused eyes scanned the neighborhoods as they sped along the dark road.

~

A sensitive Clark gathered Maysa in his arms and carried her to their pickup. He gently placed her in the passenger seat, next to her sleeping baby. He tied her sash around her, closing her wrap-around dress and wiped the tears off her dusty face. She smiled up at him, exhausted. As he stepped onto the running board of the truck, he saw, a ways down on the left, a sign flickering as the proprietor shut off its power and the capacitors emptied their charge. It was a fuel station, a quarter kilometer from them, at the south end of Lira, off the Juba Road cutoff.

~

Pitch black as a night could be, Jake steered the laboring fruit truck along the bypass route. Flickering lights from store display signs were shutting down. Only a few gaged yard lights burnt with a low orange glow. The road seemed endless.

"Jake, stop! Look. Over there!" pointed Peterson.

A one-ton dually, extended-cab pickup sat in the shadows, at the side of a brick building. It was separated from other similar vehicles and large earthmovers that bore the S&W insignia on their doors and operating arms. A light from an upper window pierced the darkness.

"I'll pull over past the yard," stated Jake. "Mac, see if you can get it going. We'll wait here."

Mac jumped out and quickstepped in and out of the shadows and uninhabited doorways until he rested against the coveted truck's bed. He looked up to an upper window—no one seemed to notice him. He quickly peeked inside the bed of the pickup and then flattened to the ground. He probed along the frame and back bumper for a spare key—nothing. Next, he proceeded cautiously to the cab—a quick glance again to the upper window. He peered inside the pickup and tried the door. It was locked.

He felt for a small pouch in his dungarees pocket and pulled out two twisted wires and inserted them into the lock. He fiddled and twisted and then the lock popped open. He slid inside, checked the visor, under the mat, and then pulled the hood's T-handle. A silhouette figure came to the upper window. Peterson and Jake waited patiently. Mac sat quietly. The figure disappeared.

Mac stepped out and lifted the hood and with his pencil-beam flashlight, he found a small, black magnetic box. He opened it up and there it was—the spare key. He closed the hood quietly, jumped into the cab, and inserted the key. The engine clicked over and purred. Two figures approached the window, and then, the silhouette bodies joined and disappeared again. Mac smiled—he knew what was going on. He placed the truck into reverse. The dually tires dug in as he pulled silently away.

Jake backed the stake truck into a flat lot next to S&W Contractors. They heaved the driver back into his seat and placed his drink container beside him. They closed the door propping the driver's head on its side post and made their way to Mac and his waiting chariot. The dual gas tanks registered full. High fives quickly left them as they headed south. They scored big time and probably did the silhouetted couple in the window. Although, come daylight, there might be some explaining to do.

~

While Clark was fueling the pickup and two 20-liter fuel cans, Maysa had transitioned from her flimsy, much worn-out wrap-around dress to a pair of cotton pants and a button blouse, courtesy of Clark's talent for 'breaking and entering'. Maysa also picked up some mangoes, tomatoes, a large pot, rice and greens of nakati and amaranth. Goat cheese was their treat as they continued to drive through the night. *I'll treat Mr. Clark to a fine feast when we find our next safe haven.*

Clark was glad to see a more uplifted Maysa as they left the fuel station. Her new 'threads' looked good on her and she laughed at his choice of words instead of criticizing their origins. She told him in Swahili, nyama meant meat, so she was going to create him a feast of nyama with mixed greens.

"If you make it, I'll eat it," laughed Clark.

"It is very good and healthy, Mr. Clark. How many obese people do you see here? Maybe Uganda is the place for me. They have plenty of fruits and vegetables that grow all year long in their fertile lands. What more do I need?

Day 5 - Sunday

South Sudan, Juba

Charlie 0545 Hrs.

Robert Blakely had secured a UN plane for Redman's reconnaissance and as they approached the tarmac in the black SUV, as requested the plane was already warmed up and waiting. Blakely bid farewell to the tough guy, Nigel Redman, who nodded just before he boarded the single-engine Mooney. Redman felt a little cramped as he buckled in. His pilot, George, sat with his headphones on and busily flipped switches before he pushed forward on the throttle. He eased the plane ahead onto the taxiing strip alongside the runway. Moments later, they sped down the runway. George pushed forward as they took flight and banked the plane in a westerly arc, flying directly over Juba.

Redman had clearly instructed that he wanted to follow the Nile out of Juba to at least Nimule. He had pulled all news stories off of the South Sudan news wire from the past week and he wanted to pinpoint them on his reference map before heading east, inland to Gulu, Uganda. He had on his agenda: a body found along the Nile; four dead men and a shallow grave of a woman; an overturned, bullet-riddled flatbed truck with an older man found inside; a reported theft at the border town of Nimule and an allegedly stolen pickup found slightly north of Gulu. Redman wasn't leaving anything to chance. Not that his 'device' was responsible for all these, but he needed clarification from the local police who investigated these alleged crimes.

The Nile was still moving swiftly north due to the end of the region's wet season. Nigel suspected it would have been tough going against the flow, but nothing a desperate, well-trained man couldn't do. It wasn't long before they flew over the small camp where a dead smuggler had been found. Redman made a note on his map. They continued to follow the lush green banks of the Nile River toward Nimule, buzzing the treetops in their Chinese-manufactured aircraft.

Before they flew over the brickyards, they spotted an overturned punt straddling between two sandbars near a Bari fisherman's hut. The fisherman was using it as a bridge as he attended his lines. Then, the brickyards lay straight in front of them just as the Nile made a sharp bend to the right. Nigel wanted to talk to the police at the border town of Nimule; they set the plane down.

Nigel wasted little time in contacting the police and the officer who handled the break-in. Nigel was told by the officer, a rear lock had been forced open and, as far as the shop owner could tell, a man's shirt, pants, flashlight, two women's dresses, and assorted children's clothes and shoes were missing. Nigel asked the officer how the scene was discovered. The officer replied, "The door was nudged open and the lock was thrown to the ground." He thanked the officer and Redman and his pilot headed back to the plane.

Nigel scratched a line through that incident. He knew his man wouldn't be so messy. Next, he wanted to check out the allegedly stolen pickup that was viewed as someone's joy ride taken from a town farther south, across the South Sudan and Uganda border, called Atiak. George guided the aircraft back onto the highway and used it as a runway; a practice commonly used when there were no official airports. As they approached Atiak, crews were busily working in the steam of hot asphalt as it was spread along from giant hoppers with S&W insignias. Three kilometers farther south, they landed on the freshly paved asphalt highway and idled to the storage yard of S&W.

The temporary office trailers were bustling with foot-traffic as employees darted in and out. Redman noticed that besides a high concentration of Chinese workers wearing white hard hats, other nationalities were quite obviously on staff. He entered the office. Politely, Nigel inquired about the pickup that ended up near Gulu, and if he might have a chance to investigate it further. He was given permission and directed to where it was located before its scheduled repair.

Nigel, with a copy of the repair manifest in hand, opened the right-hand door of the pickup. The wires had been pulled out of their loom and then roughly cut. He sifted through the red-dried dirt on the floor mat. Nothing. As he was about to close the door, the sun lit something in the disturbed dirt. Redman swayed back and forth to catch the light just right and there it was. He picked up a shell-like triangular piece. There was nothing in the area that would have been tracked into the truck that would resemble this piece. *Ceramic?* he thought. His mind raced with possible scenarios and reasons. *The embassy's clean-up crew found the lieutenant's combat knife left in one of the foxholes. The other foxhole also had cut reeds, which would have been made after he left the planted ambush. The bastard has ceramic knives with him,* deduced

141

Redman. He shook his head, *clever bastard.* He closed the door.

Out of the office trailer, a little man with a white hard hat waved a tightly held piece of paper in his hand as he came running towards Nigel.

"Redman... Redman!" he shouted in his Chinese accent. "Another truck missing. In Lira!"

. . .

The drive from Soroti, Uganda, had cost Clark and Maysa a lot of time as they maneuvered through the flooded roadways of the Awoja swamps. They had pulled off onto a dirt road just north of Mbale, leeward of Mt. Elgon, just before daybreak. They found an empty, medium-sized concrete shed with a tin roof, just beyond a small creek. Clark thought it was probably used for grain storage when in season. All in all, they had done well, but now it was time to rest before they headed to the Kenyan border later in the afternoon.

The lieutenant wasn't concerned as much with detection from the locals while driving with Maysa and her baby; it was a welcomed cover. Maysa looked very mature in her new clothes. They complemented each other and with Ateefah in her arms, they looked like a family. No—his concern was for the Morse code signal he had seen in his rearview mirror. He wondered if it was from the men he had encountered at that make-shift base camp. *But why now?* Maysa looked at him and noticed the troubled look on his face. "Mr. Clark, what bothers you so?"

Clark looked at her as she lay next to him on top of her old wrap-around dress, which was now used as padding against the hard steel. "That signal. Very strange," he said without hesitation.

"Yes. I have seen strange things as well."

"Like what?"

"Figures moving in the grass without seeing them. Funny-looking vehicles traveling silently in the same fashion," she said nonchalantly.

Clark propped his body up on his forearm and leaned into Maysa.

"You saw what?"

"Figures moving in the grass without seeing them," she restated.

"When? And where?"

"Maybe four days ago, near Atiak," she said calmly. "I know they saw me in the back of the truck. I smiled at them."

"You smiled at them? You saw their faces?"

"No, I didn't see their faces but I knew they were there."

Clark sat up against the inside fender of the pickup's bed in thought and then said, "So, you saw them twice?"

"I saw the funny-looking vehicles earlier and then later, the others in the grass beside the road."

"Which direction was the first group with the funny vehicles going?"

"West."

"And the others?"

"South."

"Okay. So we can assume there are two groups. One group is mobile and the other group, on foot." He paused. "Why on foot if they are after me? Why not in one of the Chenowths?"

"Maybe they want to travel like you."

"Like me?"

"Yes. There are many villages along the road as we have seen. Maybe the vehicles needed more cover so no one would spot them like I did."

"How old did you say you were? That's it! They wouldn't have known which way I decided to go. They were south of me to start with, so to cover their asses, one group followed the most practical route over to the Red Sea, while the other focused on me either coming down the Nile or by road. They waited for me like an ambush as we drove by."

"Why would they signal you? Why not just come after you?"

"Good point. I have been wondering about this whole thing from the start. Nothing was out of protocol but it just seemed different."

"Ah, your sixth sense," said Maysa with a smile.

"Yes...just like you. For whatever reason, you dropped your defenses when we met, and you had more reason than anyone to keep your guard up. But you didn't... you allowed me in."

Maysa laughed, "Only because you asked my name."

Clark smiled at her and combed back a fallen lock from her eye with his finger, "I hope I can keep you and your baby safe."

Maysa touched his hand. "We will keep each other safe."

Washington - Sunday

Romeo 0230 Hrs.

The room was dark and quiet with only the menacing growl that came from behind her. She found a door and heard the clicking of its paws on the tile floor as it ran through the hallway; the clicking was getting louder. She turned the knob frantically, but it didn't budge. She felt a thumb throw-bar above the handle. She turned it and the door swung open into a twelve-foot square fenced yard. She ran to the fence and took one giant leap. She clung to the chain-link fence; hand over hand, feet bravely searching for foot holds. The triple strands of barbed wire stopped her from escaping over the top. Looking down, the wolf-like creature jumped at her jacket, catching it in its mouth. It hung on, bouncing with its weight as if it instinctively knew she couldn't hang on forever. Her fingers, pinched between the wires, were cut and bleeding as she now supported her weight, plus the beast.

Out of the corner of her eye, she saw the black mane of the horse she befriended earlier. It galloped towards her. It reared on its back legs and struck at the beast, hitting it hard. The force was enough for the beast to loosen its grasp on her jacket. It fell to the ground beneath the hooves of the majestic mount as it delivered blow after blow; it snorted with flared nostrils, eyes deep and glaring. She couldn't hang on any longer and released her grip. She fell to the dirt and landed beside the wolf creature. The horse nuzzled her to get up. She lay there, and then, one eye opened as the horse nuzzled her again. She reached over to her whining phone. "Hello."

"Excuse me, Miss Marsha, for this late call... but we have another directive to move PAG," informed Paul.

She inspected her hands and then answered. "Where to this time?" she said in a sleepy, tensed voice.

"Starting south of Soroti, Uganda."

"The same quoted, 'Reliable Source'?"

"Yes, ma'am."

She took a deep breath, "Okay, Paul. You know the protocol. Have you tried the director?"

"Yes, ma'am. I left a voice mail."

"Okay, Paul. I'll inform the director. I'll see you later. Thank you."

"You're welcome. Good night."

"Good night, Paul."

"You'll inform me of what?" asked Samantha as she brushed her long black hair to the side.

"Um, another directive to move PAG," yawned Marsha.

"Reliable source?"

"Yes."

"Who is this reliable source?"

"I'm guessing here, Sam, but probably one of Tomlinson's headhunters, possibly Nigel Redman."

"How does that horse's ass know where to track this man?"

"Why did you say horse's ass? You won't believe the dream I just had." She paused. "I think he is over there in South Sudan. He said something to me about getting together when he returned to town."

"What? Why would he say that to you?"

"I think he was hitting on me," smirked Marsha.

"I guess your cover is safe."

"Which cover... being gay or ..."

"Being gay, of course!"

"That could work to our advantage, Sam. Maybe I can seduce some information out of him."

"Look, put all your humor aside, Ms. Jasmine Bond. You stay away from that animal."

"Is that an order?"

"You know I can't order you, but I can wish it."

Marsha smiled at her friend and pulled her close. "You know something is going on other than what happened to Terry, or the missing soldier. We need to find out what it is and who the ringleader is."

"Oh, I think Tomlinson is part of it. Who else is involved and how deep it goes, that I am not so sure of. But I would bet it centers on South Sudan. It's a new country with a lot of potential. Big money to be made there. China and the U.S. have been pouring in a lot of money to secure mineral rights and such."

"Yes. That I knew. It's the under-the-table and black market payoffs that concern me," said Marsha. "The country needs to establish allegiance with a superpower to be able to jump into the developing markets. They don't have enough infrastructures in place to do it on their own."

Samantha sighed as she looked up at the ceiling. Marsha looked over to her.

"What?"

"I'm going to have bags under my eyes with all this cloak and dagger stuff."

Kenya, Outside of Kitale

Charlie 1200 Hrs.

The sparse inhabitants of the desolate Rift Valley made the first part of Colonel Dimitri's relocation south from Lake Turkana, seem like a Sunday stroll. They, however, had to lay low just past the town of Lodwar, where the only crossing of the Turkwel River was over the Lodwar Bridge. They had no other choice. Each vehicle took its turn crossing, and then, took cover in the tall grass at the river's edge, and waited for the next to arrive. Once re-united, they took off down the barren road, and moved silently, with their solar packs peaked at 50 km/h. As long as the sun was shining, they were able to maintain these speeds all day. However, if they needed to get out of the way in a hurry, they had the option to fire up their gas engines.

Dimitri and his team travelled light of insignias on their vehicles and their uniforms, although in their to-go bags, Colonel Dimitri stuffed NATO stickers and patches, if needed. It was not uncommon to see NATO vehicles traveling the roads or back country. He also had a set of Kenyan Wildlife Services emblems that could be used if they encountered resistance near national parks. The Wildlife Rangers carried heavy weapons since 2002, mainly to keep up with the fire power of poachers. He doubted anyone would question his men or their fire power.

The colonel knew the Brits where training the Kenyan 'Rifles' out of Nanyuki, just east of Mt. Kenya National Park, for fear of another attack by 'Al-Shabaab', the militant Islamist group who was responsible for the massacre at the Westgate Shopping Center in Nairobi. The Kenyans believed this group was also responsible for close to 38,000 elephant deaths, sacrificed for their ivory tusks. Dimitri felt once they encountered more heavily populated areas, they would switch to gas power, and fly either the NATO flag or the Wildlife Service's insignia.

Just before Kitale and east of the 14,000-foot Mt. Elgon, Colonel Dimitri decided they all needed a much-deserved rest. Jacobs was responsible for re-establishing communication with SAS and the rest would outfit their vehicles with the 'Kenya Wildlife Services' insignias. They stood and looked at this towering mountain surrounded by a halo of black clouds with the sun appearing to perch on its peak. It was a magnificent view.

Jacobs had received two messages. One was from SAS and it reported PAG was re-directed, once again, to re-locate their imagining to south of Soroti. He also received an encrypted message from 'Hourglass' stating Redman as the 'reliable source' for PAG's re-positioning.

Dimitri gathered his men.

"Gentlemen, we are going with power from here on out." He pulled up a map of the area on his laptop. "We are here." He pointed. As he followed the road, he dragged his finger off the route to the border town of Busia, Uganda and pointed to an extraction point farther north, on Kenyan land, at a bridge over the A104 and the Malaba River. "Here, gentlemen, is our point and with any luck, our man will fall into our arms. When we get closer, I'll have Jacobs send a low-impedance ping to Jake and his men. If we are in range, they should pick it up without giving up their position. Any questions?"

"Sir, what about A109 out of Tororo towards Malaba? It looks like a straight shot."

"You're right, Vicks, it does." The colonel zoomed in on the map. "It is one of the major commercial transportation routes. Look here where the trucks are all gathered. I would say they would need to have the proper papers before continuing. And the gap between each border station is quite substantial, which would make it easy for customs to apprehend anyone. But if you look at this extraction point, there is no border station. The dirt road travels in and out of Uganda and Kenya freely before it ends in Busia, another border crossing. It's sort of like your northern states interacting with the Canadian prairies. The road C43 would be easy to jump onto from there."

"We are assuming the lieutenant knows where he is going?" added Reynolds.

"He was stationed near Kisumu on Lake Victoria. I believe he knows where he is going, sir."

"I have to agree with Jacobs. Once he gets down in this area, we might never find him. After we get out of the communication void of Mt. Elgon, we will start sending and monitoring pings to Mac. Anyone else? Gentlemen, I know it is not a perfect plan, but at the moment, we are traveling blind. Ten minutes, gents."

. . .

Clark awoke and propped himself up on his elbows. From the back of the pickup's bed, he looked through the open doorway and noticed a black ominous cloud was moving over the mountain in their direction. He quietly got up without disturbing Maysa and her baby. Standing at the doorway, he had a better view of what was in store for them. Already the black cloud had consumed Mt. Elgon's peak, disguising its majestic size, and rainwater started to flow down through its carved-out reliefs. Without warning, a flash of lightning and a thunderous boom cracked the sky startling Maysa awake. Her daughter, Ateefah, just fidgeted and gave out a long sigh as she stretched.

"What is happening?" asked a groggy, Maysa.

"Thunder clouds. It looks like we are in for a wet day. I don't think we will be able to continue on just yet."

He walked back to the pickup and looked up at the tin roof. "A few leaks but we should be dry enough in here."

"Put out the pot to catch the rainwater. Today I will make us a feast," smiled Maysa. "Can we build a fire?"

"Are you asking, if we are able or if it's a good idea?"

"Well... I guess both."

Clark opened the dented tailgate, sat on it and looked at Maysa. "I think we would be safe enough. No one is going to venture out in this today."

Clark had not been around too many babies, but he couldn't get over how good Ateefah was. She was getting bigger and stronger every day. Clark admired Maysa's tenacity; she had been through so much at such an early age and yet, she still carried herself with dignity.

The rains were coming down much harder now, so much so that Clark had lost sight of the other side of the road. And the mini monsoon had already filled the pot with water. Maysa had gathered enough dry wood from the scattering she found throughout the shed and formed them into a crosshatch to build a fire. In the center, she placed dried-out stalks of elephant grass. She looked around for some stones to strike together as Clark sat, once again, on the tailgate, playing with his boots.

"What are you doing, sir? Help me find some stones to get the fire going," she insisted as she might to a husband.

Clark laughed at her and twisted his boot's heel, and then pulled out a tiny pump flint.

"What is that?"

"Watch..." He pushed down on it a couple of times like a child's spinning-top toy. "Voilà!" he said as the straw reacted to the sparking action.

"That is amazing! Do you know how many times I have inflicted injury to my fingers trying to start a fire?"

"It has a dedicated spark, so you can aim it. But it can also give you a serious burn."

Maysa turned this ingenious device in her hand. "What is it made from?"

"High strength flint, and the case is plastic."

She smiled at him and handed it back. She looked around the shed, went to the other side of the pickup bed and stripped naked. With her knife in hand, she squeezed through a couple of broken boards and headed out into the rain.

"Where are you going?"

"Fishing! We need fish with our meal. They will be easy to catch in this rain at the creek."

Clark had almost forgotten about that lazily flowing creek. "Be careful," he shouted after her. The deafening noise of the rain battering the tin roof muffled anything he might have said to her. She quickly disappeared. Clark heard the *clang* of goat bells as Maysa passed by them. As if by internal intuition, Ateefah started to fuss as if she somehow knew her mother was gone. Clark walked over to the truck bed and picked her up. He cuddled her in his arms, swaying back and forth and whispered, "Shh, little one. Your mommy will be right back." Her eyes were bright and big as she looked up at him, smiling. "I think you should be walking by now, little one. You keep trying, so come on, let's do it." Clark held on to her petite hands as he guided her feet in short strides. The bed of the pickup made for an unobstructed level plain for her. "That's it, come on. You know you want to do this. I've seen you try."

Ateefah looked at him with questioning eyes and then flashed her big smile, followed by a giggle. With his help, she wavered on unsteady legs, and with Clark's support, she took her first steps and—whoops, faltered to her knees. She looked up with saddened eyes and a dismal grin. Not giving up, she reached for the top of the big green box and tried once more. She looked back into his eyes for encouragement and lifted herself back onto her wobbling legs. She let out excited giggles as she took a couple more steps. Clark, full of pride, picked her up laughing and danced around the shed with her in his arms. "You did it, my little one, you did it!"

As he turned, he saw Maysa, drenched, but even being water-soaked, he could see the difference in her eyes—she cried with sheer joy. She dropped the fish, her knife, and ran to join them in Mr. Clark's strange spinning dance. Clark grabbed Maysa's old wrap-around dress from the bottom of the pickup bed and draped it around Maysa to dry her. Maysa hung on to his waist with her feet on his, enjoying his peculiar dance.

Pentagon, CTA – Sunday
Romeo 0730 Hrs.

The line was full of static as Jack Tomlinson answered.

"Where are you?" shouted Tomlinson.

"Lira," a distant voice replied. *"There is a huge front coming in. Roads are already flooded past Soroti. If I don't get out now, Jack, it will be days... maybe a week before we can travel again."*

153

"You might as well come home, Nigel. Now that we have a clear direction, let's engage PAG to do its thing. Dimitri can clean things up like he is supposed to. Don't want anything hanging over us. There is a SOC (Special Operations Command) plane leaving Djibouti, I'll have them divert to pick you up."

"Roger, that."

Holding down on the disconnect button of the desk phone, Jack mumbled to himself, *That fucking PAG better do its thing.* He released the disconnect button and dialed the number for the SAS department.

"Hello, SAS."

"Hello," he said in a raspy voice. "Who's this?"

"Paul, and whom may I ask are you?"

"This is Director Tomlinson of CTA. I understand there is severe weather coming into our locating area..."

Paul interrupted the director and jumped in to boast PAG's capabilities, *"Not a problem, sir. PAG doesn't need visuals to screen for our missing person, that's the beauty of it."*

Tomlinson hesitated in replying in his usual derogatory blast, but instead assumed a polite demeanor. "Well, very good, Paul. That's what I like to hear. Keep up the good work and please let me know if anything comes up...night or day, Paul."

"Yes, sir," Paul replied politely.

"Will your director be in today, Paul?"

"I have talked with the Assistant Director Marsha Atworth this morning. She did mention she would see me later, so I am assuming they or she will be in."

"Very good, Paul. Do me a favor, let me know when either one arrives, will ya?"

"*Yes, sir, of course.*"

"Thanks Paul, nice talking with you."

"*Goodbye, Director Tomlinson.*"

The call ended.

"What a fucking schmuck," laughed Tomlinson. "And when did that bitch Marsha get promoted to AD?"

~

"What a freaking asshole. Who does he think he is kidding? I've heard how he talks to Director Jones," slighted Paul under his breath so his team members couldn't hear him.

. . .

Jack Tomlinson sat at his Virginia office desk. It was covered with 8x10 glossies of informants, friendlies and Nigel Redman's discoveries in Juba. He was startled by the ring of his in-house line.

"Hello," he said in his usual condescending manner, as if he was so busy he barely had time to speak to anyone.

"*Sir, it's Petty Officer Smyth. I just got confirmation SOC will pick up Mr. Redman in one hour and eight minutes in Lira. Also, sir, just a reminder of tomorrow's gala for the First Lady's 'Save A Day' campaign.*"

"Jesus! Not another one of those." He sighed, "What's the dress?"

"*Your whites, sir. And I have an outline of your speech sent to your email for you to proof.*"

"I have to speak?" he questioned, miffed.

"*Yes, sir. Remember you offered to inform the chamber of the wonderful things PAG was doing?*"

"Shit, Derrick, I was drunk. I got tired of hearing from all those goody-two-shoes talking about saving the whale, saving the split-tail tattle bird and the other weird shit."

"Don't know what to say, sir. Your speech is inspiring though."

"Thanks, Derrick. Does Redman have an invite? He'll be back in town. He's the only fucker I can tolerate."

"I'll make sure he is placed on the guest list with accompanying credentials, sir."

"Anything else I should be aware of, Derrick?"

"Are you referring to last year's event or the world in general?"

"You know, Derrick, sometimes I think you are just fucking with me," chuckled Tomlinson, briefly.

"Sir, I would never do that," said Derrick, sensing the director's slight humor.

The director hung up with a feeling of one-up-man-ship but his euphoria quickly left him in thought about his upcoming speech. He hated those pompous events and everything they stood for. "Fucking women getting involved were they don't belong," he muttered. He searched his email for Derrick's notes.

. . .

A nightlight offered the only illumination of a draped linen sheet that outlined two bodies nestling together. A repeated short buzz from a Blackberry that sat on a night stand, alerted Marsha of a secured message. She immediately sat up and grabbed it before it disturbed Samantha.

"I'm awake, M," said Samantha as she rolled over to face her friend. "What is it now?"

"I need to get this. Can I use your laptop again?"

"Of course," said Samantha knowing her friend needed privacy. "I'll switch on the coffee."

Samantha flipped the covers off and sleepily strolled to the kitchen. She pulled back her long black hair and twisted a scrunchie into it. She momentarily looked through the kitchen window and caught the view of the early sunrise, as it cast a long shadow of her house over her pool and herb garden. *"How peaceful."*

Marsha quickly inserted a lead from the Blackberry into the laptop. She typed in an encrypted code. The message read: "NR Romeo, ETA 2200." End of message. She signed out and set the laptop on Samantha's night table. She ran her fingers through her hair and sauntered to the kitchen where the smell of freshly brewed coffee wafted through the air. Samantha, who was already sitting at the table, was thumbing through a Better Homes & Garden magazine. She looked up at her friend as she entered.

"Everything okay?" asked Samantha.

As Marsha was about to answer, her cell phone rang.

"Hello? Hello? I can barely hear you," she said.

"Marsha, my sweet lass, it's Nigel Redman!" he yelled. *"Sorry for the noise but I'm in a transport plane heading back to Washington. It would be my honor to escort you to the First Lady's gala event Monday night."*

Marsha put her hand over the miniature microphone and turned to Samantha. "It's Redman. He wants to take me to the ball tomorrow night."

"You know my feelings about him, but I also know you have other concerns."

"Hello? Hello?" yelled Redman. *"Can you hear me?"*

"I thought I lost you for a moment. Call me Monday... Hello?" she shouted. "Lost him."

"So, our 'reliable source' is heading back?"

"Seems so." Marsha sensed a strain in Samantha's voice. She stepped to her side and put her arms around her. "I'll be okay."

"I can only hope." She looked up at Marsha. "No heroics, please."

"I'll be fine." She paused. She was conscious of Samantha's feelings and didn't want to seem inconsiderate, so she asked, "Do you want to come with me to the office? I need to pick up another laptop since mine was stolen and we need to sign off on Paul's orders for re-positioning."

"I'd better stay here. I have a speech to finish before the dinner tomorrow and also arrange for Admiral Stone to honor you with your promotion."

"Samantha, I want to thank you for everything you have done for me. I..."

"Shh. I won't hear it. You have earned every bit of recognition and it is time your peers salute you for it. If you were Army instead of Navy, I would have promoted you myself, long ago. The First Lady's 'Save A Day' is a perfect event for this."

"We do have kind of a broad spectrum of personnel here. Army, Navy, Paul is Air Force, Phillip, Carmen and a couple of the others are independent contractors. Samantha, you have really developed a special group."

"We have developed and honed this group, Miss Assistant Director. Remember, you picked them, I just reviewed their qualifications."

Kenya, Webuye – Sunday
Charlie 1530 Hrs.

The torrential downpour had the red-brown silt-filled rivers rising to mere inches of several bridges structural girders along its path as it steadily flowed toward Lake Victoria. The swollen Malaba River had overflowed its banks. This made travel across it dangerous for the citizens of the twin cities of Malaba. Their shared international border between Uganda and Kenya, a major access route for trade and commerce, was blocked by caravans of loaded trucks from Nairobi. This heavily traveled route carried trade from the west coast of Kenya to parts throughout Africa. And it was the responsibility of each country to maintain a substantial garrison of troops to try and eliminate the illegal export of endangered species.

Dimitri and his team saw the black skies to the west as they continued their movement south in the dryness of the east side of Mt. Elgin. A tributary of the Malaba River dangerously lapped at the concrete abutments as Dimitri and his team crossed. Their idea of catching up with Lt. Clark at their stated extraction point was starting to seem dimmer as they proceeded south and then west onto A104 at the town of Webuye. They hadn't anticipated this freak storm.

They pulled off the highway at a long straightaway so they could observe any traffic; Dimitri re-assigned their insignias to NATO patches. From here on out, they hoped their impersonation would save them any scrutiny from local authorities.

Jacobs sent out a low impedance ping to Jake and his men—no response. He would try later when they came out of the full influence of Mt. Elgin. They still had no idea where Jake and his team were or where Lt. Clark had eluded to. Directing Jacobs to use an open channel could simplify the matter, but one directive Col. Dimitri wasn't prepared to use quite yet. He felt there was still time to intercept the lieutenant before he got into too much trouble. Reynolds approached Col. Dimitri.

"Sir, these weather conditions have probably slowed Jake down. There are a lot of lowlands that could flood and leave them sitting for a week. If we head south as we talked about along C43 and camped at its narrowest trajectory point to the Uganda border, it could give us a strategical location for going in either direction."

"Yes, Rey. I believe you are right. By the look of the river flow so far, the lowlands of the Malaba River, where the borders cross, would probably be flooded. But I think we should still observe the area. We can't leave anything to chance, not now; we are too close to SAS's re-direction."

"Why do you think Redman was told to return home?" asked Reynolds.

"Probably for the same reason we have just re-set our mission—the rains. If he found some trail, he would have stayed on it. Having PAG as a backup and us to apprehend, maybe CTA felt he had served their purpose. Once we make camp, I'll have Jacobs contact SAS to give them our co-ordinates to use as a base line. Let's get moving; I'd rather be early than too damn late."

SAS Headquarters – Sunday

Romeo 0900 Hrs.

Marsha had just pulled up to the guard shack when her phone began to ring. She smiled at the guard, showed her ID and then the gate opened to allow passing. She juggled shifting into 2nd gear, as she held the phone in her hand eying the caller's name.

"Hello, Paul."

"Hello, Assistant Director Atworth. I wanted to inform you of a message from our extraction team regarding their new co-ordinates. Do you want us to re-position?"

"Paul, I have just pulled in. Give me ten minutes and I will be right there."

"Very good, ma'am. We will wait for you before re-positioning."

"Thanks, Paul. Bye."

Man, those guys sure do move around a lot. I hope PAG can keep up, thought Marsha.

She pulled into her assigned parking spot. *How nice.* Since Marsha's promotion, she had been entitled to some perks, one being her own designated parking spot. She whipped her little car in and then reached for her purse off the passenger's seat. With a brisk walk, she managed to grab the shuttle before it left her parking area. On entering the employee's lobby, she was, once again, subject to palm reading recognition, and an ID swipe from her card.

The halls were virtually empty compared to the weekday traffic, but nonetheless, Marsha still had to maneuver in and around meanderers to make up time from the less commanding spirits as they casually sauntered to their domains. She punched in a series of numbers, and then, once inside SAS's outer secured chamber, she rested her chin on the pad. The retinal scanner acknowledged Marsha's authorization, and the security door clicked open.

"Good morning, everyone," she hailed as she entered.

"Good morning, ma'am," they all said in unison.

Marsha walked to Paul's side.

"Good morning, Paul. Thank you for waiting."

"Mornin', ma'am. Ma'am, may I have a quick word before we engage PAG?"

"Sure, Paul," she said a little concerned.

"Ma'am, earlier, Director Tomlinson called and asked me to inform him when you or Director Jones came in. I didn't like the way he implied I had better...like I was going behind your back. I just thought you needed to know this."

"Thanks, Paul." She paused. "Paul, call him and ask him if he would like to speak to me, as I was standing near you. Let's see what he says?"

"Don't you think that will piss him off? I mean... maybe provoke his temper, shall I say?"

"Hahaha, I hope so, Paul. Oh, and Paul, use my new title."

"Yes, ma'am," smirked Paul.

"Good morning, may I speak with the director, please? Yes, I'm Paul Hawkins from SAS. Yes, I will... Thank you." Paul put his hand over the receiver. "His secretary is patching me through. Yes, good morning Director Tomlinson. You asked to let you know when Assistant Director Atworth came in. Would you like to speak to her, sir? She is standing two terminals over. Oh, okay, I'll tell her, sir. Good-bye." Paul returned the receiver to its cradle and looked up to Marsha. "I think we called his bluff, ma'am."

"Well done, Paul. What did he say?"

"Just muttered something and then said to tell you to have a good day."

"What an ass."

"Yes, ma'am," smiled Paul triumphantly.

Marsha put her work face on as she turned to the big screen. An interactive map of southeastern Uganda and west-central Kenya was displayed from an altitude of twenty miles. A highlighted blue circle pulsated just south of Soroti indicating the search pattern in process of the PAG sensors. She looked at the co-ordinates Colonel Dimitri had sent: 00°32'20" N 34°10'30" E. Paul punched these co-ordinates into his computer and zoomed in on the big screen display.

"They are in the middle of nowhere, ma'am."

"Yes. But it puts them in between Malaba and Busia. I assume they have no idea in which direction to search."

"Their message stated they were going to remain there for a time."

"Fine." Marsha contemplated for a moment before continuing. "Our sensor beam is just south of Soroti. If we move it to the Colonel's position and track north along this highway, maybe we will intercept the soldier."

"The soldier, ma'am? I thought our person who was abducted by the militants, was a diplomat?"

Marsha closed her eyes and bit her lip. *"Shit,"* she said to herself. "Paul, meet me in the director's office, please."

"Yes, ma'am."

Paul stood up from his terminal and led the way to Samantha's office. Marsha tried running several scenarios in her mind but could only come up with one—the truth. Paul was an intelligent man and therefore, needed to be treated with the respect he commanded. They stepped into Samantha's office and Marsha closed the door.

"Paul, what I am about to tell you is top secret. I need to believe you are fully committed to our team and understand completely the implications, if this goes awry?"

163

"Ma'am, if you are concerned with my allegiance to the SAS or Director Jones or to yourself, I can assure you my commission will not stand in the way."

"Thank you, Paul. I knew when we first spoke at your interview, without broaching the subject, you were loyal, and that loyalty is what we were looking for and what we are asking of you now."

"Ma'am, was Terry privy to whatever you are about to say?"

"Terry was a colleague of mine... That's all I can say at the moment. The man we have been tracking has been put into harm's way by one of our very own for their selfish gain. There are certain men who believe, as we do, that there is too much injustice in this world and the ones that wield the power have no consequence for their actions. We... and when I say we, I mean Director Jones and myself... will not be part of this; however, we also cannot sabotage our dreams or our program. We believe in this program and its ability to help humanity, not to line the pockets of certain individuals. Do you follow me, Paul?"

"Yes, ma'am and may I say, Terry was a friend of mine. He had a kind soul."

"Yes, he did, and we want the ones responsible to never be able to hurt anyone again. Colonel Dimitri is a righteous man and a man to trust. It is imperative all information goes through either me or Director Jones."

"I understand, ma'am. Would I be presuming too much to assume Director Tomlinson is not trustworthy?"

"I would say, he is of questionable intent."

"Does Carmen know?"

"No. And for her sake, she doesn't have to. She is too vital to this project for anything to happen to her. We are still doing as we were commissioned to do. So as long as we proceed in that direction, there should be no reason for anyone to doubt our cause. The end result will be out of our hands anyway, but at least we will have proven the worth of our project to our supporters and to the world, as a humanitarian resource and not just another military dogma."

"Thank you, ma'am for your honesty. It means a lot to me and that responsibility, I will not take lightly."

"Thank you, Paul, for being part of the team. Now, I would suggest we get back to finding this gentleman. Also, may I have all your paperwork on the other altered positions of PAG? I need to sign off on them."

"Yes, ma'am. Happy to."

Day 6 - Monday

Uganda

Charlie 0600 Hrs.

The rains had let up by early Monday morning, and as Clark leaned on the shed's door, he looked out through the early morning mist. He noticed their little river had dropped a couple of inches just under the bridge's wooden structure. Going across would still be treacherous and a little nerve-racking as the concrete abutments could still wash out at any given time. Clark felt that remaining where they were could transpire into a compromised situation— they must push through. He looked over at Maysa and her beautiful baby, Ateefah. They were his responsibility now, and in this short time, he had become quite fond of them. He smiled and thought back to Ateefah's first steps and the look on Maysa's rain-soaked face as she saw her baby walk for the first time. He felt proud.

Clark's instincts had kicked in; his euphoria would have to wait until later. They needed to continue on and get across the Uganda-Kenya border to where his familiarity of the land and a dash of hope, would save their lives.

He nudged Maysa and with a blink of an eye she sat up with knife in hand.

"Whoa there, missy! Just me," said Clark with raised hands as he stepped back. He admired her quick readiness response—much like his.

"I'm so sorry, Mr. Clark. I must have been dreaming."

"It's okay, Maysa. Nothing I haven't done on more occasions than I care to remember."

"Is it time to leave?"

"Yes. The river has gone down to just below the girders. We can actually see the bridge now. I want you to take Ateefah and walk across before I drive the truck over. I'm not convinced of its stability."

Maysa picked up her baby and cradled her in her arms as Clark snuffed the fire and loaded their belongings in the pickup's bed.

"Go through the passage door and be careful. I'll follow at a safe distance and wait until you are on the other side. Not too many people out at this time of day."

Maysa smiled at her Mr. Clark and did as he asked. She felt the kindness coming from his aura. She looked out the door and scoured the landscape before briskly walking to the edge of the mud road towards the bridge. The silt-filled river raged underneath as she slowly crossed the arched structure. The waters continued to slap at the abutment as the bank was held hostage to its ravaging force.

Clark, after closing the larger shed door behind him, eased the pickup through the slippery grass to the red-rich mud road. The back end of the pickup had slight traction even with the weight of the two large boxes and a few pots; however, Clark hoped the cargo added just enough ballast. He studied the situation and calculated that once he started down the road to the bridge, the momentum and the slippery conditions would outweigh any last-minute decision to not cross the bridge if a choice so declared itself.

Clark thought back to when he and a couple of buddies were being chased by the cops, and they had taken flight through a farmer's field. As they approached their old fishing bridge, they had to make the decision to stop and get arrested or take the bridge as fast as they could. They decided to take on the falling-down bridge. It was a pure adrenaline-smoking charge as they flew through the air that is until they landed on the other side. The weight of the engine forced the nose of the truck down and with its crashing came a broken nose for Clark as his face bounced off the steering wheel. One of his buddies cracked his head open on the windshield and the other broke his leg as it got jammed under the dash. And worse yet, they still got busted.

It was now or never. Maysa had disappeared on the other side of the arched bridge and Clark hoped she had continued to walk a little farther. He waited a little longer and then—he revved the engine. The rear tires sprayed a mud rooster-tail as he slipped and slid to gain momentum. Twenty more feet lay ahead of him. The engine howled. His front tires slapped the wooden boards as he raced to the top of the arch. Maysa gasped as she saw the rushing water devour the bank holding the concrete abutment in place. Wide-eyed, she screamed as Clark's truck soared from the apex of the bridge through the air. All she saw was the undercarriage as it floated towards her until the rear wheels bounced off the lonely isle of concrete sending the vehicle across the vastly decaying void. As Clark made contact with the ground, he slid sideways off the road and into the slippery, wet grass until it finally came to rest a hundred feet past where Maysa stood.

Fearing for Mr. Clark's safety, Maysa attentively ran along the mud road to his side. She slid to a stop against the truck's bed as her Mr. Clark opened the door and peered out, and with a huge grin he said, "Come on, we don't have all day."

Maysa looked at him with a glaring stare. They left behind their little safe haven, the memory of Ateefah's first steps, and an unconscionable carnival stunt.

On their way to Tororo, Clark tried to explain, light-heartedly to Maysa about the last time he attempted such a maneuver. She was not amused at almost losing her Mr. Clark.

"Come on, Maysa. Lighten up."

"LIGHTEN UP, you say! I am not talking to you, Mr. Clark," stated Maysa with folded arms.

"Look at the bright side. I would have never made it across if I would have taken it slow. The washout would have ended our transportation. And then where would we be?"

"I'm not talking!" she insisted as she sat, glaring out the window. Maysa then turned and started in on her one, and only treasured friend. "And what would I have done if you would have turned upside down and injured yourself? Run to get help as you lie there dying? How would I explain this? Oh, let me see, yes...I met this man of questionable behavior, from a foreign country who has broken into many shopkeepers establishments, and oh yes, he killed three Al-Shabaab militants to get this truck that he now lies beneath."

Clark tried hard not to smile at her embellishment and flailing of arms of her overzealous account of their meeting—if only it hadn't been true. He heard every word she spoke and also the ones she didn't say. Words he had heard before from his beloved sister.

"I'm not guaranteeing anything, but I'll try to be less flamboyant."

Maysa looked over at him with her intense blue eyes, he returned her stare. She offered up a faint smile without saying a word and returned her gaze, first to her baby and then back to the road ahead.

Twenty minutes later, a road sign stated: Tororo 1 km, elev. 1190 m.

. . .

Shopkeepers were starting to display their wares as the town began to wake up. They entered the Zenye Plaza at the crossroads of Mbale and Malakis where Clark noticed two men standing over a delivery scooter. He pulled to the side just down from where the two men who appeared baffled by their inability to start the scooter, stood.

"Why are we stopping?"

"It looks like those two guys are trying to get that bike started. Maybe I can help in exchange for money or whatever you might need. Come on; let's see if we can help."

The two stepped from their truck and headed over to the puzzled gentlemen. Maysa continued on into the store.

"Excuse me, having trouble?"

The older man, obviously the shopkeeper, and the other man, younger, probably his delivery boy, looked up at the stranger.

"Good day to you, sir. Yes, it seems our motorbike does not want to start today," said the older gentleman.

"Was it sitting out during the rainstorm?"

"My son said he had it under cover but it won't start."

Clark stepped to the side of the bike. A make-shift gas cap covered the tank's filler.

"You see, it is full of gas," said the older man.

"Yes, I see. Do you have a pair of pliers?"

The older man instructed his son to go and get a pair of pliers for the stranger.

"You can fix it?"

"I believe so. It's happened to me a couple of times," he said trying to relieve any strain between the father and son.

"He is a good boy, but sometimes he is very forgetful," offered the shopkeeper. "You are American?"

"No, Canadian."

"For the road construction?"

"Yes, safety department."

"Oh..." sighed the shopkeeper who was looking at Clark's clothes.

"We got caught in the rainstorm. We lost all our belongings trying to cross a river."

"Where are you headed?"

"Back to Nairobi, if our luck and money hold out."

The son returned with the pliers. Clark removed the spring clip off the carburetor's fuel line to let the water drain out of the tank.

He smiled and said, "Water is heavier than gas."

Clark replaced the line after he got a clean flow of gas, and then started to kick it over. On the fifth kick it started and sputtered; he kicked it again, and it coughed and choked. Clark quickly twisted open the throttle to keep it running. Finally, the sweet sound of success, much to the delight of the shopkeeper.

Maysa heard the motorbike fire up, and as she looked out to where Mr. Clark and the two men were standing, her shoulders tensed and goosebumps formed on her arms. Across the plaza a big white truck with an SW insignia slowed, she saw their curious stares. Maysa put down a pair of men's trousers she was looking at and casually walked outside to Clark's side. She put her arm around him and brought his head down to her as if she was going to give him a congratulatory kiss. Maysa whispered into his ear. The older man was very delighted and begged them to return to his store for remuneration. With a pat on Clark's back from the shopkeeper, they all turned and headed inside.

The shopkeeper, who was very receptive to the young lady's intensity, hurried behind his counter and opened his cash register. He handed Clark $50 in small bills, thanked him graciously, and then took the woman's hand and showed them the back way out. Clark turned to thank the man, but the shopkeeper gestured with a sweeping motion to hurry, and fingers pressed to his lips.

Quietly he assured the stranger, "My son will drive your truck around back. Go now."

Clark understood the gesture, smiled, and nodded with appreciation.

~

"That's him!" blurted Mac.

"Are you sure?" asked Jake.

"Without a doubt."

Peterson threw his two cents in, "Who's the girl?"

Four eyes turned and looked at him with questioning stares. Feeling foolish for his quick outburst, he confessed, "Ya, stupid question."

"I'll pull over here. Keep your eyes on him," said Jake.

Mac observed the lieutenant's every movement, and any possible indication of their discovery. He watched as the old man patted the lieutenant's back, and then ushered them inside.

"They went back inside," Mac said.

Jake wheeled the dually to the curbside, "Do you think he recognized us?"

"He never looked up. He couldn't have seen us."

"Doesn't she look like the one who we saw on the back of the flatbed?" asked Peterson trying to rebound after asking his earlier question. "She is dressed differently, but she has the baby strapped to her with the same looking sash as before. And Mac, when you spotted him the first time, you remarked he had a woman with him."

"What are you saying?" questioned Jake. "The lieutenant hooked up with the young girl from the shot-up flatbed we came across on the road?"

Mac looked at Jake, "It might be possible she is also the same girl who killed those men at the camp site."

"I don't know their circumstance, sir, but neither looked like they were the hostages of the other. They look pretty cozy," stated Peterson.

"Jesus!" blurted Jake.

"How do you want to do this, Jake?"

Virginia - Sunday Night
Romeo 2315 Hrs.

The glaring white glow of Admiral Stone's ornately opulent desk lamp—a gift from the Emir during the intense drama that ousted Russia from Afghanistan—was the only fixture illuminating his home office. He finished the final touches to his speech for the next day's gathering for the First Lady's 'Save A Day' function.

The delegation attending had been picked, screened, and would include top-heavy brass, politicians, wealthy supporters, and representatives from other invited countries. He wished there had been a positive extraction from the PAG system, not because he wanted to gloat with internal pride while facing Tomlinson but because they needed some accolades and positive reassurance while stealing the power from that war monger. SAS could only do what they could do; he knew very well of its capabilities. He had kept his level of clearance hidden from Samantha. He dared not interfere, but he took solace in the thought, anyway. It was truly the ultimate test though, tracking a man blindly who was on the move rather than a relatively educated guess to a circumscribed area. He couldn't let on he knew of Tomlinson's plans or tell Samantha as she believed he was just waiting out his years. There was top secret clearance, and then there was TOP SECRET.

The admiral had confidence in Samantha and her staff, and the last time he saw her—besides seeming a little stand-offish and stressed—she appeared almost happy. He knew she had a guest at her home, one of her staff members, and even with that burden, she had the old sparkle in her eyes. He hadn't heard of any new man in her life, so maybe her return to her old self was due to her satisfaction with her work.

Stone missed those nights they would meet in secrecy; the smell of her, the softness of her skin, and even their stimulating conversations, they now haunted him, playing over and over again in his mind. He had paid dearly for his indiscretion, but he would gladly do it again. His wife, Barbara, still hadn't returned home from a committee meeting, and as he looked at his watch, 2315 hours, he poured a small shot of scotch and threw it back. He wasn't so naïve as to think he could change the past, but the future was another story. Stone felt, in his own way, little triumphs would multiply into groundbreaking revelations. Then, at that time, one would need to be ready to take charge.

Admiral Stone was tired, his mind weighed heavy. He stood up, turned off the light, and maneuvered to the crack of light shining like a beacon beneath his closed door. He walked out into the bright foyer and adjusted the intensity of the hanging chandelier before he meandered up the swooping staircase to his bedroom. It had been years since he and his wife shared the same room—well before anything happened with Samantha. It was mentioned at his hearing that as long as he wore a uniform, there would be no divorce proceedings. It was bad for morale as he was instructed. Stone's de-commission was transcribed as being initiated by him for being allowed to resign from his active sea duties in order to be stationed in a permanent desk job at the Pentagon.

His choice was to take the de-commission or resign completely from the Navy. He was appreciative of the decision as the Navy was his way of life. Friends of his, slandered in the same situation, fared much worse. Justifiably—maybe? History will answer that question, but morally, it had no bearing on life other than Congress showing its power. Stone neatly folded his t-shirt and placed it on the chair next to his nightstand. He slipped between the sheets.

As he set to close his eyes, an intense headlight beam bounced off his bedroom wall momentarily casting long shadows from his four-poster bed.

Uganda, Tororo - Monday

Charlie 0730 Hrs.

The young delivery boy had left the truck idling as Clark helped Maysa into the cab. He closed the door softly with barely a click. He drove down the lane and turned right onto a secondary road, then left on A109. Clark headed towards A104 and Kenya as marked on the quickly illustrated shopkeeper's make-shift map.

Mac, wearing only his t-shirt and his camo pants, crossed the square with determination and headed inside the store. Peterson took off down the block and peered down an alleyway. Taillights momentarily flashed as a pickup turned out of the alley onto a back street. Peterson high-tailed it in the direction of the disappearing truck and Mac jumped down from the back of the store into the alley just before Peterson arrived.

"It's him. He turned right."

The shopkeeper and his son looked defiantly at the two men. If the two soldiers stopped to ask them for information, it would only cost them valuable time without answers—that they were sure of. On return to the end of the alley, they continued with a dedicated walk so as not to attract too much attention. Jake already had the one-ton turned around waiting for them. The two men jumped in. Jake put his foot into the gas pedal and took an immediate right at the corner instead of going left around the roundabout. He swerved barely missing an oncoming car which careened off a signpost.

"Stay left, Jake!" hollered Mac.

"Fuck. Why can't they drive on the right side of the road?" flared Jake. He zigzagged over to the left and barely missed another on-coming car. Mac and Peterson sat quietly with smirks on their faces. "Don't say a fucking thing!" Almost instantaneously, the two could not hold it in any longer and burst out laughing. Jake sped down the road gritting his teeth, and then finally conceded with a slight smile.

Mac said reassuringly, "He can't get past us now."

Jake took another roundabout. This time he stayed on the correct side as he slid their speeding truck down the dirt road, kicking up a halo of dust.

"Look!" yelled Peterson. "There he is!"

~

"Mr. Clark, they see us!" screamed Maysa as she looked out the back window. Clark floored the four-cylinder pickup.

The road from Tororo paralleled the railroad for a short distance before it circled around the border town where several custom yards were laden with shipping containers awaiting inspection. Yellow-flashing caution lights notified drivers of impending customs and slower speeds ahead.

As Clark looked at the shopkeeper's crudely drawn map, he quickly veered to the right sending a dust cloud along with it. He then jumped onto the railroad tracks and started down the bumpy ride towards a bridge.

~

"What the fuck is he doing!?" yelled Peterson.

177

Jake drifted the 4x4 to the right just as the lieutenant had done and he too jumped onto the railroad track.

~

"Oh my God! Mr. Clark, a train is coming!" screamed Maysa as she grabbed onto the window frame and seat behind her as if trying to brace herself. "It will kill us!"

"Hang on, Maysa, not yet!"

Clark barreled down the thumping tracks and entered the bridge. There was no turning back now. Right behind them, the three men followed in the one-ton dually.

~

"Jake! Are you sure we're going to fit?"

As they entered the bridge with their much wider truck, the rear fiberglass fenders were immediately torn off and the two outside rear tires began to smoke as they rubbed against the bridge's narrow rails. Fiberglass shrapnel lay strewn between the tracks while other pieces flew into the air and over the side to the river below.

At the other end of the bridge, Clark jumped the tracks again, barely missing the train as the wide-eyed conductor frantically blew the whistle in desperation. Jake jumped on the brakes with both feet and slammed the shifter into reverse just as the train caught up to their nose. Speeding in reverse, the two outside tires blew out from the heated friction. Jake didn't flinch as the rubber ripped apart. He piloted his craft off the bridge and down the mud embankment as the train whistled past.

Calmly, the three looked out their front windshield as the train cars passed them by. Not a word was spoken.

~

Maysa tried to catch her breath. "Okay, Mr. Clark...well done!" she managed to enunciate as clearly as she could remembering his words of trying to be less flamboyant.

Clark, with his precious cargo, Maysa, and her daughter, Ateefah, sped past a newly erected building that was fortified with a chain-link fence. He drove along its backside nearest the river, to where he hoped he would find a road leading to C43. Bushes lashed out, scraping the side of his truck, and twigs broke off and were released like projectiles; they pushed through with determination. Finally shedding the grasp of the maze of briars, they crashed out of the bush onto a freshly plowed field. Ahead, they spied a minor road. Dirt sprayed from under the fenders as Clark barreled over the harrowed field, they bounced onto the road, and then fish-tailed down it approaching a seemingly busier crossroad. Maysa held on in amazement as Clark wheeled his machine with precision.

"Your minor indiscretions with the authorities have now served us well, Mr. Clark," said Maysa with a hint of sarcastic humor.

Clark looked over at her and her death grip on the door's arm rest—her knuckles were white. "You can let go now, Maysa." He laughed.

Maysa looked down at her hand, swallowed hard, and released her grip. Ateefah had a look as one might see on a child's face that just got off an 'E-ticket' ride at an amusement park. She wanted more...

. . .

Mac turned around and reached into the back seat to grab his PRS. He heard the low hum as they sat there—contemplating. "It's Colonel Dimitri. We must be close to their position."

"Where are they actually?" asked Jake.

179

"They are in high brush just north of Busia on the Kenyan side, sitting tight. They were waiting until they heard from us," relayed Mac.

"Tell him our target is between us, and we believe he is heading down C43, possibly towards the Canadian training base near Kisumu on Lake Victoria," speculated Jake.

The train finally passed as it had already started to slow for the terminal in Tororo. They all stepped out of the truck to assess the damage. Other than missing rear fenders and two shredded tires, the inside tires were still holding air.

"C'mon, guys, let's get this thing back onto the tracks. No way can we hit the main road with a mess like this."

"We can look for another truck," said Peterson.

"Not around here. There are too many customs agents, police, and army personnel. The conductor has probably notified the authorities anyway. They will be scrambling to find us," stated Jake. "Mac, you are the lightest. Get in and BP and I will push."

Mac shifted the transfer-case into four-wheel drive, and with a little help of rocking the truck back and forth by Jack and BP, the tires started to get a grip, and spun up the embankment throwing a plume of dirt off of all four. Maneuvering the vehicle, Mac, once again straddled the tracks. Jake and Peterson rushed up the elevated grade, jumped in, and the three finished their bumpy trek across the bridge. Jumping the tracks as the lieutenant had done, they followed the tire tracks left by the vanishing, Lt. Clark.

Washington – Monday

Romeo 1800 Hrs.

The anticipation of the night's Gala seemed to make the day fly buy. With Colonel Dimitri's revised coordinates for PAG, everyone was bustling around at SAS. Samantha was uneasy about Marsha going to the event with Nigel Redman, something Samantha was not looking forward to. Samantha had noticed in the seating arrangement dossier, Admiral Stone and his wife, Barbara, would be at one of the front tables, whereas Samantha was two across and three down from the Stone's. She had asked Derrick if he wouldn't mind rearranging her seat so she wouldn't be staring directly at Barbara. He understood and made it happen.

Petty Officer Derrick Smyth had the privilege of matching invitations to the guest list issued from the President's office. He already knew most by sight as he also had everyone screened just to be on the safe side. Smyth thought the Secret Service had been a little lax lately and he took it upon himself to verify the guests through his means. It seemed to him to go hand in hand since he was on the team of placing certain delegates with certain senators who were poised in alignment with the President's policies. And of course, the professional fundraisers had to be placed strategically between the mix of honored patrons, businessmen and sympathizers.

What worried P.O. Smyth was the three percent he couldn't collect enough data on. Five people out of a crowd of one hundred and sixty invited guests weren't that abnormal for a function of this size. But nonetheless, to him, it was too many. He had issued a memo, pseudo-signed by Jack Tomlinson, to be circulated to all the Secret Service and Military attendees to keep a watchful eye. He knew some were delegates' wives, last minute added attaches and/or their legal advisors. He also knew everyone had to walk through the scanners, but to save time and face, not all trinkets and jewelry were required to be removed. This wasn't TSA beating up little old ladies after all. These were the well-to-do, the pillars of our society, the who's who of the world.

Keeping his thoughts to himself, Smyth stood at the check-in desk in his dress 'Whites'. He looked handsome and felt the pride of a man of color who had been honored to serve in this capacity. He watched the Secret Service, with their stern looks on their faces, hardly secretive looking. Smyth, on the other hand, had a friendly smile as he was to ease the tension of the arriving guests, not provoke hysteria.

After forty guests had arrived, two questionable names were introduced by the Ambassador of Argentina as his wife's sister and her husband. Noticing a little sidestep to their walk, Derrick smiled with delight and welcomed them in his best Spanish. They congratulated him on his pronunciation, and then, the Ambassador's wife, in English, stated how handsome a young man he was. The Ambassador laughed and shook his head commenting on his sixty-three-year-old flirtatious wife's admiration for the uniform—and wine. They headed into the grand room, laughing amongst themselves.

Three to go.

Looking between the giant, outside columns and past the rolled-out red carpet, a company car pulled up. Out stepped Lieutenant Colonel Samantha Jones. She was escorted by Paul Hawkins, her team leader of the second shift, and his wife. Samantha was wearing a black satin, form-fitting dress with a lengthy, flaring-laced train, which dangled inches from the floor. It was accented with broad draping white lapels sans sleeves and elbow-high black gloves. Derrick did not wait for them to step to his side; rather, he went to Samantha and offered his arm.

She whispered to him, "Thank you, Derrick."

"My pleasure, ma'am."

"You look very handsome tonight."

"Thank you, ma'am. You look stunning yourself, if I may be so bold to say."

"A woman always accepts a welcomed compliment," smiled Samantha.

As the two ended their private conversation, P.O. Smyth accepted their invitations and articulated in a professional manner the whereabouts of their table. He watched as the lieutenant colonel was greeted by other top officials and she in turn introduced her escorts.

For the next half hour, P.O. Smyth was inundated with the other guests and the introduction of two more of the questionable names. *One to go* echoed in his mind as a few late arrivals pulled up. From his vantage point on the upper foyer, Smyth looked over the grand salon of the East Room and saw Samantha talking with Marsha who was wearing an emerald green, off-the-shoulder dress with a golden brooch at the apex of her V'd neckline and her escort, Nigel Redman. He appeared relaxed, enjoying his usual sexist banter while the ladies politely laughed. Tomlinson was taking up residence at the bar, jovially, and at times painfully obnoxious as the Scotch neared the end of each glass. *His speech ought to be interesting*, thought Smyth.

Gleaming crystal adorned the white-linen tablecloths and colorful Birds of Paradise had been chosen for the center pieces. The entourage from South Africa added a sea of color as they mingled through the tables, as did the delegates from Egypt, Nigeria, Uganda, South Sudan and

Kenya. Everyone was lively in conversations as they waited for the arrival of the President and the First Lady.

A tone sounded alerting everyone to take their seats as the President and First Lady had arrived. Tomlinson staggered slightly as he maneuvered over to his table surprising Derrick with his dexterity after consuming glass after glass of Scotch. Samantha looked disgusted with him as he garishly bounced his chair to the side so he could sit down. He didn't seem to care or recognize her quick gripe "Must you?" statement to him, but turned and started a conversation with his buddy Nigel.

After concluding the American National Anthem, warm applauses from the standing guests saluted the performance of a visiting children's choir from Illinois. It was an unrehearsed event, which was gladly inserted into the program after the First Lady learned of their tour of the White House. To add to the children's excitement and admiration for their endeavors, each child received a White House pin as a keepsake. This improvisation was in line with what the whole night was about. *A welcomed day to remember from unexpected moments!* It promoted well-being while sharing with family and friends. The night was off to a grand start.

The Master of Ceremonies, Admiral Stone, continued the heartiness of the night with his humorous speech and finally the commission of Marsha Atworth to Lieutenant and Assistant Director of SAS. His "Act of Congress" infusion also declared the truth of the statement since it was stated in history from the 1700s that any promotion in the Navy had to be approved by Congress.

With fifteen scheduled speakers from all walks of life, from every corner of the globe, each had the opportunity to share their 'Save A Day' experience. Some were from 'Hi-Tech' companies, some from grass roots endeavors, while others shared their wildlife rescue stories. A private foundation, the Fournier Foundation from France, shared a rousing speech by the CEO along with the company's namesake, Angela Fournier—who expounded charismatically on their enterprise of bringing potable water facilities to poor, undeveloped, and barely accessible areas. Her presence added much visible delight and her charming gestures swayed over the delegates. And then as the hands of the clock made their last stroke to 2200 hours, it was time to hear from the developers of PAG.

As Admiral Stone announced the second-to-last speaker, the room, already energized by Angela Fournier, exploded with cheers. The patrons were anticipating an environment favorable for future investments. So far, the technology had not been shared with the tech community, based on a final positive outcome from SAS. Lieutenant Colonel Samantha Jones graciously stood from her table and made that long 'What am I going to tell them?' walk to the stage and then across to the podium.

Samantha had many scripts written but they all seemed to find their way to the trash can. It was true, what they were attempting was much more difficult than, say finding a lost child, skier, boater, miner or anyone else when you knew the approximate coordinates. Trying to find a man on the run, a professional on the run, was proving much more difficult.

The lieutenant colonel stepped to the podium and adjusted the microphone.

"Mr. President, First Lady Baxter, distinguished guests. We thank you for your patronage and encouragement. It means a great deal to us all at SAS. Let me first re-cap our endeavors. As you are aware, our PAG system was designed for peaceful and humanitarian applications. We feel all may benefit from this technology, once perfected. Our programmers, even now, as we enjoy this lovely event, are re-writing code as we learn the power of this advancement for human survival.

"Since time is of the essence during a tragedy, such as hurricanes, monsoons, tsunamis, earthquakes, and tornados, to mention a few, the manipulation of PAG and the training of qualified personnel are as important and as expensive as the unit itself. We have hand-picked our programmers from around the globe to ensure the equality and cooperation of all governments in this changing world. With global warming influencing more of our decisions, it is imperative, we get this right without prejudice.

"Some of our engineers have been working on the affordable inclusion into existing monitoring systems. Citizens, upon signing a release, may get screened at airports, borders, cruise ship terminals, hospitals and even at your local doctors, if they are so equipped with scanning equipment. Because this program is set up as optional and not obligatory, individuals have the freedom to be inducted into our world memory banks without the fear of governmental intervention or reprisal."

Samantha paused and took a drink of water...

"Excuse me. I must be nervous." A low hum of approval waved through the salon as they were all hanging on every word with hands ready to speed-dial their brokers. She looked over to her friend for reassurance. *Where am I to go from here?*

Samantha looked out over the room to her potential backers and government officials. She couldn't tell them they were tracking a soldier for her government's quest. She just told them this project was without prejudice or government interference.

"Our second physical test was to pinpoint a man of unknown whereabouts and unknown agenda. That is to say, he has free will to be deceptive and use whatever he deems fit to become untraceable. I know in my opening statement, I said our program was meant for mass tragedy in a known location but we felt to really test our operators and to increase our speed, we needed basically, you might say, a man on the run."

The guests became anxious as this scenario had different implications. Tomlinson leaned into Redman. "What the fuck did she just say?"

She knew she had gone too far and had to regroup.

"Ladies and Gentlemen, please. This is a controlled experiment so we can work out all the bugs..." She looked over to her table. She saw Redman escorting Marsha out along the side wall and saw Paul on his cell phone. He motioned to her frantically.

Without warning, a horrific blast from outside the building sent reverberating shockwaves throughout the East Room. Secret Service grabbed the President and the First Lady and headed out the back of the stage. The already agitated dignitaries and guests, fearful of their well-being, ran for the nearest doors—chaos ensued.

Samantha stood in amazement and watched the room's profound mayhem. She was grabbed by the pretty blonde lady, and the distinguished gentleman who delivered the foundation's speech. They rushed her to the side of the stage out of harm's way, just as Admiral Stone ascended the stairs and made his way to Samantha's side.

"What is going on?" questioned Samantha, looking at her saviors and her friend.

"I don't know, Samantha," stated the Admiral, just as concerned as she.

Samantha thanked the alertness of the visitors as they too took leave with several men attending to their needs.

"Where did Redman take Marsha?"

"I'm sorry, Samantha, I don't have an answer."

Paul and his wife, after rising from beneath their table, joined up with his director at the side of the stage.

"Ma'am, we got a ping!"

"A ping? From our missing man?"

"Yes, ma'am."

Samantha briefly felt the excitement of the accomplishment but then anxiousness took over, fearing for Marsha. She looked at Admiral Stone. "I have to go."

"But Samantha..."

She caught Barbara's longing stare as the Admiral's wife stood with two of her committee pals.

"Barbara is waiting for you, Admiral. She needs you. Come on, Paul. Please drop me off at the lab."

The three, Paul and his wife, and Colonel Jones headed for the main foyer amongst the scurry of the Secret Service and their tracking dogs. Outside, P.O. Smyth climbed the steps two at a time and met Samantha just before the huge white columns as she exited the White House.

"Ma'am, the explosion took out Miss Atworth's car and several others. They say it looks like a gas line might have burst underground. I don't have confirmation of the validity of that statement as yet."

"Marsha's car?"

Derrick saw the anxiousness about his friend's face and added compassionately, "Not just Miss Atworth's, others as well."

"Derrick, what's going on?"

"I don't know, ma'am."

"Derrick, use whatever sources you have to find out. I don't like the looks of any of this. Paul is going to drop me off at the lab."

"Is that a good idea right now?"

"I can't imagine a safer place to be, can you?"

"I will stay in touch, ma'am. And let me know when you want to leave. I'll set up an escort."

Samantha put her hand on his arm, "Thank you, Derrick." He stepped back and saluted the lieutenant colonel.

As the poised Navy valet arrived in Paul's car, Samantha hesitated and turned to P.O. Smyth. "Derrick, one more thing. Can you arrange for protection for all my staff? I need time to figure this all out."

"Yes, ma'am, already in the works. Don't worry; everyone will be safe."

A black limo with gold 'FF' script passed them as Paul waited his turn to pull out. Angela Fournier looked out of the side-quarter window.

Day 7 - Tuesday

Kenyan Outback

Charlie 0600 Hrs.

Colonel Dimitri and his men had been waiting to hear from SAS and to hopefully join up with his scouting team. Their position had been unobserved by approaching armed traffickers.

"Mac, copy?" whispered Jacobs over his PRS.

"Yes, Jacobs. What's up? Over."

"We seem to be in a bees' nest of rebels. They haven't seen us as of yet, but they are approaching uncomfortably fast. We can't move without giving up our position."

"How many?"

"Don't know. At least five trucks."

"What are your co-ordinates?"

Jacobs relayed the co-ordinates to Mac as he had done with SAS. The high plateau offered plenty of tall brush as well as wildly scattered trees in which they could remain concealed if the rebels just stayed where they were. Dimitri's team had limited ammunition as their assignment was to detain the lieutenant, not initiate a war. Besides, they had already had one gun battle; although, their surprise attack during that altercation helped to limit the amount of expended rounds.

Colonel Dimitri and his men held their position on high alert, and quietly watched the intent of the rebels. At a mere three hundred meters from their position—the length of a football field—the rebels stopped. Several of the armed guards jumped down from the back of two trucks and then motioned to whoever was in back to step out. Women and children carefully climbed down and then huddled together. The leader grabbed a couple of the women and ordered them to start cooking at a newly constructed fire pit

A young boy, with dried streaks down his face, cradled a small baby in his arms. It appeared to Mac that thirty-eight hostages were being held. Out of the remaining three trucks, the rest of the armed rebels jumped down, stretched, and then proceeded to take it upon themselves to paw at the women as entertainment. One woman tried to run but was shot before she could even leave the light of the fire. The hostages huddled in fear.

~

She woke in a whirlwind as terror set in her eyes. "Mr. Clark... did you hear that?" Maysa whispered.

"Yes, gun shot. I think higher up on the plateau about a kilometer away, maybe."

"Should we investigate? Maybe someone needs our help?"

"I think we have our own concerns, Maysa."

"But Mr. Clark... What if those men who are chasing us found someone else to torture?"

"Maysa, how did you rationalize that statement? If they wanted to shoot us they had a chance when we were on the bridge."

"We come from two different worlds, Mr. Clark. When I hear gunfire, it is always a bad thing, and usually it's someone preying on another."

"I understand, Maysa, but we need to keep moving. You and Ateefah are my responsibility right now."

"I thank you for your concern, Mr. Clark, but I cannot let my conscience rest. There have been too many atrocities committed against my people. We have all the guns and ammunition left in the pickup from those three LRA soldiers you so quickly disposed of in Gulu. Please, Mr. Clark, we have a duty."

"A duty, Maysa?" He chuckled under his breath. If this wasn't such a serious predicament already, he might have laughed even louder out loud. *How can this young refugee, laboring to care for her child, think it is her duty to help someone else? She is a remarkable human being.* "Okay, Maysa. Do you know how to use these AK47s?"

"I have watched many men execute my family and friends. I think I can handle it," said the undaunted young mother who had grown into a woman right in front of Clark's eyes.

"All right, Joan of Arc, this is how it is going to go down. We will re-conn the area on foot. If I perceive you might be in any danger, we turn around and quietly head back here and get the hell out of here. Understood?"

"Mr. Clark, thank you. You have no idea how these animals treat our women."

"Maysa, it was only one gun shot. What makes you so certain there is more to this than someone possibly shooting at a snake?"

"My gut! As you say."

After securing Ateefah in the cab of the truck with her favorite fruit in hand, the two set off armed with the weapons captured from the three LRA rebels. They crossed the grasslands with cautious speed and headed toward the direction of the single gunshot.

~

The hillside was draped in a blanket of drifting smoke as the rebels forced several women to cook for them. The rest of the women and children huddled in fear as rebels casually walked about without any care. Their obvious intimidation tactics had been observed by many throughout the outback.

"Jacobs, tell me that is not your fire we smell?"

"No, sir, Lt. Alderson, not ours."

"Where are you?"

"Northeast of the rebels," informed Jacobs.

"Okay. We are southwest. If you start shooting we might hit each other in the crossfire. Give us 10 to situate ourselves on the upside."

"Yes, sir. Hang on, sir. Colonel Dimitri wants to speak with you." Jacobs handed the PRS to the Colonel.

"Jake."

"Yes, sir."

"They have women and children. They already shot one woman. Let's see if you can take a few out by luring them away from the campsite. They will probably have to relieve themselves. Go stealth. Nice and easy."

"Yes, sir. Roger that."

Jake whispered to Mac and BP of the plan. He pointed to where they would initiate their elimination. Suiting up in their stealth ghillies, they cautiously moved between the brush and trees cognizant of where daybreak would appear and where the enemy had chosen to set their camp.

~

Lt. Clark had kept their directional path to the southwest hidden in the deep, dark shadows as daybreak would soon be upon them. Maysa froze in her step and grabbed Clark's arm. She motioned in the direction of a beat-up 4x4 truck with missing back fenders and a SW insignia on the front door. They slowly approached the vehicle, guns ready. No one appeared to be around, but it seemed to Clark this spot was an unusual place to park a truck. The cab was barren of any credible evidence of who had been chasing them.

Drifting down in the clutches of a slight breeze, the smell of smoke shifted their gaze upward. Clark motioned to Maysa of flattened blades of grass. "One path, but several footprints," he whispered. They rounded the front of the truck and decided not to take that path but headed in the opposite direction. They continued to observe without involvement or sacrificing their position. Why the men who were chasing them left their truck and trudged up the hillside to start a fire was beyond him. It made little sense. *Why abandon their vehicle here?*

Clark and Maysa swung farther west and then to the north. The lieutenant wanted to see this fire for himself, and to appease Maysa's demanding curiosity. He thought the actions of their adversaries were not in line with what they had been doing. *Were these the guys who sent those Morse codes? Was it not just a pretense to capture him? What could have altered their plan and why stop here?* Clark was as curious as Maysa—not a good combination. One of them had to be the responsible one.

As they neared the ring of trucks, Maysa picked up on the dialect coming from more than a couple of men. She whispered to Clark, "Those are the voices of traffickers."

"This must be a rendezvous with the men who are chasing us," said Clark.

"Then they are after me."

"Why do you say that, Maysa?"

"I killed several of them before we met. They want revenge."

Clark looked into the dead-serious eyes of Maysa. "I am sorry, Mr. Clark, for putting you in danger. They are ruthless and without shame. They are only interested in how much money they get for the women when they sell them off to the rebel commanders. They will keep the young girls caged in a small village until they mature a little more. Once they show signs of womanhood, they will be sold off," she stated, saddened from her experiences.

"Maysa, what happened to you is not your fault. You are the victim of antiquated laws and customs. You are a remarkable woman."

"You are so kind, Mr. Clark, but right now we need to get closer." With that said, Maysa got up and quietly headed toward the light of the fire.

"Maysa! Get back here! Shit." The lieutenant took off after her. She was quick and quiet as she stepped. Maysa moved through the tall grass as it bent with the influence of the light breeze.

~

Jake stepped into him quickly and silently. He buried his knife between a traffickers rib and thrust it upward. Jake eased him down gently. Their ghillies blended with the grass, which made them presumably undetectable.

~

Maysa stood behind him like a ghost as his piss dribbled to an end; he shook it off. Her knife slashed silently at his throat with the precision of a surgeon but with deadly consequence. Clark muffled his gurgling and lowered him to the ground. The two moved on.

Maysa's blue eyes looked almost steel grey, as if she were in a trance. She moved to another with as quick of a stroke, the hatred buried deep, but the justice tasted fresh. Clark put a choke hold on another trafficker who stood on guard on the outside of the ring of trucks and snapped his neck. Maysa needed to get to the women, but Clark grabbed her arm, stopped her, and pointed to his eyes and then across the camp's fire to the other side. She followed his direction to where they saw, from under a truck, a pair of legs went limp for no apparent reason. No one was behind him—or was there? Clark pointed to go back. Maysa looked into his eyes defiantly but then realized her friend's concern. She followed him.

Clark and Maysa wound their way down the hillside to where they saw the battered pickup off in the distance.

"The guys in the pickup are not after you, Maysa. They are after me. They are not here to rendezvous with the traffickers either; they are a special ops team. They are wearing state-of-the-art ghillies, almost undetectable. And worse, there must be more of them. That's why they stopped here. Someone must be in communication with them. Maybe the rest of their team."

"What are we to do? We can't let the women be abused by these animals nor the children to witness such wickedness."

Clark noticed Maysa's eyes had returned to her pretty blue.

"There are too many of them for us try and take out one at a time and we don't know yet our stalkers intent. Let's change our vantage point so we are on the other side and above them... that way, they are not in between us and Ateefah. If need be, we will be able to slide out of here back to our pickup."

"Mr. Clark..."

"Yes, Maysa."

"I am sorry for taking off like I did. My hatred sometimes takes ahold of me and I feel helpless in stopping its motivation."

"I understand, but you also have to be smart about your tactics. It could mean your life if not careful. We have come too far, Maysa. Come on, let's move."

Clark and Maysa headed out low and slow and within a cautious distance from the fire. They started to circle up to higher ground just as the sun peeked over the apex of the hillside. They slipped into a crevice with plenty of foliage and large rocks to protect their whereabouts.

~

Jake tapped Mac and BP over the PRS and then, pointed behind them to try and pick up any signs of movement. He had a strange feeling.

Pentagon

Romeo 2310 Hrs.

Paul dropped Director Jones off at the after-hours door at the Pentagon. She swiped her badge and placed her hand on the palm reader. The corporal handed her back her clutch purse after he inspected it.

"Late night, Director?"

"Yes, always something," shared the director casually as she hurried through the scanning arch.

Samantha had walked this hallway many times but never with such deliberation in her step.

Where would that asshole take Marsha...and why? She skipped past Tomlinson's office and headed farther down the hall, turned right, down the next hall and then finally to the secured door of SAS. She entered the inner chamber, placed her chin on the pad and looked straight ahead. A beam of light passed over her eyes and the main door clicked open. Samantha rushed inside.

"Good evening, ma'am," greeted Carmen. "We had a ping from PAG. We are closing in, ma'am. I think we have him."

Samantha looked at Carmen and her team. She saw the excitement in their eyes, but Samantha's sterling look quickly transformed their excitement into questioning stares. Samantha leaned on a terminal, hung her head, and tried to summon the correct words. Her emotional state had taken over any logical decision regarding the missing soldier. She raised her head.

"Carmen, Nina, Phillip, what I am about to say, I know is solely based on my own personal interests, but what I believe we must do. I applaud you for all your hard work in locating our missing person; however, something more pressing has developed within the last hour. You are probably unaware of the bomb that went off at the gala..."

The three responded with an escape of bewildered sighs.

"...Yes. As I was standing at the podium, a blast rocked the room. I was told Marsha's car and several others were involved, and although they are unsure of its device, someone mentioned an underground gas leak. Moments before this happened, a man named Nigel Redman ushered Marsha out of the room. I don't know what he said to her, to make her go, but I know it would not have been willingly. I know Paul has been re-writing code for PAG to lessen response time, so I ask you not as your director but as a personal favor to re-direct PAG to Washington. We need to find her. I don't want anything to happen to Marsha like what happened to Terry."

Carmen responded first as the team leader, "Ma'am, we understand the consequence of changing our orders, but I for one, have no problem in changing PAG's co-ordinates."

"Neither do I, ma'am," stated Nina.

"Nor I," responded Phillip in an authoritarian English accent. "We can refocus on the missing person's trail later. We have at least a nearby location, that is, if he doesn't jump on a plane," he said trying to ease the tension.

"Thank you all for your loyalty. How long will it take to reposition PAG?"

"About forty-five minutes. We are in the right projection of Earth's orbit," stated Carmen.

"With the earth's natural revolution going east to west, it also speeds things up. Just a matter of rotating PAG about twenty degrees northwest by west to allow for latitude adjustment from the equator to Washington," informed Phillip.

"Carmen, you'd better send a directive to Colonel Dimitri about our situation and do tell him the co-ordinates where you received our ping of the missing man."

"Yes, ma'am."

"Don't worry, ma'am. We will find the assistant director," related Nina, endearingly positive.

As Samantha was about to say something to Nina, Phillip interrupted, "Ma'am, P.O. Smyth is requesting entry."

"Affirmative, Phillip."

Outside the high tech lab, Derrick swiped his ID card and after a green light flashed of his acceptance, he entered the inner chamber. He placed his chin on the pad, the light scanned his eyes and the main security door clicked open.

He rushed to Samantha's side and put his arms around her. She accepted his gesture overwhelmingly as she tried to fight back the tears.

"Don't worry, Sam, we will find her," he said as a true friend.

"We are repositioning PAG to help us," said Samantha.

He looked at the team as they busily hammered out code.

"You have the best of the best, Samantha. They are well trained in many situations, one of them being hostage scenarios."

Samantha looked at Derrick. *What was he implying... and what was his involvement in all of this?*

"What are you trying to tell me, Derrick? Why are you referring to this as a hostage situation? Should we go to my office?"

"No need, Sam. Marsha hand-picked your whole team with the help of some very influential people. We all have been hand-picked to watch over PAG and protect its integrity...and the personnel who handle it. What happened to Terry was an unforeseen tragedy but our security has been tightened."

Stunned at hearing what P.O. Smyth just said, she quickly asked, "You are not who you say you are?"

"I am Derrick Smyth, a P.O. in the U.S. Navy; although my rank in another elite group is the same as your team. We all have been procured for our special talents, our loyalty, and our resilience to respond in strained situations. It is not my position to say any more than to assure you, we will find her."

"You are scaring me, Derrick. What is going on?"

"Samantha, without getting too involved with political fundamentals and earth's protection at this moment... basically, we have been assembled as peacekeepers, but without the naivety as from some of the other passive organizations."

"I don't know if I understand any more clearly."

"Let's just say we belong to a collective that supports the humanitarian survival of Earth's citizens."

"You mean the New World Order?"

"No, ma'am, not the Family, nor Illuminati, nor Skull and Bones."

"Then, who?" Samantha asked with a concerned stare.

"Sam, you have to trust me."

"So was PAG financed by your organization?"

"Indirectly, it's possible. I'm not totally sure if it involved the greedy Tomlinson and his cronies or his affiliates. You were privy to that private meeting in the conference room. Who do you think Tomlinson was talking to on your conference call?"

"I don't know. I had no part in who was listening. I was there clearly as the Director of SAS and to share PAG's abilities."

"Well, *THEY* believe they will take charge of PAG for their own gain once it proves to be reliable. That is not going to happen!"

"Derrick, is Marsha...Marsha?"

. . .

Jake and his team pulled back after receiving a message over their PRS that their extraction was in the immediate area. *Was he now stalking us?* The sun had started to peek above the hilltop, which would make their movement more restrictive. Their truck would have to be off-limits as well, as a rebel scouting party could be easily drawn to it. They needed to find alternative accommodations until they received intel on Dimitri's plan of attack. The safety of the women was definitely priority one.

Quietly, they drew back through the tall grass to a more wooded area. Jake and his team set their three-point position and Mac scaled a medium-sized tree that had enough foliage to cover his position. Luckily, this type of tree, the African Juniper, seemed to be prevalent throughout this high plateau as they had made note after leaving the lower plains. From his vantage point, Mac observed the rebel's camp without detection and relayed to his team. *"The rebels are digging in and look like they're waiting for others to join them."*

Dimitri thought satellite re-conn would be nice but doubted CTA would sanction such a request—the women were not their assignment. If Mac thought the rebels looked like they were waiting for others to join them, they needed to come up with a plan soon, and implement it now.

~

"Mr. Clark, don't worry. I know I can do this," said Maysa in a low voice.

"Maysa, it is too dangerous. You don't fit in anymore. You have a different look about you, a more in-charge persona. The traffickers will pick up on it in a minute."

"I know their dialect. I am the only one who can go in there and employ the trust of the women. Once I have passed the word, you set off the fireworks. We can do this," she begged of her Mr. Clark.

"Shit, Maysa..." Clark paused while he rethought the situation. "Okay, we will go back to the pickup and I'll grab the grenade launcher and that poor excuse of a sniper's rifle. You travel on the same path as we took earlier. I'll be able to keep an eye on you through the scope. I'll only have time to take out two trucks, that's it, before they re-form and start firing. You will only have a few seconds to motivate the women and children to run downhill. Go between the two trucks I take out, the two on the backside. Got it?"

"Yes, Mr. Clark. Thank you once again."

"For what, getting us killed?"

"For hope, Mr. Clark... For hope."

Clark and Maysa gathered what they needed and left the protection of the crevice and started down the hill, weaving in between the tall grass. Clark watched Maysa as she flowed with the wind. His larger frame wasn't so graceful but her instructions were better than he had learned in training camp. "Stay with the wind," she had said to him. "Watch the movement and then zigzag with the flow. It's the opposite direction of the bending grass as you pass through it that will give you away." *She should teach commando techniques,* he thought.

"Like sailing," he said. "Stay off the wind and tack back and forth."

"If that is what you know, then yes," she responded smiling.

It wasn't too far down their path before Maysa stopped. Broken grasses lead to a pathway farther to the west where an oasis of African Junipers clustered together. She carried on with Clark staying in stride. As they approached their pickup, Ateefah had woken up and was standing on the seat looking out the back window. When she saw her mother, a beautiful, warm smile flashed over her face. Even at such a young age, Clark could see her mother's charm in her little face. Clark was concerned about leaving Ateefah alone. This was not a good idea but Maysa was determined to free those women.

"Maysa, shouldn't we rethink this? Look at Ateefah. We have a responsibility to see her grow up."

"Life is harsh, Mr. Clark. If God is willing we will return to her."

"Most Americans wouldn't leave their animal like this."

"That's because they have not been kicked in the teeth by death, Mr. Clark. Africa is Africa; it can be cruel. Our people have endured pain and injustice for way too long. If we all turn our backs to protect ourselves none of us will survive. We must stand tall and be counted."

"If we get out of this, I think you should get into politics."

"What makes you so sure I wouldn't slit the throat of my opposition?" smiled Maysa.

Clark was held speechless...

Inside the cab, Maysa reached into her satchel and pulled out a couple of berries and fed them to Ateefah.

"They will make her sleep but not harm her," she said reassuring her Mr. Clark.

Clark bagged up what he needed from the LRA's green box and before Maysa took to the southern route, he gave her a hug, and told her to be careful. He handed her one of his ceramic knives. She smiled up at him for the kind gesture. Clark returned up the hill toward the direction of their previous sanctuary and observation point—at the crevasse.

Maysa moved swiftly but cautiously. She passed the abandoned truck and circled back around to where she and Clark had scouted and encountered three of the rebels. It was still early morning and the buzzards hadn't caught the smell of dead flesh, yet.

She rubbed her face with dirt and pulled out her shirt so as not to attract attention to her shapely waist. She removed her boots and set them aside. She hoped she would gather them on the way back if Mr. Clark distracted the traffickers long enough.

~

Mac watched her as she slipped in under the truck and then blended into the middle of the scared women. He tapped on his PRS.

"Colonel, we have an infiltrator. The same girl who is traveling with the lieutenant."

"Are you sure?"

"Affirmative, sir."

"Fuck! What's Lt. Clark up to? Observe Mac, we can't see her from here. One of the trucks is blocking our view."

"Yes, sir. She seems to be talking to the other women. Very low key... oh, oh..."

"What, Mac...? Over."

"It looks like she knows the young boy. It's causing a ruckus. One of the guards is approaching the women."

"Mwali, ja hapa!" ordered the guard in Swahili.

Peterson, who was lying still with Jake, heard the guard scream at the young woman and over his PRS, he translated, *"Girl, come here!"*

Maysa stepped away from the ladies, and with head down, she shuffled over to the guard. He grabbed her by the shoulder and bent over her. Peterson couldn't hear what he was saying to her but the guard then slapped her in the face. Maysa went down. He then kicked her in the butt towards the direction of the ladies. She crawled back. Another soldier came to the side of the guard and started in on him. The two were arguing and then the original guard pointed to Maysa. Her lip was bleeding as she dropped to her knees and took the young boy and his baby sister in her arms.

~

Looking through his scope, Clark said in a low voice, "Maysa, what are you doing? This wasn't the plan. Who's the boy? Jesus fuck, Maysa!"

The women slowly gathered around Maysa in small groups of two or three and then shuffled back as if they were attending to her beating. They made no other moves for fear of provoking their capturers.

~

"She is telling the ladies something," announced Mac as he continued his observations. *"A couple of them are grabbing on tightly to their belongings. They look like they are going to make a break for it."*

"That's ludicrous. It's certain death," replied Colonel Dimitri. *"Gentlemen get prepared, something is going down."*

"The girl just stepped out of the crowd with the little boy in hand. She's looking up the hill between our positions, sir."

A white vapor trail swooshed through the air. An earsplitting explosion followed by a fiery lightshow had a truck jump from the ground like a bull in a rodeo.

Seconds later, another truck exploded with the same intensity. And before the belligerent guard could take cover, Maysa was on him, her knife in hand.

Two bullets whistled by striking the other yelling man who fell to the ground with blood dripping from his head.

The demolished truck opened Colonel Dimitri and his men's view. They opened fire. Maysa and the women had already taken flight, running down the hillside. A couple of the rebels tracked in the direction of Jake and his men, trying to escape the ambush. Wrong decision! With precision, the traffickers lay face down in the tall grass, motionless.

Dimitri and his men advanced cautiously into the half circle of remaining trucks while the two trucks behind him burned. Several rebels lay face down, arms outstretched in front of them, crying, asking for forgiveness and their lives. Jake, Mac and BP walked into the circle and removed their ghillies to join their commander.

"Good to see you," remarked Col. Dimitri.

"You as well, sir," replied Jake. He looked over to the area where the young woman had peered just before the chaos started and remarked, "Well, Lt. Clark knows where we are. Maybe he will come to us."

"What do you want to do with these guys?" asked Rey.

"Peterson, come here. You want to talk to these guys. We still have three good trucks with minimal bullet holes. Let's spread out and see if we can round up the women. I think they would rather ride in safety than take their chances out here. Whoever these traffickers were waiting for won't take too kindly to what has happened," shared Colonel Dimitri.

"I assume the young mother who is traveling with Lieutenant Clark will have re-united, and now with three kids. It's going to be tough for him to stay out of sight with that many mouths to feed," remarked Rey.

Jake started to laugh. "Come on! As far as we know, he didn't know we were here, and he and the girl still took on these guys. That's some set of cojones they share. I think they're both fearless."

"Maybe not fearless, but a sense of duty or righteousness," stated Mac.

"Okay, men. Let's hope he has now seen our intent, and it has sparked his curiosity and sees us not as a vigilante group interested in capturing him. It might keep him closer. Jake, Mac, Peterson, stay with him. We will travel the high ground and keep in communication with you. What are you using for transportation?" questioned Col. Dimitri.

Jake grinned. "Well, it was a nice 4x4 dually but it has seen some better days. Not exactly fashionable but probably blends in better now. We'll scrape off the SW insignia to make it look more conforming to a used farm truck."

"There is psychological affirmation about the familiarity of seeing your 4x4 as well, which might, again help him ease his apprehension," said Col. Dimitri.

"Yes, sir."

"Peterson, how's it going with these three?"

"Colonel, they say they are simple farmers who were forced to join the traffickers. One of the women who fled is his wife but they couldn't communicate with each other for fear of being shot," shared BP after translating.

"Very, well. Get them up. But Rey, I want you to keep an eye on them. Let's see how trustworthy the women find them. Use them to help find the ladies and we will take it from there."

"Yes, sir."

Reynolds took a team and the three men to help round-up the women and get them back into the trucks. If these guys were telling the truth, it could be a lot easier to gain the women's trust and help them all.

~

Maysa nuzzled next to her Mr. Clark.

"What do you see, Mr. Clark?"

"I recognize the blond-haired guy as the commander, the young kid who led me to pick up my equipment, and two of them from the Chenowth's. Also, if I am not mistaken, the tall guy, I think, was at one of my training camps."

"Do we have them all wrong? Are they trying to help you?"

"I don't know, Maysa. It looks like three of them are heading back to their truck and the others are waiting, I gather, to find the women. They let three of the rebels up. One of the SO's was talking with them."

"SO's, Mr. Clark?"

"Special Ops."

"Who are you, Mr. Clark?"

"A patsy."

"A patsy? What is that?"

"Someone who believed he was working for the right side and was taken advantage of. It's funny. This guy I met once told me to always watch my back. *'Our line of work makes us very disposable'*."

"You are a mercenary?" asked Maysa, concerned her friend was like so many others in her country.

"No, a U.S. soldier just doing what I was told to do. That's why I have found this so strange. My orders were not definite. The commander said either, or. That is not the U.S. stand. They usually have already made allegiance to one of them and maybe they had. Maybe it was the commander who put that doubt in my mind because he knew I was being set up."

"He saved you?"

"A lot of questions, Maysa, for unknown answers, at the moment. At least, we know who has been following us, now we have to find out why. Here, take a look through the scope so you can familiarize yourself with them."

"I see one of them who is walking away with reddish hair; he is the one I saw looking out the back window of the truck at the market."

"Good. Let's get back to the kids. How do you know the little boy?"

"A family who was so kind as to pick us up, was sitting inside the cab with his father. After I was let off, I heard some gun fire up the road. When I got there, the father was dead, the boy, and the mother with her baby were all gone. I heard faint screams from a distance away. When I got there, these men were raping the woman, but the children were not there."

"What happened to the men?"

"I slit their throats and shot two. The woman shot herself out of shame."

Clark looked at Maysa. Her manner was very concise recounting the nightmare without emotional connection. But, she had just risked her life to embrace the boy and to save the other women. Clark thought he wouldn't be the only one visiting a couch when they got back to the States.

~

Jacobs felt uneasy as he approached his superior officer.

"Colonel?"

"Yes, Jacobs."

"I just received a transmission. We have lost PAG."

"What do you mean?"

"One of our own has been taken hostage and co-ordinates reassigned."

"Who did they take?"

"Code name, *Hourglass*," informed Jacobs.

"Redman involved?"

"Affirmative, sir."

Day 8 - Wednesday

Pentagon, SAS

Romeo 0120 Hrs.

The atmosphere at SAS was intense, more than usual as Samantha watched in wonderment as Derrick gave precise orders.

"Phillip, check all out-bound planes, private and any military, also bridges. Maybe we can pick up an image," said P.O. Smyth.

"Yes, sir."

"You have done this before, Derrick?" asked Samantha somewhat surprised at his calm reactions.

"Twice in France, once in Germany, and once in Syria."

"Do you have a title?"

Derrick looked up at the reddened eyes of his friend. He knew Samantha was confused but the least said the better off she would be.

"Communication Facilitator," he replied lowering his eyes to the terminal in front of him.

"So no zero-zero affiliation?"

Derrick looked up again at Samantha and broke a smile, "No... no James Bond if that's what you are inferring."

"You never answered me about Marsha's status. I mean, when she came back from her two-year deployment in Europe several years ago, she seemed different from what I remembered of her. At that time, I knew very little about her, as we really hadn't started to work on projects together. Although, when we did meet again, she seemed more mature, determined, and her soft demeanor had hardened I guess you could say. Her obvious change of hair color almost personified these changes."

"Director... I..."

"We are coming onboard with PAG," stated Carmen.

"All right, let's make this work," gleamed Derrick, rubbing his hands together as he focused his attention on the wall monitoring screens.

. . .

The room felt damp, stale, and chilled as she regained her awareness. Her throat was dry with a lingering taste of barbital. Marsha tried to move but her hands and feet were bound to a solidly staked chair, and the blindfold prevented her from forming a visual interpretation of the room. As her sensitivities became more alert, she realized she had been stripped of her evening gown—and more importantly, her golden brooch had been removed. She sat almost naked, wearing only her strapless bra and her panties.

Marsha shook her head back and forth trying to lessen the knot on the blindfold, but to no avail. She took a deep breath, and as she did, a sharp odor pierced her nostrils.

What is that? I know I have smelt that before... *Cleaning fluid like they use on-board ships,* she thought. She listened for the presence of anyone else in the room.

She couldn't hear any breathing or shuffling of feet. She was alone, she was sure. Maybe cameras had a watchful eye, but no one else.

Redman, I'm going to de-ball you, you bastard, she threatened to herself. The bindings were tight as she tried to fiddle with their plastic ends. With the little movement she had, she couldn't feel any sharp edges on the chair with her fingers.

I've been kidnapped and being held for what reason? Why not just kill me? She paused, and thought, *Exchange? That's it! Me for the soldier. Ha, who am I kidding? They'll set up the exchange, but the delivery will have us both killed.* Marsha took a hard swallow. *He must know too much, they won't stop. Fuck!* She tried to wiggle out of her bindings, but the straps around her thighs kept her still. The only noise that she heard was the sound of chains. She waited and listened.

Marsha tried to clear her mind of all things except where she was. She breathed deeply and released it slowly. Her yoga classes had helped in the past to relieve the stress of some of her assignments, and now it seemed like a good time to reinstate this philosophy. She relaxed her head and cleared her mind. She sat there and let every part of her body deflate from her situation. Marsha felt herself transcending into a state of awareness superseding pure physical limitations.

In her subconscious, she felt the presence of at least two men who had placed her there. The mixture of cologne and scotch mingled in her nostrils, and then, the smell of paint, stronger than mere house paint. Possibly paint for metal with an underlying staleness of—rust. She floated within her senses. She felt motion and water, not dripping but buoyant and pressure—pressure at the bridge of her nose, and in her ears, and it moved to the back of her jaw. Her tongue licked at her lips; it didn't taste like her normal perspiration saltiness, but more brackish-like seawater. She felt the stares.

. . .

Displayed on four big screens, Carmen and Nina plotted PAG's trajectory as they searched the Capital's eight wards that comprised approximately sixty-eight square miles. Meanwhile, Phillip was in check with all the other transportation means at his control station. He had them displayed on six lesser-sized screens, which hung to the right of the main frame. He came up empty-handed for any flights being sanctioned during the alleged time frame from his military sources, neither from commercial departures nor from the privately owned sector. He was still searching the many bridge exits leading across the Potomac River as indicated on the street grid in front of him.

"Where would they take her?" questioned Samantha. She stood with one arm folded across her chest and the other rubbing at her temples.

"Some place secure and in his network of opportunity," answered Derrick as he watched the grid work on the six monitors.

"Your answer is not very reassuring, Derrick," persisted the director.

"I'm sorry, Samantha. That wasn't very sensitive of me."

"I'm not very good with this cloak-and-dagger stuff," admitted Samantha.

Derrick was preoccupied with watching the digital recounting of I-695 as it crossed the Potomac and almost ignored the director.

She sighed. "What about a speed boat to the coast?"

"What?" Smyth looked up at Samantha as if a light bulb had turned on.

"A speed boat. Wouldn't they think about all the traffic cams and traffic jams? It seems to me, if I wanted to make a hasty escape, I would jump onto the Potomac, not drive over it with everyone else."

"Samantha, that is brilliant! I thought you said you weren't very good at this cloak-and-dagger stuff?"

"So you were listening," smiled Samantha, briefly.

"Phillip, there has to be hundreds of webcams. Government...possibly the Marine Corps Base at Quantico, the Naval Academy, river restaurants, even boat clubs. Make me a list and I will help you," engaged Derrick.

"We only have two more wards to scan, Derrick, and they are in the north part of D.C. Do you want us to travel down the Potomac?" asked Carmen.

"I believe the director is on to something." Derrick looked up at the Washington, D.C. clock, which hung on the wall immersed between the other twenty-four clocks of Earth's time zones. "We've been at this for about two hours with forty-five minutes getting here from the gala, an hour plus to relocate PAG, and it's about a hundred miles down the Potomac to Chesapeake Bay from here. Let's say, so as not to arouse too much suspicion, they cruised around 15 knots. At this time of night, I don't think such a speed would be practical to sustain, but hypothetically speaking, let's go with it. It would take them a little more than six hours to get to the mouth of the Potomac as it drains into the bay. Carmen, set PAG at the mouth of the Potomac and Phillip, let's pull up web cams in the surrounding area. We might get lucky."

Kenyan Outback

Charlie 1100 Hrs.

The five huddled together—Lt. Clark, Maysa, and three children—harbored between large boulders and tall grasses, shaded from the near noon-day sun. They were eating leftover maize and drinking fresh goat's milk that Maysa so kindly obtained. The young boy was so traumatized, he couldn't remember his name when asked by Maysa or why he held on so tightly to this baby girl. He just did. Maysa decided to call him 'Mosi', a traditional name for a boy meaning 'first born'. The little girl, who was near Ateefah's age, she would call, 'Jamila' for 'beautiful'.

"For our family's growing size, you look less tense, Mr. Clark."

He looked over to Maysa and watched as she tended to the children. "I guess knowing who has been on our tail has eased my anxiety a little. I'm still not comfortable with the fact, but at least we both know what they look like; that is giving us an edge."

"Should we approach them?"

"Not yet, Maysa. Let's keep an eye on them to see what they are up to. We know one thing...they aren't carrying heavy weapons otherwise they would have taken out the traffickers. It seemed to me, they were waiting for some kind of diversion before jumping into the mix."

"Is it safe for me to go into that village we saw, to gather more food?"

"We are going to have to do something soon."

"I'll take Ateefah with me. The boy will not leave the side of his sister and I don't think he could handle the walk without giving us up out of sheer fear."

217

"Yes, probably better he remains with me. He needs to regain the feeling of trust from a man. I'll try to bond with him by building something small just to occupy his mind."

"You are a kind man, Mr. Clark, even if you do make trucks explode into the air."

Clark chuckled at her slight of a compliment. The boy, Mosi, timidly looked up at Clark's smiling face and then back down to the ground. The young boy twirled grass blades between his fingers.

Maysa stood up and went over to Mosi and told him in their Nilo-Saharan dialect of what she was about to do, and for him to stay with the smiling man. He barely nodded a reaction, just remained twirling grass, lost in his own mind.

"Maysa, I don't have to tell you to be careful and watch your back, do I?" He knew very well, he did not.

"Mr. Clark, I believe you just did. I will be careful, no need for alarm. I will keep my knife hidden," said Maysa with a smile.

"Here is some money the shopkeeper gave us."

Maysa gathered Ateefah into her wrap and realized, soon she would be too big to carry. She was getting stronger every day and as Maysa had noticed, more endeared to her Mr. Clark. As Clark watched Maysa walk down the hillside, he thought about how Maysa, even though she had been through horrendous misfortunes and was of such a young age, she was still such a good mother. He admired her.

. . .

Colonel Dimitri knew that UN camps were very portable. Some sprung up out of nowhere and could relocate just as fast, to get away from approaching rebels. The larger ones, however, sometimes fell prey to rebel and trafficking mercenaries, who seized the opportunity to raid these sanctuaries of hope.

Colonel Dimitri had commandeered the traffickers' trucks and promised to escort the women and their children to the safety of a UN camp. He was discussing his plan with Jake over their PRS.

"We're going to have to find a UN camp nearby and soon. The women need..." Colonel Dimitri was cut-off by Mac's transmission.

"Colonel, I spotted the young woman with her baby."

"What is she doing?"

"Looks like heading back to that small village we just passed."

"Okay, stay with her but out of sight. She is as cunning as the lieutenant. We'll stop here and wait for your observations," stated the Colonel.

. . .

Clark picked up a handful of grass and moved a little closer to Mosi. The boy's eyes opened up with fear. Clark tried to reassure him with hand signals he was in no danger. Clark began to weave what appeared to be a giraffe for the boy's amusement. And then another four-legged animal, which also looked like a giraffe. He placed them in between him and the boy. Clark motioned for him to pick them up, but the boy hesitated several times and then crossed his hands once again. Clark made another, and then another, but this time, the fourth one had bent knees and he positioned them in a circle with the mother giraffe in the middle amongst her family. The boy looked up at Clark and tears misted his eyes. Clark handed him a smaller version, which the boy removed from Clark's outstretched hand and held it next to his heart. The young boy then picked up the make-believe mother, and brought it over to his sleeping sister, and placed it by her side.

Clark had seen many children in war-torn countries react differently to too many atrocities. Stoic faces wandered around aimlessly through abandonment from slaughtered parents to seven-year-olds waving AK47s like a toy stick; some of the guns bigger than the ones carrying them. But nothing wrenched his gut as much as watching Mosi lay the grass giraffe alongside his sister. Clark's symbolic family had somehow touched Mosi. He came over to Clark, sat down beside him, and rested his head against Clark's chest.

SAS Laboratory
Romeo 0500 Hrs.

Carmen and Nina engaged PAG near the mouth of the Potomac. They still hadn't picked anything up on Marsha's whereabouts. Phillip, however, was zinging along on his keyboard. Stroke after stroke, his excitement prompted multiple exclamations. Finally, he found what he had been searching for. Unable to contain himself, and with his eyes fixated on the screen, he informed everyone of his find.

"I've searched a lot of web cams along the way down the river, but most turned out to be just live feeds for their customers' viewing. I thought about contacting Quantico but decided it would take an act of Congress and forms after forms, so I looked up ATM machines in the area and found one from the Potomac Federal and Savings that faced the Potomac. I hacked into their mobile web feed from their backup tape machine. Look at this!"

Phillip reversed his stolen recorded footage for everyone to see. "Now, watch the bow of this boat turn up the water into white foam as it breaks into view. Now, watch the wake it has created when it leaves our view." He reversed it. "Now watch the time stamp..." It appeared at 0430.32.1 to 0430.35.7. "It's a fairly wide-angle lens, and it only took them 2.6 seconds to pass through the view of camera. Whoever it was, was hauling ass."

"Can you get a registration off the bow?" asked Derrick.

"I tried to enhance it but the lens isn't of any real quality. It gets muddy in the pixelization. And the overhead light overpowers the background."

"I'm amazed you were able to get what you did, Phillip. Well done," congratulated the director.

"So, are we still assuming this boat is related to our problem?" asked Carmen.

"Yes, but who at this time of night...or morning, I should say, would be going balls out?"

"You English do have a way with words," remarked the director.

"Sorry, mum."

"Where do you think they are going?" asked the director, still trying to debunk her cloak-and-dagger status.

"If I were to guess, I would say, Norfolk."

"Why there, Derrick?" asked the director.

"Where better to hide out but in the middle of everything? Everything is there for their use, NAS, Langley, Joint Chiefs, Air Force and Naval bases, everything and enough places to stash someone out of sight."

"All they would have to do is flash their credentials and no one under a General or Admiral would question their intentions," added Carmen.

"Besides, we aren't allowed to scan our own bases or military installations," shared Nina, who had been sitting quietly listening to all the assumptions. "We would need to contact Vandenberg's AFSPC to get authorization wouldn't we?"

"Yes, Nina, quite right... and possibly the President," responded the director.

"Do we even know if PAG can scan through layers and layers of metal and electronics?" asked Phillip.

The director sat down in one of the rolling chairs with her head in her hands. Dismayed, she looked up at her team. Questions swirled around in her mind, all of them running into closed, locked doors.

. . .

At 0715 hours East Coast time, a shuffle of feet, an inserted key, and the squeak from a heavy metal door awoke Marsha from her yoga trance. A woman's voice softly addressed her.

"Ma'am? I'm sorry I am not allowed to remove your bindings, but I brought you some water and a bit of food if you would like?" politely asked Seaman Apprentice Alicia Gifford.

"Yes, thank you. That's very nice of you."

Marsha heard the top of a water bottle break its plastic ring as the S.A. unscrewed it.

"I've put a straw in it for you."

She held it to Marsha's lips who took a much needed draw of water. It soothed the scratchiness and the bitter aftertaste from whatever they had given her.

"Would you like some scrambled eggs and ham?"

"Yes, thank you, miss...?"

"Sorry, ma'am. I'm not allowed to tell you my name."

The S.A. knelt beside her, placed the metal plate of food onto Marsha's lap, and began to cut the ham.

"Are you from Mississippi?" casually asked Marsha, detecting a southern accent.

"No, ma'am, Louisiana."

The S.A. put the egg and ham mixture to Marsha's lips. Marsha chewed slowly absorbing as much of the taste as she could.

"So, how do you like the Navy?" asked Marsha on her final gulp.

"Oh, I love it, ma'am. Been to lots of exciting places."

"I bet the weather was hard to get used to here?"

"I like the snow. It's so different than back home."

"Yes and I bet the dampness mixed with the cold is different than Louisiana as well?"

"That's what my mama asked when I told her I was stationed in Virginia."

"I bet your mama is very proud of you."

"Well, thank you, ma'am. Sure is nice of you to say."

"I appreciate your kindness in bringing me the food and water. I feel a little embarrassed sitting here in my underwear while others can watch me. You understand don't you?"

"Yes, ma'am, but the men are not allowed to view you. That wouldn't be right. Just us women who have remained onboard."

"Thank you, I feel very relieved to hear that. Is your crew not all here then?"

"We just have a skeleton crew while in port."

"When do you deploy?"

"I believe in another week. Then we head for the South Pacific."

"Wow, how wonderful! Will you get liberty at your next port?"

"I'm due, but I'm a little nervous about going to the beach in Panama."

"Oh, you will love it. The sand is white and silky."

"Yummy, that sounds so nice, thank you. Truthfully, I'm not sure my bathing suit will fit anymore?"

"Oh, I'm quite sure the men will love you in it."

"I have no interest; they all seem crude and rude."

"I know what you mean. I'm sorry, but you have been so kind to me, I feel like I am being so impolite without being able to address you properly."

Still on one knee, the young S.A. twisted slightly and whispered into her ear, "Seaman Apprentice Alicia Gifford, ma'am."

"Thank you, Alicia. You are very sweet. And when this hideous mistaken identity comes to light, I will make sure you receive accolades for your charming attention." Marsha continued her cunning questioning of the un-expectant seaman. She now knew that she was still in the States and probably Norfolk and possibly, Alicia was gay.

"Thank you, ma'am. I better take these back now."

Alicia stood and was almost at the door when Marsha asked her one more question.

"Alicia, how do I inform you when I need the head?"

"You are scheduled for a potty break in two hours, ma'am. Will that do?"

"Yes. Thank you once again for being so kind."

"You're welcome, ma'am. See you in two."

Outback of Uganda

Charlie 1530 Hrs.

The afternoon sun was high in the sky and the breeze had stalled as Maysa finished up at the small, local market. The array of fruits, goat cheese and bottled water, plus spices and greens were well appointed. The seller stated rumors were being spread around of a fearless young woman who had risked her life to save the lives of a group of captured women and their children. As she was a stranger to the area, the seller asked if she might be the one. Maysa denied she had anything to do with that rumor.

"How could I? As you can see, I am carrying my child." But she confessed she had heard the very same thing a few kilometers west from where they stood.

As Maysa headed back in the direction of her Mr. Clark, in the stillness of the air farther up the hillside, she noticed the tops of the tall grass were moving. She stopped. She put her bag of fruit down and pretended to adjust Ateefah in her wrap as she thought of what to do. She couldn't go back to their shelter and chance giving up their concealment. Maysa looked through her bag of fruit as if she had forgotten something and then turned around and headed back to the fruit stand.

The seller's wife had just pulled up to the fruit stand in their battered Toyota pickup as Maysa turned the corner of the shack. She talked with the woman emphasizing Ateefah. The woman smiled and motioned for Maysa to get into the truck. They headed down the red dirt road through their fields of fruit trees and disappeared over a berm.

~

From further up on the hillside, Mac pinged his team over his PRS.

"I think she made us."

"How could she? We are too far away," stated Jake.

"I don't know, but she went someplace with the other woman in her truck."

"Maybe to get something for her baby? Let's hang for a while to see if she comes back."

"We can always follow the truck to the berm to see if she is anywhere in sight," added Peterson.

"We are getting jumpy. Time to chill, boys."

"Yes, sir, but I feel like she is hanging us out to dry while she circles back around to the lieutenant."

"She was heading east, Jake."

"Okay. Peterson, head back and get the 4x4. Pick us up down at the fruit stand. Let's see where she went."

"Yes, sir."

"I think you are making the right decision, Jake. This woman is something else. Cunning, loyal, and deadly!"

"Yeah. Sort of makes you think twice about making contact. Maybe we should show our colors so we don't get ambushed. She is a phantom among the grasses and with that knife of hers, makes her dangerous. Come on, Mac. Let's get down there."

~

Maysa asked the woman to take her through the orchard to beyond the rolling hill out of view from anyone that might stand on the upper hillside. Maysa wished no harm to the woman and thought none would occur. Besides, the woman had done enough. Maysa asked one more thing of the woman, "Please don't tell them in which direction I'm headed."

Maysa walked quickly in the shadow of the hill and between the stalks of grain that were planted on the other side of the orchard. She had no reasoning for why the soldiers were following her and her daughter. *They had to know Mr. Clark knew who they were. Why not kidnap me and force me to take them to him? Why were they hesitating if they were friendly? They, however, did witness the talents of Mr. Clark when he took out the convoy's trucks and then the other trafficker. Maybe they were afraid to get too close for fear of being shot? It didn't make any sense.*

Maysa came up to another red dirt road grooved with deep, water-runoff veins and headed north. She shared the roadway with other women who were walking in their own directions. Although they were moving at a much slower pace than she, at least she wasn't alone. Ateefah was getting too heavy for this strenuous walking, but she had to prevail. No one was going to get *her* Mr. Clark without a fight.

. . .

Clark heard the U.S. convoy as it slowly approached above his rock sanctuary. The convoy stopped and sat still as if it were waiting for something or someone. Clark was blind to what was going on. If he came out from behind the rocks, the soldiers would certainly see him. He had to remain quiet and still.

All of a sudden, the U.S. convoy started moving and passed him by without detection. *Where was Maysa? She should have been back by now. Did they capture her and that is why they started to move?* He chuckled to himself, *It would be a cold day in hell before she would give up any information.*

He waited. Minutes seemed like hours. The young one, Jamila, was starting to stir and the boy, Mosi, lay quietly with his grass animals. *What if she starts crying for food? What am I going to do? Other than Ateefah, I've never even held a baby.* He looked in one of Maysa's bags and pulled out the last mango. He thought if she made a fuss, he would simply cut it apart and feed it to her. Ateefah loved plums and mangos, so with any kind of luck, this little one would as well.

From outside, an unsettling sound startled Clark. A sound that he had heard before while lying prone during an exercise in Kenyan. A blend of loud mooing, hissing, and gargling; a hyena had picked up their scent. *Shit.* He got up onto his knees and crawled out of his little cave. The caravan was still within hearing distance; he couldn't shoot it. He had to wait until the hyena thought it was safe to seize its prey. If he stood tall, it would probably scare the animal away—but then someone might see him. If he stabbed it then the anguish of the animal might divert stares his way.

Just then, little Mosi crawled out of the cave and reached for a piece of a fallen branch, and placed it on top of his head. He stood tall and still. The hyena raised its head and sniffed the air. Mosi stood his ground. The animal lowered its head and made like a bull, kicking at the dirt and then took off running while it squealed with its unusual laughter. Mosi, dropped the branch, grabbed Clark's hand, and took him back inside their little cave. Clark was speechless.

By the time Maysa returned, Clark was dividing the mango up between Mosi and the now awake Jamila. She smiled when Maysa entered the cave with her new playmate, Ateefah. Ateefah took a long stretch before she waddled over and sat down beside her little friend. Together they shared another fresh peeled mango from Maysa's sack. Maysa noticed the grass animals and the boy as he sat beside Mr. Clark. She smiled.

"Where have you been?"

"I saw them again. They were watching me from the hillside. I had to distract them away from following me here. I lead them on another roundabout. I see you have made a friend."

"Yeah, quite innocently I might add. And he saved our hides from a hyena as well."

"Really?"

"Yes. He scared the thing off by putting a tree branch on top of his head. I couldn't believe it."

"Never underestimate the ancient knowledge of Africa, Mr. Clark. We have been around a long time before the white man brought guns."

"I'll try to be a worthy student," said Clark with a smile. "The caravan passed just above us. I believe they will need to find a permanent shelter for the women so they can continue on their mission. The three who are following us are probably in communication with the leader and they are dragging the net. I think it is time for us to turn the tables and start to follow them. What do you say?"

"What do you mean, dragging the net?"

"Every so many yards or so, maybe a hundred, they will drop a man back, in this case, a Chenowth, and move in a V formation. They can cover more ground visually and physically while staying in a fairly tight formation. We'll stay far enough back so they can't hear or see us... hopefully, that is. As soon as they establish a safe place to drop off the women, the game changes once more."

"And what about the children, Mr. Clark? We can't abandon them again."

Clark looked at Maysa and the young children. He understood full well the pain of abandonment.

~

Frustrated, Jake and his team acknowledged that Maysa had given them the slip. Mac had the task of calling it in.

"We lost her again, sir," said Mac over his PRS.

"Well, you better join the rest of us. We know where she will be if we ever find the lieutenant," said Col. Dimitri.

"On our way, sir."

Virginia – Secured Location

Romeo 0915 Hrs.

Marsha heard footsteps approaching the metal door. A light tap assured her it must be Alicia, as promised, to take her for her assigned head break. The door creaked open and a sweet southern voice announced, "Ma'am, it's me. I have some fatigues for you."

Marsha's mind swirled with what-ifs. She didn't want to hurt this young S.A., but Marsha needed to get out of there.

"You are so kind. Are you alone?" asked Marsha.

"There is a guard in the passageway, but I can help you get dressed."

"Thank you, Alicia. You have no idea how much I appreciate your help."

"You're welcome. Okay, ma'am, I'm going to release your restraints and then help you to stand. You are not violent are you?"

"Of course not, Alicia. Like I told you, someone mistook me for someone else. Truly, a case of mistaken identity. You know, wrong place at the wrong time. I have no idea why I am here."

The concerned S.A. cut the plastic straps from Marsha who let out a sigh of relief. "Thank you, that feels so much better."

"They had these pretty tight," stated Alicia as she rubbed Marsha's thighs to get the blood flowing.

"You are a gem. That feels really nice."

Alicia ran the palm of her hands up and down on Marsha's marked thighs; her color started to return.

"There is no reason to be cruel to people, ma'am. I wasn't raised that way."

"The last we spoke, you only mentioned your mother. Is your father still with us?"

"The last time I saw him, he was drunk and beating on my mother. I was eight, and it was the last time I ever wanted to see him. We left the next day while he was sleeping it off. Mother and I have been on our own ever since."

"I'm sorry to hear that. Maybe after all of this, we can become friends?"

"That would be nice, ma'am. I don't make true friends easily. I don't want others to feel awkward being seen as my friend. You know how people make up stories?"

"Yes, I do. Are you allowed to remove my blindfold? It might be easier for us to maneuver my foot into the pants."

The S.A. stood in front of Marsha as she untied the blindfold. Marsha could smell her lightly scented body as she lowered her head into the S.A.'s bountiful chest. It gave way to ease of accessing the well-tied knot.

"You smell nice," Marsha said softly as she plotted her escape, and she lightly pressed against the SA's thicker leg with hers. Alicia felt a flush of embarrassment encompassing her darkened face. She removed the blindfold slowly from her charge's eyes and gazed into the face of a pretty, blue and green-eyed woman. Marsha squinted from a caged globe that shone immediately above her. As she got accustomed to the light, she looked up into the natural deep brown eyes of her keeper.

"You have beautiful eyes, Alicia. I can see the kindness in them."

"Ma'am... I..."

"It's okay, Alicia. I understand. I've had to hide my personal life throughout my career as well."

"Ma'am, I am sorry for what they have done to you."

"It will be all right, I promise. Can you help me with the pants?"

"Yes, ma'am."

The young SA squatted down and rolled the pants so Marsha could slip her bare feet into the legs. She went behind Marsha and released the chain that held her bound hands to the chair.

"Let me help you up. You can lean on me if you feel like you are losing your balance."

Marsha stood and one at a time, she placed each foot into the rolled pants. Alicia began to raise them past her curvy calves, past her strong thighs, to her waist. Holding on to each end of the waistband, she brushed her hands along Marsha's flat stomach and pushed the button through its loop. Alicia hesitated and looked into Marsha's sparkling eyes. She unconsciously licked the side of her lips as if to catch an unwanted drop of moisture and then lowered her eyes to the zipper. With the back of her left hand still up against Marsha's stomach, holding on to the waistband, she reached for the zipper. Alicia looked up into Marsha's eyes but did not say a word. The zipper rose slowly.

"I'm sorry they are so baggy on you, ma'am, but they are a pair of mine."

Marsha noticed Alicia's uniform had no identifying badges or rockers that were usually sewn in at just below the shoulder seam.

"They'll do just fine. And knowing they are yours means a whole lot more to me."

"Ma'am, they have ordered me to put these shackles on your ankles. I do apologize. I thought we were done with slavery."

"It's protocol. I am quite sure whoever brought me here told the commander I was a dangerous criminal of the state."

"No one said anything to me. But I did see a big man with a funny accent talking with a CPO."

"Not the Commander?"

"Not that I am aware of, ma'am. I was topside greasing a winch when they spoke. Then moments later I was instructed to watch over you." Alicia paused. "Ma'am..."

Marsha interrupted Alicia in mid-sentence. "I'm sorry, but could you call me Marsha? I would really like that."

"Yes, ma'am... I mean, Miss Marsha. Um, I feel so awkward doing this, but I need to remove the bindings on your hands to put on your shirt."

"Do what you need to do. I promise I will be good."

"Thank you ma'... ah, Miss Marsha."

"So, are you in engineering?"

"No, Miss Marsha. Actually, into computers. But we are doing whatever they need of us while we are in port."

The young SA removed Marsha's bindings. Her arms were indented as were her legs; her arms felt like lead ballast. Alicia rubbed Marsha's arms to help recirculate the blood, and then Alicia guided them into the sleeves. While Marsha's arms hung still at her side, Alicia began to button the shirt. Marsha's heightened awareness poked through her strapless bra, which caused Alicia's hands to fumble with the second to last button that would have obscured her view. Marsha raised her pins-and-needle arms and placed her hands upon Alicia's. She pressed them to her chest through her opened shirt. Alicia gasped.

"Have you never touched another woman?" tempted Marsha in a soft tone.

"No, ma'am... I mean, Miss Marsha. I have always wanted to but have been afraid to approach anyone on the subject. I'm not very aggressive, and I don't think my female friends would understand."

Alicia looked up into Marsha's caring eyes and as she reluctantly slid her hands from under Marsha's, she shone with a slight mischievous glow.

"You better chain up my hands, Alicia. Otherwise, they might ravish your body," smiled Marsha as she held them out to tie with the adjoining bindings on her ankles.

"Miss Marsha...I..."

"Shh, it's okay. We will get through this." Marsha paused. "I was wondering why you don't have your rocker displayed on your uniform."

"We were ordered to remove all identification, ma'am."

"Any reason given?"

"No, probably above my pay grade."

"I understand. All of us grunts are the last to know anything. Now, who is standing guard?"

"Ensign Jenkins, ma'am."

"Is he nice?"

Alicia leaned to Marsha's ear, "He is an asinine redneck."

"Unbutton the top two buttons of my shirt and push up my titties. A little distraction might be in order."

"Yes, Miss Marsha." She smiled.

Uganda Outback

Charlie 1630 Hrs.

Mosi looked up to the tall man who had made him the grass animals. He didn't understand what he was saying to the young woman who had saved his life, but felt he was in safe hands. He wondered who this white man was with the hairy face. He remembered another woman. She had sat in the back of a truck while he had sat inside, and then something awful happened. He rubbed his head where a deep-purple bump still protruded. *Where am I? How did I get here? Where are my mother and father? Why can't I remember anything?*

Clark held out his hand to his little friend who responded favorably by grabbing two of Clark's fingers with his small hand. He took the young boy outside to help him remove the brush that camouflaged their pickup. The young boy followed Clark's lead and neatly piled his smaller branches to one side. Clark picked him up and placed him inside the bed of the pickup before returning to the cave to help Maysa. They gathered the two young girls and supplies, and they turned to leave. In the entrance, a young boy stood—waiting.

"I think he thought you were going to leave him." Maysa reassured young Mosi everything would be all right. He stood to the side as Maysa crawled out and he waited for Clark before following him.

"I don't think he realizes what happened."

"I believe you are correct, Mr. Clark. He has not asked about his father or mother. I wish we would have exchanged names so I could keep their memory alive for him."

"We might never know their identity or their position in life. They had a truck, as you said. They had to have money to buy it, which would have meant they were prosperous somewhere. It's always the innocent who suffer when greedy ambitions, held by the few, have no accountability."

"It has been our way of life for centuries. And thank you, Mr. Clark, for caring to know my name."

"You are most welcome, Maysa. We'd better get these kids in the cab; we don't want to be too far behind the SO team."

After they put their supplies in the pickup's bed alongside their arsenal, Clark in turn, helped Mosi step in and showed him where to sit—next to him. The two young ones took up residence next to Mosi and all three crowded

Maysa into her passenger door. Clark looked over and smiled at Maysa, who despoiled any sign of discomfort and began to play a clapping game with the children. *No one would believe this back home.* Clark started the truck and took the high ground following the tracks, well behind the caravan.

PAG – Nowhere to Hide

P.O. Smyth went to Samantha's side and placed a hand on her tense shoulders. He had just received a private message and needed to answer it.

"Ma'am, let me make a call. Can I use your office?"

"Yes, by all means, Derrick."

Derrick entered the director's office and closed the door behind him. He wasn't afraid of the rest hearing his conversation, but he knew Samantha's office was free from any bugs. He dialed a series of numbers and momentarily waited. The call was almost immediately acknowledged.

"Be patient... Hourglass is on the move," said the voice at the other end. "I will contact you when I learn more." The line went dead.

Derrick felt a little relieved but, *How can I tell Samantha what I just learned? I know it isn't much, but someone must be in contact with her...somehow.*

Derrick stepped out of the office. All eyes were on him. He casually walked over to the terminals as if he was putting together a decisive plan.

"Phillip, can you pick up any footage at the docks along where we think Marsha might have been placed aboard that boat? And Carmen, can we set PAG maybe to the entrance of James River?"

"I'll see what I can find, Derrick," said Phillip.

"Why do you ask?" inquired the director. "Who did you call?"

"I learned nothing of consequence from the phone call, but I just had a hunch if you consider Redman's background and Tomlinson's ties and authority."

"You think Marsha is somewhere at a Naval base?"

"Just a hunch, Director. How long before the target?"

"Ten minutes," stated Carmen.

Okay, a little breathing room without Samantha breaking down.

"We'll find her, Samantha. We just need to relax a bit and let technology work for us," stated Derrick, hoping his friend would not take what he said too personally.

"You're right, Derrick. Please forgive me. I can't imagine what Marsha must be going through. And thank you all for your loyalty and determination. I would be at a loss without you all."

. . .

The heavy steel door swung open and the tethered woman stepped into the passageway. The guard, Ensign Jenkins, grabbed Marsha's arm and walked her down toward the head with the S.A. in tow. They walked past a fire station but only the ship's code number stenciled in black was visible behind her guardsman; Marsha stumbled. As the guard lifted her up, her opened shirt displayed her shapely form to him. He paused.

"Like what you see, handsome?" smiled Marsha.

"You're not gittin' me in trouble out here, lady," snapped the guard gruffly.

"You have a better place in mind?"

He rushed her down the passageway, with her chains scraping the floor like tin cans strapped to a car's bumper; he pushed her into the head's door.

"Here you are. Git in there."

"Oooo, so forceful," replied a sultry Marsha. "I might need some help with these chains, my stallion."

"I ain't your stallion and you sure don't want me in there helping out. Now shut the fuck up and do your business," blurted the Ensign. He looked back at the shy S.A., "Hey, you! Git in there and help her, will ya?"

Alicia walked around the raging guard and went through the door.

"Shit, help her out. I'd help me out with a little of that. Dumb bitch, who she tryin' to impress?" Uttered the guard under his breath.

. . .

Phillip stopped typing on his computer as his search had turned up more questions.

"Derrick, you need to see this!" called out Phillip.

"What do you have?"

"I traced the timeline back and found the boat in question in the ATM's footage at the docks at the Washington Navy yard on the Anacostia River. I got a clear shot of its name. It is registered to Admiral Stone."

"That's impossible!" blurted the director. "He wouldn't harm Marsha! There must be a mistake."

"Ma'am, I said I traced back the boat we saw in the video footage. And when I further reversed the footage, I couldn't see any person of Marsha's stature getting on board."

"Who did you see?" asked Derrick.

"Several men and...I'm not positive, but it looked like a woman with long blonde hair."

"Then, what does this mean?" questioned the director very intently.

"Maybe they were chasing..." And before Derrick could finish his sentence, the phone in the director's office rang. It startled them all in the intensely still room. The director quickly maneuvered around the other terminals anticipating good news.

"Hello... Yes, Director Tomlinson..." She listened—her face went white. "What! Nooooo!" The phone dropped out of her hand as she wavered. Derrick and the others ran to her side, just in time to catch Samantha before she hit the desk.

"Samantha! What is it?" questioned Derrick as he cradled her in his arms. She slithered to the floor.

Her eyes were glazed as she looked up at Derrick and then at each member of her team. She was barely able to summarize Jack's words.

"That was... Jack Tomlinson," she choked. "He said... early this morning... there was a fiery boat crash... and they believed Marsha... my Marsha... perished in the blaze. He said something like... her escort, Nigel Redman, was found unconscious, and... they believed it was a terrorist plot, and that it was possibly linked with the explosion at the White House dinner."

Carmen and Nina gasped! Their hands tried to suppress their anxiousness and horror as clear eyes turned red and teary. Phillip and Derrick shared dubious stares of betrayal.

"I don't believe a word, ma'am," stated Phillip.

"Neither do I," added Derrick. "Come on, Samantha, let me help you up."

Phillip joined in and they managed to get their devastated friend to her couch. Nina ran to the office fridge and grabbed a bottle of water for her. The director was visibly shaken and incoherent with arms flailing about. Nina doused a paper towel and placed it on the director's forehead and then poured a small amount of water into a Dixie cup.

"Take a drink, Director."

She managed to take a sip and then flopped into the back of the couch. Her mascara forged lines of black down her face; her eyes—red and swollen.

. . .

The close quarters of the muted grey, single head was barely enough room for one. Alicia pulled out her key from her breast pocket and started to unlock Marsha's bindings from around her waist. Marsha still needed a hand undoing the waist button as there was no slack in her chains to bend her wrist. They were as close as any two could be without physically touching. Alicia unzipped her friend's pants and let them drop. Marsha looked at her and smiled as she now had to lower her panties; she helped to guide her to the head. Over the echo of the stainless steel head, Marsha engaged.

"Listen, Alicia... we don't have a lot of time. I didn't want to say anything in the interrogation room just in case, well you know, but you have to believe me. There is a group of really bad men who will stop at nothing to get what they want. I believe I am being held as a pawn in exchange for a soldier who defied their orders on an assassination attempt of a small African country's leader. I work for a project that we thought was for humanitarian gain but have learned the contrary. I need your help. I know I am aboard a destroyer and where it is going after Panama, is anyone's guess. I am assuming on a black ops mission since all of your rockers have been removed. I need you to send a message to my superior. Can you do this for me?"

"Well...I don't know? Won't I get into trouble? I mean..."

Marsha sensed her hesitation.

"No. This message would be out of normal channels and no way of tracing it. It's just a series of numbers and hash tags as if you accidentally placed your hand one key to the right. Once you hit 'enter', your history is deleted automatically. I need you to do this for me... Will you help me?"

Jenkins banged loudly on the door. "Hurry up in there."

"Oh, Alicia, one other thing..."

Step Into My World

Charlie 1730 Hrs.

As Colonel Dimitri and his team descended the backside of a knoll, off in the distance, they viewed scores of wafting smoke furls. They cautiously approached. As they neared, they observed gaping holes in the chain-link fence with precariously hanging bullet-riddled signage bearing UN's unmistakable ensign.

He waited for all his men to arrive, and then they set in a semi-circle outside the carnage. He instructed the Sudanese drivers to stay with the trucks and to watch over the women and children as his team geared up and methodically investigated.

The smell of burnt bodies and dismembered torsos abound the dusty roadway as they eased each step through this sordid slaughter. Ripped clothing exposed the naked, battered bodies of women as they lay beside their slain babies, and the saturated soil attempted to swallow more of the spilled red fluid. Huts smoldered in the deluge of destruction without consciousness. The barbarity sickened the soldiers as they reconned the area for any semblance of life. Nothing was left untouched—as if an atomic bomb had been dropped. But this was obviously the brutal force of betrayal against humanity by man's hand.

After they swept the area, the body count was eighty-three women and one hundred and sixteen children all under the approximate age of ten. Inside the UN office, four men in white lab coats were splayed like fingers on the floor, but no women staff was found. They had escaped the savagery of death outside but not their demise.

Jake and Mac entered the office and reported they could only find a few bodies outside of the fenced area.

"I think these people thought that whoever did this was on their side or wore badges declaring so in order to get this close without mass hysteria. Most are gathered outside their huts as if they knew nothing of what was going to go down," stated Jake.

"Pretty ballsy, sir. The leader must have a heart as cold as a Montana winter night," remarked Mac.

"Yes. Maybe even a Siberian night. Pass the word for everyone to keep a sharp eye...even the ladies in the trucks. And Jacobs, send a communication to HQ of what we found. Tell them I suspect them to be Al-Shabaab fighters like we crossed on the road last week up north.

There must be a company, a hundred plus men to do this much damage so quickly."

"Yes, sir."

"What do you want to do with the bodies, sir?"

"Nothing we can do. We have three trucks loaded with women and children who are still alive, and I plan on keeping them that way. Let's head out, and Mac, tell Peterson to speak to the drivers and instruct them to stay on the south side of the fence so the women won't see so much of this."

"Yes sir, Colonel."

The men left the UN office the way they found it and as they stepped over the carnage in the main yard, Jake inquired, "What about the lieutenant?"

"Ha, you're kidding, right? You know he is watching us. Let's hope he has our backs. Let's stick in tight formation. It will be dark in a few hours and I don't want, any of us to get separated... not now."

"Yes, sir."

Virginia - Cold and Stiff

There was no need for Marsha's blindfold, not now after going to the head. She knew exactly where she was—well, she knew the chair was still hard, but also what type of ship she was on. The location was dubious but it had to be docked at one of the many locations throughout the Navy's dockyards. She imagined they would transfer her to a smaller holding tank so they could use the one she was in for supplies. *Had they found the soldier? Where would they make the exchange, if truly that's what they were going to do? Had Alicia managed to get my message out? Fuck, I hope so!*

Marsha's train of thought quickly vanished when she heard the key enter the lock. There was no knock as Alicia had previously done. She watched the door partially open, Jenkins quickly stepped inside and dogged it down.

Marsha knew his kind would take the bait. He shouldn't be in the Navy—prison would suit him better.

"Miss me, bitch?"

"Oh yeah, you studmuffin."

"Quit with the names. I don't want to hear a word from you." He walked behind her and ran his hand along the top of her shoulder and across her back to the nap of her neck. He circled her. Standing over Marsha he looked at the bindings secured to the floor, his ball cap shaded the glare from the light above her. He stared at her luscious titties and then ripped open her loose-fitting shirt and tucked it behind her arms.

"So you like your women tied up and submissive, do ya?"

"Shut the fuck up."

Jenkins slowly touched her skin, directing his fingers from the roundness of her breasts to the top of her bra. He traced a line following the curvature of the lace to the single side band and started to pull it down. Marsha swiftly kicked Jenkins square in the groin. As he bent over in pain, Marsha rose from her chair, and with straightened arms, she whirled them around. With a clenched chain rolled up in her fists, she pummeled his ears. She lifted his head in one hand and delivered a powerful punch to his nose, clearly breaking it—he fell backward. The chains dropped to the steel deck with a *CLANK*.

In agony he muttered, "You fucking bitch."

"So, how do you like me now, asshole?" she said sternly.

Jenkins struggled to get to his feet, but a round-house kick caught him in the side of the head, sending a stream of blood spewing from his mouth and down he went on all fours.

"You like picking on harmless women do you?" Marsha went on the attack; this time to his mid-section with a precise kick, which lifted his 200-pound frame off the floor. Jenkins gasped with escaping air. His survival mode rolled his body away, and as he sat on his knees, dazed, he reached for his side-arm. Marsha planted another kick to his head; Jenkins tumbled backward and unconscious.

Marsha stood there in a fighting stance anxious to get it on. Her adrenaline was pumping, and her fists were drawn to her chest as she waited to unleash their full fury. He remained still. Trying to calm herself down, she began to walk around in circles, shaking it out and considering her next move.

Stopping, Marsha stood over him, bent down, and removed his side-arm. She threw it to the bulkhead away from his reach. Grabbing Jenkins by his shirt, she dragged him over to her waiting chair. Lifting his dead weight, she plunked him down, gathered her bindings and chained him up. Marsha reached for her blindfold from the deck and formed a gag wrapping his bleeding mouth. She then reached into Jenkins' shirt pocket, removed his keys, and gave him one last punch just for the women he had probably abused before.

Tucking in her ripped shirt to look a little more presentable, she wrapped her hair in a bun, reached for his ball cap, and stuffed her hair under it. She then picked up Jenkins' side-arm and belted it on. Marsha looked around, and then stared at his boots. *No way will they fit; I need to find me a pair of Bates. I can't ask Alicia... she has done too much now. I'll have to take my chances. They must have started to stockpile supplies for their deployment. I just got to find it.*

Marsha unlocked the door of her holding cell and stepped out, barefoot and all. She closed the door behind her and secured it. She thought she must be on the bilge deck as she continually heard pumps operating. She looked up at the bull's eye stamping above the door: 4-47-6-A. The only ship she had been on was a communication frigate, which was part of a training deployment of two months, based out of San Diego. She tried to remember the sequence.

Fourth deck, 47 frames aft of the bow, sixth compartment outboard to port from mid-ship and it is a supply room. That I know, but where is the stockpile of provisions that they have already brought on board?

Climbing up a ladder and through a hatch, Marsha reached Deck 3. Carefully she eyed each passageway for any indication that could direct her to the storeroom. Too mechanical she deemed. Up the ladder again she went and landed as the signage posted: Deck 2. *More like it.* She could smell coffee wafting through the passageway. She spotted more signage: 'Provision Issue Room' to her immediate left but it was right out in the open to the mess hall. She had no choice; she had to go for it.

Marsha slid along the room's bulkhead and stopped short as two men sat having coffee. Luckily their backs were to her. She rounded the corner and tried the handle—the door was locked. But next to it, was a room with signage rendering: Foul Weather. As before, with her back against the bulkhead, she slid along and kept close observation of the two men. Marsha also kept an eye out for any discovery from the galley as she now came into their view. She tried the handle and the door jarred open into her, nudging her forward. She backed in and closed it quietly. Looking around, the only thing she spotted was rubber deck boots—two sizes too big. She also grabbed rags, a mop, and a rolling bucket where she concealed her weapon. Marsha's plan was sketchy but the only thing she could think of at the moment. As she pushed open the door, she felt the stares of the two men. She pushed along staying to the port side past the scullery to the next bulkhead. Lifting the bucket through the hatch, she encountered another ladder but going down. She needed to find one going topside.

Marsha rolled past more mess tables and berthing compartments as she headed forward. *Where's the damn door?* From behind one of the curtains she heard, "Hey, quit with the rolling, I'm trying to get some shuteye."

"Sorry," she squeaked out. Between two rows of berths, past a pea coat locker, she crossed to the starboard side, bucket in hand. Finally, another door. She dogged it open and stepped through. There it was, straight ahead, a ladder going topside. Just then, a forward door opened from the C.P.O.'s quarters, and stepping through, talking in a deep brogue, she saw her dear friend, Nigel Redman with a commissioned officer. Marsha stopped in her tracks. There was nowhere to go. She grabbed a rag and turned inward facing another door leading into the mess area of A-204L. She started wiping down the door as if she was totally involved and didn't notice the men coming toward her. Nigel passed and then the C.P.O.

"Nice job, seaman," announced the C.P.O.

Marsha quickly turned and acknowledged her superior. Disguising her voice somewhat, she saluted, "Thank you, sir."

"Carry on," he said, and then he noticed her ill-fitting boots. "And go get some better-fitting boots."

"Yes, sir." She prayed Nigel wouldn't turn around. He did not—below his concerned level. No, Marsha Atworth was on his mind.

"Are we going to lollygag all fucking day?" cracked Redman.

"Has anyone ever told you, you are an asshole?" returned the C.P.O.

"All the time. Come on, I've got work to do."

Through the bulkhead and into the next compartment they passed, and from there it would not be long before they would discover her 'checkmate'—the battered guard. Even once on topside, she still had to figure out how to get off the ship without being noticed. Marsha thought, with all the new crew and supplies being stowed away, it could be in her favor. She didn't know how far she could continue with this charade before she got caught. Then what?

Marsha held onto her bucket and mop and went topside and through the hatch to the main deck. To her surprise it was bustling with activity. She was immediately approached.

"Thank you, seaman, for coming so quickly. The spill is down by the port gang plank. About four dozen eggs broke from their tether. Clean it before it gets all over the ship."

"Yes, sir." She rolled her bucket in the direction of the gang plank. *Okay, this works, but how do I get off?*

Men were trying to side-step the spill but the gooey slime stuck to their boots, causing several to slip onto their asses. She hurried to their rescue.

~

As Redman approached the secured lockup, his rage flushed his face. "Where's the fucking guard?" he blasted. He tried the door—it was locked. "You got keys?"

The C.P.O. snapped a ring of keys off his belt loop. He searched for the right one and inserted one. It didn't fit. Redman was anxious. He tried another and the lock *clicked*, he jarred the dogs open. Redman rushed past the C.P.O. and as soon as he spotted the bloodied guard chained up, his rage spiked. Within an instant, that rage turned to murder as he snapped the neck of the guard before the C.P.O. could view the exchange.

~

Marsha stepped to the duty officer and said, "Sir, it will take me an hour to dig through the supplies that are arriving to clean this properly. I can hit the commissary and get what I need and be back in a flash before this muck gets everywhere."

He looked at her yellow sticky hands and the steady stream of seamen and the dock workers bringing supplies onboard. "Go, seaman, and hurry! It's a fucking mess...and don't touch anything."

"Yes, sir."

~

Redman placed his fingers on the guard's neck checking for a pulse as if he was concerned.

"She killed him! I told you that bitch was dangerous."

Instantly, the C.P.O. rushed to the passageway and grabbed the intercom, "Code Zebra, Code Zebra!" he shouted.

A horn blasted with a Code Zebra as Marsha scampered in her oversized boots, midway down the gang plank.

Uganda - Aftermath

Clark and Maysa pulled up into the same tracks as their predecessors. The carnage was obvious without leaving their pickup. Maysa shied away with her hand covering her mouth. Clark reached for her other one, the one that was tenderly wrapped around Ateefah; he squeezed it tight. She returned her look from her passenger window to Clark.

"Why do our people have to suffer like this? It is senseless. Do you have conflict in your country like this?"

"Depends who you talk to. We have very prejudiced people who still haven't accepted the equality concept. Minorities are put down, victimized, sent to prison for years on unsubstantial evidence, and then twenty years later find out they're innocent. It happens all the time and especially, it seems, if you are of color."

"But do they get massacred?"

"Well, the white man did it to our native Indians only a couple hundred years ago, and more recently to our Blacks in the 60s. Now we just give guns to others to do it for us."

"So all of this is part of someone's grand scheme?" Maysa asked.

"Ah, now you are suggesting a conspiracy."

"Well?"

"Well what? You could be right...above my pay grade."

"Someone sent you here to kill one of our officials. Is that not a conspiracy?"

"Not to the U.S. Government. They rationalize it as being 'peacekeepers'. Granted, they do supply troves of aid but you can bet there is always an underlying agenda."

"Which is?"

They hit a rut in the road near the end of the chain link compound before Clark had a chance to answer—they bounced upward. Maysa could still feel the heaviness of the still air as she held onto the children.

Clark continued his assessment. "Anything. Oil, minerals, drugs, alliances, or just plain greed; someone's pockets getting lined with cash or favors."

"I don't know, Mr. Clark. I pray Ateefah lives in a better world."

"By the way, when did you find out about my mission? I never told you."

"Whispers at the UN camp before we left Gulu."

"You knew a week ago and never said anything?"

"Not my business, Mr. Clark. You have been kind to us, that's all that matters. Sometimes, we do things for which we are not proud of, but do anyway, out of what is right in our mind."

"Some of us have accountability, but not necessarily politicians."

"True... or elders. They lie to protect their station, their self-indulgent integrity even if others know they are lying."

"Judicial law. The one with the best lawyer wins, not necessarily the one who is innocent."

"I can attest to that one." She looked down at Ateefah, "But look what I have beside me." She smiled. "Shall we continue, Mr. Clark?"

SAS Headquarters

Petty Officer Smyth's blackberry buzzed as they all tried to comfort Samantha.

"Excuse me, Director, I need to get this. I'll be right back," reassured her friend.

Smyth stepped out of the office to one of the terminals and entered a series of strokes. A message then popped up: <Hourglass on the move>. Message terminated.

He looked confused. *Why did Tomlinson say she was dead? Maybe he thought they had her but has since escaped.* He quickly signed out and then just sat there for a moment. *Just because she is on the move doesn't mean by her own free will. They could be moving her somewhere else. Okay...let's see if we can spot her if she is out in the open.*

Derrick rushed to the director's office and looked down at his devastated friend. He needed to bring her back slowly.

"Ma'am, I think we should still scan the area. Tomlinson could be wrong," he stated sympathetically. "Phillip, see if there were any boat crashes. This would be a newsworthy item. Carmen and Nina, if you would set PAG in the general area above the Naval shipyards..." he paused. "But first get a list of any outbound vessels...say leaving port in the next few days to a week out."

"Yes, sir," they affirmed.

"Samantha, just rest. Let us confirm what Tomlinson has reported. Personally, I don't believe him or trust him with any words coming out of his mouth. Sorry for being so disrespectful, ma'am."

Samantha formed a brief smile and turned her head away without saying a word.

"I'll close the door so we don't disturb you, Sam." The P.O. shut the door softly and briskly stepped over to his counterparts.

"I received a text from the Swan's associate. It indicated Marsha was on the move. Now, I don't know how he knows this, or whether or not of her own accord, or if someone is transporting her. So, my friends, it is up to us to find her. Use all your resources you trust. Let's get to work."

"Derrick, I checked with different news stations in the area and it seems there was a collision early Tuesday morning between two watercraft, and bodies were found. What is strange to me though, instead of the Coast Guard investigating, the incident was held by the Navy. The story doesn't mention which department."

"Very good, Phillip. That's what I am talking about. Normal channels are being bypassed, so we know Tomlinson is controlling all of this. He's trying to cover his tracks but what he is doing is opening our door wider. Keep digging everyone."

Nina blurted out, "Bingo!"

"Go, Nina. What do you have?"

"Sir, the USS Bulkeley is scheduled to deploy this Saturday with one known stop to the Bocas Del Toro Islands in Panama."

"Where is it berthed now?"

"Naval Station, Norfolk, Virginia, sir."

"YES!" Derrick spun around snapping his fingers, doing his version of the rumba.

"Carmen, can you hover over Norfolk to see if we can get a ping?"

"I've already sent a message to Vandenberg requesting permission for an exercise exploratory. We have clearance."

"How long to get in position?"

"In five, four, three, two, one! We are over top, Derrick. Scanning..." She types some more, "Scanning..." The room hushed when a *PING* sounded over the SAS lab's speakers—in stereo.

"YES!!!" Rang out from all their lips and high fives were set in motion. Quickly they re-grouped and began to zoom-in on their friend's position in real time.

. . .

Jacobs, after speaking with the female UN camp director over regular channels, now spiked his PRS and stated to his team there was another UN camp 30 kilometers away.

Colonel Dimitri, who was sitting in the lead Chenoweth, spiked his set, "It will be dark when we approach the camp. Keep your eyes peeled. We don't know for certain who Jacobs spoke with, or is in fact, the real camp director, or one of the hostages taken from the last camp. Sorry, guys, just a little suspicious of everything."

"Sir, when we get closer, do you want my team to check it out?" asked Jake.

"We'll stop one kilometer away, but only recon, no engagement no-matter-what. I want us all to have a clear and informed response if there is a situation."

"Yes, sir."

. . .

As Marsha approached the end of the gang plank, two guards with drawn M4A1 Carbines stopped her access. She instinctively raised her yellow-dripping hands. She looked at them and then back to the duty officer. He waved his hand for her to proceed. The mess was getting everywhere. They stepped aside and she took off running to the commissary. She carefully opened the door and stepped inside.

Redman scanned the room—her perfume still lingered in the water-tight chamber. *Her perfume?* He rubbed his nose. He had complimented her on her perfume at the gala. *Her perfume...that fucking bitch! That fucking mop-toting, bucket-rolling bitch. It had to be her.*

"Fucking bitch! She's the one you were lollygagging with. Come on!"

Redman charged out of the chamber and pushed the door so hard, it bounced with an echoing *clank* off the bulkhead and shut closed.

"Call your duty officer and tell him not to let anyone off this ship until I get there, understood?"

The Chief Petty Officer had orders from a higher command than his own Captain. He wished this asshole would disappear from his sight; otherwise, he just might have to shoot the bastard. He acknowledged Redman's request.

~

Marsha looked around in desperation for another way out. She ran down a side aisle to the back freezers and then across their frosted faces to where a sign pointed to 'washrooms'. Down the hallway she went, hoping it didn't dead-end. She dodged staff who were hurriedly replacing stock as fast as they could. She knew any second now, Redman would be busting through the doors. It wouldn't be pretty.

She burst through the ladies' lavatory and scanned for anything to help her—nothing. Marsha jostled out of there and pushed through to the men's. A smallish window almost seven feet up, next to the last stall, brought hope. She swung open the stall's door and hoisted herself up on it—the window had a wired screen on the outside. "Fuck!" she screamed. She kicked the small chain that held the window partially open, and as it fell, she kicked at the wired screen with all she had. Again and again, she hammered it. It broke from its anchors and fell to the outside ground—but as she withdrew her foot, a piece of wire broke off and had embedded through her rubber boot and straight into her foot. She muffled her scream.

Redman popped his head out the hatch and ran like a mad bull to the duty officer—behind him, the C.P.O. He noticed the mop and bucket propped up between the hose rack and a deck locker on the exterior bulkhead.

"Where did she go!?" yelled Redman.

"Who, sir?"

"The bitch with the mop, fuck face."

The duty officer looked at the C.P.O. who nodded to him.

"The commissary."

Redman charged down the gang plank almost knocking some of the crew into the cold water below. The two guards stepped aside as he hit the end of the gang plank. Swinging around the hand railing, Redman ran across the hard deck approaching the commissary. He blasted through the doors knocking a seaman on his ass.

On top of the commissary's roof, the hatch flipped open and a young woman in fatigues with yellow rain boots passed through and then she quietly closed it behind her. Without saying a word, the CPO and duty officer watched from the height of the main deck as she limped along the roof-top of the commissary to the other adjoining warehouses. The duty officer saluted the C.P.O. as he turned to leave this moment of reckoning. His concern was below deck where he needed to investigate the recorded footage of the collateral damage left by the indiscretion of this belligerent man and to secure the identity of the man chained to the chair.

~

"There she is!" screamed Carmen. "She's limping and on a roof!"

~

Redman stepped from the commissary with phone in hand obviously frustrated by the loss of his prisoner.

"I don't know, Jack, through a back window." Redman looked around and then up at the duty officer who gave him a middle finger salute. "Look, now is not the time. I'll discuss it with you when I see you. It's not over. I'll get that skinny bitch; she can't be far. There is blood on the window frame where she went through. No, I didn't see any other access. The warehouse door was locked. They keep everything locked around here because of all those thieving bastard E2s; you pay them monkey wages. What! Hell no. There is a mile of warehouses. I'll get my SUV and go around back. She has to leave a trail with as much blood as I saw. Right, talk later."

From the forward port hatch of the ship, a familiar face, carrying a gallon container of concentrated detergent, raced across the main deck in double time toward the duty officer. She glanced at a hurried figure hobbling across the rooftops, as a large man who stood on the tarmac was oblivious to his captive's movement. Alicia smiled from within as the figure disappeared behind a large air conditioning vent.

Marsha felt her foot slipping within the oversized boot as she crossed the roof of the commissary and now, after clearing the firewall between the two buildings, she took refuge undercover offered by some large ductwork. She thought she would stay put until dark; plus, it gave her a chance to ease out the ten gauge wire that was stuck in her foot.

"UGH!" She muffled her outer voice as she removed it through the yellow boot. Marsha quickly removed her holstered gun from beneath Alicia's gifted shirt, pulled out the tail and ripped a section to wrap her foot. Easing her foot out of the boot, she thought it looked like something you would see in a Scorsese movie.

Marsha bound the throbbing foot tight and let it rest for the time being. Tonight, she would have to replace the boot and find the nearest phone before Redman found her.

Iceman Cold

Dimitri stopped his caravan a kilometer from where the coordinates indicated the next location of the UN camp. As they had discussed, Jake, Mac, and Peterson continued on to recon the camp in order to avoid any chance of being caught in an ambush. The colonel was not taking any chances after what they had just witnessed a few kilometers back.

The three stepped from their Chenowth, donned their ghillies, and headed out into the darkening night. Within thirty minutes they were belly down and had eased closer to the fenced compound. They split up so they could cover more ground. As they got closer, nothing looked out of place. People were milling around, children were playing and pots sat on their open fires. The three men all sent their impressions back to the colonel who then had Jacobs radio the UN camp director. An aid answered and politely asked if he may put the receiver down to fetch the director. Jake and his team watched as a man ran from a building beckoning the whereabouts of the director. Soon, she rounded a tent and came to the aid's side. They spoke and he pointed to the office.

"Hello, this is Amelie Thorsten."

"Hello, ma'am. This is Corporal Jacobs. We spoke earlier today."

"Yes, Corporal. How can I help you?"

"We are approximately a kilometer away and would very much like to call upon your assistance with the three trucks of IDP's we came across."

"They are always welcome, Corporal. Not much room left, but I am quite certain we can fit them in."

"Thank you, ma'am. We will be there shortly."

Amelie Thorsten, a thin, blonde lady of 5'-9" stature, hailing from Copenhagen, Denmark, stepped from her office and spoke to her personnel of new incoming souls. Jake relayed a message to the colonel that everything looked above board and secured. The caravan set in motion.

~

"Why did they stop?" asked Maysa.

"I don't know. They have been in a tight formation for the last thirty kilometers. Maybe they expect trouble from the ones responsible at the last camp."

"Do you think they have found another one?"

"It's possible. I'll scout out their camp after they settle in. Maybe we can get a feel for what they are up to?"

"I feel a little skittish." Maysa rubbed her arms. "I don't think we should light a fire tonight."

"I thought it was just me," smiled Clark. "We'll find some decent cover first and then I will take a peek. How does that sound?"

"Very well, Mr. Clark. I trust your judgment."

~

The gates swung open as the caravan approached the UN camp and much to the director's surprise, perched out front waved an American flag. Colonel Dimitri pulled to the side so the three trucks carrying its valuable cargo could stage in front of the office. The other vehicles closed in tightly behind them—the gates closed. His men helped the ladies disembark with their personal belongings, the little they had, and then the children.

One of the truck drivers hurried out of his cab and excused himself as he hunted for his wife. On their encounter of seeing each other, tears rushed to their eyes as they embraced deeply. It had been the first time during this whole ordeal they could finally show their affection.

Colonel Dimitri stepped from his buggy and walked over to where the camp director was standing and joined in the celebration. He introduced himself.

"Mrs. Thorsten, I am Colonel Dimitri."

"It is 'Miss', and it's Amelie. A pleasure to have you Americans here. A little unusual to see you I might add, but nothing surprises me anymore. Welcome." She held out her hand to his.

"We had no choice. We had to get these ladies to some semblance of safety. Are you aware of the trouble at the camp not far from here?"

"At Dr. Mathews' camp?"

"I don't know his name, but a horrible massacre took place. We just came from there."

"Oh my God! I have not heard a word."

"Were there any women nurses?"

"Of course, maybe six or seven... I can't believe it." The director sat on the step of one of the large transport trucks and shook her head.

"I'm sorry to have to bring you bad news, but it was a much smaller camp than this one. I hope just the sheer numbers would negate any plan to attack your sanctuary."

"If we are dealing with Al-Shabaab, they have no reason for what they do. It is just for the pure sake of killing. We had the Westgate Mall a couple of years ago. What was the sense of that? I just heard they tried attacking a garrison of Kenyan soldiers. No, I am afraid if they are around, we are in trouble."

"We'll do our best to keep everyone safe tonight, but we will be off in the morning."

"I appreciate having you here," replied Amelie holding onto Colonel Dimitri's arm.

"I'll get my men situated, and our rigs out of sight. Do you have UN decals we can place on the doors of the trucks we just brought in?"

"I'll see what I can find," smiled the director.

Amelie returned to her office as Dimitri instructed his men on the placement of vehicles and where to set the perimeter. He instructed Jake and his men to come in for some food but afterward, they will need to find a strategic spot to observe beyond the compound's fence for the evening.

~

Clark brought the scope to his eyes and searched the camp, then its perimeter, and then... he quickly removed his scope from his eye to gain a better visual of the area, and then raised the scope once more.

"What do you see, Mr. Clark?"

His face turned 'Iceman' cold.

~

Mac couldn't believe his eyes.

"Incoming, sir," announced Mac over his PRS, who was perched high on a sturdy limb of a Juniper tree, and well hidden by the foliage. *"And, sir, if I am not mistaken, it is our phantom woman carrying a young child in front of her, another strapped to her back, and a toddler hanging on to her shirt tail. She just came out of the shadows."*

A posted sentry raised his weapon as he eyed a figure as it came into the light of the overhead halogen's cast. As they approached, he radioed the Colonel and identified the figure as a young woman carrying a couple of kids with one next to her walking assuredly toward the gate.

"Let her pass, soldier, and then bring her to me."

"Yes, sir."

The soldier lowered his weapon, removed the padlock and chain, and swung the gate open so the woman could pass. He motioned her to stay put, and then he re-padlocked the gate.

"Ma'am, do you speak English?" he politely asked.

"Yes."

"I've been instructed to escort you to my Colonel, ma'am."

"Is he the one in charge?"

"Yes, ma'am."

"Good... and please hurry. We don't have much time."

Virginia, Norfolk

Romeo 2000 Hrs.

An orange glow flickered off the tarmac as the halogens began to come alive. Carrying a seemingly empty container, Alicia fell in behind the other sailors, down the gang plank, and headed directly to the brightly lit commissary. The bustling would continue for the next thirty-six hours as they prepared for deployment. She entered through the double passage of propped open doors where draped heavy clear plastic curtains shielded the frosty air from escaping the warehouse. The sailors spread out to their shelved merchandise.

Alicia scanned the large warehouse space and found a utility room where an encased firehose was mounted on the outside and walls that extended to the roof trusses. Casually, she looked about and then entered. Mounted on the concrete firewall that portioned each warehouse space was a steel-rung ladder leading to the roof access. She lowered her bin, opened the blue and tan flaps, and pulled out a pair of Bates. Tying the laces together, she draped them over her shoulder and began the thirty-foot climb.

The hatch easily opened. Alicia eased her body through and quietly re-closed the lid. The shielded halogens left the roof in darkness as she followed her friend's path. Over the adjoining firewall she slipped, unobserved from the towering destroyer. Alicia stepped softly as she approached the large air conditioning ducts where she had last seen her friend disappear. Just as Alicia was about to call out Marsha's name, a figure jumped out of the darkness and stuck Alicia in the shoulder propelling her sideways along the gravel roof. Marsha jumped out of the shadows and pinned the intruder down. Marsha could feel the softness of her intruder as their hips pressed together. The scent of slight perfume eased Marsha's elbow from her intruder's throat and she heard, "Miss Marsha!"

The familiar voice stopped Marsha in mid-swing and she collapsed, soaked with perspiration, onto her friend's body.

"Alicia?"

"Yes."

"What are you doing here? I could have killed you."

"I'm here to help you."

"That is so sweet, but you can't get involved. This is much more dangerous than you think."

"I saw you limping so I brought a first aid kit and a pair of Bates for you."

Marsha hugged her. Alicia could feel the sweat coming from her friend's drenched clothes and reached up to feel her forehead.

"You have a fever."

"I got a piece of rusty metal stuck in my foot. I'll be alright."

"Oh yeah, you are as tough as nails," sarcastically claimed Alicia. Marsha slipped off Alicia and lay beside her. Alicia's eyes had adjusted to the moonless night's sky and she felt the bulky-wrapped foot. She pulled out a small service kit from her dungarees.

"Sit and be quiet while I dress this properly."

"Wow, for my sweet little southern girl, you can be pretty bossy."

"You have no idea," she muttered as she pulled the stained wrap from Marsha's foot.

"I've got some powder here that might take your breath away, but it will cauterize your wound."

As she shook the powder on, Marsha tensed up.

"Ugh! I hate that feeling."

"You've had this before?"

"A couple of times. Still, it does take your breath away for a split second."

"Here take these two pills; they will help with your fever."

Alicia felt around on the gravel roof and found a shoestring. She pulled them to her side. "I guessed at your shoe size, so I hope these fit." She handed the Bates to Marsha.

"Okay, the wrap is as good as it is going to get. Now try the boot."

Marsha struggled with the boot on her injured foot but the other slid on almost perfectly.

"You are so sweet, Alicia. Thank you for everything. Now, help me up so I can get out of here and you can get back to your ship."

"Not so fast, my friend," stated Alicia.

Marsha froze and quickly gazed at Alicia... *Fuck, have I been set up by this sweet innocent thing?*

Alicia looked at her watch. "Come on; put your arm around me. We need to get to the other roof."

"What do you mean?"

"Look... over there... past the second firewall."

Marsha peered through the darkness to where her friend had indicated. She could barely make it out, but it looked like a figure was being lowered down to the adjoining rooftop. Above, the blades of a helicopter barely made a whirring sound.

"Come on. Use me for balance; we don't have much time."

"Who are you?"

"Marsha, there will be time for that... but right now, you need to get out of here."

Alicia helped Marsha over the firewall and then within a few more steps, they approached a blacked-out military-dressed soldier.

"Are you 'Hourglass', ma'am?"

"Yes."

"Please, stand next to me so I can put this harness around you. The soldier slipped the straps around Marsha and adjusted them securely. "How's that? You feel secure, ma'am?"

"I believe so."

The soldier spoke over his PRS; they started to rise in silence.

"Later, my friend," promised Alicia.

. . .

The group at SAS sat in wonderment as they witnessed their friend's heat signature from PAG's live feed being extracted from the rooftop.

"Who are they?" asked Carmen.

"I don't know. Maybe another team was near and they were sent in," replied Derrick.

"We need to get the director up. That sedative should be wearing off by now," said Nina.

"I'll go in," insisted Derrick. "She'll be asking a lot of questions, you can damn well bet."

"Ease it to her, Derrick. The shock and all."

"Will do, Carmen. Mr. Compassionate... here I go."

Derrick turned from the big screen and walked up the three steps to the director's office. He lightly rapped on the director's door and then opened it. "Samantha, it's me, Derrick."

She wrestled with her drowsiness. "Come in, Derrick."

"Ma'am, we have some great news. We found Marsha, she is alive... PAG identified her." Derrick knelt beside the couch.

"What?! How? I mean... Jack said she was dead." Samantha offered her hand to Derrick to help her sit upright. She swung her legs out over the couch and sat with the back of the couch supporting her.

"I think he was assured she would be, but someone intervened."

"Who?"

"We don't know as yet."

"Derrick, what are you not telling me? Wasn't it Admiral Stone's boat you said helped in her kidnapping?"

"Samantha, listen. We have only partial knowledge of what went down. Phillip retraced the Admiral's boat, but we now believe it was chasing whoever was responsible for Marsha's disappearance, not the cause. Footage shows it wasn't the Admiral or Marsha. We don't know who was powering the craft, but possibly the same people who rescued her."

"Derrick, this is all so very confusing."

"It is for us, as well, but the good news is, Marsha appears to be safe."

"Can't we still track her with PAG?"

"We believe as she entered the helicopter, and this is only speculating, it's some type of stealth engineering, we lost her aura's index."

"We have such a thing as a stealth helicopter?"

"As far as I know, the stealth models were only developed against detection from radar. It must have a Faraday cage of some type to stop PAG. So, I guess the answer is, yes, ma'am."

"So what do we do now?"

"Wait..."

Day 9 - Thursday

Uganda, UN Camp
Charlie 0300 Hrs.

The office door of camp director, Amelie Thorsten, closed behind the young woman and her three children. She now stood before a blond-haired man wearing a military uniform and beside him, a white-faced lady.

He out-stretched his hand to her. "Hello, my name is Colonel Dimitri, and this is the camp Director, Amelie Thorsten."

Maysa hesitated and drew back, appearing to be afraid.

"No need to alarm yourself," he said in a strange accent she had never heard. "Why do you want to speak to me?"

"You know who I am?"

"We have a pretty good idea... Why don't you tell me?"

"I have information but first, why do you hunt Mr. Clark?"

"Ah, Mr. Clark... That is Lieutenant William Clark I believe you're referencing to."

"Yes, you know... Why?"

"Well, we are not hunting him; we are trying to save his life."

"With three guys who go invisible and trucks you see and then they disappear?" Maysa said hotly.

"You are very perceptive, aren't you? We are a special team..."

"Yes... Special Ops."

"I see Lt. Clark has taught you well. We are just trying to protect him from an agency that betrayed his loyalty. Unfortunately, when word gets out, we will be at risk as well. Now what information do you have for me?"

"First, I want assurance no harm will come to Mr. Clark."

"You have my word no harm will be inflicted by us... Miss...?"

"Maysa," she countered confidently.

"And are there any other requests?"

"Yes. If I die tonight, you deliver my daughter to the house of my mother. Also, please tell her that I am happy and that her granddaughter's name is Ateefah."

"And the other two?"

"The boy I call Miso and his sister, Jamila. Their parents are dead."

Colonel Dimitri thought that was a strange request but he handed her a pad and pencil to write down the pertinent information.

"Thank you," she said leaving the pad on the Director's desk. "Mr. Clark said a large company of Al-Shabaab troops have stopped just outside striking distance of your camp. He thinks you are not well equipped to handle this many and offers eight RPG's."

"Why does he think we are not equipped?"

"Because of your hesitation at the last scrimmage."

"Your Mr. Clark is well trained in warfare. May I be so bold as to ask if he has a plan?"

"For me to gather the three who have been chasing us and then strike Al-Shabaab hard and fast before they have a chance to re-organize. We then back up to help defend the camp."

"Are you sure that is exactly what he said?"

"Yes."

"He didn't send you here with your children to be out of harm's way?"

"No!" she said crossing her arms defiantly. "Besides, I am the only one who can direct your men to where Mr. Clark is without setting off Al-Shabaab. You might think your men to be invisible, but I can see them with their movement."

"You are cunning, from what I understand, but I can't allow a young woman to throw herself into battle; especially when you have children to care for."

"You have no choice... me, or die!"

The Colonel bucked at her remark. *Who is this young woman with steely blue-grey eyes glaring at me, puffed like a banshee?* He turned to the camp Director. "Miss Thorsten, can you look after this young woman's children and see to her wishes if anything happens to us?"

"Yes, Colonel. And by-the-way, these young warriors, like Maysa here, would do anything to help their fellow man."

"So I see. Come on Maysa, let's get this ball rolling."

Maysa hugged the little boy and placed his hand into the Director's. She removed her sashes and placed the two little ones into wooden chairs that were situated in front of the Director's desk. She bent to them and hugged and kissed them both; she turned quickly and charged the door with Colonel Dimitri following suit.

In the compound, Dimitri summoned Jacobs and told him to radio Jake and his team to come in and meet him at the front gate, pronto. He added, "Have the rest of the men here as well."

"Yes, sir."

. . .

Derrick helped the director glide down the steps leading to the main lab. She was still a little wobbly but insisted on sitting with the rest.

"Are you feeling better, ma'am?" asked Carmen.

"A little shaky, but relieved knowing Marsha is alive."

Just then, Derrick's Blackberry rang. He went over to a terminal and typed in a series of keystrokes and then a message popped up: "*Hourglass is safe—at sanctuary.*" Message ended. Derrick glared at the blank screen and then logged out. He lifted his head to the questioning stares of his teammates.

"She is safe!" he announced joyfully.

They all broke out in a harmonious cry of relief.

"Thank God!" shared the director. "Or whoever they are."

"Shall we turn PAG back to our missing soldier?" queried Nina.

"Yes, by all means. Let's try and save someone else if we can," gleefully added the director. Samantha let out a sigh of relief and shared with everyone. "Thank you all for this long day...night... whatever time it is, for all your hard work. I am indebted to you all."

"You are welcome, ma'am," they shared in unison.

Carmen and Nina busily started to re-position PAG to the last known co-ordinates of the missing soldier before Marsha's abduction. Derrick wandered over to Phillip and in a low voice, asked him to research sanctuaries in the area. He had no idea what was meant by that last transmission on his screen, but he was going to find out.

. . .

The Colonel waited along with the rest of the squad and a slim, blue-eyed young woman, for Jake and his team. Maysa noticed dust kicking up and a weird shimmering pattern moving toward her. They removed their ghillies and looked at their young phantom. She slowly walked over and touched their disguises and then quickly drew back.

"Jake, this is Maysa," introduced the Colonel.

Jake held out his hand, she hesitated, and then met his.

"So you are of skin and bone," joked Jake. "I thought you were just a mirage who we kept seeing."

"And likewise of you," she countered.

"How could you spot us? These are the latest techno-camo out there."

"I couldn't see you, but I knew where you were."

"How?"

"The way you moved through the grass. At this time of year we have two waves of wind: in the late morning and late evening. The rest of the time it is fairly calm. As the breeze blows over the knolls, you must zigzag like in sailing as Mr. Clark explained his interpretation of my instructions. If you break the grass against the wind, it looks out of place, but if you zig, it looks like a wave of air."

"How did you learn this?" questioned Jake.

"I live in Africa."

The men smiled as they understood her meaning.

"Okay, gentlemen, here is the plan," offered the Colonel to his collective team as they formed a circle. "Maysa is going to guide Jake and his men to the lieutenant and with his help they will spur on the first wave of attack before the Al-Shabaab have a chance to organize. With any luck, and with the lieutenant's list of arsenals, the company will be reduced in size and we will be able to defend this camp. I know it is not much of a plan, but we have no other choice. They out-man us at least four-to-one. Any questions?"

The Colonel looked around at his men's faces. "Dig in men and do your best. You are the best, so let's show them what we have."

"Yes, sir," they collectively acknowledged.

"Mac, keep us informed with what is going on."

"Yes, sir."

Maysa turned to lead her team of avengers toward the fields of compassion and treachery, of life and of death, past the silent Junipers, confronting the savagery of man. Her young mind crippled by languish of plight, instilled by the predators of flesh, who had amassed this night into a solitary collective to rid her darkness, if her god so willed. She stopped suddenly...

Her steel-grey eyes sharpened intensely on the tips of the lush green grass. She drew her knife, and as a face appeared between the blades of greenery, she thrust her ceramic blade deep into his throat and muffled his mouth as he gurgled in repeated shudders. Jake and his team spread around her, watching her... learning. She moved ahead, slithered through the grass, and then lay still. Another appeared and was quickly brought down by Jake... another sprung from the moving grass but without success as his time had run its course. Maysa wiped her hand on his shirt and moved closer to her friend hoping she was not too late to lay eyes on him one more time.

Maysa quickly bolted behind a boulder, down a crevice, and up the other side to where she saw the back end of their pickup as it sat quietly amongst a dense clump of elephant grass. The three men cautiously approached as she scanned for intruders, her eyes misty as fear invaded her mind.

Lt. Clark watched as the tips of the grass, bent in defiance... he sprung forth, blanketing his prey. He raised his knife to plunge it deep... suddenly he heard, "Mr. Clark... NO!" His stroke was swift, without discourse and careened to the side narrowly missing his object. Another dove onto his body and tried to calm him.

"Lt. Clark... it's Jake. We met at a training camp," he managed to say while wrestling his friend down.

Maysa ran to his side and dropped to his chest in tears. "Mr. Clark, I thought they had killed you."

Clark's adrenaline was pumping and his breathing intense, he struggled with Jake's hold.

"Calm yourself, man. We are here to help you," insisted Jake. "I'm going to let go." Jake eased his grip and toppled off Clark. Maysa still hung on, moving with his breathing. He sat up and grabbed Maysa strongly, "What are you doing here? I told you to stay at the camp until this is all over."

Clark looked into her teary blue eyes and then hugged her close. "I'm sorry, Maysa."

"Lieutenant, you are a hard man to follow... and if it wasn't for this brave young lady, I don't think we would have ever caught up with you."

Peterson stood above the two men and outstretched his hand to help them up. He bent to Mac. "You okay?"

"Yeah... thank you Miss for calling out. I didn't see him coming."

"Sorry about that..." said Clark offering his hand to the stranger.

"Mac, sir," he offered.

"I'm Peterson, sir. We are glad to see you."

"Nice to finally meet you all. I must admit I envisioned a totally different scenario to our meeting than this," smiled Clark.

"What's going on, Lieutenant?" asked Jake.

"Three crept up to the pickup only moments ago. I thought you guys were part of them. They are like ants crawling around here."

"We ran into a couple as well. Actually, your friend here spotted them before we did. The outcome might have been different."

"How many do you think?"

"I would say, at least a hundred or more."

"I need to check in with the Colonel, to let him know we made contact," interrupted Mac.

"Go ahead, Mac. So what's in the pickup?"

"RPG's and extra 7.62 x 39 Bimetal mags for AK-47's. I got three guns stockpiled from my three bodies. Sorry but there was only one poor-excuse-of-a-sniper rifle in the box."

"Yeah, well, we have seen its damage," smiled Peterson.

"Lucky shots..." returned Clark.

"Jake, the Colonel wants a time."

"Okay, what do you say, Lieutenant? It's your show."

"Let me see your watch." Jake turned his wrist to Clark. The low fluorescent dial stared back at him.

"Is this your usual watch?"

"No, similar, we were given these at the beginning of our mission. Why do you ask?"

"They gave me one, just like yours. I dumped mine into my foxhole with the rest of the garbage given to me. It wasn't minutes later before three guys showed up with guns drawn creeping into my position. Have you activated the GPS yet?"

"No, we were told not to engage until we had completed our mission."

"And that meant... finding me?"

"Affirmative. We assumed so we all could get a ride home."

"Right... a ride home... in a pine box."

"What are you saying?"

"I don't think any of us are supposed to survive this. We are all being set up. They want a clean slate with no loose ends. Who else knows our location?"

"PAG, sir," informed Mac.

"PAG?"

"It's a new Particular Aura Generation system to find, basically whomever, if lost. It's a satellite system that can pinpoint an individual so rescuers can locate them faster and easier."

"And one of these has been following me?"

"Well, not exactly, sir. They only recently got a ping, from what I understand."

"But they know where you all are at this precise moment?"

"We stay in contact with command, sir, so that is affirmative."

"Okay, I got an idea. If what I think is true regarding your watches, give them to me. I'm going to circle around behind their camp, set the GPS and then get the hell out of there... because gentlemen, fireworks are going to happen."

"And if it doesn't?"

"I'm not a God-fearing man, but pray it does; otherwise, we are going to die."

"Mr. Clark... let me do this. You know I am the only one here who has any chance at all. You are all too clumsy and will surely die. Set your rockets like we talked about.

You are now four...that's two rockets each. Let me place the watches."

"Maysa, I can't protect you. I will have no line of sight if you get in trouble."

"Mr. Clark, you know as well as I do, my life on this planet has endured more than most, yet I still live. I owe it to my fellow man so they may prosper... so my daughter will be able to grow up and be proud of me. I need to do this, Mr. Clark, please... I beg of you."

. . .

PAG zeroed in on its known target.

"Ma'am, we got a ping! I'll zoom down," declared Carmen excitedly.

"Where is he?"

"Approximately the same coordinates as Colonel Dimitri and his men."

"They found him before we did?" questioned Nina.

"Maybe they haven't yet come face to face?" interjected Derrick.

"We'd better inform Tomlinson. This is his show," stated Samantha. "Although I despise that bastard, he still is our commander on this mission."

"Ma'am!" alerted Carmen. "There seems to be a lot of gunfire going on, and our man is moving from one spot to another very quickly."

. . .

The chaos was extreme—beyond what anyone could imagine.

"Move back!" yelled Jake over his PRS. *"They are breaking through on my right. I can't contain them."*

"Me too... Motherfucker, take that!" shouted Mac.

"Colonel, we are taking heavy fire. We are moving back as quickly as we can. I have no idea where the lieutenant is. Peterson where are you?"

"Fuck, man... Took one in the leg."

"I got him, Jake. We are falling back."

A flurry of bullets zipped by as the injured Peterson and Mac hobbled backward in preparation to defend the camp. Over his PRS, Jake heard, *"Mac... Look out!"* A rustling of noise and the agony of pain vibrated through his headset, the transmission went silent.

An armored truck laden with some heavy explosives went from orange to almost translucent white. Rays of light shot skyward in a rainbow of color and the molten red-hot steel showered down. Jake knew it was Lieutenant Clark. *He's still alive.* Jake backed up to the now, darkened compound. A bullet zipped by and creased him in the side of the head... he went down only feet away from the gate. From the other side of a machine gun mounted Chenowth buggy, one of his team darted out and pulled Jake to safety. The machine gun rattled at the incoming—100 meters away. Bullets riddled the trucks and the walls of the camp director's office. The director, covered in blood, crawled through the compound's dirt to the fallen Colonel. She rested her hand upon the open wound of his chest.

Streaks of fire filled the sky as men howled with the instinct of an animal's cry. The warriors advanced closer to the compound through the middle of the darkened hours.

. . .

Tomlinson, after hearing about the whereabouts of his devise, immediately picked up the receiver and made a call.

"Commander, I want every fucking plane with every fucking nuke sent to the exact coordinates you received! I want it to be the fourth of July. Do you understand me?" demanded Jack Tomlinson.

"Yes, sir. They have already taken flight and we should be getting a response momentarily."

"Good, Commander. I appreciate your diligence in handling this matter for us. This rogue soldier could have made an international incident with his actions."

"Yes, sir. Sir, just received an update: 'Elmer Fudd' terminated."

SAS Horrified – UN Camp
Charlie - After Midnight

PAG's heat indexing screen exploded with traces of light—white, red, and yellow blended, crisscrossing past their eyes through the night sky. The director and her team sat in silence watching the inferno displayed before them as the violence ensued through the darkness. The intensity from the heat waved like a Texas highway on a summer's day, as machinery melted into a river of liquid iron and bodies vaporized into thin air. Samantha, unable to continue watching the horror of destruction, reached past Carmen and shut PAG down. The screens went black. They all stared into the darkness.

Day 10 - Friday

Uganda – UN Camp
Charlie 0630 Hrs.

The hissing of expanded metal from the intense heat spat at the morning dew. The continued snapping of burnt wood with their rising plumes of smoke, greeted the wafting of the pre-morning breeze as dawn broke over the hills. Muffled cries by the victims' kindred as they buried their heads into their loved ones' chests, and moaned their loss as precipitant tears vanished before hitting the ground.

A few wandered in the wake and a few who were cognizant assisted the needy as the field next to the compound reeked of smoldering bodies and burnt rubber. Twisted machinery lay in unrecognizable abstract mounds while adolescent fires erupted through unspent energy without guidance.

Propped up against the office wall, wrapped in a midriff bandage, Colonel Dimitri's eyes opened to each and every sound. He sat as others acknowledged his authority and presence. His breached Berretta lay to his left while his over-worked doctor, Amelie, spared a moment to lay to his right. His breathing was laborious but she assured him of many more days.

Jake, with his cyclops head-bandage, was inspecting the perimeter fence, when he came across two of his teammates displayed with white sheets soaking up their blood next to a giant hole. Farther on he saw his pals, Mac with bandaged hands and a gauzed chin and Peterson with binding encircling his thigh. He felt a sad relief as others didn't fare as well. He was told that one of his teammates, Reynolds, was still fighting for each breath—but they had hope.

Jake removed his hand from his aching head, grabbed the chain-link fence, and faced his buddies. "Are you going to be okay?" he asked.

"They say I won't be able to play the violin, but with proper rehab I will still be able to pick a lock," smiled Mac. "I think that is pretty good."

"How about you, BP?"

"They told me no dancing for a while. The bullet just nicked the bone and went straight through. Lucky on this one."

"What about you, Jake?"

"Bullet creased my orbital socket just above my eye. Didn't break it but dislodged a splinter. Thank God, they managed to get it out. Possible double vision for a while and headaches. I'm good to go."

"What about the colonel? I saw him lying over there by the doctor's office; not looking too good," shared Mac.

"Amelie said at least two months of rest but didn't advise return to active duty for another couple of months after that. I kind of got the feeling he's going to be listening to her for quite a while."

"Anything on the lieutenant?" asked Peterson.

"Nothing yet. Just before I got hit, I saw one of the ammo trucks go up, so he was alive and in the field then. But after the incoming barrage... I can't say."

"Has the girl showed up?" asked Mac.

"Haven't seen her either. I saw her kids being taken care of... so fucking sad! ... I truly believe if it wasn't for her guts and the lieutenant's intuition with the watch thing, we wouldn't be having this conversation."

"They will be two of the unsung heroes. This camp and the world need to remember," shared Peterson.

"Yeah, buddy, you're right," remarked Jake, patting BP on the back. "We need to set up a search team and comb through that mess out there."

"I can still walk, just can't pick anything up," volunteered Mac.

"Mac, BP, you have done enough. Some of the other guys are a little better off; although, I didn't see anyone who hasn't been through some triage. Come on, let's go see the colonel."

The three turned and slowly walked back to the main gate. Civilians were helping the medical staff lay out the 'not so lucky' under a canopy out of the sun's morning rays. Last count, two hundred civilians were hit, and mostly by stray bullets from the militants. It could have been much worse.

They dragged their weary bodies to where the Colonel was sitting; Amelie had already gone back to the operating table. He looked up at them, smiled, and hailed in French.

"Mes Les Trois Mousquetaires."

"Pretty good for a Russian," laughed Peterson.

"Hey, we can speak multiple languages, unlike most Americans," he said returning Peterson's quip. "Come on, help me up."

"Are you sure you should be moving, sir?"

"I can't lie around all day in the dirt. I have a reputation," smiled the Colonel, who was more humorous than usual.

"Sir, it might be the drugs speaking," added Mac concerned.

"Nonsense, come on Athos, Aramis, and Porthos... heave me ho."

Jake went behind the Colonel and grabbed him under his arms, making sure Peterson could steady them with his good leg before lifting.

"Ahhgg, okay, good. I'm up."

Mac maneuvered a chair through the blown-out wall of the director's office using his elbows.

"Sir, maybe you should sit in this for a while until Airvac gets here."

"Thank you, Mac... appreciate it. Where's Jacobs?"

"Trying to piece together communication, sir," relayed Mac. "I would help him..." he held up his hands, "...but he said he had it covered."

"Have you done any recon yet?"

"We were just discussing that, sir. I'll put together some able bodies and make sure they have enough ammo just in case. Don't want anyone else to go down."

"Good, Jake... sorry I'm not much help. Any word on the lieutenant and his lady friend?"

"Nothing, sir. We are hoping they are out there somewhere and safe."

"Your lieutenant is a good man and she sure is gutsy. A real firecracker," added the Colonel.

"You know, sir... it was Maysa who took our watches and set the GPS signal. The lieutenant was pissed at her for even coming back. But she insisted on taking them."

"Somehow, gentlemen... and this stays between us... their lives will not be for nothing. I swear I will find the truth!" He coughed.

"Sir, just relax... we are all on the same page here," stated Jake.

"You know, we all were meant to be vaporized along with the lieutenant. I would imagine the press will be eating this up soon and it won't be as it went down. Say nothing that might raise concern until we are all fit... then by God!"

Colonel Dimitri's eyes rolled as the pain medicine finally took hold. They secured him to a righted buggy facing the carnage as he insisted. He went in and out of consciousness, sucking up the pain to maintain control. Jake retrieved the Colonel's weapon, loaded a fresh mag, and holstered his side-arm. They in turn saluted him and then searched for a running Chenowth along with eight more teammates to find their missing friend.

One of their teammates, Taylor, just finished attaching the negative battery cable to a recommissioned battery confiscated from one of the previously seized trucks. He turned the key and it came alive.

"Good job, Taylor," commended Jake.

"Sir, we don't have any stealth power, but otherwise, she is purring." Taylor looked at the three men who stood in front of him. They looked worse for wear but he didn't want to sound insubordinate, and suggested, "Sir, um, please don't take this wrong but, you can't see, Mac can't hold a steering wheel and BP can't engage the clutch."

"So what are you saying, we look like the three stooges rather than the three musketeers?" smiled Jake.

"No, sir, I would never imply that."

"Ahahah, right. We get your drift. How about you chauffer us around?"

"I think that would be wise, sir."

"Come on 'Larry' and 'Curly', climb aboard."

Jake helped Peterson swing his leg in and take the machine gun post, then steadied Mac as he sank in beside the ammo cans. Jake then bent awkwardly under the roll bar and took the front seat.

"Take it slow, Taylor, we don't want to miss anyone."

"Yes, sir."

They crept along, weaving around objects, distorted bodies impaled with twisted munitions. The destruction was half a kilometer in length and as much, wide. If the coordinates relayed were moved east by a fraction of a degree, there wouldn't be a compound. They were lucky to be alive.

Dimitri's men were out in the field picking through the rubble making sure any surprises were dealt with. A couple of rat-a-ta-tats humanely put a few insurgents out of their misery and pain. Jake and his men passed a subtle line of destruction where the impact was the heaviest and as the buggy's front tire turned the ash, a half-moon fluorescent watch face lay on edge. Jake bent over and picked up the only remnant visible. He placed it in his shirt pocket.

Mac coughed and spat out the stench of the smoldering debris. Jake looked back at him.

"The Colonel tried to explain to me one day the taste of war from when he was stationed in Sarajevo. I now understand," he reflected solemnly.

They reached the wavering edge of destruction and bodies still dotted the landscape to their west.

"Keep going, Taylor. Let's make a broad loop."

They went down a ravine and up the other side, past some boulders to where a half-burnt pickup stuck out of the cinders of elephant grass. Jake asked Taylor to stop the buggy so he could get out. He scanned the area.

"Anything?" asked Mac.

"Nothing," he sadly replied. He slid back into the Chenoweth, and they continued their loop, pushing through greener grass and fresher smells. Scanning the devastation from the machine gun post, BP, all of a sudden yelled out, "Stop! Look over there, Jake."

Jake stood up in the buggy and looked to where Peterson was pointing, "What? I don't see anything."

"That's right, my friend. Taylor, ease the buggy to that slight clearing. There's no reason for the grass not to grow there."

The buggy eased closer and broke the rim of the clearing. Two dead Al-Shabaab lay with burnt backs and beside them—a skinny, blistered, and bloodied arm poked from underneath. Taylor immediately stopped the buggy and climbed out. Jake joined in, while the other two waited impatiently.

They carefully removed one of the bodies and noticed his slit throat. They laid him to the side. Next, they lifted the other out of the way. Staring back at them with wide-open eyes from a shallow foxhole was the blistered, blood-soaked body of Maysa.

"She's alive!" yelled Taylor.

Jake and Taylor bent to her.

Her eyes were blinking like a faulty turn signal—rapidly. She stared back at them who looked down on her.

I see two men lowering to me saying something, but I cannot understand them. One is bandaged around the head with only one eye glaring at me, the other, appears friendly but concerned in his manner. I feel them; their hands surround me; their strong fingers support my back and others wrap my thighs. I feel them lifting me to the light; the grass is green and alive. I feel... Aagghh!

"She's in shock!" shouted Taylor.

"Aagghh!" cried Maysa again. Jake and Taylor lifted her out. She took a deep breath and another, bucking in their grip as she gasped for air.

"Lay her over me!" insisted Mac. "I can cradle her. Take it easy, Maysa, I got you."

"Taylor, get us to the doctor as fast as you fucking can!"

"Yes, sir."

White House Press Conference Room

Washington, D.C.
Romeo 1000 Hrs.

The news agencies were all gathered at the White House's request for an update on the latest operation from the fighting of the war-torn areas of South Sudan and Kenya.

"President Baxter will be arriving momentarily to share the latest in the fight against the Al-Shabaab militants," shared the press secretary.

"Ladies and Gentlemen, our President..."

"Good morning, Ladies and Gentlemen. It is not often I can address you with good news on what is happening with our mutual friends in Central Africa. But today, I am pleased to announce, through the diligent work of our CTA Director Jack Tomlinson and his agency, they thwarted an attack on a UN camp that housed over one hundred thousand refugees, mainly displaced by the division of our planet's newest country, South Sudan. Two years after its induction in June 2011 as the 193rd country to be recognized by the UN, it has been in bitter turmoil.

"Their President, Salva Kiir, a Dinka, and his ousted Vice-President, Riek Machar, Nuer, have been battling without accountability to the citizens of South Sudan since this date. Their indiscretions have caused thousands of deaths, rape of young girls, castration of young boys, and numerous other atrocities against its people because of two men from different tribes. This oil-rich nation could be one of the front runners of democracy and social awareness, but instead, chooses to violate human decency with their Neanderthal thinking.

"Under past President Bush, the American people donated one billion dollars for infrastructure to help this newly formed country compete with hydroelectric plants, oil refineries and road construction. I stand disgusted at their inability to harness a cease-fire; especially after the help of the combined efforts of their neighboring countries, notably, Ethiopia, Kenya, and Uganda.

"The violence has been so extreme, it has forced its citizens to make the treacherous journey to neighboring countries, at the risk of encountering human traffickers, rapists, and murderers, for any semblance of existence.

"Gentlemen, this needs to stop here and now. Our CTA team proved we have the stopping capabilities to ensure those freedoms, and I might add that we will not hesitate to beat back the criminals who harass or maim the freedom of these individuals.

"Again, Ladies and Gentlemen, I want to thank Jack Tomlinson, Director of CTA, and all his team, for the fine work of terminating the influence of this cell of Al-Shabaab before they slaughtered more innocent people. Good day, and God Bless America." The President gathered his notes, waved, and left the podium.

The camera swung to a news correspondent.

"Ladies and Gentlemen, you have just heard from our President regarding an undoubtingly huge blow to the Al-Shabaab who is a jihadist terrorist group based in Somalia, who has pledged its allegiance with Al-Qaeda. They have been crisscrossing the border between Kenya and Somalia since 2012, inflicting hundreds of deaths in the name of Islam. We will have more to share on our nightly report as soon as we can establish a link. I am Carrie Southerland with Eyewitness News 8."

. . .

Samantha opened her door and bent down to gather her evening newspaper. She had slept all day except for getting up once to pee and to fetch another box of tissues. She was tired of crying and tired of friends and loved ones disappearing. This wasn't what she signed up for.

She poured herself a cup of coffee out of habit and opened the newspaper to the 'Political Arena' section. It was always fun to read to see who got what wrong or whose foot was stuck in their mouth for an off-color comment. But tonight, staring out at her was the smug face of Jack Tomlinson shaking hands with the President. Samantha shook her head. *Am I dreaming still?* She began to read the article.

She slammed the paper down. "What kind of fucking hypocrisy is this? That bastard murdered American soldiers! How can they laud him as a hero?"

Heading: Due South

Romeo 0800 Hrs.

Marsha awoke in sweat-drenched pajamas, lightly rocking in a luxurious cabin aboard a yacht, and with a large bandage wrapped around her foot. Her fever had broken; she felt like a mess. At the foot of the bed, neatly folded, was her strapless bra and clean panties. She scanned the room and noticed the sunken decorative lights, built-in dressers with wall-to-wall mirrors, and then down to the crafted wood floors accented with plush rugs. The tinted portholes indicated *they*, whoever they were, were moving.

Where the fuck am I?

Marsha noticed a pair of crutches resting near the elaborately carved door. She swung her legs over the bed and hopped over to them, secured them under her arms, and then went back and checked her bra. The homing device was still embedded in the fancy flowered rosette between each cup. She hobbled with the help of the crutches to one of the floor-to-ceiling cabinets and opened the polished door to a handful of clothes—even a slinky cocktail dress hung all pristine.

Damn, nice taste. She looked inside to read the label. *AD Fashions!*

A knock startled her. "Um... yes?"

"You are awake then, ma'am," offered a muffled English female voice.

"Yes..." She wanted to know who was asking, "Please, come in."

"Good morning, ma'am... I'm Jackie. If you need me for anything, just pick up the telly and press my name and I will be right here. I will be looking after your needs while you travel with us," she informed, polished and politely.

"Um... Jackie. Who is the 'us'?"

She smiled. "Miss Angela is in the upper salon and is waiting to meet you. Well, officially that is."

"Miss Angela?"

"Yes, ma'am."

"May I have a shower first?"

"But of course, ma'am. Miss Angela guessed at your size..." she walked over to the cabinets and opened all the doors, "... so whatever you would like to wear. There are more selections in the drawers for you. Shall I pour your bath, ma'am?"

Jackie helped Marsha maneuver into the glass-enclosed shower sans bathtub. An English saying Marsha gathered. Jackie covered Marsha's dressing with a plastic bag so she wouldn't get it wet. Jackie then helped Marsha pick out a pair of white stylish shorts and a form-fitting Lorna Jane sports top. Marsha's new ensemble accented her shapely figure.

"What do you think, Jackie, am I presentable?"

"You look just fine, ma'am," smiled Jackie as if she would say anything to the contrary.

"How do I get to the upper salon?"

"Take the elevator with the circular door up two levels. It opens at the grand salon, ma'am."

The elevator door slid around behind her as it stopped on the upper level. Sitting at a high-polished teak table, a very pretty lady with long flowing blonde hair, dressed in lounging pajamas, sat in front of her computer. A freshly brewed carafe of coffee sat next to her. She looked up at Marsha after hearing the elevator door swish open, stood, removed her red-framed glasses, and smiled with an extended hand.

"Good morning, Marsha. I am Angela. I trust you are feeling better?"

Marsha hobbled to her and accepted her hand. "Yes, thank you..." She stared at her momentarily and then said, "...we have met, haven't we?"

"Yes, at First Lady Baxter's Gala dinner. I was one of the speakers with the Fournier Foundation."

"Yes, and if I recall, you had the crowd in your hands."

"Ah, you are so kind. Please sit. Coffee?"

"Please and thank you."

"Well, Marsha, I'm not the kind to mince words... and I don't think you are either. So you are undoubtedly wondering what you are doing here. Sugar?"

"No, just a touch of cream, please."

"Shall I say, we have mutual friends and when their hands got tied in red tape, we were requested to step up and help if we could? Your homing device was brilliant, by the way, and I believe conjured with the help of Admiral Stone, is that correct?"

"Yes, I went to see him late Sunday night before the Gala and he gave me the brooch with the inlaid decoy camera. When they ripped it from my dress, it activated the smaller device."

"Sorry, but it's not active any longer, for your own sake. My friends and I borrowed the Admiral's personal craft and followed you and your assailant to the USS Bulkeley. They put on quite the show I might add... boats colliding, fireworks and all. It looked very convincing; I imagine faking your death. But once you were on board, we had no way of knowing how to reach you. Oh, excuse my manners, croissant or eggs?"

"Croissant would be nice."

Angela typed into her computer and hit enter.

"We hoped we could rely on your intuitiveness to react if a possibility came up. Oh, here's your croissant and someone wants to say hello."

Marsha turned to her right...

"Hello, Miss Marsha," said Alicia.

"OMG! What the...?"

Marsha stood, supported by the chair, and reached out. The two friends hugged.

"What are you doing here?" asked Marsha.

"I work for Miss Angela."

"And all that scamming I was trying to lay on you."

"I was very flattered," smiled Alicia.

"So the scammer got scammed," laughed Marsha. "Who were the guys in the helicopter?"

"They also work for the Foundation," responded Angela.

Marsha sat down in amazement. "So, you know who I am and who I represent?"

"We don't need to know everything about you, only where your allegiances lie. It's best for everyone if some things remain unsaid. But, in saying that, we are true believers in your PAG system and its humanitarian implications. That was one of the reasons we agreed to, shall I say, entertain the troops at the Gala... it was to meet you, Director Jones, and your team. You see, we have poured millions into your research."

"I thought it was all the CTA's doing?"

"Oh, Jack would love for you to believe that...but frankly, he has no idea where the money came from... like most politicians. You see, Jack had his own agenda, which directly interfered with our investments in sustainable energy and water solutions. We have interests in Ethiopia, Kenya and Uganda to supply potable water to the many drought-stricken areas of these nations. Warfare is big business and greedy men get greedier. And of course, there's the oil. When the U.S. backed a rebellion against Omar al-Bashir's Sudan, through the now President of South Sudan, Kiir, who was then the rebel leader, they invested billions to secure his presence.

"So now, depending on which newspaper you read, al-Bashir is sending arms to Machar, the ousted VP. So Tomlinson was getting anxious and sent in a loyal soldier to take out one of them. They would have preferred to keep Kiir, because he was already in their back pocket, but they would have negotiated terms with Machar, no doubt. And this is where PAG came in. We couldn't stand by and watch a man be sent to his death under those circumstances."

"So, how did you get Jack to agree to use PAG?"

"I believe a little birdy planted a seed."

"Hahaha, you?"

"I really am not at liberty to say," smiled Angela.

"Let's back up. How did you get Alicia on board a U.S. destroyer that was about to deploy?"

"Well, once we knew on which ship you were being held, Admiral Stone was quite resourceful. And how could anyone deny those sparkling brown eyes?"

"I just got on board and was bent over a winch when I was asked to watch you. I hadn't been below as yet and only had time to quickly familiarize myself with the ship's layout before we left," remarked Alicia.

"Who was the asshole?"

"One of Redman's associates, I presume. Definitely not Navy."

"I left him pretty bruised up," said Marsha with a smile.

"He's dead."

"What?!"

"Not by you. Alicia turned on the monitoring camera after she left you the second time. The footage clearly shows Redman snapping his neck while in a rage of finding you missing."

"Wow! Angela, I thought I had an interesting life. Is this what you do? I mean, you float around solving world problems?"

"No, not exactly. I have a wonderful husband, a mischievous little girl, two art galleries, and a fashion design firm in L.A."

"The slinky piece below?"

"Yes, that is one of my, well... *our* creations. One of my cohorts now runs my design house, another, the galleries and I am working my way into the family business, so to speak... the Fournier Foundation."

"What's your husband do to try and keep up?" joked Marsha.

"His love is finding missing children and reuniting them with their families... but his company does take on other assignments. In fact, my husband will meet up with us later," shared Angela.

"Where might that be?"

Angela paused and looked directly into Marsha's eyes, and then with a single response, she said, "Africa!"

Offices of CTA

The door of Jack Tomlinson's office was shut tight and locked. He left strict instructions he didn't want anyone to disturb him. His only ally sat in the chair in front of him, downing bourbon.

"What do you mean she just vanished?" questioned Tomlinson, annoyed at his friend's response.

"Vanished... as in nowhere to be found. I checked out behind the commissary and only found a dribble of blood on the outside wall. Nothing in the shipping area beyond that."

"Who do you think has her?"

"Don't know. I have my sources checking everywhere and nothing has come up yet, but I will find her."

"You better! We can't have any loose ends. What's the word from Kenya? They all dead?"

"I got an agent heading that way. Either way, Jack, you come out the hero. Nothing has to be mentioned of us locking on the coordinates of their watches. We'll use PAG as the source," smugly implied his henchman, Redman.

"Yeah, I've requested the footage from Jones to prove our case," eased Tomlinson, as he leaned back and took a sip as well. In thought, he savored a puff of his cigar and blew a smoke ring. After a brief pause, he asked, "What about the guy on the Bulkeley?"

"I blamed Atworth; she'll take the fall. Is the ship still headed to Somalia?"

"That's their orders. They've been there before on rescue missions. It seemed our plan was going to work in our favor having her onboard but plan B worked just as well. Let me know what your man finds out. We need to wrap this up nice and clean."

Brentwood Walker
Charlie 1300 Hrs.

The whirring noise of the Huey's blades seemed to back off as the pilot eased up on the stick. They could see a huge burnt field with melted wreckage and beyond that rows and rows of tents with UN insignias displayed on their sloping pitch. Two male passengers yelled above the noise as most of the ride they sat in silence.

"You say you are from the States, do ya, lad?"

"Yes. I managed to secure a contract to handle, you might say, propaganda for the UN. I finished my photojournalism course a couple of years ago, but this is really my first assignment. I'm a late bloomer," smiled the enthusiastic Jeff Miller. "You say you are with Reuters?"

"That's right, sonny, out of Istanbul," informed Brent Walker, a stocky, balding Englishman, dressed in wrinkled linen pants and short-sleeved shirt, wearing a Panama Jack hat.

"Don't take this wrong, but you look like you belong in a ring," joked the young man, who himself was in solid shape.

"Ha, that's funny, lad. You might say I cut my teeth working the IRA stories. You had to be tough as them Irish to gain any respect," said the man as he held his binoculars up to his eyes and scanned the burnt fields.

The helicopter threw up a dust field as it descended down to just outside of the camp's main gate. The burly man jumped out like a pro, even at his age, while the newcomer waited for the craft to settle.

"How long are we going to be here?" asked the young man of the pilot.

"Sorry, sir. A change of plans. I got to take some of the injured back. I'll catch you on the next trip to take you to Nairobi to the UN Headquarters."

"Okay, thank you!" loudly replied the young reporter.

Miller followed behind the seasoned reporter to the open-walled office of the director of the camp. An assistant, who was working on repairing the damage, told him the camp director was in the 'OR' and without listening to the assistant's plea to wait, Brentwood Walker trudged through the debris, past a soldier who stood beside a Chenowth, to the medical tent. Standing outside, he heard.

"Maysa, I'm going to give you a sedative so you can relax. I have to bandage your forearms to keep infection from getting into your blisters. Do you understand me?" said Amelie Thorsten.

Maysa looked around at the three injured soldiers who stood beside her and then to the woman dressed in a blood-spattered lab coat. She nodded approval.

"Good, Maysa. You'll be just fine," said Amelie.

"We got a tent for you and your family," said Jake. "We'll bring you your babies as soon as the doctor is finished. We promise, Maysa."

She looked up at them with scared, big eyes as the men turned and walked out, almost bumping into a big man sporting a sweat-stained hat.

"Excuse me gents. Looking for the director," he inquired.

"She'll be with you when she finishes with the girl," stated Jake.

"Right then. I'll just wait for her."

"Outside," ordered Jake.

"Yeah, that's what I meant, of course." Brentwood walked with the three soldiers to the waiting buggy. "So, what can you tell me for our readers? Looks very nasty," he said, trying to win their favor.

"Who are you?"

"Brentwood Walker ... Reuters."

"How did you get in here?" asked Jake.

"Well, when you've been in this business as long as I have, you meet people who know people, that sort of thing," smiled the pompous man as he offered his hand. "You can call my Brent."

"Well, Mr. Walker, this is a restricted area."

"Oh, come on guys... help a guy out here. Your president already held a news conference. This is news and no one is covering it except me. I need a big story like this."

Jake looked over at the young man standing by the office. "He with you?"

"No! A newbie. On his way to Nairobi. He hitched a ride until we found all this. A puffer, if you ask me," said

Brentwood Walker as he leaned over to the soldier doing all the talking. "Are you in charge?"

"Second in command."

"Well then, can I speak with your commander to straighten this all out? Just trying to do my job."

"He's not receiving guests right now, but I'll check with him in a bit. Come on guys, mount up."

"Hey, well can I just look around? I promise I won't touch anything."

"Just stay out of our business."

"Right-O."

Taylor pulled away from the tents and the pushy news guy. They needed to find the lieutenant before anyone else did. As they slipped through the gates, past the helicopter and the medical staff loading seriously wounded civilians, they headed back out to the destruction, while Brent Walker hoofed it to the fields with phone in hand. The doctor came out of the tent and walked over to where Jeff Miller was passing the time.

"Are you the reporter?" she questioned somewhat disgruntled.

"I am, but I think you are referring to that gentleman over there. My name is Jeff Miller and I am on my way to Nairobi to the UN Headquarters to receive their assignment on which camp to document first."

The doctor's tone changed and with a smile, she said, "Well, sorry about the insinuation. Nice to meet you, Mr. Miller. What will you be doing for us?"

"From my conversation with them, they want to raise awareness of the complexity of horrors people in the surrounding areas endure and to present these at the summit talks. I had no idea your camp was in such dire straits."

"We are pretty much the standard; over-crowded, under-funded, and poorly equipped...until yesterday. Then all this happened." The doctor opened her hands, fingers pointing downward, and then spun slightly around guiding the reporter's view of the disaster. "Now we are worse off. Well, if you are here to learn, this place is as good as any to get started. It will be a few days before you will be able to continue on your journey, anyway."

"Anything at all to help, ma'am. I am at your disposal."

"That is very kind of you, sir. As you can see, my staff is very busy at the moment. Can I get you to help me with my last patient? She has suffered greatly throughout her young life by the indications marking her body. She has three small children that we will be placing in her tent with her after she wakes up. You have a kind face. Do you have any children, Jeff?"

"A baby girl, ma'am."

"Wonderful. And do you participate in caring for her needs?"

"Diapers and all, ma'am," smiled Jeff.

"Good. You are just what the doctor ordered, then. Come on, but first let me check on Maysa, and then I'll introduce you to her family so you can get better acquainted."

Amelie and the young UN reporter, Jeff Miller, returned to where Maysa was still sleeping. Jeff noticed her clothes were covered in blood but only her arms were bandaged and a couple of fingers had sutures sticking out.

"Wow... that's a lot of blood she lost."

"Not hers. The soldiers said they found her on the other side of the field of destruction with two Al-Shabaabs lying over top of her. They surmised she was hurriedly digging a hole with her bare hands when they came upon her and she managed to, somehow, slit their throats and then use them as cover just before the bombing started. We will know better after she calms down as to what happened."

"That mess out there from bombings?"

"Yes. Thankfully they missed us and hit the Al-Shabaab, who was bent on hell to murder us all."

"The Al-Shabaab was after the soldiers?"

"No... It was fate that brought them here and saved us. I'll have one of my female staff clean Maysa up and get her new clothes. In the meantime, shall we go meet her family?"

On their way to the children's play area, Jeff commented on Maysa's involvement and asked why she was on the other side of the burnt field. The doctor informed him of her arriving at the compound, offering information, and securing safety for a friend of hers called Mr. Clark, who the Colonel seemed to know. Jeff politely inquired of the friend's whereabouts. The doctor said, "They haven't identified him yet."

~

Brentwood Walker, even as a seasoned reporter, couldn't believe the destruction.

"Holy fuck...! What did you guys send over here?" said Walker over his SAT phone. He walked a few more feet into the debris. "Everything is melted together, crisp like bacon... Oooo fuck... two guys look like they're Siamese twins."

An inaudible voice questioned Brentwood Walker.

"The Colonel... No, haven't met him yet. The second in charge seems like a badass but he's half blind and the rest are pretty ragged." Walker listened and then replied.

"No, I only count a handful. Four took off in a buggy. I can see them but they're a ways away," said Walker as he perused the carnage looking for any signs of Lieutenant Clark.

"I don't think they have found him yet. But how could you tell anyone's identity?" He left the caller somewhat hopeful.

"Yeah, I'll see what I can dig up."

SAS Headquarters

The Director, Samantha Jones, had been out of the lab all day while her team, led by Paul, had been vigorously mapping the whereabouts of their missing soldier. Jack Tomlinson had requested the footage of the previous night's aerial activity that took place in Kenya and recorded by PAG. Paul had called the director before complying and then relinquished the time-stamped footage with coordinates. It was all Jack Tomlinson needed and as far as he was concerned, PAG's mission was over.

Samantha was pissed after seeing the article in the evening post. She quickly brushed out her long black locks, wrapped them in a bun, and high-tailed it to SAS. Something didn't sit well with her, and she still hadn't heard from Marsha. As Samantha entered the lab, she immediately apologized for her non-professional appearance of her usual perfect make-up and dress. Paul was glad to see her even without her explanation. He gave her a compassionate hug.

"How are you, ma'am?"

"Holding up. Life would be better without this cloak and dagger crap. I know you all thrive on it, but it is too much for me."

"We are here for you and to keep PAG safe, ma'am."

"Yes, I understand your dedication, Paul, from the little information Derrick would give up. So, what are we working on?"

"Raj is finishing off Phillip's search into 'sanctuaries' near Norfolk, ma'am. There were sixty-seven listings for bird sanctuaries, ten for names of church groups, ninety-five were wildlife, and a realty office. So it is taking time."

"Humor me, Paul. Why did Derrick request that information? My head has been spinning."

"I assume it had something to do with finding Marsha's whereabouts."

"Okay. Keep it up. If she is safe somewhere, don't you think she would have contacted me... us?"

"Well, maybe she is letting time pass a bit. Maybe to let those involved feel they have the power again."

"Like I said, Paul, I'm not trained for this; I get too anxious."

"Yes, ma'am, and that's why you have us."

"Paul, you are starting to sound like a broken record, but I do appreciate what you are doing even if I don't understand it," smiled the director for the first time in days.

Raj hung up the phone obviously laughing to himself. The Director and Paul noticed and looked at him, questioningly. He looked up at them.

"Sorry, Director, but they thought I was from USA Bell call center doing a marketing interview. Boy, we sure get a bum rap. Not all of us from India do telephone solicitation."

They all joined in on Raja's comment with a much needed relief of laughter.

"But, I have good news. It seems the owner of a boat marina, called Sanctuary Bliss, remembered seeing a mega yacht leave the bay late last night as he was making his final rounds. It was called 'Claire's Sanctuary' with a French registration. Upon delving further, I located its owner of registration to be the Fournier Foundation."

"Fournier Foundation?" queried the director.

"Yes, ma'am."

"They were at the Gala and she gave a very rousing speech."

"You're right, ma'am, I remember her quite well. She was very pretty as my wife pointed out with a kick under the table as I was glued to her...um, speech," remarked Paul.

"I think she had three quarters of the room in a spell," smiled the director thinking back to her reaction. "And they were the ones who brought me off the stage to the side wings. She had an entourage of beefy men with her."

"Booty guards?"

"Okay, Paul, let's leave it at that." Samantha certainly caught his drift. "But what do they have to do with Marsha? They don't know her as far as I know. I mean, Marsha didn't indicate to me she knew them. What do they have to do with all of this?"

"It could be a coincidence, ma'am... the name and all," offered Paul.

"Ma'am, there's a 'Claire's Sanctuary' listed in New Hampshire, as well...," informed Raj, "...a thousand acre protected preserve."

"Okay," sighed the director. "You're right, Paul... just a coincidence."

"Ma'am."

"Yes, Raj."

"It's funded by... Fournier Foundation!"

Uganda - Outside UN Camp

Jake and his team slowed at every charred figure and every clump of debris and found nothing that would indicate Lieutenant Clark's state. Rising gasses still escaped as they flipped and dislodged wreckage, stinging their eyes. They left the burnt field and continued with their loop from where they had found Maysa. *Maybe he also covered himself with bodies as the field lit up,* thought Jake. *Their only defining indication of proof would be the lieutenant's civilian clothes since everyone else was in uniform.*

Parting from the team's straight line loop, they zigzagged and re-crossed—still nothing. They decided to head back to camp and ask for volunteers to help them the next day. Maysa was a miracle, and for anyone else to survive just seemed to be too survivalist in thinking. He was good, but after Jake saw the ammo truck explode, the lieutenant would have been too close to the center of destruction.

The reporter, Walker, was still milling around in the debris as they drove by. They watched him with his phone out, snapping pictures and then attaching a hand-held SAT phone and uploading them.

"Gruesome following he must have," shared Mac.

"Shocking News at 7," uttered BP.

"A lot of sick fucks out there, gentlemen," added Jake.

Taylor wheeled the buggy to the left, past where the helicopter had landed, through the gates, and parked beside the barely standing office of the camp's director.

"Taylor, grab some grub and then gather the rest of the guys. Say we meet here around 2100 hours and we'll draw straws for four hour watches. I'm going to check on the Colonel and then see how Rey is doing."

"Yes, sir."

"We'll come with you, Jake."

The three trudged over to the medical tents where they expected to see the Colonel lying down or at least relaxing. He wasn't there. Jake, concerned, stopped an orderly and asked his whereabouts. He pointed to the children's play area. Confused, they hobbled as quickly as they could to see what was going on. It seemed as though the young reporter, Jeff Miller, was entertaining the children using the five woven-grass giraffes that Clark had made for Mosi. The children in the area—combined with wounded patients who could still walk—the Colonel, who sat beside Amelie and others, were all enjoying this would-be correspondent. His audience clapped on as he took his final bow.

"Well done, Jeff," congratulated Amelie as she stood to shake his hand. "We all needed that, thank you so much."

"You are welcome, ma'am. It was my pleasure," smiled Jeff as he handed the giraffes back to Mosi.

Jake went over to the Colonel.

"You all right, sir?"

"I might need another couple of stitches after watching this young man, but other than that, it is going to take more than a little shrapnel to keep me down."

"Dimitri!" flared Amelie.

"Oh, yes... right, Doctor. I promise to take it easy."

"We are on our way to check on Rey."

"He's doing fine... considering," shared the doctor. "He is better at taking orders than your colonel."

"Yes, ma'am," acknowledged Jake with a smile. "Colonel, we are gathering at 2100 hours with the rest of the team at the doctor's office to organize a watch tonight."

"Very good, Jake. How's the eye?"

"No pain, really... just the headaches."

"Tonight, I will give you something for that," offered Amelie.

"Thank you, ma'am."

The young reporter who was carrying two young girls and a boy who trudged through the dirt with his hand grasping onto the reporter's pocket, stepped up to the men.

"I'm taking the kids over to Maysa. Will you join us?"

Jake looked at BP and Mac.

"We'll walk with the Colonel and meet you over there."

"I'll go with Jeff. See you all in a couple of minutes. Here, give me one of these little darlings," said Amelie.

The two set off as the others hung back.

"Who is that Miller guy?" asked Jake.

"You know as much about him as I do," stated the Colonel.

"The other guy is still shifting through debris. I don't trust him either. He's looking too close."

"Well, Jake, your intuition has never let me down... follow it. As far as the younger one, he seems harmless."

"He looks a little too buff to be a reporter," stated Mac.

The Colonel slowly turned to Mac. "Well, boys, I'll say one more time. I trust your intuitive nature. We are a team. You know what to do."

"Yes, sir."

"Obviously nothing on the lieutenant?"

"Not yet, sir. I want to organize some volunteers tomorrow and take a wider swath around the area."

"Has Jacobs got us communication, yet?"

"I'll check, sir."

"Maybe PAG can still locate the lieutenant, if he is still alive."

The soldiers, who were standing at the doorway to Maysa's tent, overheard the doctor talking to her. As they entered, Maysa—who also overheard the men talking outside—looked up into their eyes. She knew they had not found the lieutenant and she broke into an uncontrollable rage of tears. Mosi, identifying with Maysa's sadness, took one of his giraffes from his pocket and walked over to her bed. He placed the biggest giraffe into her hand as if trying to console her while Ateefah stretched away from the reporter's arms with little fingers grabbing for her mother. The three brave soldiers, with all they had seen, looked away from Mosi's actions to maintain composure.

Day 11 - Saturday

Uganda – UN Camp
Charlie 0730 Hrs.

The next morning, as Jake briefed the gathered volunteers, the Airvac slowly descended. Another reporter, Gillian Perkins, a young, physically fit, square-jawed redhead with cropped spiked hair, braless with a jersey T-top and dungaree shorts, jumped from the chopper as her predecessor had done the day before. She landed sure-footed with a bag flung over her shoulder. Jake watched as she charged the opened gates proceeding directly to where she deemed to be the camp's office.

"Camp director available?" she gruffly asked loudly, upon entering a seemingly vacant office.

Stepping from the office's storage room, Amelie acknowledged her presence.

"I'm the camp director, Amelie Thorsten. How may I help you?"

"I pulled this assignment to get the low down on what happened. Baxter's speech was pretty lame and transparent."

"And you are?"

"Gillian Perkins, AFP ... Paris... you've probably heard of me. Anyone else here of importance?"

"You certainly are quick to the point."

"Ma'am, no disrespect, but I'm here for the news, not a tea party."

"To answer your poignant question, two gentlemen of your peers are already here."

"Fuck... how'd they get here before me? I was promised an exclusive."

"I am sure I don't know that answer."

The reporter quickly searched her bag and pulled out a recorder.

"So, ma'am, when did this all happen?"

"I really don't have time for this. Maybe you would like to speak to Lieutenant Alderson. He is in the yard right now, and if you hurry, you might catch him."

"Right. Thanks."

The woman turned abruptly and headed directly to the soldier who was instructing his volunteers of what not to touch. He also advised that if anything came into question, to get the attention of one of his men. Unlike her usual prying gait, she waited until he was finished and had divided his volunteers into teams of four. She stepped up to him.

"Excuse me, sir. I'm Gillian Perkins, AFP. Do you mind if I tag along and maybe ask you some questions?"

"Uh, Miss Perkins, you might stand with your counterpart over there."

"I would rather not, sir. No offense, but I work alone and don't need an old man to nurse maid."

"I doubt he would see it that way, but if the two of you drop back and let us do our job, we won't have any problems. Understand me?"

"Yes, sir. Like a mouse, you won't know I'm here."

"I rather doubt that but..."

"What, may I ask, are you looking for?"

Jake, stopped and looked at her.

"Any survivors from our camp."

"They all look pretty crispy to me."

"That's why we are looking, ma'am."

"Right. Gotcha."

Jake paired each of his men with the team of four making up eight teams. Each team leader issued latex gloves and masks and was given a plot plan to dissect and a sheet to add body count to. Peterson went with Jake and Taylor in the Chenowth while Mac hung back with Jacobs to try and resolve the communication problem. The seasoned reporter, Walker, hung back at the camp base as well, while the young woman reporter took up after their heels, picking up bread crumps.

He, Brent Walker—who had overheard the conversation outside of Maysa's tent the previous night—casually walked over to the open-walled tent where Jacobs and Mac had displayed the guts from their main communication enclosure. They snipped and re-soldered, stole parts from their PRS's that sat on the table and re-attached diodes and microchips.

"Are these all of them?" asked Mac.

"All I could find. Jake's headset was destroyed when he took the bullet to the head, yours has the blade through it, so..." he counted, "...that's eighteen, two down for sure...

is twenty, four counting the Chenowth's and the armored supply truck... that's funny... one seems to be missing."

"Your missing friend, perhaps?" piped up the seasoned reporter.

"What are you talking about?" asked Mac.

"Come on, gentlemen, who do you think you are trying to kid here? I've been in way too many situations not to notice you are looking for someone not something."

"It's best to stay out of Military business and stick with what you know, sir."

"The young woman in there, the one crying her eyes out, she lost someone dear to her. You can't hide that."

Mac straightened up from being bent over the table and confronted the man. Even with his bandaged hands, they rose to the occasion.

"Look, buddy. Don't be printing anything your big mouth can't support."

Just then, the young reporter, Jeff Miller, stepped out of Maysa's tent, which was right next to where this conversation had been taking place.

"Mr. Walker, maybe you should back down and let these soldiers finish their task in peace."

"What's your take on this, newbie? If you want to be a war correspondent, you need to ask the difficult questions. What are you hiding? You're running around here like you're part of a USO tour, not a reporter. What school did you say you graduated from?"

"I didn't... but if you must know... Parson's in LA and then Berkeley."

"Well, excuse me. So you learned how to smoke pot and then how to grow it," laughed the obstinate man, Walker. "When you put in your dues, kid, then have something to say. Otherwise, stay out of my business and go back to babysitting."

The older reporter stomped off as Jeff stood with the two soldiers.

"A real asshole, isn't he?" remarked Mac.

"I guess war hardens someone's sensitivity," shared Mr. Miller.

Atlantic Ocean

Romeo 0100 Hrs.

The night was clear as the ship sailed south charted for their first stop, Fort Lauderdale. Marsha stood on the main aft deck watching the surf churn from the powerful propellers. Alicia approached after seeing her through the large double sliding doors from the galley. The doors opened with a slight swoosh... Marsha turned to see her friend.

"Hey there. Beautiful night, isn't it?"

"Hello, Alicia. Yes, almost surreal. A couple of days ago, I was chained up in a stinking hold debating my life... you staring me in the eyes... and now we stand in the moonlight on a luxury yacht."

Alicia put her arm in Marsha's and leaned her head on her shoulder.

"Life does offer us interesting avenues."

"If you don't mind answering, how did you get mixed up in this? Not that 'this' is a bad thing..."

"Well, when my mom took sick, I really got into, shall we say, hacking... using the Navy's computers. I was trying to find the right medicine and knew we couldn't afford it on E2 wages, so I found ways of shipping it to us, already paid for. When I got caught for stealing a doctor's identity, the story broke over the internet and became viral. Before I was even in front of a military judge, I had a visit from a lawyer who said he represented a humanitarian corporation that would take up my case if I talked with one of its founders. What choice did I have? So I agreed.

"This distinguished gentleman and his friend met me privately. I signed some papers and next I knew, I was learning a more legitimate form of hacking and my mom was taken care of. A win-win for me. Since I didn't appear in front of a tribunal, my rank was never withdrawn. And from what I understand, I am listed as being on special assignment... indefinitely. How about you? How did you manage to get put in chains?"

"Long story... But what I can tell you is that I'm also Navy, and my Navy identity is Marsha Jean Atworth. My real name is Jenna Rose Atworth. Marsha was my twin sister."

"Was?"

"Yes. She was an attaché in Europe and I believe implicated by association as being an infiltrator in a drug smuggling cartel from Russia. When she was found in a cargo hull of a Navy ship, she was chained to a chair with her throat slashed. Of course, this is all unofficial for diplomatic reasons."

"Ohh! I am so sorry for your loss," said Alicia sorrowfully. She slid a finger across her eye repressing a tear and added, "But that sounds like a reoccurring M.O."

"Exactly... and until I unravel her murder, if you please, continue calling me Marsha. When I was approached with this horror, I was asked to retain her identity and was replaced as her. So, I... as you, Alicia...

had based my career in computers and was introduced, at that time, to this lady, a Lieutenant Colonel, and became her assistant. Over the years, we developed PAG and a friendly relationship. Similarly, like you, those who approached me probably have the same philosophy, just different and militarily based, to handle whatever needs to be handled outside of normal channels. So who is Angela?"

"Oh... she is awesome. She really hasn't said much more than what she told you today, but I wouldn't want to work for anyone else. She is caring, compassionate, precise and deadly."

"Deadly? She looks so... 'Hollywood'!"

"Hahaha, that's funny. Don't let her pretty face and gorgeous body throw you off. She is tough as nails. You'll probably get to see her spar with one of the crew. There is no holding back from either... well, not to the death, but..."

"Really...?"

"And she can handle weapons as well. She is grooming me, and I love it. She says I have that innocent face and when properly trained, I could probably get an audience with the Queen by just flashing my smile."

"You sound very loyal to her."

"With my life... I owe her everything."

"Now that's funny. I have heard me say the same about my friend. When do you think I will be able to call her? She is probably worried sick."

"That, you will have to ask Angela. Not that I am purporting to know Angela's every whim, but I would venture to say after we leave the port of Fort Lauderdale. Oh, and tomorrow, I would also set Angela straight with your story. She is a stickler for allegiance and would do anything for her friends."

"I will, my friend, and thank you for everything you did for me, even knowing I was trying to play you."

Alicia lifted her head from Marsha's shoulder and looked her in the eyes, "Truthfully, you were making me wet."

Uganda – UN Camp
Charlie 1800 Hrs.

The soldiers along with their civilian volunteers had only completed half of the assigned plot plan by the end of day, but Jake was still happy with the progress. His volunteers were thorough and he was glad to see that. One hundred and eight confirmed deaths on the west side went into the report. After a congratulatory speech of the day's proceedings by Jake, his volunteers dispersed and he joined his teammates at the re-arranged mess hall. Also included were the three reporters who sat at the far end of the adjoining tables. The soldiers' conversation was minimal but the talk from the reporters was unexpectedly lively after they gathered each other's identities.

"So you're the arrogant bastard who stole my story in Latvia," spurned the young woman reporter.

"Ha... stole your story... Listen, you chippy little dyke, I was there, dug into a foxhole with three dead, a scared kid with a rifle, and bullets eating away at the sandbags days before you showed up. When you learn how to mix with men and write objectively about how they perceive war, maybe then you'll become a writer. Always draining the cum from them before you assess the reason and the horror they see..."

"You pompous, fascist pig! It's guys like you who vindicate the atrocities of war just for readership... The apex of hard-ons, grabbing your own dick with inflated scrotums like bull's balls, but it is meaningless piffle... jabber babble bullshit. Do you know those words? Check them out in the dictionary, if you own one."

Jeff Miller dared not interfere with this charming discussion but their egos were way too infuriating to sit by – mannequin-ish-like.

"You two no doubt share a certain... eloquence for the term 'dinner talk'. Perhaps duct tape and a pointed dunce hat sitting in the corner would curtail your personal flamboyant persiflage and allow us to enjoy a peaceful meal."

"Oh wow," said Walker sarcastically. "Berkeley has a vocabulary."

"Enough down there. We don't need to hear your dribbling, save it for your newspapers, you are just guests here. I have no problem escorting you out. By God, I don't know who would want to read the shit that comes out of your mouths," instilled Lieutenant Alderson. "I'll shoot you both if we hear anymore. Understand me?"

The young woman got up from the table and moved to another spot. Another man imposing his will over her—they needed to take her seriously... *They have no idea!*

The rest of the evening's dinner was uneventful and as the camp quieted down for the night Jeff Miller thought he would check on Maysa and her children before taking a late-night stroll around the camp. She lay peaceful, as did her children, so he slipped back out quietly and headed over to the camp director's office. Most of the walls had been repaired but the door still was not installed. He knocked softly and entered. He thought the doctor might have been in as the lamp over her desk was still on. He sauntered over and peered down to a partially burnt pad with a note from Maysa. He read it.

As he stepped out the door, he quickly glanced in each direction before continuing in the shadow of the building and then, leaving its safety, he stepped into the brightness of the camp's overhead halogens. He continued to walk onward, but glaring from the shadows of the tents, a figure moved swiftly without notice. As the reporter rounded one of the corners to a secondary interior road with a makeshift sign with 'Peace' written on it, he almost bumped into the doctor.

"Oh! You startled me," said Amelie.

"Sorry, I was just taking a walk, listening to the sounds of nature and the campfire songs."

"Their music is truly beautiful. Very rhythmic and rich in culture."

"Sort of soulful, almost calypso... Makes you want to shuffle your feet," smiled the young man.

"Are you getting anything for your assignment?"

"I have talked with some of your staff and had a few conversations with the ladies. I am amazed at the distance they have travelled on foot to escape the fighting and then end up here with this tragedy."

"Yes, well, let's say we were lucky and now it is time to heal. I hope you will be able to persuade those who make the big decisions to send more relief. I don't think the other two have that same concern, do you?"

"We are on different sides of the desk, so to speak. They have deadlines and need to get in quick and fast while I can linger longer to formulate my theories."

"I was told about their heated conversation at the mess hall. Rivals, I guess?"

"Seems so. I didn't think it was called for; especially after everyone trying so hard to find Maysa's companion."

"Well, let's hope tomorrow will be a brighter day. I'll say good night, Mr. Miller."

"Good night, Doctor."

Day 12 - Sunday

Florida - Dockside

Romeo 0530 Hrs.

The dock master was standing on the bridge with the captain of 'Claire's Sanctuary' as they maneuvered between its bow and aft thrusters to gently glide the mega yacht into its Fort Lauderdale slip. Lines had been cast and their main M.A.N. turbo engine hissed off. The sun had broken the sky and all but the deck hands that were scurrying about, lay still asleep, that is, all except Angela.

She had put her hair in a ponytail, slipped on tights and sports bra, grabbed a protein shake from the galley, and sat down at her computer in the grand salon. Angela retrieved a message from her husband and started to set things into motion for him. The VP of her clothing design business was on L.A. time and wouldn't be up for hours, but her partner in 'Angileen Arte' Galerie in Paris was a few hours ahead. She fired off several emails, including one to her foundation at La Défense, Paris.

She downed her drink, signed off her computer, and then headed for her daily workout in the Yacht's gym. This was her time to unwind and refocus before her day started. Angela missed 'Pooky', her nine-month-old little girl, but she was in good hands with their dear friends and husband's partner, the Thoroughgoods. The miles rode by on the stationary bike as she listened to the song that her husband had proposed to. That was a magical night.

By the time Marsha limped to the gym's door, Angela was already on the mats with a toned suntanned man. Marsha peered through the porthole of the door first before going inside. Breathing heavily, Angela acknowledged her standing there.

"Good morning, Marsha," she squeezed out before blocking a kick. Angela spun, faked a high kick and came back with the ball of her foot square into the sparring partner's jaw. He rallied with a swoop that took out her legs, and then as he came in for a death punch, she clasped his fist between her legs, grabbed his Gi and flipped him behind her. He rolled to the side and as he sprung to his feet, one foot stepped off the mat. He smiled. They both bowed and met in the center.

"Très bien, Angelique. I thought I had you on the punch." Antoine, chef and martial arts teacher, bowed in respect.

"So did I. That was purely instinctive, I assure you," she laughed.

Angela walked over to where Marsha was standing and grabbed a towel from a nearby bench.

"Very impressive, Angela."

"Thank you, Marsha. Just trying to stay sharp. Sometimes these long trips can wear on your body. Come; walk with me to my cabin."

"I have to admit, when I met you yesterday, I thought you were just another pretty California blonde."

"And today, Marsha... What has changed?"

"I talked with Alicia last night...and now, after watching you in action, I would be proud to stand beside you."

"Well, thank you, Marsha." They stood at Angela's cabin door. "Come in, take a seat on the bed. I won't be long."

The room was laid out much like Marsha's with highly polished, blonde Teak cabinets and glass-enclosed shower. Angela disappeared into her dressing room and then reappeared naked, and she stepped into the shower. Marsha admired her shapely body.

"I don't know much about you," loudly stated Angela over the noise of the rain-head shower while she shampooed her hair.

Marsha got up from the bed and took a seat on an ottoman closer to the shower.

"Well, originally from Madison, Wisconsin. I have an older brother who still lives there, a younger sister trying to break into theater in New York, and I had a twin sister."

"Had?"

"Yes, she was killed."

"Oh, so sorry to hear that, Marsha. So, how long have you been with PAG?"

"Since its inception. Samantha and I designed the protocol, and with help from a dedicated team, we have struggled with the priorities of programming, but I think we have solved some of its initial faults."

Angela rinsed her hair.

"Well, we found you with your system's help, so I think you and your team have now accomplished what you set out to do."

"I hope so. We have an assignment from CTA to find a missing soldier, and as far as I know, we haven't been successful."

"That mission has ended," said Angela as she dried her body and whipped her hair into a towel. "Marsha, could you be so kind and hand me my wrap?"

A white silky robe hung by itself from a series of wall hooks that protruded from one of the marble walls. Angela, who had been standing on a mat, waited as Marsha removed the robe and flared it open; Angela slipped it on.

"Thank you, sweetie."

"What do you mean the mission has ended?"

"Jack has terminated your mission."

"But why? Have they found the soldier?"

"There was a raid by the Al-Shabaab at a UN camp in Kenya. Jack ordered a missile strike that took out the militants, but also some American lives were lost. The camp housed over 80,000 refugees, mostly women and children and with the dedicated coordinates of PAG, saved those lives. You should be very proud of this accomplishment."

"The soldier was one of them?"

"I'm not privy as to who didn't make it."

Marsha walked over to Angela's bed and sat down, thinking. She had a stressed look on her face.

"Angela, there is more I feel I need to tell you about myself...but first, when do you think I will be able to contact Samantha?"

"We will only be in port for a few hours... I would feel more comfortable after we make-way. Right now, with the main engines down, our shields are also. This makes us vulnerable to hacking."

Angela noticed Marsha's concern. She walked to her side and put her arms around her. Marsha felt the warmth from Angela's body through her robe and rested her head against Angela's stomach.

"Don't worry, we are here to help in any way we can," said Angela softly as she comforted her new friend.

Uganda - UN Camp

Charlie 1400 Hrs.

Maysa had slept late, and by the time she had taken care of the children with her limited dexterity, the sun had slipped into the afternoon. Jake and his volunteers were still canvasing the eastern side of the destruction. She noticed the young reporter who was kind to her children, talking with several women. Maysa approached him.

"Kind, sir," she interrupted.

He looked up. "Yes, Maysa? And please, call me Jeff."

"Yes. Well then, Jeff, may I summon your help?"

"Of course. What do you need?"

"Please, will you come with me?"

Jeff excused himself from the ladies and promised to return to finish their conversation. He walked alongside Maysa as she left camp for the direction of the last known whereabouts of her friend. Jeff, although sensitive to Maysa's concerns, questioned her intent.

"Maysa, Lieutenant Alderson, and the volunteers already scanned this area."

"That might be so, but I haven't," she said determinedly. "You don't know him as I do. I survived because of him, I owe him this courtesy. Can I trust you, Mr. Jeff?"

"Of course, Maysa."

"Then why were you in my tent last night?"

"Uh... just checking on you to make sure you and your children were all right. I thought you were sound asleep."

She looked up at him. "You don't know me either, Mr. Jeff."

"Then why did you ask me to join you, if you question my intentions?"

"I needed for us to get away from the others so I could feel your sincerity."

"And do you?"

"Your eyes are kind and your words speak truth. Your actions will be proof."

"Boy, you are hard-nosed," smiled Jeff.

Maysa stopped in her tracks and grabbed Jeff's arm with her battered hand.

"I've learned from a young age how to survive on my own and care for my daughter. Mr. Clark has been the kindest man I have ever met. I will not accept his death until I see him with my own eyes."

"I understand, Maysa. I will help in any way I can... you have my word."

"Good."

Within another two hundred yards of walking, Maysa saw the back end of their pickup truck still nestled between rocks and a clump of burnt grass. She quickened her step in anticipation. The tires were flat and still smoldering, the front glass was blown out, and the seats were burnt. She had Jeff open the charred lids on the big boxes in the pickup's bed; they were empty. The grass had been trampled, probably by the volunteers, but she still looked for more.

The driver's door was partially ajar and as she gazed around at the burnt-out interior, her face lit up. Maysa bent down to the floor mat and picked up a flattened grass giraffe. She held up the novelty and blew the ashes from its pristine body.

"How many giraffes did Mosi have?"

"Five," answered Jeff.

"Yes, five... one for me, one for Mr. Clark, and three more... one for each child, Mr. Jeff."

"Yes?" said Jeff as he held onto the driver's door with a questioning look on his face.

"Mr. Clark made five... our little family befriended a scared young boy."

"Okay... I don't understand. What you are getting at?"

"Here... Mr. Jeff is number six."

Washington, D.C. - SAS

Romeo 0930 Hrs.

Samantha heard her office phone ring and dropped her clipboard onto Paul's desk as she scurried to answer it.

"Hello, Director Jones speaking."

There was an eerie stillness over the line, then a click and then, *"Samantha... it's me!"*

"Oh, my God! Marsha, I've been so worried!" cried the director. "...we all have been. How are you? Where are you?"

"I am fine... Well, recovering nicely. And as far as where, I can't currently say."

"I've missed you so much," wept Samantha.

"I've missed you as well, Sam."

"When are you coming home?"

"Ah... that might be awhile. Who's on duty?"

"Paul is here."

"May I speak with him briefly?"

"Yes, of course." Samantha was a little confused by her friend's request since they barely had time to reunite. She stepped to her office door as everyone sat in anticipation from the director's outburst.

"Paul, Marsha wants to speak to you."

He ran to the phone, smiling.

"Hello, Marsha... you okay?"

"Yes, fine Paul. Listen, I need you to do some things for me." Marsha informed Paul of what she needed.

"Yes... okay, no problem... Yes, I can do that, and Derrick as well. I'll handle it... Okay, take care. Here's the director."

"Marsha, is everything all right?"

"Yes, Sam... I just needed Paul to handle a few loose ends."

"When are you coming home?" pleaded Samantha.

"I can't right now, but Paul will get you hooked up so we will be able to talk more often. What's happening with PAG?"

"Nothing... well, I mean, our mission for CTA is done. I imagine we will downsize to a skeleton format."

"You have a new mission and it is being financed by Fournier Foundation."

"What! How can that be?"

"Not to worry, they are extremely friendly to our cause. I'll be in touch with the particulars as soon as I learn more. I've got to go, Samantha."

"Marsha ... I just wanted to say... I miss holding you."

"Soon, Sam. Soon all will be righted." Marsha ended the call.

The director turned to Paul and said, "I suppose you can't tell me what your conversation was about?" Paul looked at her with sealed lips. "Never mind, sorry to pry," sniffled Samantha.

"It's okay, Director, but I do need to get you hooked up with your own Blackberry and your own personal code. I will get with Derrick this afternoon."

"Should I be watching more James Bond or Bourne Identity?" smiled the director.

"We are far more advanced than both of them, ma'am."

"So... it looks like Marsha does know this Fournier Foundation after all." She shook her head. "I love you all... whatever you do. I know in my heart you are here for me, and I trust that... Thank you."

"You are welcome, ma'am."

. . .

Angela felt an overpowering understanding upon hearing her new friend's story.

"Thank you, Angela. She is not as strong as the two of us, but she is pretty remarkable."

"Do I detect a fuzzier feeling for the director?"

"You could say that... it's kind of complicated. I didn't want her to get involved with my life but she... it evolved shall I say."

"Understand completely. Your secret is safe with me. We all have another life to our business face and thank you for sharing yours. Well, now that we are underway again, what do you want to do? We have a home theater room where we can stream any movie you want, and of course, the gym but I wouldn't recommend any exercising until your foot heals a little further. We could enjoy some pool time and the sun on the upper deck?"

"Do you have a swimsuit to fit me?"

"Honey, we don't wear suits up there. Don't you know... tan lines spoil a girl's choice of what to wear!"

Kenyan Outback

Charlie 1930 Hrs.

The street was dark with only one small light on in a store window that displayed a newspaper with photos of Kiir and Machar with headlines reading *"Nairobi Next to Stage Talks – War or Peace for South Sudan?"*

~

Walker had received a note telling him to meet someone at the far corner of the camp, away from prying eyes. There was no name or other information, but Walker showed up as requested. Out of the shadow, a voice startled him.

"What do you have to print?"

"I'm not telling you. Who are you?"

A newspaper landed at his feet and the seasoned reporter gazed down. "Your interest is in these two clowns?" said the reporter.

"They need to be punished for their war crimes. They have committed atrocities against these people by the tens of thousands. They have allowed the young to be slaughtered, raped, and then burnt alive. They have forced citizens from their homes to follow a path of desolation and despair. There is your story, not here."

"You might be quite right but that was not my assignment. You see, that is old news and here, right now, is new news."

The reporter bent down and picked up the paper. "Why do you want me to follow their story?" he asked.

Walker waited for a reply. "Are you there?" He stepped into the shadow from where the voice had spoken to him. He searched—nothing.

Walker carried the paper under his arm and went to the gathering spot—the mess hall. Faces were grim as the volunteers and military personnel had found nothing of the remains of the young woman's friend. He sat down beside Lieutenant Alderson, the one who had threatened Walker's life the night before.

"I just had an interesting conversation," said Brent Walker.

"Oh yeah?" responded Jake less than enthusiastically.

He produced the newspaper and placed it in front of Jake. "I think it was your friend who gave me that. Are you interested now?"

Jake looked at him. "What are you saying?"

"Look, I've been around a long time... No evidence of a body means there is hope. And did you see the young woman's face when she and that pretend-to-be reporter came back in from the field. I would bet my last dollar they uncovered something."

"Did you see this guy?"

"No, he was in the shadows."

Jake casually opened the paper and on the third page, a black charcoal circle surrounded President Baxter and Jack Tomlinson shaking hands. The reporter's eyes opened wide.

"Is this the story your man was talking about?"

Just then, Jeff walked through the draped canvas door and headed to where Lt. Alderson and Brent Walker were engaged in a private conversation. He sat down and with a bright smile. He placed his out-stretched folded hands on the table.

"What's up, gentlemen?"

Jake looked at the young reporter's freshly washed hands. "Cleaning up, are you? Washing charcoal off your hands?"

"Pardon?"

"Your hands?"

"What about them?" defensively questioned Jeff.

"Did you just wash charcoal off them?" Jake flipped the paper over to Jeff so he could see the black-smudged circle.

"What? You think I did that?"

"Just answer my question."

"I just had some maize and chicken dip with Maysa," he retorted. "Besides, where would I get this paper?" He flipped to the first page. "It's yesterday's. It hasn't come to the camp yet."

"That's what I want to know," flared Jake.

Jeff put his arms up in the air as if surrendering.

"I have no idea. You guys are barking up the wrong tree."

"We'll see," added Brent Walker.

"Why are you trying to play me? Where's the girl?"

"The dyke?"

"Yeah, whatever," said Jeff Miller.

"Haven't seen her. Maybe she's doing her job gathering newsworthy stories from the camp's women," barked Brent Walker.

"What did you find out there? Your man here said Maysa looked a little brighter when you came back," asked Jake.

"Nothing really... Just one of Mosi's giraffes. I guess it touched her."

Jake stood to leave. Jeff looked up at him and said, "Oh... by the way, before I went to wash my hands, Mac said to tell you they got a radio working."

"Thanks... sorry for the third degree."

"We're cool." Jeff waved off the questioning and then turned to the reporter after Jake left. "What's this paper got to do with anything?"

"Nothing, I suppose. It was how it was delivered."

Pentagon - SAS

Romeo 1300 Hrs.

Derrick had brought in a Blackberry for the director's use and instructed her on how to unencrypt messages using her computer and her chosen personal code. She was entering their 'spy ring' as she called it; she felt a little more secure and not as vulnerable. Samantha was thrilled to have talked with Marsha and just knowing she was safe, eased her mind. They were still waiting for data from this welcomed ally, Fournier Foundation, so the director had her team clean up all the questions that plagued her.

First on the agenda: back footage of who piloted the Admiral's boat and stepping it back even further to find Marsha's assailant, since they were now certain she was taken by boat. Next: PAG's timestamp on the rescue of Marsha—the usual questions, who and how? And third: PAG's timestamp on relocating the soldier's ping and the following destruction. The director expressed concern to her team about the timing. Samantha felt it was way off for the military to coordinate a strike using their sequencing. How did Jack obtain intel about the militants invading the camp as they barely had PAG in position before the strike occurred? And why had he shut them down? Didn't he want to know the outcome of the soldier... or at least to know the whereabouts of the soldier after spending several million dollars of taxpayers' money?

Derrick and his fellow team members were also concerned with what the director questioned. The three operators each took a task and started to delve deep into the memory banks of PAG.

As the director paced up and down in front of the terminals, her concentration was broken by her vibrating

Blackberry. Samantha looked around. Paul smiled and lifted the cell phone up off his desk.

"Yours, ma'am."

"Who knows me?"

"Do as I showed you," replied Derrick.

Samantha grabbed the phone from Paul and quickly punched in a sequence of numbers. She then went to a computer and typed in another sequence, this time with Derrick's help. A digital file opened—it was Marsha sitting in the middle of a room, chained to a chair. A man dressed in Navy attire came into view. They watched as he started to caress her shoulders and then stepped in front of her. They saw Marsha's foot come up between his legs and as she stood up, they noticed her ripped shirt exposing her bra. She then unleashed swooping arms with chains wrapped around her fists and slammed them into each side of the perpetrator's head.

"Wow, go girl!" raved Paul.

After a series of kicks and punches, the man sprawled on the floor. They watched as she disarmed him and then dragged him to the chair and chained him up. Marsha then disappeared out of view. The images continued to roll with the time-stamp noticeable in the lower right corner. The man started to shake his head and fought with the chains, but to no avail. Then, another man entered the room and with his back to the camera, made a quick motion with his arms, and bent into view as his fingers... his fingers... Redman's fingers checked for pulse. He then disappeared out of view.

"Holy fu...dge!" declared Derrick as he raised his hands to his face.

"We got him!" chanted Paul.

"We certainly do," smiled the director smugly. "I think I like this Blackberry thing. But why did it come to me?"

"I programmed a few numbers into your phone, Sam. If SAS wants legal counsel to prosecute, it would be best to initiate it by a higher command."

"Okay, Derrick, I can understand that, but tell me why I would not want to prosecute and most importantly, who sent it to me?"

"Sometimes leverage is a better solution and 'who', someone much higher than all of us, one with powerful connections."

"The President?"

"No, ma'am... even above him."

"There's someone above him?" Samantha raised her eyebrows dubiously.

"Yes, ma'am. Unbiased, ideological and without limiting strings of governmental bureaucracy."

"God?" she said somewhat sarcastically.

"No, ma'am," smiled Derrick.

"Have you met him?"

"Not that I am aware."

"So you might have but didn't know it," quizzed the director.

"That is possible."

"Just one man?" asked the director, even more confused.

"Well, I can't attest to that either. Maybe they are a consortium of different men and women, humanitarians, military advisors, businessmen, or even clergy. I really don't know, but I do know they are concerned for the Earth's well-being and its citizens."

"Okay, I need a break from thinking about alien superpowers. What do we do with the footage?"

"We'll make a copy and hide it within PAG and I'll transfer this one into a secured server."

"How would I access it, if I needed to show someone?" asked the director.

"The same way you just accessed this one. I'll prioritize it so if someone tries to hack it, it will go viral."

"You can do that?"

"Yes, ma'am."

Uganda – UN Camp
Charlie 2115 Hrs.

Finally, Mac had turned his gifted talent into a positive scenario. There hadn't been much to celebrate.

"Mac, I hear you have some good news?"

"Yes, Jake. We got the radio working and have already sent a message to command."

"What about SAS? Send them anything yet?"

"Thought we would wait until we hear back. I relayed what happened here with the Colonel's approval."

"Good. Let's see what they want us to do now."

As the two men conversed, Jeff slid into Maysa's tent, unnoticed from the outside, that is.

"Maysa, please take that knife away from my throat," pleaded the young reporter.

"Don't you knock or something before you enter someone's tent?" she said softly.

"I didn't want to attract attention."

"Silly, man... I could've cut you."

"I'll be more careful next time, I assure you. Listen, I just came from the mess hall where Lieutenant Alderson and Walker showed me a newspaper he received. They thought I gave it to him..."

"He is alive!" voiced Maysa with a quiet but enthusiastic tone.

"I believe you might be right. Now, they have not seen the woman reporter for a while. That tells me she is not who she seems or has an alternative motive for being here."

"Why do you say that, Mr. Jeff?"

"Because, I have been around this camp and have talked to a lot of people. No one besides me has asked any questions. Granted it is a large camp, but I think I would have met someone who has talked with her. They mention seeing the older reporter but not the woman. After today, I'm not sure of the soldiers' plans but I'm going to go out into the fields away from the destruction and see if I can spot anything out of place."

"I'll go with you."

"I think it best if you stay around here. They also commented on your seemingly brighter face when we got back. I told them you found one of Mosi's giraffes."

"It might not be safe for you to go by yourself, Mr. Jeff. My Mr. Clark is well-trained and might take you for an intruder."

"I'll have to deal with that. I have no weapons to imply a threat."

"Just being a white man implies threat, Mr. Jeff. If you try to sneak out of camp, they will know we know

339

something. If I go with you, we are just going for a walk. Maybe ask them if it is okay first...gain their trust."

"Where did you learn all this?"

"I'm a young woman with a baby, Mr. Jeff. I've had to do things."

"Why don't you want to tell the soldiers what you believe?"

"If it was just the soldiers here, I would. But the other people, I don't trust. In our country, knowledge breeds information and that information goes to the highest bidder. If Mr. Clark was still alive and believed we were safe, he would have come in. He still must distrust someone to stay away, probably for my sake."

"All right, Maysa. We will meet up tomorrow, casually, and take it from there."

"Good night, Mr. Jeff. And thank you for believing me."

~

She saw the broken lock and how it had been replaced to look like it hadn't been tampered with. The single light, with its acorn metal globe, shadowed most of the small store in deep darkness. *What had he wanted here?* She thought. *And by how much time had I missed him?*

She looked around at the assorted merchandise. It could have been almost anything. Then she saw it, even in the darkness—a dust ring glared at her and behind that, triple antibiotic ointment for livestock. She picked up the ointment and shifted it around to read the label: lacerations, bites, bruising, and burns. She looked further— a large package of bandage wraps—gone. *So, Lieutenant Clark, you're hurting a little?* she smugly said to herself.

Leaving, she replaced the lock as she found it. She headed down a goat's path and then veered off guided by the glow of the camp light that peered through the thick brush and into the starless night.

He removed the scope away from his eye.

Quebec Time Zone
1400 Hrs. 26.1333° N, 65° W

Alicia adjusted her watch from the time change and joined the ladies poolside after her 2 pm shift ended. Marsha was already showing signs of too much sun on her D.C. white body without enough applied sunscreen. It had been a perfectly relaxed day with spirited conversation between Angela and Marsha. The openness of Angela amazed Marsha and she understood why Alicia loved working for her. Alicia had brought up a bottle of champagne, three glasses, and chilled grapes as a prelude to dinner, which was set just like every day, at 6:30 p.m. Claire's Sanctuary's chef, Antoine D'Artois was very punctual and demanded respect for his dinner schedule from all onboard, no matter what their schedules dictated. The other meals were handled by his sous chef and bartender, Nicolette, who was more than happy to bend to others' wishes.

Angela relocated a lounger next to them as Alicia popped the cork, poured each lady a glass, and placed the grapes between each chair.

"Cheers, ladies!" saluted Alicia.

"Bienvenue, mes amis," shared Angela.

"To charming company," added Marsha.

They each took a sip of the expensive champagne and savored the taste.

"So, Angela, you speak French or just a few catch phrases?"

"Fluent. With a last name like Fournier, I better be able to," she laughed.

Surprised, Marsha asked, "You are actually a Fournier?"

"Oui... a long story of which I still haven't completely grasped, but the short of it is, I was adopted by my mentor, Gilles Fournier, and hold both a U.S. and French passport. My business partner, Jamison Starkney, was mentored by Gilles from when he was a little boy, and when Jamison took over the reign from Gilles, he developed the company into what we have today. Jamison is teaching me the family business so to speak as I fell into this unexpectedly a little over a year ago. Along with my auntie, who is a cloistered nun living in Belgium, and me, presumably through the adoption, are the only living relatives of Gilles and the Fournier Foundation."

"I thought the Fournier Foundation was merely a corporate identity, not a family name?"

"Trust me. As you know, I am very much tangible," laughed Angela, thinking about Marsha putting sunscreen on her early on the upper deck.

"Yes, you are right there. So where is Jamison?"

"Brussels."

"Where the summit is going to be held next month?"

"Actually in two weeks."

"Damn... he must be connected."

"You could say that."

"Ladies, another round?" asked Alicia.

"By all means, Sweetie," said Angela. "We better leave time for pampering and powdering before dinner. Antoine is a stickler."

"Is it casual?" asked Marsha unaware of the ship's customs.

"Not dinner," shared Angela. "I know Jackie placed some cocktail, semi-formal, and formal wear in your closet. When on the seas, cocktail wear is appropriate, first night in port will be semi-formal, and depending on the guest list, formal attire will be required, unless it is more of a meet and greet."

"I have to admit, I've never been part of anything like this. Here we three lie stark naked on the most incredible ship, then just to eat dinner, we don fancy cocktail dresses?"

"I know... it takes some time to get it all straight," laughed Angela.

"Ah, in a few days, it will be old hat to you, Marsha," shared Alicia.

"Aahhh, you southern damsels enjoy these dress-up parties. I'm from Wisconsin... hunting, meat and potatoes, and cold beer out of the back of a pickup truck."

Angela laughed. "Marsha, you are a crack-up."

"Hey... and let me live my black dream. I love all the dress-up... feeling real nice as the silk teases my body," said a smiling Alicia as she cuddled herself in her lounger.

"I meant no disrespect, Alicia."

"Oh, none taken, Marsha, trust me. I am living the dream here with Angela. You know how many women, black or white would cherish this job?"

"I feel like raising my hand," laughed Marsha sinking down in her lounger.

The sun and the champagne had the three giggling like long-time schoolgirl friends. Angela was pleased with their decision to help Marsha out, even with their pressing schedule. She admired Marsha's frankness and dedication and trusted her own intuitiveness after spending a relaxed day with her. But now, it was time to head below to get ready.

"Cocktails at six, ladies."

~

Before Angela joined the ladies in the grand salon for cocktails, she had checked her incoming email. She had news for Marsha that she needed to relay to SAS regarding their new mission.

Marsha's foot was healing nicely; maybe the relaxed day had something to do with it, she surmised. She left her crutches in her cabin and wore a form-fitting elastic brace guided into a black-blingy, two-inch heel shoe. Her cocktail dress, designed by AD Fashions, draped across her breasts in a deep V with a plunging backline to the crest of her butt with a length barely covering her unmentionable. She pulled back her hair to one side and with a rosette matched to her shoes, she pinned it in place. She looked killer.

Marsha took the elevator to the grand salon where Alicia, who looked equally sexy, was standing at the bar waiting for Nicolette to finish making her martini.

"Wow... look at you!" exclaimed Alicia as the elevator door opened.

"Phew, girl you look so hot too. Is that one of Angela's designs as well?"

"Who else could make this body zing with less fabric than one of my bras?"

"Yeah... she sure likes nothing left to the imagination," laughed Marsha.

"Martini?"

"Sure... whatever you are having."

"Nicolette, another please."

"Yes, Miss Alicia."

"Is everyone always this polite?"

"Angela demands respect for everyone by everyone. She doesn't take friendship for granted."

Nicolette set Marsha's martini down on the Italian marble bar on top of a linen coaster with FF initials embroidered in gold.

"Cheers!" They clinked their glasses and took a sip.

"Mmm delicious, Nicolette!" remarked Marsha.

"Thank you, ma'am."

Angela, sporting a grand smile, entered the salon from a forward cabin wearing her signature Sapphire dress.

Marsha nearly choked on her martini as she watched Angela flow as she approached her.

"My God, Angela... I thought you looked beautiful naked but... WOW! That dress on you is just... captivating."

"Thank you, Marsha, and I'll say the same about you two HOT ladies!"

She gave each of them a hug.

"My usual, Nicolette, please."

"Yes, ma'am."

"Obviously, you designed that dress as well."

Angela sashayed to the bar.

"Actually, no. My VP and long-time friend, Gina, designed this years ago, but occasionally I like to wear this recreation to make me feel warm and fuzzy and blessed to have the friends I do."

"Well, cheers to that, Angela," shared Marsha.

"Sorry, ladies, I don't want to distract from all this beauty in front of me, but I have information for Marsha. You will want to share this with your PAG team," said Angela as she handed a piece of paper to Marsha. "They're coordinates for your team to start your search. My source is convinced your soldier is still alive and needs our help."

"Is that why we are heading to Africa?"

"Yes."

"So, you knew about this mission before you rescued me?"

"Yes. We were about to depart for Africa when we were asked to help out if at all possible. So we got a little side-tracked to work on the logistics of extracting you from the Bulkeley. And I am glad we did." Angela took Marsha by the hand and they stepped to the other side of the salon's centered bar where her computer was sitting on the bar's lowered sit-down counter.

"We need to hurry before Antoine serves dinner. Here, use my Blackberry and computer to send the message. I'll give you your privacy."

"Thank you, Angela."

Angela sauntered around the bar to where Alicia was sitting in a tall, leather-backed swivel chair. Her dress looked more like a belt, baring her strong thighs. Angela placed her hands on them, slowly and lightly, she scraped her nails zigzagging flirtatiously to Alicia's knees. Alicia shuddered. "Oh, Miss Angela, you're making me tingle."

Angela bent to her ear and whispered. "When we get to Mombasa, don't let Marsha out of your sight. I fear she still is not out of danger." She smiled and gave Alicia a kiss on the cheek.

"Yes, ma'am, I understand completely," she whispered back.

Marsha finished with her transmission and couldn't help but notice the intimate moment shared by her new friends. *Lucky girl.*

The white dinner jacket crew started to file in as Nicolette rang a dinner bell for the ladies to take their seats. Angela sat at the head of the table and her two friends on either side. Antoine, Jackie and Nicolette served dinner and then took seats at the opposite end of the table. The room flowed with chatter and boisterous laughter as they toasted and consumed another perfect creation by Antoine.

Marsha leaned into Angela and whispered, "Antoine certainly doesn't look like your typical chef. And all these chiseled crew?"

Angela smiled and took another spoon of her Bouillabaisse.

Day 13 - Monday

Uganda – UN Camp
Charlie 0730 Hrs.

The young reporter, Jeff Miller, was sitting in the mess tent, preoccupied with typing his notes into his laptop when he heard a noise and looked up. The Colonel, who was feeling much better, Jake, Mac and Peterson with the seasoned reporter, Brent Walker, came in and sat down. They seemed brighter after coming from the recovery tent of their fellow soldier, Reynolds, who cursed and wanted to get out of bed. Jake's head bandage was only a couple of strips of tape and gauze, but his face was still black and blue, with streaks of yellow surrounding his massively red eye. Mac also seemed to be recovering with fewer wraps and more fingers exposed; Peterson had ditched the crutch. *Tough sons of bitches,* thought Jeff.

"Good morning, gentlemen."

"Morning," said the Colonel for all of them.

"You all look a little fitter today," said Jeff smiling, trying to gain an understanding with them.

"We're healing," remarked Jake.

"So, what are your plans? Am I going to be able to get a ride to Nairobi?"

"Command wants us to stay put and rest up for a couple of more days. Sorry, I forgot about you wanting to go to Nairobi. Hasn't been exactly on my mind. I'll have Jacobs send a message to see when the chopper is coming this way," said the Colonel.

"Well, there is plenty to write about this place and the people here. It's a sad situation but at least they are alive, thanks to you gentlemen. So, Mr. Walker, I guess you will be staying as well?"

"Not if I can help it. As soon as passage comes this way, I'm heading out."

"What about your lady friend?"

"What about her? Haven't seen her... And I thought we were having a civil conversation," gruffly remarked Walker.

Jeff smiled. He started to close his laptop when Maysa entered the mess tent. She was bombarded with "Good mornings." She, in kind, shared their salutation.

"Colonel, I have just spoken with the camp director and she tells me there is a small hardware store over the ridge about a kilometer away where I might find some treats for my children. I would very much like to go there. Do you have any objections as she insisted I check with you first?"

"We haven't reconned that area that far over, maybe not a good idea at this time."

"I am quite capable of looking after myself, Colonel."

"No doubt, Maysa, but not bandaged as you are."

She turned to the young reporter.

"Mr. Jeff, would you be so kind as to be my escort as the Colonel believes I am incapable of defending myself?"

"Well..." He looked at the Colonel for permission. "It's up to the Colonel, Maysa."

"You know how to handle a weapon, young man?"

"I've shot a few rounds in my life."

"Jake, give him a 9mm."

Jake hesitantly stood up and offered one of his 9mm handguns to Jeff. Jeff dropped the mag, removed the safety, slid the barrel, and caught the ejected round. He then re-inserted the round back into the mag, replaced the mag into the frame, and set the safety.

"I would say more than a few rounds there, Mr. Miller," smiled the Colonel.

"Okay, Maysa, your writer friend seems capable enough to handle a situation. Just be careful. And if you spot trouble, haul your asses back here and I'll send out a patrol."

"Yes, sir, and thank you," Maysa said politely.

"I will expect you back no later than 1000 hours... Are we in agreement?"

"I'll have her back here, Colonel," remarked Jeff.

The Colonel started to laugh.

"If you can control her, you are a better man than I."

The two took leave and as soon as they were out of sight, Jake voiced his opinion.

"Sir, was that wise to give that guy a gun?"

"Jake, I was just going on your intuition. I don't believe he is any threat to Maysa but I am curious as to why the charade of asking my permission even if Amelie had told her to do so. Are you forgetting the way she came into this camp...all brimstone and fire, demanding her friend's safety and all? No, those two are up to something. I'm more concerned with the woman reporter. Where has she been?"

It took Maysa and Jeff fifteen minutes just to reach the back end of the camp. The rear gate was still precariously hanging from its pins, although men were working on mending the fences ravaged by the invasion. The field grass was green and getting taller and as they reached the top of the knoll, the valley opened up to them. Jeff thought it was majestic as junipers dotted the landscape and shrouds of elephant grass grew to almost ten feet tall. Maysa found a goat's path headed in the direction of the dirt road at the bottom of the hill.

Maysa stopped Jeff several times on their way down as she noticed smaller and lighter footprints in the red dirt pathway.

"A woman's print," she said.

"How can you tell?"

Maysa bent down. "Look at the boot imprint. The heel doesn't dig in as far as a man's and the sole doesn't lift the sand as high." She looked around for any other clues.

"Look over here on the side of the berm. She went down towards the road here and her stride is shorter and unsure as if she was spying on something or someone, or maybe was anticipating seeing someone. Coming up, her stride is longer and more determined."

"Why do you say unsure?"

"There is more weight on the outer ridge of the boot."

"How do you know this stuff?"

"Have you ever tracked a lion, Mr. Jeff? You want to know if it is circling around behind, hunting you, rather than you hunting him. It's easy to get disorientated in the tall grass."

The reporter began to step lighter as he looked at the footprints and signs of the grass. He thought of himself as knowledgeable in being able to gouge out the truth with minimal evidence, but Maysa had opened his mind even further. They continued to walk.

Jeff felt fairly safe with the 9mm tucked in the back of his pants and his Hawaiian-flowered shirt offered coverage from concerning eyes. His tattered backpack carried his essentials: computer, paper and pencils, duct tape, shaving kit, his media credentials, his passport, and sewn into seven hidden stays, a King's ransom, with one of them empty.

When they arrived at the hardware store, they were surprised to see all the interest. Several men were milling around while another complained loudly to all who would listen. His arms flailed about like an orchestra conductor, stopping briefly, pointing, and then resuming their musical score.

Jeff leaned into Maysa and asked what he was saying.

"Someone robbed him the other night."

"What did they take?" asked Jeff, concerned for the man's future well-being.

Maysa interrupted the wailing man.

"He's complaining about the broken lock and a bottle of livestock ointment, a box of gauze and... a missing bag of fertilizer."

"That's it, and he is carrying on like this? I thought they might have cleaned him out for this theatrical performance," said Jeff smiling as he turned away from the man's observance.

"Mr. Jeff, don't laugh... This is very important to the shopkeeper."

"I guess. Do we send flowers with a condolence card?"

"Stop it! You sound just like Mr. Clark."

"You're right, I'm sorry. Ask him how big a bag was the fertilizer?"

Maysa translated Jeff's question.

"He said ten liter."

"Ten liter. That is like a size for house plants."

"Well, I don't know, but he is very upset."

"I think we should find something for the kids and head back. Hey... look at this front page news. Looks like the talks didn't go so well in Nairobi. Let's grab a paper as well."

~

Jeff and Maysa returned to the camp as instructed and on time. Mac and Peterson were sitting at the benched table when they walked in. Maysa excused herself in order to share her treats with her children and Jeff sat down with the two men and placed the newspaper on the table.

"Looks like it didn't go so well with the negotiations on the weekend," said Jeff Miller.

"Anything else of importance?" asked Peterson.

"Don't know... haven't looked through it yet," remarked Jeff. "But what was interesting was a break-in at the store."

"Is that right," shared Peterson, unimpressed.

"Yeah. Livestock ointment, gauze and... fertilizer."

"Really?" piped up Mac.

"Yes... I thought you might be interested in that. Someone knows the ingredients for a ..."

"A bomb?" questioned Mac.

"Yes, that's what I was thinking."

"How much?"

"Not a lot... ten liters of fertilizer."

"No, that's not much, but it is enough to startle someone to get the drop on them or even set a delayed fire or explosion," stated Mac.

"A delayed fire?" asked Jeff.

"Yeah. You would place the fertilizer mixed with dried grass or other combustible, then stretch the gauze over it and add the ointment onto the gauze. As the alcohol or acetone bleeds off through the gauze and drips down to the mixture below, it would act like an ignitor."

"What about burning someone?"

"Just the ointment alone could do that, but mixed with the fertilizer and wrapped, it could..."

Jeff interrupted Mac this time. "It could give the illusion of a badly burnt body without the effects of burnt out lungs or internal injuries?"

Mac and Peterson looked at Jeff with questioning stares.

A rustle of the tent flap had all three men looking up and directly at Jake. He saw a bewildered look on his two friends' faces and a smile on the other.

"What's up?" he asked.

"We have been listening to an interesting theory," stated Mac.

"Hypothetical, I would say," added Jeff.

"Okay, a hypothetical theory. It seems the store had been broken into and some merchandise of interest was stolen; fertilizer, ointment and gauze," related Mac.

"Yeah, okay."

"The ingredients could make a bomb or could disguise a body to look like it was badly burnt; especially to an untrained eye."

"Okay, so you are saying that our lieutenant splashed this shit on himself to appear he was badly burnt to blend into the burnt bodies of the Al-Shabaab? And why would he do that?" questioned the doubting Jake.

"To give him more time?" inserted Jeff.

Jake looked at him.

"More time for what? And where is my gun?"

"Sorry." Jeff reached around to the small of his back, pulled out the pistol, and handed it to Jake.

"Thank you. And my question still stands... More time for what?"

"If I may..." Jeff stood up and leaned into the men, and softly stated.

"He obviously was not too sure about you guys and especially with the watch thing..."

"How do you know about the watches?" flared Jake.

"Maysa told me. He must have felt there would be others coming here to check out the situation, like Walker and the woman..."

"And what about you?" Jake added gruffly, interrupting.

"Okay. You might think that, but I don't see anyone else coming up with any ideas."

"This could be a ploy?"

"Are you sure your name isn't Thomas?"

"Look, you little prick. I don't have time for this shit. What are you getting at?"

Jeff could tell he was winding Jake up. That really wasn't his intention. He calmed down his attacks.

"Maybe he is watching us, just biding his time to see who shows up. From what Maysa told me, he thought you guys were chasing him. If he is around Maysa, it could mean danger for her as well and I don't think he wants her to be involved in anymore injustice."

"You are assuming he is still alive?"

Jeff looked around. "Where's Walker?"

"A delivery truck came by when you were on your little walk-about and he hitched a ride," informed Jake.

"Okay. I'll level with you if you answer me one question."

"Shoot."

"Why were you chasing Lieutenant Clark?"

Just then, the Colonel walked into the tent and had overheard the men talking.

"We weren't," he answered from the entrance. He joined the men in the discussion.

"We felt he had been set up and although we followed strict protocol, we might have left a little doubt in the lieutenant's mind. I had Jake and his men attempt to find the lieutenant and then help in any way possible to secure his safety. He eluded us several times, and probably with Maysa's help. She is very cunning for a young girl. We all finally met up about thirty clicks from here when a small caravan of soldiers transporting women and children had stopped, we assume, to rendezvous with those you see out there. For whatever reason, Maysa became immersed within that camp and then all hell broke loose when the lieutenant fired several RPG's. We were able to save the women and brought them here."

"But your mission was to terminate him if he did whatever he was assigned to do?"

"Correct to a point. Authorities were supposed to capture him and then make it seem he was a rogue soldier acting as a lone wolf, but we were not going to let that happen," said the Colonel.

"I had met him at a training camp... He is a good man," stated Jake. "We couldn't let him go out like that."

"Does he know all of this?"

"Not the whole story... We didn't have time when we met face to face," remarked Jake.

"I was lucky to not get my throat slashed," uttered Mac raising his hands feeling his neck. "If it weren't for Maysa stopping him... well, I wouldn't be sitting here."

"So, gentlemen, there I say again...he is protecting Maysa from any danger associated with him. And I, um...

we believe the lieutenant is alive. When we searched their pickup, I said we found one of Mosi's giraffes, well that wasn't quite true. The lieutenant had made five, which Mosi had... we found a sixth on the floor of the pickup without any burn marks. It was his clue to Maysa that he still lived."

"Why would you keep this from us?" asked the Colonel.

"Maysa's wishes. I guess she has her reasons, one of which, she doesn't trust others around here. Too much corruption, she had stated to me."

"So, Mr. Miller, who the fuck are you? You are not a reporter on an ambassadorship type assignment for the UN, are you?" asked Jake.

"Gentlemen, I..."

Jacobs, ran into the tent with a surprised look on his face, and interrupted Jeff.

"Sir, PAG picked up a ping on the lieutenant. He's just outside of Nairobi."

French Guiana, South America
Papa Time Zone 0600 Hrs.

Angela knocked on Marsha's cabin door.

"Marsha, you got fifteen minutes. You got everything?"

"Everything I'll need," she said opening the door dressed in ominous black.

"Okay, let's go. The plane is waiting for us at the Aéroport de Cayenne."

Marsha flipped her bag over her shoulder and entered the passageway with Angela.

"I got to say Angela, brilliant move in having us dock here in French Guiana to fly over to Africa."

"Merci, ma chère. Since I am a French citizen and our ship is under French registration, it was our only solution to take the 'Sanctuary' down to a French territory. We couldn't trust flying out of any U.S. airports for fear of you being questioned and Jack getting notice from your passport. We've secured passage on a UNMISS flight to Mombasa where our sister ship 'Toujours' will be waiting."

"Toujours?" asked Marsha.

"Always," smiled Angela. "It's part of my husband and mine's contract that we...we consummated one night in Belgium."

"I imagine a story lies beneath that," gleamed Marsha. "We have a problem though, Angela... I don't have my passport."

Angela placed her hand on Marsha's arm and was about to say something when the door of the elevator rotated open; the two women stepped in.

"Angela, you are like a chameleon, one minute you are fussy and sweet, then sultry and sexy, and then you're beating the shit out of someone."

"I do take that as a compliment, shouldn't I?" said Angela batting her eyelashes.

"See!!!"

Angela and Marsha were still enjoying a hearty laugh when they met up with the others in the grand salon. Angela's team all looked very serious as they checked their equipment and secured bags with the French Diplomatic tags attached.

"Okay, ladies and gentlemen..." Angela raised her arm with her military watch. "...let's synchronize our watches. We will be going to Charlie time when we land. We will meet up with the rest of the team aboard 'Toujours'. You know our assignment and you know who to watch out for. Ready... set."

"I knew Antoine was more than a chef."

Angela smiled at her new friend, "Oh...I have something you will need from now on. Here's your passport."

Marsha looked at her wondering how she got a hold of it. She opened it.

"Jenna Rose Atworth..." She returned her gaze toward Angela but didn't say a word.

"By the way, how's your foot, Jenna?" asked Angela.

"Feels great, kick-ass ready... and I love these boots," replied a confident and resolved Jenna.

"Israeli," shared Angela.

. . .

The phone rang in the darkened room. He looked at the clock's red-dial face to see what time it was.

"Yeah, this better be good to call me at four in the morning."

"You need to go to Kenya to help her out. I've got a plane waiting for you at Norfolk. And... Nigel, you need to end this now."

UN Camp - Can I Buy Passage

Secured and reliable information was vital for their mission. Jacobs remained vigilant and timely.

"You say he is in Nairobi?" questioned the Colonel.

"That's what PAG just indicated," replied Jacobs.

"How can that be?" The Colonel looked at the young reporter. "We need to have a serious talk, Mr. Miller. But first, Jake round everyone up, prep all our vehicles that still run, maybe even grab one of the transporters. Gentlemen, why I came in here was to tell you we have our new assignment... to protect the lieutenant at all costs, and this time, officially, right from Command." The Colonel shifted his eyes to Jeff. "But you knew this already, didn't you, Mr. Miller?"

"What about Rey, sir? I don't think he is in any shape to travel, even if he thinks he can," voiced Peterson.

"We'll set up a bunk in the transporter. I'm not leaving anybody behind and you know Rey wouldn't hear of it either."

"And Maysa, Colonel? Lieutenant Clark's her friend. If we leave, you know she'll follow, even if it is on foot," remarked Jeff Miller. "Remember, she saved all of your asses."

"We are a military team, not babysitters. We can't take the children with us; it's too dangerous," bellowed the Colonel.

"Can I buy passage, Colonel?"

"Just stay out of our way. You can ride in the back of the transporter and keep Rey company."

"Thank you," accepted the young reporter.

Jake passed the word to all his team to get ready to deploy. Colonel Dimitri sauntered over to the camp director's office and knocked on Amelie's door.

"Come in."

"Amelie, good morning. My men and I have to ship out as soon as possible. There should be a squad of NATO troops coming to stay with your camp on a permanent basis. I just want to say thank you for all you have done for me and my men."

"Dimitri, why now? I thought we would have more time together. You shouldn't travel with those broken ribs. Doctor's orders," she said forcing a smile.

"I thought we would have more time as well, but we have a new mission. It seems our missing lieutenant has made his way to Nairobi... I don't know how since all indications pointed to him still being out there somewhere observing us. But I believe that our young reporter, Mr. Miller, might have some answers for us when I get time to pin him down."

The doctor moved past her desk and rested her hands gently on Dimitri's chest.

"You take care of yourself. The sutures should come out next week. Don't make any sudden movement with your arms or lift anything heavy. It will take a while for your ribs to heal." A tear formed in her eye. "I... it was a pleasure to meet you, Dimitri, and I hope you will think about me when you can."

She cupped his face with her hands and placed a kiss on his waiting lips. "Just something else to remember me by and maybe a little enticement."

"Amelie... I haven't been involved with anyone for many years; I lost a special friend who was brutally murdered. I have a sworn vendetta I need to avenge before I can be free, but my lovely one, I promise, we will meet again."

Amelie's hands slid off his body and Dimitri turned and headed for the door. He stopped, looked back at her one more time and flashed a smile.

Jake had the trucks and Chenowths lined up as they loaded up with minimal supplies and remaining weapons. The two fallen soldiers from Dimitri's team had already been transported via the helicopter. A cot was placed for Rey to relax on. As Jake rounded the front of the transporter, Maysa came stomping out of her tent heading directly toward the Colonel. Mac and Jake watched with compassionate interest from behind the truck as she tore into him with a vengeance, and then, this independent woman madly left him and headed steadfast into the camp office. They smiled and continued to go back and forth loading the vehicles.

A few came out to say their goodbyes as the patrol slowly motored out of the camp. The camp director, Amelie Thurston, stood with her fellow doctors and nurses and waved as the caravan made a final turn. But, before the last transporter disappeared, out of the tarped back, the young reporter waved, and next to him stood Maysa who was blowing kisses to her daughter. Ateefah was cradled in the arms of Amelie. The little girl waved while Mosi held up one of his giraffes.

Jeff and Maysa returned to the bench where one other soldier sat while Rey lay in his cot muttering under his breath rolling with each sway of the truck.

"I'm not even going to ask you, Maysa, how you convinced the Colonel to let you come. I barely secured passage."

"Mr. Jeff, not only do you need to learn about Africa... but about the persuasive power of women."

"Oh... I know exactly about the persuasion and reasoning of women. I might not understand it, but trust me, I am well aware. I am married, you know."

Maysa smiled as they rocked and rolled down the road heading en route to her friend and Nairobi.

In the front Chenowth, Jake just had to ask, "Sir, I'm curious on how..." And before Jake could finish, the Colonel knew by his tone of voice what he was going to say.

"Lieutenant Alderson, don't say a word..."

"No, sir." The three men started to laugh and the Colonel turned to them with a smile, hoping he didn't make the wrong decision, and then said, "I can't wait to meet Lt. Clark."

Colonel Dimitri and his team of battered men, with a young woman and a secretive reporter, turned off the camp's bumpy road and motored down past the Kakamega Forest to just north of Kisumu on Lake Victoria to where they turned east onto C34 past the Mustang Bar with its stone walls and high-peaked thatched roofs, past the Mamboleo market, and quickly approaching Chemilil. At a quick stop at the Excel Petrol Station, they were able to load up with petrol, local favors, and much-needed supplies, paid for by the generosity of Mr. Miller. A kilometer down the road had them following a turn-about, and then straight on until the road T'd where the shopkeeper graciously told them to make a left onto highway B1. This would take them directly to A109, the major highway to Nairobi.

The road had stunning views of vast valleys. "The Rift Valley," said Maysa to Jeff, "has its lowest elevation around 1400 ft. below sea level and rises to a height of 6,000 ft." They drove past flocks of pink flamingos leisurely feeding at Lake Nakuru. No one seemed to be bothered by the military fleet as they headed south in their caravan, nor as they mingled with the heavier stream of traffic while approaching the city of Nairobi.

~

For Lieutenant William Clark, the journey had been long and arduous with constant changing of buses, half lazy stares and multiple well-wishers as they gazed at his tattered body and half burnt clothes. He appeared as a man of desolation in need of medical attention. He suffered through their insistent bantering of antidotes of their abusive tribal hostilities. They felt compassion.

The bus driver pulled his blue, over-crowed Isuzu bus over to the side of the road at the Waruku stop. This was across the roadway from a *Brightstar-Petro* station on A109, where the blighted man could hail a cabby to take him to the Canadian Embassy. Clark thanked the bus driver for his kindness and as he stepped down, the passengers chanted, *"Kuwa vizuri, kuwa vizuri."* "They say, 'be well'," translated the bus driver. He smiled and held up his hand as they pulled away. He slipped his backpack over his shoulder and crossed the roadway's twin lanes to the safety of the median. He waited until a man of slower means could safely cross.

There were several cabs waiting as the bus driver had said; it was a busy area for transferring before getting into the center of Nairobi. From a distance, a cabby watched an injured man as he trudged toward his car, where he immediately jumped out and offered assistance. "To the hospital, my man?" he offered.

"No... Canadian Embassy."

"Right away."

The cabby jumped into his car and headed with screeching tires out of the parkway onto A109 and streaked across the busy roadway. Clark noticed the many billboards dotting the roadway, all advertising their wares. 'Nairobi' in big green letters with white and yellow accents and below in quotation marks 'Green City in the Sun', elevation 5,889 ft., population 3.8 million, and coordinates 1° 17' S 36° 49'

E. Other signage claimed fast food chains; while others had sponsorship from Coca-Cola, IBM, Citibank, Goodyear, General Motors and Toyota. There was no lack of commercial-related billboards and as they got closer, they seemed to multiply with redundancy.

"I go the quickest, but the road is bumpy."

"Fine. Just get me there."

"As you say."

"What's your name?" asked Clark.

The cabby looked in the rearview mirror. "George, sir. But my friends call me Gee-gee."

The cabby slid left onto Westlands-Red Hill Road link, a dusty dirt road that went up a hillside. They dodged and bumped and banged through. The driver with his shirt stained with the warm day's sweat, apologized at each occurrence. Gee-gee barely touched the brake as they flew onto Red Hill Road heading east. As they approached the transition onto Limuru Road, many embassies' flags dotted the roadway ahead. The cabby made a quick left, then swerved around a car in the opposite lane and jolted out onto Limuru. As they approached United Nations Avenue, directional signs pointed to the Embassy of the United States of America and the UN buildings. Finally, he slowed and turned right into the parking lot of the Canadian Embassy.

"How much?" asked Clark.

"In dollars or shillings?"

"In U.S. dollars."

"Twelve dollars, please."

"Here's fifty... Wait for me."

"All night if you'd like. Thank you, sir. Do you need help?"

"Thanks. I got it, Gee-gee."

"I'll be here waiting." Gee-gee smiled brightly as his passenger stepped out.

The lieutenant looked up at the Canadian flag; it swayed lightly in the modest breeze. He slowly made his way to the front door. The inside guard, dressed in a formal uniform, watched, as a muscular, bearded man with obvious injuries reached for the door. The soldier stepped toward it and opened it for him.

"Sir, may I help you?" said the guard, concerned for the man's obvious appearance.

"Passports, please," said Clark.

"You'll have to check your bag on the other side of the arch, sir."

"How about I let you hang on to it, Corporal. No need in setting off alarms, and I am in no mood for interrogations, if you catch my drift."

Clark handed the bag directly to the soldier with an out-stretched arm.

"Sir, I can't..."

"Yes, you can, soldier. I know the drill."

"Umm... I'll put it behind my desk, sir."

"Good man."

Clark stepped through the security arch. From there, he was shown to the information desk. He slowly shuffled forward but was still in ear shot of the humbled soldier when Billy announced, "Lieutenant William Clark, JTF2, I need to get a message to my ex-commander."

The Corporal's eyes widened when he heard the statement by this torched man.

"His name, sir?" asked the pretty attendant.

The lieutenant bent down and grabbed a pencil from her desk and ripped off a piece of paper where he wrote,

"Alouette... need help. Canadian Embassy, Nairobi. Passports for five. Signed, Iceman." He then wrote a series of numbers and directed the message to Trenton, Ontario, Canada.

"Please, send this off while I wait," he asked of the young attendant.

She looked up at the twenty-four clocks on the wall, "Sir, it's only 0430 hours there. You'll have to come back for a reply."

"Fine. Please send it."

"Yes, sir."

The receptionist did as she was asked and then started to hand back the man's scribbled piece of paper when a young paperboy came through the arches. He courteously smiled as he dumped the evening's 'Daily Nation' newspapers on her desk.

"Tomorra," he said, grinning with a perfect white smile as he turned away.

As Clark's eyes glanced down at the front page, a man dressed in a white short-sleeved shirt and dark trousers, noticed the unkempt, bloodied, and tattered man, and stepped to the receptionist's desk.

"Joyce, everything okay here?" he asked staring at the man.

"Yes, Mr. Berry. Everything is handled."

"Sir... Sir, may I be of assistance?" he asked intrusively.

Clark remained glued to the newspaper and picked one up. He looked at the front photo and read the headlines: 'Brave Young Woman Saves UN Camp.' Byline by

Brentwood Walker. It was a picture of Maysa. *Fuck! What am I going to do now?* he thought.

"Sir. May I help you?" insisted the man in a louder voice as if Clark were deaf.

Clark looked up at him with a void look on his face.

"Sir, are you all right? I mean other than the obvious."

"May I have this?" he asked of the young attendant.

"Yes, of course, sir."

Clark placed the paper under his arm and turned to leave. The man called out after him, but Clark continued through the arches to the Corporal who was holding on to his bag. The young soldier saluted him and handed him his belongings.

"Sir, is there anything I can do?"

"Tomorrow, soldier... Maybe tomorrow."

The lieutenant left the building and hobbled to where Gee-gee was waiting who quickly opened the door for the limping man.

"Where to, my friend?"

"Some place close to here."

They drove out onto Limuru Road.

"There is a very nice place called 'Tribes' just up the street."

"That's fine. Oh, and Gee-gee, I need a phone...a throw-away type. Know of any place around here?"

"Yes, sir. Leave it to me. Sir, how about a doctor? I know of one who is very discreet."

"Phone first, then room, then your doctor friend. Thank you. I will need some clothes, too... Can you do that for me as well?"

"Yes, sir. There is a market close by 'Tribes' that has everything."

"I'm only going to be here a couple of days. How about I hire you, say five hundred dollars a day?"

"I'll sleep with my dog to be at your beck and call, kind sir," said Gee-gee smiling as he looked into his rearview mirror.

"Good... we have a deal then, Gee-gee. Also, keep your ears open for any talk among your friends from anyone asking about me."

"Yes, sir. Phone-Mart," he announced. "Do you want me to go in?"

Clark smiled and handed his cabby another one hundred dollars. Clark couldn't remember when he had seen this much money; he was thankful for old friends.

The hotel was more than Gee-gee described. More like a resort with its four-story vaulted entrance with glass and stainless steel, waterfalls, and African art displayed in unique floor–to-ceiling black tubes. His standard room had frosted glass open-styled bathroom with a stand-alone tub and a rain-head shower. He thought of the movie, "Out of Africa", and wondered what Miss Blixen would think of Nairobi, if she were writing her book today.

He threw the paper on the desk, stripped off his blood and pus soaked clothes, and stepped into the welcoming shower. The water stung at each intrusion as it cleansed, but it still felt divine. Next, he placed the lather upon his beard and dragged the hotel-supplied razor down his face. He even found a piece of metal dug into his cheek that he hadn't felt before. He must have frightened the poor young secretary at the embassy. Maybe that's why she was so nice to him.

Clark hadn't heard Gee-gee at the door but noticed his cell phone vibrating next to the newspaper. Gee-gee already had program his cell number into Clark's new phone as requested. Clark wrapped a towel around himself, peered through the peek-a-boo peep hole, and saw Gee-gee with a large bag and another man who nervously looked around.

Clark opened the door of room 214 and the two entered. "Sir, this is my doctor friend I told you about."

The doctor looked at Clark's riddled body and wondered how any man could survive such punishment. As promised by Gee-gee, the doctor carefully pulled out three bullets and a bowl full of shrapnel. The doctor then doused the wounds with antibiotics and he proceeded to stitch them up. Clark's self-inflicted burn blisters had all popped while he was showering so the doctor added ointment and bandaged them as well. Clark remarked that he looked like a turkey target at a country fair. The doctor barely raised a smile and gave him a shot of antibiotics. Gee-gee had lain out the man's new clothes on the bed while the doctor was attending to his patient. The sight of blood, although Gee-gee had seen plenty, was not on his top ten list.

Before they left, the doctor gave the unknown man more bandages and ointments to help the healing of the burns. Gee-gee also asked, "Sir, what shall I call you?"

"Clark," he informed him. "Just... Clark."

"Is there anything else I can do for you, Clark?"

"Not tonight, Gee-gee, and thank you for everything you have done. How about meeting tomorrow morning here at 7 a.m. for breakfast?"

"I'll be here as you wish."

As Gee-gee and the doctor headed out the door, room service brought in some fresh fruit and a twelve ounce steak. Clark had lost fifteen pounds and if it wasn't for Maysa, he might have lost more.

Yes... Maysa. What am I going to do now that you have become a celebrity?

Clark's plan had been to say he got robbed and left to die. His wife and the two girls were theirs together, as they were as close as one could tell at their age of being twins, and the boy was from a failed arrangement. This was going to be his story to obtain passports to return to Canada. But now, he would have to rely on his contact to come up with something creative.

Clark went over to the bed to lay down and read the article written by Brent Walker about an amazing young woman. She was called only by her first name: Maysa.

"In all my years of being a war correspondent and reporting from war-torn countries around the world, the desolation and horror that follows and the atrocities against the innocent, I am sometimes surprised by the diligent nature of those special people who spring forth during such crises. One such is a young woman called Maysa. Although only in her mid-teens, she has endured rape—resulting in a child and forced to leave her village, beatings, stabbings, and hardships that followed such injustice.

"Her remarkable young life has taken many roads— some not so desirable for anyone of any age. A few short days ago, she again, shone in the eye of her comrades as she led a few good men into battle against the notorious, Al Shabaab. The devastation was unparalleled by anything I have ever witnessed or care to see again. And yet, this woman, this Maysa was dug out of the rubble, spared to fight another day. And believe me, this feisty young woman, a champion to some, deserves the respect of a decorated soldier and humanitarian. I tip my hat to her and all she stands for. You have earned this old man's respect."

Clark laid still as a tear rolled down his face. He shut his eyes.

Day 14 - Tuesday

Coord: 1°16′33″ S 36°51′46″ E

Charlie 0600 Hrs.

Out of the dark and cloudy early morning sky, a private jet was cleared to land at Moi Air Base, Nairobi, Kenya. The tires barely raised a puff of smoke as its thrusters slowed and they taxied to a government held hangar. The United States of America ensign was proudly displayed as Nigel Redman looked out the port window.

A woman with spiked red hair stood by a blacked-out SUV and next to her was a man in a blue uniform with gold applets and a sewn on *Customs* badge. The gangway swung down and Nigel stepped out and toward her.

"Did you find him?" he quickly asked above the whirl of the jets shutting down.

"Not yet..." She paused as Nigel approached the Customs agent. He lifted his bag to the agent and showed him the diplomatic tag drawn across it.

"Is this all, sir?"

"Yes, not planning on being here long."

"Very good, sir. Enjoy your stay."

"Thank you, I'll do my best."

Nigel opened the SUV's door and Gillian Perkins stepped in and slid over to the other side. The agent returned to his office with clip board in hand.

"I put the word out with some sympathizers. We will be meeting up with them shortly. Our man hasn't checked in with the U.S. Embassy."

"Okay, what about back up?"

"When we have our meeting, we can arrange for whoever we want and fire power. They have guaranteed me they can get anything we request."

"Good. We've got to end this now." He ripped off the diplomatic tag, unzipped his bag and brandished a .45 caliber Smith & Wesson with a screwed on silencer. He put three 10 shot mags into his pocket.

"Who's our driver?"

"Simon. He knows the area well and is our contact with the underground," she said matter-of-factly.

"Good, then we should be all set. What time is the meeting?"

"Seven."

"What about our other business?" asked Redman.

"Whenever you want to set things up. They are a little concerned about the route."

"Fucking wimps! I told them it's secure."

"They're out of their element; different country and all. It might take them a couple of runs."

"All they have to do is get the shit to Mombasa. Jack doesn't want to use Moi anymore. The Valdez brothers from Argentina and the Los Valles from Honduras cartels will take it from there."

"I'm still amazed to how you got them to cooperate with each other."

"We've done business with both of them for years. They know the drill and they know which side their bread is buttered. We had some exchanges when I was in Russia. Money talks and bullshit walks, missy."

Kenya, Mombasa
Charlie 0617 Hrs.

The UNMISS plane hit the tarmac with a subtle bump. Angela had arranged for nondescript, white lorries to pick them up at the airport and take them to 'Toujours' for a brief rendezvous with the rest of her team before heading to Nairobi. Just before embarking, her cellphone vibrated in her chest pocket.

"Hello. What! Fuck... thank you, Tom."

"What is it, Angela?"

"Redman has beaten us to Nairobi. He just arrived. Okay, a change of plans. Tom, my security director, has arranged for a Sikorsky helicopter. Let's load everything into the lorries and have them take us over to where the helicopter is waiting. We will divide into two teams. Antoine will take a team and extra gear in the lorry to Nairobi. Its seven plus hours by road..."

"Je vais faire en quatre heures," interrupted Antoine.

"That I don't doubt, my friend. Ladies, you will be with me."

"The Sikorsky can hold all of us," stated Jenna. "I've been in them."

"Yes, but from what I understand we are going to have civilians as well on the return. We will be under the guise of women hunters going on safari. Antoine, we will be staying at the 'Tribes.' We should arrive in a little over an hour."

"Bien entendu, ma chère, Angelique."

The cargo plane opened its rear door and Angela and her team rushed to the quickly approaching lorries. They loaded the trucks and headed for the waiting helicopter. There, Antoine and his men loaded the ladies' equipment and then they bid their farewell. Antoine sped along the tarmac and exited the airport.

"He'll probably beat us there," laughed Angela. "Come on ladies, we got a bull to put down."

. . .

Dimitri and his courageous but battered soldiers left their vehicles in the rear of the U.S. Embassy. From the basement, the team replenished much needed supplies both personal and military from the bulk storage containers that officially didn't exist. Dimitri had the young reporter and Maysa in a private office pinning down Jeff and what he knew.

After a lengthy discussion, Dimitri stood and opened the door. In walked Jake, Mac and Peterson. With favorable intel, they formulated a plan.

. . .

Gee-gee was waiting downstairs standing near the restaurant at exactly 0700 hours as the man known as Clark stepped out of the elevator onto the slick marble floor. He was looking much better than the previous day when Gee-gee had picked him up. Just his clean-shaven face made his eyes seem bluer. Gee-gee waved and flashed a friendly smile as Clark approached.

"Good morning to you, sir. You look rested."

"Good morning to you as well, Gee-gee. Yes, thank you. I feel... at least alive, thanks to your doctor friend. Shall we sit?"

The hostess guided the two men to a well-appointed table overlooking the pool area where some guests, with towels in hand, had already gathered to catch the early sun before the later hours blazed down on them.

"So, Mr. Clark, have you decided what we are about to do today?"

"Yes, but first... any word on the street of anyone asking about me?"

"I haven't heard as yet, but I informed my associates to keep an ear open and to contact me immediately, discreetly of course, if someone does."

"Good. The embassy opens at 8:15 this morning, so I would like to be there as soon as it does to see if I received a message from a colleague."

A waiter approached ceasing their conversation. He took their orders after he filled their cups with freshly brewed Kenyan coffee. Gee-gee watched the waiter intently as if he were the house detective.

"You never know who is spying on you here," he said returning his friendly gaze to Clark from his not-too-subtle stare.

"So I have been told by a close friend of mine," shared Clark, thinking of Maysa's awareness. He felt comfortable and lucky that his first contact in a desperate city like Nairobi was someone who had his interests at heart. Clark decided to lighten up their 'who-done-it' tone for a more personal vibe.

"So, Gee-gee, are you married?"

"Very much so. Seven kids to brag about. My eldest boy is a teacher at twenty-five years old and my next is a girl who works at the 'Nairobi Press' who has delighted us with three of her own. We have two more at the University and my youngest boy who is sixteen is a national soccer hopeful. And the other two girls are in intermediate school. How about you, Mr. Clark?"

"Not as fortunate of a man as you, I'm afraid. You might say business has kept me from enjoying the family life."

"But you have money. Why would you not have a wife and family?"

"It's complicated, Gee-gee. As you have seen, some days I never know if I'm going to wake up. Not a very promising future to offer someone."

"Well, my wife has ordered me to have you attend dinner with our family tonight. She will not accept anything but your appearance."

"That is very kind, Gee-gee, but I'm not sure your invitation is a good idea considering the circumstances."

"You don't know my wife... she is very persistent. Besides, she doesn't believe a generous man gave me all this money. She thinks I was gambling, so I need to save face."

"Ahhh, I understand, my friend. I will be honored to meet your family... and your wife."

"Oh, thank you. I will get to sleep in my bed tonight."

. . .

Simon, the driver, slowly drove their SUV through the crowded streets of Kibera, past cardboard and corrugated tin-roof huts, to a modest brick building with lime green wooded trim work, half peeling. The heavily built brown door had a steel-caged peep window. Simon stepped out and went over to the door applying two quick knocks and then another. The peep window opened then quickly closed. The door creaked opened to a slit of light, then opened wider to accept their guests. The three entered. Nigel and Gillian stepped to an obtrusive table while Simon stood on one side of the entrance with his hands clasped in front of him. He watched intently.

There were four heavily armed men watching them as intensively; the modest dirt floor room was nearly filled to capacity. Another interior door opened and the two were allowed to pass through it, and then down a dimly lit hallway that led to a surprisingly cheery and airy office.

"Mr. Redman I presume?" said a casually-dressed man, outstretching his hand.

"Yes. And you must be Amir," he cordially stated.

"I am. Please sit. Good day to you as well, Miss Gillian."

"Good morning, Amir."

"Would you like some tea or coffee?" offered Amir.

"We just had a bite, Amir, but thank you," declined Gillian.

"Let's get down to it, Amir. How many trained men do you have?"

"Well, Mr. Redman. I have a small army of government-trained loyalists who have now pledged their allegiance to me and our cause."

"And their readiness? How soon can they be deployed?"

"We are very efficient, Mr. Redman. At our base, we have all the modern technologies and resources. Our façade here is merely that. We keep it low-key as not to arouse suspicions, yet still to be able to acquire necessary intel from valued informants."

"I like what I am hearing, Amir. But... and I don't mean any disrespect, I would like to see your operation."

"Let me ask you this first. What do you need?"

"About ten efficient men who can follow orders."

"That is it?"

"No. Vehicles plus armaments, a safe house and a place where an extraction can disappear without a trace."

"This is Africa, Mr. Redman. We have plenty of those places," smiled Amir. "Now for your request. How about I set up what you have requested..." he looked at his Gucci watch, "Come by here in two hours... And Mr. Redman, come in a cab. Your SUV is not very subtle in this neighborhood. He will leave from here. I think you will be impressed. We can discuss payment and where to wire the money at that time."

"Okay, Amir... two hours. I hope you impress the hell out of me."

. . .

Clark and Gee-gee finished their breakfast and still had time for one more cup of Java Joe's coffee. Clark savored the smell and taste for as long as he dared as the clock's hands spread to 7:53 a.m.

"We better head out, Gee-gee. It's almost time for the embassy to open."

"Right, Mr. Clark. Let me bring the cab out front before you step out. Better to be on the side of caution."

"Very astute, Gee-gee. I believe you have done this before. Perhaps, dignitaries sneaking out of the hotel in the wee hours of the morning?"

Gee-gee laughed.

"Who is the one who is astute now? I'll be right back."

Clark eased his way to the all-glass front entrance and watched as Gee-gee wheeled his cab in front. Baggage sat to the side as the new guests were arriving while others were waiting for tour buses. Gee-gee stopped, jumped out and opened the door for Clark. Side-stepping excited guests, Clark made his way to the opened door.

"Seems busier today," commented Clark.

"Tuesday is when most of the tours leave for a two day caravan. Wednesday you will see the wannabe hunters lined up to go farther inland to the 'canned' farms. The hotel will be a ghost town on Wednesday."

Clark remained silent. He remembered his first exposure to poachers when he was stationed at the Canadian training base. He loathed the idea of it all; destroying some of earth's most beautiful creatures—and for what? Someone's enlarged ego and a place on a wall.

The two men pulled onto Limuru Road, took the gradual curve to the left, past the signage for the U.S. Embassy and the United Nations, through another gradual curve, this time to the right, and arrived at the unmistakable flying red leaf. Gee-gee guided his cab to as close as he could get to the front door. A well-dressed Clark stepped out of the cab at precisely 8:15 a.m.

Clark approached the embassy and as he neared the doors, the Corporal from the day before recognized him, flashed a friendly smile and graciously opened the Embassy's door.

"Good morning, sir. You look much better today."

"Thank you, Corporal. I feel much better."

"No bag today, sir?"

"My cabby has everything I need."

Clark approached the young secretary.

"Good morning, Joyce. Do you have anything for me?"

The receptionist couldn't believe her eyes that who was standing before her was the same man who could barely walk the day before.

"Yes, sir," she said in amazement. "Let me ring my boss."

Joyce dialed a series of numbers and replaced the receiver. She smiled back at Clark. "One moment, sir. He will be right down."

Clark looked over to the sound of a *ding* as the elevator door opened. Out stepped a man, not the nosey one from the previous day, but a man dressed in a Canadian Armed Forces uniform with Major stripes dressing his applets and just below his shoulder, a badge with the initials CANOSCOM. He walked with an air of authority and stepped to Clark with his hand out-stretched.

"Lieutenant Clark. I'm Major Strafford. Please, come this way."

They headed back to the waiting elevator where an armed soldier turned a key and pressed a blank button. At the authorized floor, the door slid open and the soldier removed the key, stepped out and joined another armed soldier who stood at the opposite side of the elevator. The Major guided Clark to a door prepped with a palm reader. The Major pressed a series of buttons and then placed his hand on the pad. The door popped open.

"Please, Lieutenant... after you."

Clark stepped inside to an array of monitors and computer terminals.

. . .

Nigel and Gillian returned to the waiting SUV and closed the door. In the tranquility of the SUV's interior, insulated from the hustle and bustle surrounding them, Nigel said to Simon, "I need a drink... someplace quiet."

"Yes, sir."

Simon nudged his SUV through the streets of the Kibera slums, past the curious eyes of its residents and local hawkers, to Mbagathi Way and then eased onto Langata Road, where they jumped onto the A104 North and then merged to A2. He quickly turned off A2 onto Kiambu Road and took the driveway to the Muthiaga Golf Course.

"It should be quiet here, sir. It is past tee-time...a couple of hours before anyone starts to come off the first nine."

"Good thinking, Simon. I like your style."

It was as Simon had said. Nigel and Gillian sat comfortable as Simon stayed alert watching the entrance from the far end of the bar. The bartender brought over a couple of Glenlevits straight up for Redman and Gillian.

"What do you think of Amir?" asked Gillian.

"Think? We'll see how he performs. I judge a man's merit by what he can do for me...nothing else."

"A little narcissistic, aren't you?"

"Ha... you should talk. For a trained journalist, you are the most narrow-minded dyke I have ever met."

Gillian slightly raised an eyebrow and laughed off Nigel's disparaging comment. She read him like a book.

She knew her worth. She threw it right back at him and said, "Is that why you asked for my help on this?"

"Let's put it this way... I trust you are not going to sleep with the enemy and then fall foolishly in love and then stab me in the back, Lass."

"You know, a girl does what she needs to do."

"Is that right? I would love to see some guy try to make a move on you. You would cut off his balls."

"No I wouldn't. I would shoot him in the head first... and then maybe cut off his balls."

"Hahaha, agreed!"

Redman raised his glass to toast Gillian.

"How long have you worked for Jack?" asked Redman.

"He recruited me straight out of journalism school, when Bush was still President."

"You've got some pretty impressive assignments, haven't you? Exclusive interviews, first on the scene, some great bylines to add to your hat."

"Yeah... so?"

"Let me ask you this... several years ago, maybe four or five, who supplied the intel on removing that young attaché from the consulate in Russia?"

"I don't know. It wasn't me, if that's what you are inferring?"

"You do remember though?"

"I was covering another story at the time. I remember the girl from a press party. She looked too innocent to have any knowledge of the cartel's business. Why do you ask now?"

"A couple of things. She was linked with having an affair with a Russian Colonel, named Dimitri, who was heading a Special Forces team to curtail the drugs from entering or leaving Russia."

"I never heard that... the affair I mean. I knew about the Russian Colonel but had never met him."

"Well, like I said, that's what I was told."

"What's the other?"

"I met her again, a couple of weeks ago. Although, I know it wasn't the same girl, just one who looked like her. I had her in my grip but incompetence got in the way and I lost her before I had the chance to beat the truth out of her."

"An imposter?"

"She went by the same name."

. . .

After being dropped off at a private helipad, Angela and her team gathered their equipment and shuffled their gear into the waiting Tribes lorry. Fifteen minutes later, they arrived at the hotel's concierge.

"Come on, ladies. Gather your personal gear and let the porters take the rest."

"Wow, Angela, this place is awesome," remarked Alicia as she stepped out of the lorry to the front of the four story rise of glass.

"Ma'am, may I take that for you? It looks very heavy," asked a porter.

"No, thank you. I've got it," said Jenna as she hoisted her pack up.

The ladies walked into the main foyer and went over to the reception desk where Angela proceeded to check in.

"Angela Fournier. I have reservations for two, 2 bedroom adjoining suites. I believe my secretary requested rooms 211 and 215 and across the hall, 214 and 216."

"Yes, Miss Fournier, as you requested...except the other adjoining suites has a guest in 214 until Thursday. We can split them and give you 212 until then, if that would be satisfactory?"

"Not a family with screaming kids is it?"

"No, ma'am. A quiet, single gentleman."

"Very good. May I have the keys for the other rooms as well? I'm not sure what time my friends will be getting in and we want to surprise them. Come, ladies; let's settle in. Big day tomorrow."

A concierge ushered Angela and her entourage to the elevators while the porters took the service elevator with the rest of their gear. Getting off at their floor, he led the way to their adjoining rooms. Angela noticed that room 214, where the quiet gentleman would be staying until Thursday, was directly across from hers. She smiled as the concierge swiped her key card and then swiped room 215. Stepping inside, he unlocked the bypass door and offered the magnetic cards to the ladies. Angela pulled out a tip and the concierge graciously exited. Moments later, a slight knock had the rest of their gear safely stored in their rooms.

"Well, ladies, how is your room?"

"Beautiful. It is huge!" stated Alicia, a little naive.

"Nice clear view over the main pool and upper deck," remarked Jenna.

"I've got the front entrance and patio," related Angela. "The other rooms across the hall should have the back and service area. How about the fourth floor bar?"

"Plants and shrubs hiding the railing," said Jenna.

"Well then, let's go for a drink to see what we can see. But first..." Angela opened one of her bags and pulled out a small device with a ribbon cord and a card dangling from the end. She slipped it into both of their door mechanisms, re-coded the locks, took their cards and placed them into the machine entering the new code. She also did it to rooms 212, 214, and 216.

"Angela, you weren't asking about the décor of the room, were you?"

"You'll learn, my sweets. Alicia, could you be so kind as to take this card to the front desk and tell them you found the card outside of room 214. Suggest maybe the occupant might have dropped his. Then meet us on the fourth floor bar."

"Yes, ma'am."

. . .

Simon handed Redman and Gillian a pack of cigarettes and a lighter before they stepped into a cab.

"Keep these on you," he said. "I'll be able to track your movement from the SUV's onboard system."

"RF signal?"

"No... GPS," stated Simon. "Nothing to activate to send a signal, so nothing to scan if one was so inclined."

Redman looked at him with a smirk on his face, "Nothing like the old days where everything became personal during a hunt. Mano a mano."

"Also, if you light the cellophane wrapper, it will cause a mini flash and then create a smoke screen. You will have two seconds before it flares."

"Anything else, Q?" grinned Redman.

They stepped into a cab that Amir had asked for and left Simon on the outskirts of shanty town in his SUV. They weaved through the streets and came across an old woman who sat on a stool, peeling fruit, and then added them to a liquid-filled jar. She poured this mixture over an iced cone, shrouded in a paper cup of similar shape. Passersby dropped coins into a basket that was set on a small table under a colorful umbrella. She glanced at the cab as it made its way through the crowded street. As a wave, the people filed in behind the cab while it moved forward. She returned her gaze to the peeling of fruit. Redman noticed.

The cab stopped at a sturdy door with a caged peep hole. They stepped out. Inside, they were once more, led down the hallway to Amir's office.

"Right on time, Mr. Redman."

"I like to be punctual."

"Well, then, let us proceed."

Amir lifted the lid of a cigar box and hit a concealed switch. The walls started to *clang* together as steel panels locked in place. Redman and Gillian watched as the room fell into darkness. A red light began to flash and the floor started to lower. A moment later, it stopped and another side panel *swished* open to a lit tunnel.

"Come, just a short distance to our garage," said Amir.

A Humvee sat with opened doors waiting for them as they exited the tunnel.

"Please, after you," proudly said Amir.

"Very nice so far, Amir," complimented Redman who was a bit taken back by Amir's wizardry.

The steel-bar gate lowered into the concrete floor. They slipped out of the garage, onto a back street and headed toward Amir's compound.

. . .

Major Strafford ushered Lt. Clark past uniformed personnel who were attending flickering terminals to a set of glass doors with automatic shades sandwiched between two panes of glass. The room was large with a substantial boardroom table surrounded by leather-cushioned chairs. Three sat around the table. One was casually dressed in a polo shirt, a woman in dungarees with Colonel stripes and the one at the helm, dressed like the Major, but with stars on his applets. He also wore the same shoulder patch as the Major – CANOSCOM.

"Lieutenant," welcomed General Helmuth. "This is Colonel Cici Carruthers, and this is Pete Timmins, Canadian Embassy. Stand at ease, Lieutenant. Sit. We're here talking in an unofficial meeting that never took place. You seem to have friends in very high places; otherwise, we would not be sitting together, entertaining an operative of the U.S. Military. I see from your dossier that you are still a Canadian."

"Yes, sir. Born in Aylmer, Ontario. I still have family there."

"How can we help you?"

"Well, sir, I need passports and safe passage for a friend of mine and her three children, who have escaped the terror of the civil war in South Sudan. She is an incredible woman, especially for her young years."

Colonel Carruthers pulled out a newspaper clipping from the dossier that sat in front of her.

"Are you referring to this woman called Maysa?" she asked, sliding the photo over to Clark.

He stopped it, looked down, and turned the photo right-side up facing him.

"Yes. It was not my intention of her getting on front page news but when I saw that, I was at a loss on how to help her," said Clark, somewhat embarrassed.

"According to the article, Lieutenant, she has become a voice of the suffering. Are you sure she wants to go to Canada?" asked Pete Timmins.

"No, I'm not sure. I haven't talked to her about it. The last time we spoke... Well, let's say, more immediate actions were necessary."

"What about you, Lieutenant? What are your needs?" asked the General.

"I think my line of work was definitely compromised. I'm not certain, but I believe Maysa is not safe around me."

"Why is that?"

"Whoever set me up knows I am alive. They will not stop until I have been terminated."

"Why didn't you contact the U.S. Embassy?" asked Timmins. He reached for Maysa's photo and turned it to face him, and then picked it up.

"I feared whoever framed me would take out the Embassy and then blame it on terrorists. These are ruthless people. That air strike at the UN camp was meant for me, not to save the camp or to take out the Al-Shabaab."

"Are you certain of that? According to your President, it was their surveillance that tracked the Al-Shabaab."

Clark sat straight in his chair and leaned forward. He could taste the betrayal.

"Excuse me, sir, but it was the tracking device in the extraction team's watches that sent in the rockets. I was instructed to activate the GPS to receive support and then a military helicopter would extract me from my location in

Juba. What I figure is that they, whoever they are, planned to take out the extraction team as well. No loose ends."

"Are you at liberty to say what your mission was, Lieutenant?"

"To take out either one of the two opposing party leaders in South Sudan."

Clark sat back into his chair while the three looked at each other in disbelief.

"That's not all. There is a woman who has been trailing me since the UN camp. She knows I am here."

"Would her name be Angela Fournier?"

Clark raised his hand to his temples and gave them a rub in denial trying to remember the woman's name.

"I don't know her. The one I am talking about disguises as a reporter, but I believe, works for the same man who wants me dead."

"Gillian Perkins?" asked Colonel Carruthers.

Clark perked up upon hearing the woman's name and said, "Yes. I believe that is her name."

"That all makes sense now," stated Timmins.

"You know her?" asked the lieutenant.

"Our paths have crossed, shall I say," remarked Carruthers.

"Lieutenant, we will see what we can do, diplomatically of course. By the way, where is Maysa now?" asked Timmins.

"I guess still at the camp."

"Lieutenant Clark, I suggest you go back to your room and wait to hear from us. Where are you staying?" asked the General.

"A place called Tribes."

"Very well, we will be in touch."

"Lieutenant... If Maysa needs sanctuary, I can help," stated Timmins.

"Thank you, sir, and thank you all."

. . .

Angela and Jenna canvassed the fourth floor roof-top bar, the 'Loft', for in and out passages plus the overview of the pool area below them. Satisfied, they took seats under a colorful umbrella. The bartender brought over a couple of drinks.

"So what do you think, Jenna? Can we defend this place if necessary?"

"I think with a well poised group we should have no problem. I hear Wednesday is very quiet around here."

"Good, we can hold the press conference around the pool and have eyes up here," stated Angela.

"Still haven't got quite used to using my real name. It's been three and a half years that I have been using Marsha's name. I was told to be patient and now I feel it is coming to an end."

"That's why this plan has to work. I feel your pain, Jenna, for the loss of your sister, but we need to see this through together. No cowboy stuff. There are legal consequences."

Jenna released her tightly spun hair, shook it out into a flowing wave, smiled and raised her glass to Angela's.

"Thank you for all you and your team have done." She paused. *I just want Redman's last look to be of me, the fucking bastard.* "I will do as you say."

Alicia's smiling face lightened the conversation as she came in and sat down.

"The desk clerk was very thankful for our keen eye. They will make sure the gentleman gets his key card."

"Well done. A mojito?"

Angela motioned for the bartender to bring another mojito for their friend. He returned to his post just as the Loft's door opened, and four men dressed in military fatigues marched in. Two stayed at the door while the other two approached the ladies. Jenna casually reached into her backpack and held her hand inside. She looked across the table to Alicia and hoped the new intern would sense a need to defend herself if a situation arose. The doors swung open once more, showcasing a good-looking, well-built man with a young woman. They followed the two who approached the table. Angela noticed Jenna's concern. Angela placed her hand on top of Jenna's.

"Jenna, it's okay."

Angela stood and outstretched her hand blocking Jenna's view of whom she was addressing.

"Colonel Dimitri, hello."

"Angela. A pleasure. This is Lieutenant Jake Alderson."

"Ma'am," acknowledged Jake.

The two men stepped aside. This time, the angled umbrella benefited Jenna's view. The couple closed in behind the soldiers. Jenna again, looked at Alicia with a quick glance; her hair flowed across her face. Jeff smiled, as did Angela, and then, Angela rushed into his arms. Jenna and Alicia were paralyzed with amazement but stood for the occasion. Jenna released her grip on her Glock.

"Baby, I missed you so," passionately teased Angela.

"It is so good to see you, my love," whispered Jeff Malardo—alias Jeff Miller, Angela's husband.

"Miss An-gel-la?" queried Alicia in her slow, southern drawl.

"Ladies, this is my husband, Jeff. Jeff darling, this is Jenna, and our newest recruit, Alicia."

"Ladies, it is a pleasure to finally meet you all."

"Angela, you were definitely holding out on us," laughed Jenna, as her tension eased.

"Well, he was also holding out on us too... I mean about who he really was," stated Colonel Dimitri, a bit clumsy as his eyes came into contact with the woman who stood behind Angela. Dimitri stepped back noticeably.

"He was too smooth," remarked Jake with a smile.

"Angela, it is my pleasure to introduce you to, Maysa. Maysa, the lady I told you about, my wife, Angela."

"Oh, Mr. Jeff... I mean, Mr. Mal... Malardo. You didn't say how beautiful she was. Only that she was stubborn like me, as you put it."

Angela laughed.

"Thank you, Maysa. And during our conversations, I have to confess, he failed to mention your natural beauty. You have gorgeous blue eyes."

Maysa bowed her head and accepted the compliment.

"Gentlemen, Maysa, please sit with us."

"Thank you, Angela, but I'm not sure how much time we have," said the Colonel without taking his eyes off Jenna.

"About fifteen minutes, and then Lieutenant Clark will be back in his room," informed Angela.

"And you know this how?" questioned the Colonel.

"Friends in high places, Colonel," smiled Angela.

Jake placed chairs around the table so all could be part of the discussion. Angela placed her cell onto the table.

"So... the plan... the one Jeff told us," stumbled the Colonel. "I'm not too comfortable with."

"Colonel, are you alright?" questioned Angela.

"Yes... fine... uh, sorry."

"I understand your concern but we need Maysa to do the press conference and have the lieutenant stand just behind her. We need to draw out the bad guys. I'll have my team here and with whatever help your team can supply, there should be no harm come to either," stated Angela.

"Where are you going to hold this?" asked Jake.

"In the pool area. Wednesday, they say, is very quiet here. Besides, the terrorists won't be able to organize that quickly to come here during that time frame. We can state a dedication will be held later that day in the park, which will further reduce any collateral damage. You can set up your men in the park and I have been guaranteed a team of JFT2 force will be available from the Canadians."

"You are assuming the lieutenant will go along with this?" remarked Dimitri as he regained his composure.

Angela turned to Maysa.

"What do you think, Maysa? You know the lieutenant better than the rest of us."

"His concern will be for me that I am sure..."

"I agree," interrupted Jeff. "He won't want to put her in harm's way."

"Yes, Mr. Jeff, but don't you forget, we have a responsibility to catch these criminals who are bringing harm to my Mr. Clark," claimed Maysa determinedly. "This is MY Africa... I will not be held hostage!"

"Gentlemen and ladies, I rest my case. I know how determined Maysa is, and I also know how determined my wife is, so let's do it," announced Jeff as he looked at his watch. "It's almost time, people. We need to get Maysa into the lieutenant's room to keep him calm."

Angela lifted her vibrating phone from the table and looked at it and remarked, "Okay. And Antoine is about an hour away; he just texted me."

"Colonel," said Jenna, "you and your men look a little worse for wear. I understand what your team went through, but these are ruthless people as you already know. Will you be up for the task?"

"I assure you, Jenna, these men are the best of the best. We will be ready. I'm sorry if I seemed a little confused, but have we met?"

Jenna hesitated. *He looked at me as if he knew me. Does he know my sister? Was he responsible for setting my sister up? That can't be... Everyone spoke so highly of him.* "Not that I recall, Colonel... unless it was at one of the White House press parties? Although, I do know of you and your team. I worked for SAS."

"Really? I don't recall anyone there by that name," he said rather adversarial.

Angela looked at Jenna. *This isn't going well!* "Colonel, I can vouch for Jenna. I promise you, she is who she says she is. In fact you might say, we just didn't pick her up out of thin air to join us," said Angela with a smile, making light of the fact that they actually had.

Alicia could not contain herself and blurted out, "That is really funny, Angela." She looked around as all eyes were on her. "I guess you had to be there, kind of thing. You know...helicopter, ropes and such."

"Come, ladies and gentlemen, we need to proceed with the plan. Jenna and Alicia, could you escort Maysa to room 214? I want to speak to my husband for a moment."

"Certainly Angela," said Alicia. "Come, Maysa, the room is beautiful."

As soon as the ladies disappeared through the Loft's doors, Angela turned to the Colonel.

"Colonel, for all this to work, I need to know what that was all about. We need to be unified and anything that could possibly interfere has to be dealt with now."

"I apologize, Angela. I was taken aback by Jenna's looks and I thought I knew most of the staff at SAS, at least their first names."

"You know the director, Lt. Colonel Jones?"

"Yes... well, actually only by sight."

"And do you know her Assistant Director?"

"I believe her name is Marsha, but I don't know her last name."

"How about 'Hourglass'?"

"Yes, of course. I was told that she was kidnapped."

"Well, Colonel, who do you think Jenna is?"

"I had no idea. I really need to apologize to her. But I can't get over her likeness to a late friend of mine."

"Would her name be Marsha Jean Atworth?"

"Yes. How do you know that?"

"Jenna is her sister."

"Her sister?!" exclaimed the Colonel as he took a seat under the umbrella.

"Her twin sister to be more precise."

The Colonel was astounded to hear this news. He didn't know his lover had a sister, but their encounters were more about their needs since time always seemed to dictate their meetings. He thought for a moment in disbelief.

"That's why Redman wanted her. I know he killed Marsha, and now it is time to settle the score."

"Colonel, our mission is the lieutenant. No grandstanding, not at this time," insisted the level-headed Angela. "It could jeopardize everything. Are we in agreement, Colonel?"

"Da," he said in Russian as he slowly composed himself.

. . .

The dusty backroad lined with tall grass and Juniper trees opened to well-placed bunkers with razor wire that acted as barriers before they reached a concrete-blocked compound. The solid steel gates swung open as the tall guard shack decked with 50 caliber machine guns, received a signal on their operation module of Amir's pending approach. Amir's Humvee maneuvered the maze and through the gates and stopped outside of an open air pavilion that showcased the main house. Rows of barracks and larger-sized equipment buildings extended throughout the expansive compound.

"Very nice," remarked Redman as he stepped out onto the brick-inlayed courtyard.

"Thank you, Mr. Redman. Please come inside."

They walked up the hand-honed steps, across the natural granite floor, inlaid with ivory pictographs; through the eight-foot African mahogany slatted doors, past podiums of Ironwood sculptures, to a large couch-enshrined room, dressed as if it was the Taj Mal with gold-threaded pillows. It overlooked a Romanesque-statued pool with cascading waterfalls and lush gardens.

"Judging from your epicurean tastes, Amir, you live very well," stated Gillian.

"We like to indulge, shall we say."

"Indulge me, Amir. How about the ten men I asked for and a show of their expertise," grumbled Redman.

"You are a man of few words, are you not, Mr. Redman?"

"I'm not here to party, Amir. Not in this sense."

"Very well. Let's get on with it."

Amir stepped to one of his bars and opened a laptop. He punched in a series of strokes and closed the lid. A man dressed in dungarees came in moments later.

"This is Captain Paituk. He will take you to one of our practice ranges."

The Captain ushered Gillian and Redman to where a waiting SUV transported them to a hundred foot limo-tinted, glass-enclosed tower serviced by an outside elevator. The observation deck was furnished with military grade computer terminals and operating them were several programmers who overlooked a four square block town.

"Everything is computerized for our tactical maneuvers. We can re-set all the charges within minutes once the initial attack has finished and re-programmed for a hostage siege. Please sit and watch."

One of the programmers initialized one of the stored scenarios. A light turned green on top of the tower. The attack began.

A team of six men ran, jumped, dodged, and crawled between the buildings as live ammo burst through the air, and hidden explosives discharged. Paituk stood with a stopwatch as his men gathered twenty minutes later unscathed, except for a couple of minor flesh wounds at the base of the tower.

"Very impressive, Captain," congratulated Redman. "I think we are good here."

"Then I shall take you back."

Amir sat on one of his opulent couches rolling a cigar between his fingers as Redman and Gillian walked in.

"Well... did I impress you, Mr. Redman?"

"I think we can do business, Amir. Now, how much?"

"Ten men, as you requested, at one hundred thousand a man, equals one million U.S. dollars, Mr. Redman."

"Done. Where do you want the money wired?"

Amir handed Redman a business card and on it, was an account number.

"As soon as I receive the deposit, you can have your men. Where would you like the Captain to drop you so your man can pick you up?"

. . .

As the lieutenant and Gee-gee entered the hotel's main lobby, an attendant shuffled over and announced, "Mr. Clark... Oh, Mr. Clark! Your card, sir. It was returned to the front desk by a young woman who spotted it on the hallway floor next to your room."

"Do you know her name?"

"No, sir, but she is with the Angela Fournier entourage."

Angela Fournier? That is twice now that her name has come up. "Thank you. I must have dropped it earlier this morning." Clark noticed the attendant's name badge and said, "By the way, Percy, in what room is this observant guest staying so I may send an appreciation note?"

"They have suites 211 & 215, so I am not sure which is hers."

"Thank you, Percy. I appreciate your service."

The two men walked through the lobby to the free-standing floor-to-ceiling glass elevator.

"You dropped your room key, Mr. Clark?" asked Gee-gee.

Clark reached into his pocket and felt his key.

"No, I have mine."

The door slid open and they stepped inside. Clark slipped his hand into his backpack and clutched his 9mm.

"Are you packing, Gee-gee?"

Gee-gee reached to his back and pulled out a .38 from his waist band.

"Always, Mr. Clark. This is Africa."

"Ha-ha, not just Africa, Gee-gee, in America, too."

The elevator quietly dinged. They stepped out onto the balcony that partially surrounded each floor. Clark peered down his wing. It was deserted. They silently crept along until they reached room 211. Clark placed his ear to the door and listened. He heard indiscriminate talking. He then crossed the hallway as Gee-gee backed up to the side of room 211. Clark listened at his door, not a sound. He then tried his original card key, slowly slipping it in. Nothing happened. He then took the card key handed to him by Percy and inserted it. The lights blinked green. He opened it and the two men rushed inside with guns drawn.

"Mr. Clark!" screamed Maysa as she jumped off the bed.

. . .

Simon watched the two little blue dots on his inboard computer screen as Gillian and Redman left the compound and started down the dusty road. He sat at the cross hairs of the main road and the two-mile stretch to the compound; it was as close as he dared without being observed. He decided to return closer to town so whoever was driving his colleagues wouldn't think they had been followed. He sat at an Echo's gas station and waited. Redman called and Simon informed him of his position.

As soon as Redman and Gillian were seated in the SUV, Redman hand Simon Amir's card and said, "One million dollars to this account, Simon, ASAP." They sped off.

. . .

Maysa stood at the podium with Lt. Clark behind her, in subtle view, at the press conference that was being held poolside at Tribes. Gee-gee had arranged with his daughter to gather all the news groups to be on hand as the hero of 'Camp Inferno'—as it was being dubbed—hit the air waves. Flashes flared as cameras digitized her image for eternity.

Above, marksmen scanned the attendants as three women peered out of their hotel suites with binoculars chanting coordinates over their headsets to the marksmen's spotters.

~

"Shit!" exclaimed Gillian as a text crossed her phone of the engaged press conference.

"What is it?"

"That young woman, Maysa, is holding a press conference right now." Gillian flipped through the incoming photos. "Fuck..." She zoomed in on the photos that flickered past off of each post. "Is that the lieutenant standing behind her?"

Day 15 - Wednesday

Kenya, Nairobi

Charlie 1200 Hrs.

The newscasters had been jubilant as they announced the dedication and support rally that was scheduled to be held that afternoon next to the World Agroforestry Center, which was located off ICRAF Road and United Nations Avenue, the rim of Karura Forest. Maysa's status was being glorified as only news agencies 'can do': quick to report and then lost in absurdity as notoriety blended into indifference.

Angela and her expanding team had staged the area with well-placed eyes, and arms to handle any situation. A show of local troops lined the streets as the masses started to assemble, but buried in the rim of the forest were the elite teams to keep Maysa safe. The unexpected crowd grew to five thousand supporters and well-wishers, all eager to listen to this angel of mercy.

Chairs that had been set in rows and placed in blocks and patterned in a semi-circle out from the stage, now held little consequence as supporters and their families edged closer to spread blankets on the freshly cut grass, as this peaceful demonstration of support started to form.

The three ladies, Angela, Jenna, and Alicia, nudged their way through the crowd of diverse well-wishers, of all nationalities, as cosmopolitan as Nairobi itself, lay, stood, sat, and waited.

Finally, Gee-gee's daughter, Narfinia, took the microphone and welcomed everyone. Then, it was time for Maysa to step up and enlighten her people.

Maysa looked out over the crowd. Her eyes misted as she scanned the smiling faces. She was only one young girl from a village high in the north of South Sudan who no one cared about, and now, all knew her name.

"Thank you all for coming," she said over the microphone. She held up her scabbed hands to quieten the cheers from the crowd. "You all have been so kind in giving up your time to be here for this dedication of this newly planted tree. It will be forever remembered as the 'Tree of Wisdom', in hope, for all reconciliation and understanding from our individual countries' leaders. I see, as I gaze out, we are all different in skin and in tongue but we are united in the color of our blood. We are a single species called Humankind who must adapt, and share all the wealth of earth, and protect those who cannot.

"We slaughter each other in the name of religions, out of greed and hold adulteress ambitions for political gain, and yet sacrifice the very ones we gain to control. My country, South Sudan, suffers from this senselessness as children have weapons thrust upon them barely before their lips have ceased to suckle. And today, after nearly six years of turmoil, and families who have been ripped apart, and thousands of wasted lives, the two responsible have signed an agreement to where they stood years ago. Where is the..."

~

Antoine radioed, *"Jenna, ten o'clock, third row in… now!"*

Jenna pushed past bystanders with minimal annoyance. She grabbed the rising gun being pulled from under the shooter's jacket. Two silenced rounds fired, and then Jenna settled the shooter slowly down to the ground, none the wiser as all eyes were on Maysa.

~

"… wisdom in that?"

~

Behind the billboard stage; another set of silent rounds split the airwaves as two breast bones exploded in red spurts while they tried to leave a Land Rover. *"Two down,"* announced Mac over his PRS.

~

"Can we continue to let these atrocities mount while the killers walk freely? They stand on the very ground where rape and murder stain the earth and pledge peace while their generals slaughter more of us. We, the people…"

~

A cab nudged its way down ICRAF Road. Gee-gee stepped to the driver's side. "You can't be here."

"Who the hell are you, mon?"

"I'm the cabby inspector, don't you know."

The cabby seemed nervous and then the rear window partially rolled down. A muzzle quickly appeared and a shiny projectile hit Gee-gee in the side. "Ahhgg!" he screamed as he rolled to the ground. Gee-gee raised his .38 and shot through the rear quarter window at the face peering out—the back glass shattered. The passenger slouched over.

404

"And take your garbage back to where you found it," he said to the cabby as he managed to stand.

~

"... need to stand together, to rise above the corruption..."

~

A skirmish on the back road to the right of the stage sent a stray, unexplainable rip through the billboard's paper backing, just missing Clark. He moved closer to Maysa as four JFT2 members exchanged silenced gun fire with three men and a driver. They radioed, *"Four count."*

~

"... so please join me in walking over to the United Nations where we will pledge our allegiance for the freedom of the people of the world and the abolishment of tyranny."

Clark stepped to Maysa and whispered, "What are you doing? That's not the plan."

"Mr. Clark, thank you for all you have done for me, but these are my people. This is for my country because this is my Africa."

The crowd rose to their feet, raised their arms, and chanted, *"Freedom for all! Freedom for all!"*

"What is she doing, Lieutenant?" questioned an astounded Angela.

"She wants to rally the people over to the UN building," replied Clark.

"Stay with her. Colonel, see anything?"

"Nothing..."

"Ma chère! Rifle, four hundred meters to the northwest, behind a monument. I don't have a shot! I'll scare him into taking one. Lt. Clark, get down!" Antoine quickly unscrewed

his suppressor and took a shot. The un-muzzled rifle-shot rang out. The bullet hit the corner of the granite monument causing an explosion of fragments. The crowd spun around in disbelief.

Clark took Maysa to the ground as the bullet whistled past and split the 'Y' in the creative advertising script that haloed Clark's head. The worked-up crowd charged the monument before another shot could be made.

~

A spiked red-haired woman, Gillian Perkins, stepped beside a Black woman who stood to the left of the stage. Gillian watched as the dispersing crowd abandoned a couple who was lying on the platform. She pulled a silenced 1911 from her pack and raised it. Alicia looked over at the red-haired woman and, without thinking, Alicia slammed her elbow into the woman's face, breaking her nose and sending her to the ground. Gillian's missed shot hit the treetops. Alicia stood rubbing her elbow as two JFT2 soldiers subdued the women.

A large man, Nigel Redman, stepped from a Humvee and pointed his weapon at an easy target. Running at full tilt down the sloped grounds, Jeff kicked the gun out of Redman's hand but the trained saboteur spun a solid punch to Jeff's chest, sending him to the ground. As Redman raised his foot to crush Jeff, Angela laced him in the side of the head with a back kick.

Redman staggered against the side of the truck, boiling inside, anger flushed his face.

"You fucking bitch!"

Jeff rolled to the side and stood up ready to take on Redman.

"Get in!" yelled Captain Paituk.

A seasoned combatant knew when to retreat, for another day would manifest itself. They took off and crested the edge of the forest as Angela fired two shots that ricocheted off the door's window frame. While Jeff looked around for a vehicle, Gee-gee came bouncing over a curb and slid to a stop beside them in a confiscated cab.

"Don't mind the body in the back. Just throw him on the floor."

Angela took the front seat while Jeff rearranged the back. They crested the forest with all wheels off the ground and then landed in a sideways slide. Gee-gee hammered the throttle and pulled it out swerving left then right. Through the driver's side window, Angela saw Jenna as she ran with all her might, gun drawn, and fired round after round at the fleeing Humvee. Empty, Jenna stopped and caught her breath as the cab streaked by.

The Captain wheeled the Humvee through the forest's backroad, slid into a right-hand turn along Family Trail's walking path, and then screeched to the left, just missing a florist's truck as they landed on Limuru. A potted tree ready to be delivered toppled to the side and spread across the opposite sidewalk.

Gee-gee came off the dirt road with a less fashionable spin and had to swerve to miss the parked truck and gathered looky-loos. Ahead, the Humvee flew past the Austrian Embassy and took the round-about to its left, which landed them on Muthaiga Road, heading straight for the A2 Auto-Expressway.

The Humvee pulled away easily from the laboring yellow Kia 'Cube' and disappeared in an 'S' curve. By the time the Kia came out of the curve and slowed at the entrance to the Expressway, the Humvee was nowhere to be seen. Gee-gee stopped the cab. Frustrated, they opened their doors, stood alongside, and watched the passing traffic.

Suddenly, Gee-gee screamed, "Look, the lower ramp on the other side of the freeway. They're headed for Eastleigh. Let's go!"

"What's Eastleigh?" asked Angela as she jumped back in.

"It's the second worst area in all of Nairobi, very old and derelict. Beware, pretty lady, it is very nasty and dangerous. Lock your doors. If they try to roll our cab, shoot them."

. . .

A kind gentleman helped Clark and Maysa up; his eyes seemed sincere. As the crowd gathered around to protect them from any further incidents, Antoine continued to scan the area through his scope. He watched as two of his fellow teammates helped Alicia subdue Gillian Perkins, cuffed her and lead her to a waiting lorry. So far their plan had worked. Now, only Redman needed to be apprehended and he hoped Angela and Jeff were on it.

"Maysa, are you all right?" asked a concerned young man.

"Yes, thank you."

"I believe with all my heart in every word you just spoke."

"You're most kind," she said. "I'm sorry but we need to lead this rally. I am in good hands with my friend here."

The young man looked up at the lieutenant.

"Yes, I can see but..."

The crowd pushed Maysa and Clark through, separating them from the young man who got lost in the chanting crowd. Antoine followed his intent as the young man pushed his way closer to this rising star. Antoine dropped his finger through the trigger guard; the cross hairs aligned. The young man was determined; he pushed through to just behind where Maysa and Clark now stood.

"Maysa!" he yelled over the noise.

She turned and as she did, the young man reached inside his shirt... Clark pulled out his Glock and pointed it at the young man.

The young man screamed, "No!... No!" and pulled out a colorful ribbon.

"No, Mr. Clark!... It's my family's colors."

Clark eased his gun back into his pack and Antione, from his perched position, removed his finger from the trigger.

"Where did you get this?"

"Your mother. I saw your picture in the newspaper... I had to come and find you. You do not remember me?"

Maysa hesitated. Her village was but a long distant memory. His eyes were deep and brilliant, and as she recalled, his smile warmed.

"Josef?"

"Yes, Maysa. I've longed to find you and any news at all would have been gratifying, but I heard none. That is until I saw your picture... I could not wait any longer."

"Walk with us, Josef. I need to hear the words of my family."

. . .

The Humvee sped down the frontage off-ramp and then fishtailed onto Northview Road nearing the Eastleigh ghetto. The yellow Cube followed a thousand meters behind. The Captain barely kissed his brakes as he darted between approaching cars on Juja Road and jumped onto Muratina Street. The crumbling buildings were but a blur as they hurtled down to Sergeant Kahande where he made a left then four blocks up, took a right onto Eastleigh First Avenue. His eyes scanned his mirrors as he quickly made a left onto Seventh. He pressed a red button and before Redman turned back around, the Captain grazed the roof of the opening over-head warehouse door as he slid inside. The Captain pressed the button again, and the door dropped down blocking the sunlight, and the noise that reverberated between the buildings from the Eight Street Market.

"Where are we?" asked Redman.

"Safe house. Most of these old buildings used to house supplies for the British Air Force base. There are many underground catacombs that lead to the airfield. Tonight, I will lead you to the edge of the tarmac where your plane will pick you up as it taxies to the runway."

"What about our mark?"

"Don't worry, I have one of my best still engaged."

~

"We've lost them. I don't see them anywhere," shouted Gee-gee as he scanned the area.

"That Humvee would stand out like a sore thumb. I can't believe this!" said Angela.

"Just drive around slow, Gee-gee. Something has to give. Angela, do you remember when my secretary was kidnapped by Micholanetti, and Tom and his team found her in the old warehouse district of L.A.?"

"Yes, that was the first test of PAG," recounted Angela.

"Well, okay... but how did Tom find her?"

"Your old boss, Harry, had every one of his staff screened... including you. He arranged with Tom who sent the values to PAG. Our Foundation had invested a lot of money into the research so they were excited by the opportunity to help us."

"I would imagine Tomlinson would stay clear of anything like that for his operatives. Gee-gee what is at the end of this street?"

"Moi Air Base."

Angela looked at Jeff and knew exactly what he was thinking. "Escape route?"

"No doubt! Gee-gee, what were these old buildings used for?"

"Housing for supplies when the RAF opened the base. I heard a maze of tunnels used to connect to the outer hangars. But they are long gone since they lengthened the runway."

"I think we should check to see if anyone has filed a flight plan for tonight. Which end of the runway do the planes take off from?" asked Jeff.

"At this time of year, the wind is blowing away from us so they will be taxiing right close to this fence here."

"All right. Let's check on the others and then come back here tonight and stakeout close to where the planes taxi."

"But the hangars are now all down at the other end," insisted Gee-gee.

"I don't think Redman would chance going to a hangar. He'll jump on as close as he can get to take off."

As they turned around at the end of the street, Angela noticed a red-soaked stain covering Gee-gee's side. Gee-gee reassured Angela he was fine and it was a mere scratch. After they disposed of the body in the back seat, Gee-gee contacted one of his allies for the cab to be sanitized.

Angela arranged for another vehicle, and as the blacked-out SUV pulled up, the driver stepped out and opened the doors for his passengers.

"Everything go well?" asked Angela as she secured her straps in the back seat.

"Without a hitch. Redman has the transponder." He lifted a street navigation screen and a portable unit popped out. "And there he sits."

Angela smiled. "Back to Tribes please, Simon. Well done."

Day 15 - Midday

Nairobi – Tribes Hotel
Charlie 1800 Hrs.

Simon dropped off Angela and Jeff at Tribes and then took his friend, Gee-gee to see their mutual friend, the doctor. As Angela and Jeff approached their room, 211, Jeff instinctively put his ear to the door—only minor undiscernible chatter. He swiped Angela's card and they entered the suite.

A hush enveloped the room as they stepped in. Alicia rushed to her and gave her a big hug.

"I was so worried, Angela. It's been over an hour," reprimanded Alicia in a motherly way.

Angela smiled and as she hugged back, she felt a cold compress on Alicia's elbow. "What's this?"

"Gillian's nose," laughed Antoine.

"Do we have our man?" asked Dimitri, who was sitting on the couch holding Jenna's hand.

Angela raised a dense black case, opened it, and shared the blinking blue dot.

"We know where he is and we suspect his plan," informed Jeff.

"I've called the authorities. They will pick him up and extradite him to the States where I imagine he will be arraigned for murder, conspiracy, drug smuggling, and who knows what else. The press will have a field day, I am sure," stated Angela.

"Doesn't seem quite enough," Jenna shared sadly.

"He's out of our hands, Jenna, I'm sorry to say. Our security policy that is Fournier Foundation's policy, only applies to recovery and defending. We are not allowed to be judge and executioner. Our mission was to extract the lieutenant, safely. If we would proceed any further, we would be negligent of our legal liabilities and responsibilities. I know it is hard to accept but let's be thankful no one else will suffer from this mad man."

"Yes... sorry, Angela. You and your team have done wonders. I thank you all," said Jenna.

"Speaking of which... how did you pull this off, Angela?" asked Clark.

"I wish Tom, our security director, was here to enlighten you all... but I'll try. We knew something was going down the night of the First Lady's 'Save A Day' event. Admiral Stone served with my father many, many moons ago. In fact, on the day of my dad's funeral, I was nine at the time; he came to pay his respects. I remember seeing him there, but I was too emotionally distraught to remember anything else.

"My mentor, Jamison Starkney, was asked if the Fournier Foundation would be interested in sponsoring a portion of PAG; this was back in its infancy. During a fundraiser, the Admiral approached me and we chatted and then he remarked on my resemblance to an old friend of his. Well, you can imagine my amazement as my life had completely changed. We've kept in touch over the years. Uh... sorry for digressing.

"The Admiral was the only one who knew Jenna's true identity and when she called him about the 'date' with Redman, he invited her over to his place where he gave her the mini transponder that fit into the rosebud of Jenna's bra disguised as a broach. I assume, when Redman ripped Jenna's dress off, it pulled apart the broach and activated our signal. We sent Alicia in undercover to keep an eye on her and to help in her escape."

"She was very delectable. Thank you, Angela," laughed Jenna.

"I was so nervous... and you didn't make it any easier. I was having heart palpitations," added Alicia, waving her hand in front of her face.

"We also knew Jenna had assumed her twin sister's identity to get closer to the one who had Marsha killed," continued Angela.

"And I believe, by Redman's reaction, he knew he murdered the wrong sister," stated Jenna.

"You had me going too, Jenna. I completely lost it when I saw you sitting at the table when we were upstairs at the bar," shared Dimitri.

"I understand Jenna's involvement, but how did you set this all up to save my sorry ass? And more importantly, what was this all about?" asked the lieutenant.

"We originally thought Jack Tomlinson's interest was in the rich oil fields but quickly surmised it must have been drugs all along. He was probably paying off one of the two leaders for safe passage along South Sudan's route in order for them to finance their militaries. The Colonel here and your biggest supporter, Lt. Alderson, whom you had met at a training camp, felt you were being set up unjustly. You might say they went rogue to find you and help you escape out of South Sudan. Erroneous coordinates were sent back to PAG to where they thought you might be headed, for Tomlinson's sake, but the Colonel actually had Jake, Mac and BP to try to intercept you and bring you safely to an extraction point," informed Angela.

"The one snag was you meeting Maysa. No disrespect, Maysa, but you were very cunning. You kept us on our toes," laughed Jake.

"And your bravery saved a lot of lives, Maysa," endeared the Colonel.

"Now I need to ask, Lieutenant, how did you manage to get to Nairobi?" asked Jake.

"I'll let Jeff answer that one."

"While Angela was taking care of rescuing Jenna, I flew to Nairobi and then headed back to the UN camp. We made it possible for Brent Walker to cover an exclusive and also be a distraction as I posed as a journalist. Washington assumed but could not prove as of yet, of Gillian Perkins' involvement in espionage. Of course, Tomlinson had to send her before anything actually had happened, so we knew then she was working for Tomlinson. We also leaked the story to the White House to put Tomlinson on record with the President.

"The first night I was at the camp, I met the lieutenant out in the fields, and lucky for me, my best friend and co-worker, 'Goody', trained Clark and gave him his first pair of Israeli boots... and the nick name 'Billy the Kid'. I'm glad it wasn't any longer or I might not be here to tell this part of the story," smiled Jeff.

"Lucky you are a pretty tough cookie as well there, Jeff," laughed Clark.

"I told the lieutenant we needed to get word to Maysa, and when I shared the story of playing with Mosi's giraffes, Clark came up with the idea of making another and giving it to her. I thought if I did that, everyone including Perkins would know he was alive. We needed more time. So, I put it in their burnt out truck so Maysa could discover it. I then broke into a small store and stole some bandages and ointments for Clark's burns. I thought Gillian had tracked me but the next day, Maysa pointed out from her tracks where she must have lost me. I also gave Clark money to get the hell out of there."

"What about the fertilizer?" asked Mac.

"Oh, I was just having some fun. I always wanted to make a small explosion from the time I was in high school. It had nothing to do with anything," laughed Jeff.

"How did the cabby get involved?" asked Jenna.

"He works for a joint task force made up of several governments who are involved in stomping out all the illegal drugs and poaching coming out of Kenya, Uganda, and several other nations. Since my mentor is heavily involved in drug-related talks that are being held in Belgium, we were given Gee-gee as a contact here in Nairobi. We knew exactly where the lieutenant was by keeping in contact with PAG, so we had Gee-gee waiting for him as the bus pulled to its stop," shared Angela.

"What happens now?" asked Clark.

"I think you will all agree, this has been a very productive day," said Angela as she looked at her watch.

"It's well past cocktail time. Shall we head upstairs to the Loft?"

~

It was a beautiful starry night as they chatted and cemented friendships on the fourth floor of the open-aired bar, drinking their favorite martinis. Angela and Jeff sat arm in arm as Clark and Maysa carried on with a discussion of her returning to her home village. Dimitri commented that Maysa could accompany him as far as the UN camp where Dimitri hoped someone special was waiting for him. Maysa could then recover her children and with the courtesy and appreciation of the U.S. government, hitch a ride by helicopter, home. Jake, Mac, Peterson, and the rest of the squad were going to take much-needed R&R before getting back in touch with Angela and the Fournier Foundation for a possible new assignment.

Alicia already knew where her home was and she would join Antoine and the rest of the team for a flight back to Claire's Sanctuary, which was waiting in port in French Guiana. Angela suggested to William Clark that he was welcome aboard while things settled as his past assignment was sure to be questioned by Congress. Angela and Jeff needed to get back home soon as some *"compromised interests"* had been put on hold.

Jenna put down the phone after talking with her friend. Samantha couldn't wait to rekindle their friendship without fictitious names.

All of a sudden, Clark jumped up. "Shit... I promised Gee-gee I would have dinner at his house tonight! His wife is a little suspicious and thought his newfound wealth was due to gambling."

"Let's all go!" cheered Angela. "That should put her mind to rest."

"Yeah, having all of us over would surely do it for me," laughed Jeff.

"He needs us to explain to her how he got his wound."

"You are such a shit disturber, Babe."

The Colonel and his three officers declined, but the gang led by Angela jumped into the lorry and made the trek over to the house of a surprised Gee-gee. He most graciously asked them all in and introduced them to his family and caring wife, Giselle. Antoine took it upon himself and offered his services to Giselle, in adding the additional meats and condiments while Narfinia chatted with Maysa on state issues and her future political agenda.

They ate, they drank, and they painfully moaned with laughter. Angela, stepping over to Gee-gee, put her arm into his and pulled him aside. "You know, when we contacted you to look after the lieutenant, you weren't supposed to get shot up," she said, concerned.

"Part of the game... we all know the rules. Besides, it has been a pleasure, other than this, to be part of this operation... and, a pleasure to finally meet you, Angela."

"We can't have our best contact riddled with bullets, Gee-gee. You're our eyes and ears to Amir and his gang's drug trafficking. Washington would be pissed at me if anything happened to you."

"I know you speak from the heart, Angela, and I appreciate it. I know Amir takes his cut for providing protection along the trade route, and it will only take time before we will be able to bring him down."

Giselle, eavesdropping, smiled with a new pride.

Across town

The Captain drove the Humvee through a dimly lit tunnel. His precious cargo was good for Amir's business. As they started to rise from the depths below, the roar of engines blasted off down the tarmac. The Captain looked at his watch.

"The pilot said he was third in line. We wait here."

"Shit... I forgot my cigarettes and lighter on your desk. I guess a gift to you, Captain."

The authorities and their tactical team hammered down the steel cargo door of a building on Seventh Avenue, Eastleigh district and rushed inside to an empty building furnished with only a desk, a small lamp, a couple of wooden chairs, a pack of unopened cigarettes and a flashy lighter.

One of the plain-clothed forensic officers slipped on a pair of latex gloves and picked up the lighter. He flipped the cap and rotated the wheel. It didn't light. He shook it and tried it again. A little fluid dripped out and fell onto his glove. Unaware of the drip, he rotated the wheel; the lighter flamed and ignited the drip. He quickly peeled off his glove and threw it down, landing beside the cigarette package. The flamed glove ignited the cellophane.

A tapestry of color lit the room ablaze!

The boarded windows blew out and fell half-way into the street; the wood beams crackled and fell like match sticks as the floor reverberated like an earthquake. The instant inferno waved through the tunnel towards the expectant duo. As Redman and the Captain looked back at the approaching fireball, the Captain gunned the throttle and catapulted out the partially sealed escape route. Their Humvee slid along the tarmac to the opposing thrust of the military jet's engines as the pilot revved for take-off. The side glass shattered, pelting Redman and the Captain, and the overheated tires of the Humvee exploded destabilizing any recovery.

Redman kicked open the blistering door and fell to the ground. With his face potted with blisters and his hands steaming with melted flesh, he picked himself up and staggered to his waiting plane.

Redman clambered up the Lear's stairway and collapsed onto the plush carpet. "Simon, you motherfucker! ... Only a flash, you said!"

Italy - Two Months Later

While sitting in a restaurant in southern Italy, Nigel Redman had his cellphone pressed tightly against his ear having a private conversation with his friend Jack Tomlinson, Director of CTA.

"No fucking way, Jack. I'm loving this town."... "Where you ask? You sure we are secure?"... "In Italy, on the coast. It's called Sorrento. I told you, I'm sending you Duncan Sinclair. He's tough as nails... a good man. He'll do us well until I can get back."... "What? You my mother?"... "Having spaghetti at a place called Zi'Ntelli."

A black and silver Ducati pulled up onto the small sidewalk on the north side of Via Marina Grande. A motorcyclist dressed in grey leather and a matching helmet with a black face shield stepped off the bike and grabbed the red carryout bag off its back rack. The delivery driver stepped into the restaurant, where—sitting at the front family-sized table—a large man was talking on his cell and eating pasta. His scarred face caught the grey form's interest as they entered with the red bag hung to the side.

As the motorcyclist passed by Redman and headed toward the kitchen, the grey figure paused, reached into the red bag, and pulled out a ceramic knife. Silently, the figure stepped to the back of Redman, held his head tight against their chest, and slit the surprised man's throat with precision.

Redman dropped his cell phone. "Hello... Hello?" shouted Jack Tomlinson as he heard faintly from the open line as the cell hit the table. The assailant walked to the front of the table as Redman gasped for air. Clutching his blood-spewing laceration, Nigel Redman looked at the assailant with glaring eyes as he slowly slouched forward. Removing her helmet, she shook out her long wavy strands, smiled at him, and into her headset, she said, "Dimitri, it's done."

Austria - One Week Later

"Hello, Amir? This is Duncan Sinclair."

The Author — John F Russo

I stand humbled for the plight of the South Sudanese people and for all people who have been put on a horrifying path and for what they must endure. Unfortunately, they are not alone in the atrocities being committed on nations in our little world. As this book goes to press, we have just witnessed the Paris attacks, and on our own soil, the San Bernardino terrorists' murders. These are troubling times, no doubt!

. . .

Thank you to my wife, Lori, for her support as I am able to fulfill a lifelong dream of writing fiction. I love empowering women as I live with my inspiration every day. She is the softness around my—sometimes—rough edges; she is the sensibility to my rashness, my anchor to my kite, and my passenger on my pedal trike who pushes the wind through our hair.

My journey, our journey, is what has fed the stories and characters, and sometimes gathered through many conversations with friends, sometimes friends themselves, and sometimes what I see and read on all our devices. With you, my friends, and our lifetime journey together, you have made these words come together and have created the characters you read on my pages.

To all my friends, a sincere – thank you!

Interesting Facts

There have been so many interesting tidbits I came across while researching this book, "Darkness After Midnight". I will list some of them so you can do some research yourself. I also use wire services from around the globe to verify information.

USS Bulkeley (DDG-84) commissioned: 12-8-2001 and still serving our country, whose name was taken from Vice Admiral John Duncan Bulkeley.

USS Slater (DE 766) is retired and being restored, which you can donate to the fund. It served as my deck plan for Marsha's detainment and final escape.

Tribes Resort in Nairobi, Kenya is a beautiful paradise located just north of the United Nations and the U.S. Embassy.

The Special Operation Forces that exist from different countries; their equipment, weapons, communication and skills are unbelievable. www.defense.gov

Railroad track metering system: In Africa, because of the different influences from other neighboring industrial countries, their rail gauges are different. A Meter gauge is 1000 mm (39" wide) while Broad gauge is 1435 mm (56" wide). These widths make a difference in the construction of bridges and the constant re-adjustment of freight. The narrowed gauge allowed Clark and Maysa to escape in their slimmer Nissan while the 1-ton dually barely made its way through.

I have hundreds of 4x6 recipe cards that I use to track plot, props, places, characters, and research for the continuity of the story in my recipe card holder. I have pages of taped-together maps, room layouts, deck plans—some four feet long.

Military Time Zone

Romeo (Washington Area)				Charlie (Central Africa)	
0100 Hrs.	1 am	x	8 hours	0900 Hrs.	9 am

Wikipedia ® explains the use of military time zones as:

Going east from the prime meridian at Greenwich, England, letters Alpha through Mike (skipping 'J') are used for the 12 time zones with mainly positive UTC offsets until reaching the International Date Line. Going west of Greenwich GMT (UTC – Zulu) letters November through Yankee are used for zones with negative time offsets.

Plus: Alpha A – UTC+01:00, Bravo B – UTC+02:00, Charlie C – UTC+03:00

Negative: November N – UTC−01:00, Oscar O – UTC−02:00

In Darkness After Midnight, Washington, DC lies minus five zones from Greenwich and South Sudan lies plus three zones ahead of Greenwich. The time difference is 8 hours.